KU-733-209

FRIENDSHIP ON FIRE

JOSS WOOD

ON TEMPORARY TERMS

JANICE MAYNARD

MILLS & BOON

First Published in Great Britain 2018
by Mills & Boon, an imprint of HarperCollinsPublishers,
1 London Bridge Street, London, SE1 9GF

Friendship on Fire © 2018 Joss Wood
On Temporary Terms © 2018 Janice Maynard

ISBN: 978-0-263-93611-7

51-0718

MIX
Paper from
responsible sources
FSC® C007454

This book is produced from independently certified FSC™ paper to ensure responsible forest management.

For more information visit: www.harpercollins.co.uk/green

Printed and bound in Spain
by CPI, Barcelona

Joss Wood loves books and traveling—especially to the wild places of Southern Africa. She has the domestic skills of a potted plant and drinks far too much coffee.

Joss has written for Mills & Boon Modern and, most recently, Mills & Boon Desire. After a career in business, she now writes full-time. Joss is a member of the Romance Writers of America and Romance Writers of South Africa.

USA TODAY bestselling author **Janice Maynard** loved books and writing even as a child. But it took multiple rejections before she sold her first manuscript. Since 2002, she has written over forty-five books and novellas. Janice lives in east Tennessee with her husband, Charles. They love hiking, traveling and spending time with family.

You can connect with Janice at
www.janicemaynard.com
Twitter.com/janicemaynard
Facebook.com/janicemaynardreaderpage
Facebook.com/janicesmaynard
and Instagram.com/janicemaynard.

FRIENDSHIP
ON FIRE

JOSS WOOD

Prologue

Callie...

As she'd done for nearly thirty years, Callie Brogan kissed her daughter's sable-colored hair, conscious that nothing was guaranteed—not time, affection or life itself so she took every opportunity to kiss and hug her offspring, all seven of them.

God, no, she hadn't birthed them all. Levi and the twins—Jules and Darby—were hers. The Lockwood brothers—Noah, Eli and Ben—were the sons of her heart. Biologically, they belonged to her best friend and neighbor, Bethann Lockwood, who had passed away ten years ago. Dylan-Jane, well, DJ was another child of her heart.

The life Callie had lived back then, as the pampered wife of the stupendously wealthy, successful and most powerful venture capitalist in Boston, was over. Her beloved Ray was gone, too. She'd been a widow for three years now.

Callie was, *gulp*, alone. At fifty-four, it was time to reinvent herself.

So damn scary...

Who was she if she wasn't her kids' mom and her exuberant, forceful husband's wife?

At the moment, she was someone she didn't recognize. She needed to get to know herself again.

"Mom?"

Callie blinked and looked into Jules's brilliant eyes. As always, she caught her breath. Jules had Ray's eyes, that incredible shade of silver blue, incandescently luminous. Callie waited for the familiar wave of grief, and it washed over her as more of a swell than a tsunami.

Damn, Callie missed that man. His bawdy laugh, his strong arms, the sex. Yeah, God, she really missed the sex.

"Mom? Are you okay?" Jules asked, perceptive as always.

Callie waved her words away. She considered herself a modern mom but telling her very adult daughter that she was horny was not something that she'd ever do. So Callie shrugged and smiled. "I'm good."

Jules frowned. "I don't believe you."

Callie looked around and wished Noah—and Eli and Ben—were here. Eli and Ben had excused themselves from Sunday lunch; both were working overtime to restore a catamaran. And Noah was in Italy? Or was it Greece? Cannes? The boy used jet travel like normal people used cars.

Would Noah ever come back home to Boston? The eldest Lockwood boy wasn't one to wear his heart on his sleeve but his stepdad's actions after Bethann's death had scarred him. He had far too much pride to show how wounded he was, to admit he was lost and lonely and hurt. Like Bethann, he saw emotion and communicating his fears as a failure and a weakness.

Noah's independence frustrated Callie but she'd never stopped loving the boy...the man. Noah was in his midthirties now.

Her own son, Levi, sat down on the bigger of the two leather couches and placed his glass of whiskey on the coffee table. "Right, Mom, what's the big news?"

Callie took her seat with Jules next to her, on the arm of the chair. Darby and the twins' best friend, DJ, bookended Levi.

Jules rubbed her hand up and down Callie's back. "What is it, Mom?"

Well, here goes. "Last Tuesday was three years since your dad died."

"We know, Mom," Darby murmured, her elegant fingers holding the stem of her wineglass.

"I've decided to make some changes."

Jules lifted her eyebrows, looking skeptical. Jules, thanks to Noah's desertion and Ray's sudden death, wasn't a fan of impetuous decisions or change. "Okay. Like...?"

Callie looked out the picture windows to the lake and the golf course beyond. "Before you were all born, Bethann's father decided to turn Lockwood Estate into an exclusive gated community, complete with a golf course and country club. Your dad was one of the first people to buy and build on this estate and this house is still, apart from Lockwood itself, one of the biggest in the community."

Her kids' faces all reflected some measure of frustration at the history lesson. They'd lived here all their lives; they'd heard it all before. "It's definitely too big for me. The tenants renting the three-bedroom we own on the other side of the estate have handed in their notice. I'm going to move into that house."

Callie could see the horror on their faces, saw that they didn't like the idea of losing their family home. She'd reassure them. "When I die, this house will come to you, Levi, but I think you should take possession of it now. I've heard each of you talk of buying your own places. It doesn't make sense to buy when you have this one, Levi. The twins can move in here while they look for a property that suits them. This house has four bedrooms, lots of communal space. It's central, convenient, and you'd just have to pay for the utilities."

"Move in with Levi? Yuck," Darby said, as Callie expected her to. But Callie caught the long look her daughter exchanged with her twin sister, Jules, and smiled at their excitement.

Callie knew what was coming next…

"DJ could move into the apartment over the garage," Jules suggested, excitement in her eyes.

She loved this house; they all did. And why wouldn't they? It was spacious, with high ceilings and wooden floors, an outdoor entertainment area and a big backyard. It was close to Lockwood Country Club's private gym, which they all still used. The Tavern, the pub and Italian restaurant attached to the country club, was one of her kids' favorite places to meet, have a drink. The boys played golf within the walls of the pretty, green estate where they were raised, as often as their busy schedules allowed.

It was home.

"I don't want to live with my sisters, Mom. It was bad enough sharing a childhood with them," Levi said.

He was lying, Callie could tell. Levi adored his sisters and this way, he could vet who they dated without stalking them on social media. Levi's protective streak ran a mile long.

"It's a good solution. This way, you don't have to rent while you're looking to buy and, Levi, since I know you and Noah sank most of your cash into that new marina, it'll be a while before your bank account recovers."

Callie wrinkled her nose. Levi probably still had a few million at his fingertips. They were one of Boston's wealthiest families.

Levi shook his head. "Mom, we appreciate the offer, but you do know that we are all successful and you don't need to worry about us anymore?"

She was *Mom*, Callie wanted to tell him. She'd always be *Mom*. One day they'd understand. She'd always worry about them.

"Are you sure you want to move into the house on Ennis Street?" Jules asked.

Absolutely. There were too many ghosts in this house, too many memories. "I need something new, something different. Dad is gone but I'm still standing and I've made the decision to reinvent my life. I have a bucket list and so many things I want to do by the time I turn fifty-five."

"That's in ten months," Darby pointed out.

Callie was so aware, thank you very much.

"What's on the bucket list, Mom?" Jules asked, amused.

Callie smiled. "Oh, the usual. A road trip through France, take an art class, learn how to paint."

Jules sent her an indulgent smile. God. Jules would probably fall off her chair if Callie told her that a one-night stand, phone sex, seeing a tiger in the wild, bungee jumping and sleeping naked in the sun were also on her to-do list. Oh, and she definitely wouldn't tell them that her highest priority was to help them all settle down...

She wasn't hung up on them getting married. No,

sometimes marriage, like her best friend's, wasn't worth the paper the license was written on.

Callie wanted her children to find their soft place to fall, the person who would make their lives complete.

But, right now, Callie wanted Noah home, back in Boston, where he belonged.

How was she supposed to get him to settle down when he was on the other side of the world?

One

Noah...

Noah pushed his hand into her thick hair and looked down into those amazing eyes, the exact tint of a new moon on the Southern Ocean. Her scent, something sexy but still sweet, drifted off her skin and her wide mouth promised a kiss that was dark and delectable. His stupid heart was trying to climb out of his chest so that it could rest in her hand.

Jules pushed her breasts into his chest and tilted her hips so that her stomach brushed his hard-as-hell erection...

This was Jules, his best friend.

Thought, time, the raucous sounds of the New Year's party receded and Jules was all that mattered. Jules with her tight nipples and her tilted hips and her silver-blue eyes begging him to kiss her.

He'd make it quick. Just one quick sip, a fast taste. He wouldn't take it any further. He couldn't. He wanted to, desperately, but there were reasons why he had no right to place his hand on her spectacular ass, to push his chest into her small but perfect breasts.

One kiss, that's all he could have, take.

Noah touched his lips to hers and he fell, lost in her taste, in her scent. For the first time in months his grief dissipated, his confusion cleared. As her tongue slid between his teeth, his responsibilities faded, and the decisions he'd been forced to make didn't matter.

Jules was in his arms and she was kissing him and the world suddenly made sense...

He was about to palm her beautiful breasts, have her wrap her legs around his hips to rock against her core when hands gripped his shoulders, yanked his hair.

Surprised, he stumbled back, fell onto his tailbone to see Morgan and his dad looking down at him, laughing their asses off. His eyes bounced to Jules and tears streaked her face.

"Bastard!" Morgan screamed.

"That's my boy," Ethan cooed. "Blood or not, you are my *son."*

And Jules? Well, Jules just cried.

Another night, the same recurring dream. Noah Lockwood punched the comforter and the sheets away, unable to bare the constricting fabric against his heated skin. Draping one forearm across bent knees, Noah ran a hand behind his neck. Cursing, he fumbled for the glass of water on the bedside table, grimacing at the handprint his sweat made on the deep black comforter.

Noah swung his legs off the side of the large bed, reached for a pair of boxers on the nearby chair and yanked them on. He looked across the bed and Jenna—

a friend he occasionally hooked up with when he was in this particular city—reached over to the side table and flipped on the bedside light. She checked her watch before shoving the covers back, muttered a quick curse and, naked, started to gather her clothes.

"Do you want to talk about it?" she asked.

Hell, no. He rarely opened up to his brothers or his closest friends, so there was no chance he'd talk to an infrequent bed buddy about his dream. Without a long explanation Jenna wouldn't understand, and since Noah didn't do explanations, that would never happen. Besides, talking meant examining and facing his fears, confronting guilt and dissecting his past. That would be *amusing*...in the same way an electric shock to his junk would be *nice*.

He tried, as much as possible, not to think about the past...

Noah walked over to the French doors that opened to the balcony. Pushing them open, he sucked in the briny air of the cool late-autumn night. Tinges of a new morning peeked through the trees that bordered the side and back edges of the complex.

He loved Cape Town, and enjoyed his visits to the city nestled between the mountains and the sea. It was beautiful, as were Oahu or Cannes or Monaco. But it wasn't home. He missed Boston with an intensity that sometimes threatened to drop him to his knees. But he couldn't go back...

The last time he left it nearly killed him and that wasn't an experience he wanted to repeat.

Noah accepted Jenna's brief goodbye kiss and walked her to the door. Finally alone, he grabbed a T-shirt from the chair behind him and yanked it over his head and, picking up his phone, walked onto the balcony, then perched lightly on the edge of a sturdy morris chair.

The dream's sour aftertaste remained and he sucked in long, clean breaths, trying to cleanse his mind. Because his nightmares always made him want to touch base with his brothers, he dialed Eli's number, knowing he was more likely to answer than Ben.

"Noah, I was just about to call you." Despite being across the world in Boston, Eli sounded like he was in the next room.

Noah heard the worry in Eli's voice and his stomach swooped.

"What's up?" he asked, trying to project confidence. He was the oldest and although he was always absent, his hand was still the one, via phone calls and emails, steering the Lockwood ship. Actually, that wasn't completely true; Levi buying into the North Shore marina and boatyard using the money he inherited from Ray allowed Noah to take a step back. Eli and Ben were a little hotheaded and prone to making impulsive decisions but Levi wasn't. Noah was happy to leave the day-to-day decisions in Levi's capable hands.

"Callie called us earlier—a for-sale sign has gone up at Lockwood."

"Ethan's selling the house?" Noah asked.

"No. He's selling everything. Our childhood home, the land, the country club, the golf course, the buildings. He's selling the LCC Trust and that includes everything on the estate except for the individually owned houses."

Noah released a low, bullet-like curse word.

"Rumor has it that he needs cash again."

"Okay, let me assimilate this. I'll call you back in a few."

Noah sucked in his breath and closed his eyes, allowing anger and disappointment to flow through him. Ten years ago he'd taken the man he called Dad, a man he adored and whom he thought loved him, to court. After his mom's death he discovered that the marriage that he'd thought was so perfect had been pure BS. The only father he'd ever known, the man he placed on a pedestal was, he discovered, a serial cheater and a spendthrift.

Stopping Ethan from liquidating the last of Lockwood family assets, passed down through generations of Lockwoods to his mom—a legacy important enough to his mom for her to persuade both their biological dad and then their stepdad to take her maiden name—meant hiring expensive legal talent.

Noah ran his hand over his eyes, remembering those bleak months between his mother's death and the court judgment awarding the Lockwood boys the waterfront marina and the East Boston boatyard and Ethan the Lockwood Country Club, which included their house, the club facilities, the shops and the land around it. Ethan was also awarded the contents of the house and the many millions in her bank accounts. All of which, so he'd heard, he'd managed to blow. On wine, women and song.

Fighting for his and his brothers' inheritance had been tough, but he'd been gutted by the knowledge that everything he knew about his mom and Ethan, the facade of happiness they'd presented to the world, had been a sham. A lie, an illusion. By cheating on his mom and choosing money over them, Ethan had proved that he'd never loved any of them.

Why hadn't he seen it, realized that his dad was actually a bastard, that every "I love you" and "I'm proud of you" had been a flat-out lie? Faced with proof of his father's deceit, he'd decided that love was an emotion he couldn't trust, that marriage was a sham, that people, especially the ones who professed to love him, couldn't be trusted.

And Morgan's actions had cemented those conclusions.

The year it all fell apart, he'd spent the Christmas season with Morgan and her parents. Needing something to dull the pain after her parents retired for the night, he'd tucked into Ivan Blake's very expensive whiskey and dimly recalled Morgan prattling on about marriage and a commitment. Since he'd been blitzed and because she'd had her hand in his pants, he couldn't remember what was discussed...

The following day—feeling very un-Christmassy on Christmas morning thanks to a hangover from hell— he'd found himself accepting congratulations on their engagement. He'd tried to explain that it was a mistake, wanted to tell everyone that he had no intention of getting married, but Morgan had looked so damn happy and his head had been on the point of exploding. His goal had been to get through the day and when he had Morgan on her own, he'd backtrack, let her down gently and break up with her as he'd intended to do for weeks. He'd had enough on his plate without dealing with a needy and demanding girlfriend.

Yet somehow, Ivan Blake had discerned his feet were frozen blocks of ice thanks to his sudden engagement to his high-maintenance daughter. Ivan had pulled him into his study, told him that Morgan was bipolar and that she was mentally fragile. Being a protective dad, he'd done his research and knew Noah was a sailor, one of the best amateurs in the country. He also knew Noah wanted to turn pro and needed a team to sail with, preferably to lead.

Ivan had been very well-informed; he'd known of Noah's shortage of cash, his sponsorship offers and that there were many companies wanting to be associated with the hottest sailing talent of his generation.

Ivan had known Noah didn't want to marry Morgan…

He'd said as much and that statement was followed by a hell of an offer. Noah would receive a ridiculous amount of money to sail a yacht of his choice on the pro circuit. But the offer had come with a hell of a proviso…

All Noah had to do was stay engaged to Morgan for two years, and Ivan would triple his highest sponsorship offer. Noah's instant reaction had been to refuse but, damn…three times his nearest offer? That was a hell of a lot of cash to reject. It would be an engagement in name only, Ivan had told him, a way for Morgan to save face while he worked on getting her mentally healthy. Noah would be out of the country sailing and he only needed to send a few emails and make a couple of satellite telephone calls a month.

Oh, and Ivan had added that he had to stay away from Jules Brogan. Morgan felt threatened by his lifelong friendship with Jules and it caused her extreme distress and was a barrier to her getting well.

A week later he'd forgotten that proviso when he kissed the hell out of Jules on New Year's Eve…the kiss he kept reliving in his dreams.

Not going there, not thinking about that. Besides, thinking about Jules and Morgan wasn't helping him with this current problem: Ethan was selling his mom's house, his childhood home and the land that had been in his family for over a hundred and fifty years. That house had been the home of many generations of Lockwoods, and he'd be damned if he'd see it leave the family's hands. His grandfather had built the country club and was its founding member. His mom had been CEO of the club and estate, had kept a watchful eye on the housing development, limiting the estate to only seventy houses to retain the wide-open spaces.

Think, Noah, there's something you're missing.

Noah tapped his phone against his thigh, recalling the terms of the court settlement. Yeah, that's what had been bugging him...

He hit Redial on his phone and Eli answered. "In terms of the court settlement, Ethan has to give us the opportunity to buy the trust before he can put it on the open market."

"I don't remember that proviso," Eli said.

"If he wants to sell, he has to give us three months to buy the property. He also has to sell it to us at twenty percent below the market value."

Noah heard Eli's surprised whistle. "That's a hell of a clause."

"We had an expensive lawyer and I think it's one Ethan has accidentally on purpose forgotten."

"Then I'll contact our lawyer to enforce the terms of the settlement. But, No, even if we do get the opportunity to buy the trust—"

"We *will* get the opportunity," Noah corrected.

"—the asking price is enormous, even with the discount. It's a historic, exceptional house on a massive tract of land. Not to mention the club, the buildings, the facilities. The golf course. We're talking massive money. More than Ben and I can swing."

Noah considered this for a moment. "We'd have to mortgage it."

"The price to us should be around a hundred million," Eli said, his tone skeptical.

"We'd need to raise twenty percent." Under normal circumstances he would never be making a financial decision without a hell of a lot more due diligence. At the very least, he'd know whether the trust generated enough funds to cover the mortgage. He didn't care. This was Lockwood Estate and it was his responsibility to keep it in the family.

"Ben and I recently purchased a fifty-foot catamaran which we are restoring and that's sucked up our savings. We'll be finishing it up in a month or two and then we'll have to wait a few weeks to sell it. Even if it does sell quickly, the profit won't cover our share of the twenty-million deposit. Do you have twenty mil?"

"Not lying around. I invested in that new marina at the Boston waterfront with Levi. I'll sell my apartment in London, it's in a sought-after area and it should move quickly. I'll also sell my share in a business I own in Italy. My partner will buy me out. That would raise eight million."

"Okay. Twelve to go. Ben and I have about a million each sitting in investments we can liquefy."

Thank God his brothers were on board with this plan, that saving Lockwood Estate meant as much to them as it did to him. He couldn't do it without them. Noah ran through his assets. "I have three mil invested. That leaves seven. Crap."

Noah was silent for a long minute before speaking. "So, basically we're screwed."

Damn, his head was currently being invaded by little men with very loud jackhammers.

Eli cleared his throat. "Not necessarily. I heard that Paris Barrow wants to commission a luxury yacht and is upset because she has to wait six to ten months to get it designed. If you can put aside your distaste for designing those inelegant floating McMansions as you call them, I could set up a meeting."

"What's the budget?"

"From what I heard, about sixty million. What are your design fees? Ten percent of the price? That's six mil and I'm sure we can scrounge up another million between us. Somehow."

Noah thought for a moment. He had various projects in the works but none that would provide a big enough paycheck to secure the house. Designing a superyacht would. At the very least he had to try. Noah gripped the bridge of his nose with his forefinger and thumb and stepped off the cliff. "Set up a meeting with your client's friend. Let's see where it goes."

"She's a megawealthy Boston grande dame, and designing for her would mean coming back home," Eli said softly.

Yeah, he got that. "I know."

Noah disconnected the call and stared down at his bare feet. He was both excited and terrified to be returning to the city he'd been avoiding for the past ten years. Boston meant facing his past, but it also meant reconnecting and spending time with Levi, Eli and Ben, DJ, and Darby.

And Callie. God, he'd missed her so much.

But Boston was synonymous with Jules, the only person whom he'd ever let under his protective shell. His best friend until he'd mucked it all up by kissing her, ignoring her, remaining engaged to a woman she intensely disliked and then dropping out of her life.

She still hadn't forgiven him and he doubted that she ever would.

Jules...

Jules frowned at the for-sale sign that had appeared on the lawn of Lockwood House and swung into the driveway of her childhood home—and her new digs—and slammed on the brakes when she noticed a matte black Ducati parked in her usual space next to the detached garage. Swearing, she guided her car into the tiny space next to it and cursed her brother for parking what had to be his latest toy in her space.

Jules looked at the for-sale sign again. She was surprised that the Lockwood boys would let the house go out of their family but, as she well knew, maintaining a residence the size of the houses on this estate cost an arm and a leg and a few internal organs. Jules shoved her fist into the space beneath her rib cage to ease the burn. She'd spent as much time in that house as she had her own, sneaking in and out of Noah's bedroom. But that was back in the days when they were still friends, before he'd met Morgan and before he'd spoiled everything by kissing her senseless.

It had been a hell of a kiss and that was part of the problem. If it had been a run-of-the-mill, *meh* kiss, she could brush it aside, but it was still—*aargh!*—the kiss she measured all other kisses against. Passionate, sweet, tender, hot.

Pity it came courtesy of her onetime best friend and an all-around jerk.

Jules used her key to let herself into the empty house. It was still early, just past eight in the morning, but her siblings would've left for work hours ago. Thanks to efficient workmen and an easy client, her Napa Valley project had gone off without a hitch and as a result, she'd finished two weeks early, which was unexpectedly wonderful. Since winning Boston's Most Exciting Interior Designer award five months ago, she'd been running from one project to another, constantly in demand. For the next few days, maybe a week, she could take it a little easier: sleep later, go home earlier, catch her breath. Chill.

God, she so needed to chill, to de-stress and to rest her overworked mind and body. Despite her business-class seat, she was stiff from her late-night cross-country flight. Jules pulled herself up the wooden stairs, instinctively missing the squeaky floorboards that used to tell a wide-awake parent, or curious sibling, she was taking an unauthorized leave from the house.

Parking her rolling suitcase outside her closed bedroom door, and knowing the house was empty, Jules headed for the family bathroom at the end of the hall, pulling her grubby silk T-shirt from her pants and up and over her head. Opening the door to the bathroom, she tossed the shirt toward the laundry hamper in the corner and stepped into the bathroom.

Hot steam slapped her in the face. A second later she registered the heavy and familiar beat of the powerful shower in the corner of the room. Whipping around and expecting to see Darby or DJ, her mouth fell open at the—God, let's call it what it was—*vision* standing in the glass enclosure.

Six feet four inches of tanned skin gliding over defined muscles, hair slicked off an angles-and-planes face, brown eyes flecked with gold. A wide chest, lightly dusted with blond hair and a hard, ridged stomach. Sexy hip muscles that drew the eye down to a thatch of darker hair and a, frankly, impressive package. A package that was growing with every breath he took.

Noah...

God, Noah was back and he was standing in her shower looking like Michelangelo's *David* on a very, very good day.

Jules lifted her eyes to his face and the desire in his

gaze caused her breath to hitch and all the moisture in her mouth to disappear. Jules swallowed, willed her feet to move but they remained glued to the tiled floor. She couldn't breathe. She couldn't think. All she wanted to do was touch. Since that was out of the question—God, she hadn't seen him in ten years, she couldn't just jump him!—she just looked, allowing her eyes to feast.

Noah. God. In her bathroom. Naked.

Without dropping his eyes from hers, Noah switched off the water and pushed his hair off his face. Opening the door to the shower cubicle, he stepped out onto the mat and placed his hands on his narrow hips. Jules dropped her gaze and, yep, much bigger than before. Strong, hard…

Were either of them ever going to speak, to turn away, to break this crazy, passion-saturated atmosphere? What was *wrong* with them?

Jules was trying to talk her feet into moving when Noah stepped up to her and placed a wet hand on her cheek, his thumb sliding across her lower lip. He smelled of soap and shampoo and hot, aroused male. Lust, as hot and thick as warm molasses, slid into her veins and pooled between her legs. Keeping her hands at her sides, she looked up at Noah, conscious of his erection brushing the bare skin above the waistband of her pants, her nipples stretching the fabric of her lace bra.

Noah just stared at her, the gold flecks in his eyes bright with desire, and then his mouth, that sexy, sexy mouth, dropped onto hers. His hands slid over her bare waist and down her butt, pulling her into his wet, hard body. Jules gasped as his tongue flicked between the seam of her lips and she opened up with no thought of resistance.

It was an exaggerated version of the kiss they'd shared

so long ago. This was a kiss on steroids, bold, hotter and wetter than before. Noah's arms were stronger, his mouth more demanding, his intent clear. His hand moved across her skin with confidence and control, settling on her right breast. He pulled down the cup of her bra, and then her breast was pressed into his palm, skin on skin. She whimpered and Noah growled, his thumb teasing her nipple with rough, sexy strokes.

Jules lifted her hands to touch him, wanting to feel those ridges of his stomach on her fingertips, wrap her hand around his—

Holy crap! What the hell? Jules jerked away from him, lifting her hands up when he stepped toward her, intent on picking up where they left off.

Jules slapped her open hand against his still-wet chest and pushed him back. Furious now, she glared up at him. "What the hell, Lockwood? You do not walk back into my life and start kissing me without a damn word! Did you really think that we would end up naked on the bathroom floor?"

"I'm already naked." Noah looked down at her flushed chest, her pointed nipples and her wet-from-his-kiss mouth. "And, yeah, it definitely looked and felt like we were heading in that direction."

Jules opened her mouth to blast him and, flummoxed, couldn't find the words. "I— You— Crap!"

Noah reached behind her for a towel and slowly, oh, so slowly, wrapped it around his hips. He had the balls to smile and Jules wanted to slap him silly. "So, how much does it suck to know that the attraction hasn't faded?"

Jules glared at him, muttered a low curse and turned on her heel and walked toward the open door.

"Jules?"

Jules took her time turning around. "What?"

Noah grinned, his big arms folded across his chest. "Hi. Good to see you."

Jules did her goldfish impression again and, shaking her head, headed to her bedroom. Had that really happened? Was she hallucinating? Jules looked down and saw that the fabric of her bra was wet, water droplets covered her shoulders and ran down her stomach.

Nope, she wasn't dreaming the sexiest dream ever. Noah was back and this was her life.

So this was her punishment for finishing a project early?

Unfair, Universe. Because all she wanted to do was catch a plane back to Napa Valley and Jules hunted for a reason to return to the project she'd just wrapped up. Jules ran through her mental checklist and, dammit, she'd definitely covered all her bases. The workmanship was exemplary, the client was ecstatic and his check was in the bank. There wasn't the smallest reason to haul her butt out of this house and fly back to California.

Balls!

After three months in California she'd desperately wanted to come home, to unpack the boxes stacked against the wall and to catch up with Darby and DJ, her best friends but also her business partners. Darby, her twin, was Winston and Brogan's architect. Jules was the interior designer, and DJ managed the business end of their design and decor company. She spoke to both of them numerous times a day but she wanted to hug them, to be a part of their early-morning meetings instead of Skyping in, to share an icy bottle of wine at the end of the day.

Jules scowled. It was very damn interesting to note that during any one of those many daily conversations one of them could've told her that Noah was back in Boston.

Five words, not difficult. "Noah is back in Boston."

Or even better: "Noah is back in Boston, living in our house."

He was tall and built and it wasn't like they could've missed him!

Jules sat down on the edge of her bed, her feet bouncing off something unfamiliar. Looking down, she saw a pair of men's flat-heeled, size thirteen boots. Lifting her head, she looked around her bedroom. A man's shirt lay over the back of her red-and-white-checked chair, a leather wallet and a phone were on her dressing table. No doubt Noah's clothes were in her closet, too. Noah was not only back in her life, he'd moved into her bedroom and, literally, into her bed.

Jules frantically pushed the buttons on her phone, cursing when neither Darby nor DJ answered her call. She left less-than-happy messages on their voice mails and she was about to call Levi—who hadn't shared the news either—when her phone vibrated with an incoming call.

"Mom, guess what I found in the house when I got home a little while ago?" Jules asked, super sarcastic. "Guess you didn't know that Noah was home either, huh?"

"Damn, you found him."

In the shower, gloriously, wonderfully naked. *Spectacularly naked and I must've looked at him like I wanted to eat him up like ice cream because, before saying a damn word, he kissed the hell out of me.* "Yeah, I found Noah."

"I told your siblings to tell you," Callie said.

Hearing a noise coming from her mom's phone, Jules frowned. "Where are you?"

"At a delightful coffee shop that's just opened up next to the gym at LCC," Callie replied. "Amazing ambience and delicious coffee—"

"And the owner is really good-looking!" A deep voice floated over the phone and was quickly followed by Callie's flirty laugh. Wait…what? Her mom was flirting?

"Is he?" Jules asked, intrigued enough to briefly change the subject.

"Is he what?" Callie replied, playing dumb.

Really, they were going to play this game? "Good-looking, Mom."

"I suppose so. But too young and too fit for me."

"I'll admit to the fit but not to the too young. What's ten years?" the cheerful voice boomed. "Tell your mom to accept a date from me!"

Well, go, Mom! Despite her annoyance at her family in general, Jules laughed, listening as her mom shushed the man. "Maybe you should take the guy up on his offer. Might be fun."

"I'm not discussing him with you, Jules," Callie said, and Jules was sure she could hear her blushing.

Since Callie normally shared everything with her daughters, Jules knew this man had her unflappable mom more flustered than she cared to admit. Now, that was interesting. Before Jules could interrogate her further, Callie spoke. "So, how do you feel about Noah being back in Boston?"

Sidewinded. Horny. Crazy. Flabbergasted.

Not wanting her mom to know how deeply she was affected by this news—hell, the world was Jell-O beneath her feet—Jules let out an exasperated laugh. "It's not a big deal, Mom. Noah is entitled to come home."

"Oh, please, you've been dreading this day for years."

Jules stared down at the glossy wooden floors beneath her feet. "Don't be ridiculous, Mother."

"Jules, you've been terrified of this day because you'll no longer be able to leave your relationship with Noah in limbo. Seeing him again either means cutting him out of your life for good or forgiving him."

"There's nothing to forgive him for." Okay, she had a couple of minor issues with that gorgeous, six-foot-plus slab of defined muscles. Things like him getting engaged to a woman he didn't love and kissing her on New Year's Eve while he was engaged. And then for remaining engaged to Morgan, disappearing from her life without an explanation—she was still furious that he dropped out of college without finishing his degree—and not trying to reconnect with her when he and Morgan had finally called it quits.

In the space of seven years, the two men she loved the most, her best friend and her dad, had dropped out of her life without rhyme, reason or explanation. Her dad had been healthy, too healthy to be taken by a massive heart attack but that was exactly what happened.

Jules doubted there was a reasonable explanation for Noah abandoning her and their lifelong friendship, for not being there at her dad's funeral to hold her hand through the grief.

Okay, maybe that last one wasn't fair; Noah had been in the middle of his last race as a professional sailor at the time.

"No more coffee for me, Mason," Callie said, snapping Jules out of her wayward thoughts.

She grabbed her mom's words like a lifeline. "Mason is a nice name. Is he hot? If he's too young for you, can I meet him?"

"He's far too old for you and not your type." Well, that

was a quick reply…and a tad snappy. Did her mom have the hots for Coffee Guy? And why not? It was time she started living for herself again.

"I don't have a type, Mom," Jules replied, and she didn't. She dated men of all types and ethnicities but none of them stuck. She didn't need a psych degree to know that losing the two men she loved and trusted the most turned her into a card-carrying, picket-sign-holding commitment-phobe.

"Of course you do—your type is blond and brown-eyed and has a body that would make Michelangelo weep."

She hadn't said anything about Michelangelo, had she? How did her mom know that? "Why do you say that?"

"I'm old, not dead, Jules. The boy is gorgeous."

Noah, wet and naked, flashed behind her eyes. *Goddammit.* Like she needed reminding.

"You need to deal with him, Jules. This situation needs to be resolved."

Why? Noah had made his feelings about her perfectly clear when he dropped out of her life. She'd received nothing from him but the occasional group email he sent to the whole clan, telling them about his racing and, after he retired from sailing, his yacht design business. He didn't mention anything personal, instead sharing his witty and perceptive observations about the places he visited and the people he met.

His news was interesting but told Jules nothing about his thoughts and feelings and, once having had access to both, she wasn't willing to settle for so little, so she never bothered to reply. For someone who'd had as much of his soul as he could give, she'd needed more, dammit…

"Mom. God, just butt out, okay?"

There was silence on the other end of the phone but

Jules ignored it, knowing that it was her mom's way of showing her disapproval. "Mom, the silent treatment won't work. This is between Noah and me. Stay out of it."

Jules rubbed the back of her neck, feeling guilty at snapping. Her mother had mastered the art of nagging by remaining utterly silent. How did she do that? How?

"Mom, I know you love me but I need you to trust me to do what's best with regard to Noah." Not that she had any bright ideas except to avoid him.

"The problem, my darling, is that you and Noah are so damn pigheaded! Sort it out, Jules. I am done with this cold war."

Jules heard the click that told her Callie had disconnected the call and stared at her phone, bemused. Her mom rarely sounded rattled and considered hanging up to be the height of rudeness. But as much as she loved her mother, she was an adult and had to run her life as she saw fit. That meant leaving her relationship with Noah in the past, where it belonged.

Jules looked up, waited for the lightning strike—her mom, she was convinced, had a direct line to God—and when she remained unfried, she sighed. What to do?

Her first instinct was to run…

Jules heard the bathroom door open and, hearing Noah's footsteps, headed down the hallway in her direction, flew to her feet. Grabbing her bag off the bed, she pulled it over her shoulder and hurried to the door. She pulled it open and nearly plowed into Noah, still bare-chested, still with only a towel around his waist. *Do not look down, do not get distracted. Just push past him and leave…*

"I'm going out, but by the time I return, I want you and your stuff out of my room," Jules stated in the firmest voice she could find.

"Levi said that you were away for another two weeks.

He insisted I stay here when he picked me up from the airport yesterday. I'll find a hotel room or bunk on the *Resilience*."

His forty-foot turn-of-the-century monohull that he kept berthed at the marina. The yacht, commissioned by his great-great-grandfather was his favorite possession. It was small but luxurious, and Noah would always choose sleeping on the *Resilience* over a hotel.

"How long are you staying?" She needed to know when her life was going to go back to normal. With a date and a time, the Jell-O would, hopefully, solidify into hard earth.

"I'm not sure. A month? Maybe two?"

Great. She was in for four to eight weeks of crazy. Like her life wasn't busy and stressful enough. Jules rubbed her forehead with her fingers. God, she did not need to deal with this now. Today. Ever. Seeing him created a soup of emotion, sour and sticky. Lust, grief, hurt, disappointment, passion…

All she wanted to do was step into his arms and tell him that she'd missed him so damn much, missed the boy who'd known her so well. That she wanted to know, in a carnal way, the man he was now.

Jules shook her head and pushed past him, almost running to the stairs. *Sort it out, Mom?*

Much, much easier said than done.

Two

Callie...

After a brief and tense conversation with Levi, Callie dropped her forehead to the table and banged her head on the smooth surface. Levi reluctantly admitted to her that none of them told Jules that Noah was back. Nor had they informed her that Noah was sleeping in Jules's bedroom at her old house.

Really, and these people called themselves adults?

Aargh!

The whisper of a broad hand skated over her hair and she lifted her head a half inch off the table to glare at Mason. With his dark brown hair showing little gray, barely any lines around his denim-blue eyes and his still-hard body, the owner of the new coffee shop looked closer to forty than to the forty-five he claimed to be. Yes, he was sexy. Yes, he was charming, but why, oh, why—in a room filled with so many good-looking women, most of them younger, slimmer and prettier than her—was he paying her any attention?

Mason slid a latte under her nose and took the empty seat across from her. Callie glared at him, annoyed that he made her feel so flustered. And, holy cupcakes, was that lust curling low in her now-useless womb? "Did I invite you to sit down?"

"Don't be snippy," Mason said, resting his ropy, muscled forearms on the table. "What's the matter?"

Callie thought about blowing his question off but suddenly she wanted to speak to someone with no connection to her annoying clan. "I'm arguing with my daughter." Callie sipped her coffee and eyed Mason over her mug. Because his expression, encouraging her to confide in him, scared her, she backtracked.

"She asked if you were good-looking, whether she could meet you. She's gorgeous, tall, dark-haired with the most amazing light silver-blue eyes."

"She sounds lovely but I have my heart set on dating a short, curvy blonde."

Callie looked around, wondering who he was talking about. His low, growly laugh pulled her eyes back to his amused face. "You, you twit. I want to take *you* on a date."

"I thought you were joking."

"Nope. Deadly serious."

Okay, this was weird. He seemed nice and genuine, but what was his game? "You don't want to date me, Mason."

"I've been making up my own mind for a while now and you don't get to tell me what I do and don't want." Mason's tone was soft but Callie heard the steel in his voice and, dammit, that hard note just stoked that ember of lust. Man, it had been so long since she'd felt like this around a guy, she didn't know what to say, how to act.

For the first time in thirty-plus years she wanted to kiss someone who wasn't her husband, to explore another man's body. The problem was, while he was a fine specimen for his age, she was not. Her boobs sagged, she had a muffin top and lumpy thighs. Despite her wish for sex, a one-night stand, that was more hope than expectation. And if she found the courage to expose her very flawed body to a new man, he wouldn't have the lean, muscled body of a competitive swimmer.

Mason made her feel insecure and, worse, old. There were, after all, ten years between them and, God, what a difference ten years could make. Age, the shape their bodies were in, and then there was the difference in their financial situations.

She was, not to exaggerate, filthy rich. Mason, she'd heard, was not. Did he know how wealthy she was? Was he looking for a, *ugh*, sugar mommy? What was his angle?

"Tell me about your daughter," Mason said, leaning back in his chair.

Yeah, good plan. When he heard about her family he'd go running for the hills. "Which one? I have two by blood, one by love. I also have four sons, one by blood."

Mason blinked, ran his hand over his face and Callie laughed at his surprise. "Do you have kids?"

"Two teenage boys, fifteen and seventeen."

"My youngest, Ben, is twenty-eight," Callie said, deliberately highlighting the differences in their ages again.

"You old crone." Mason sighed, stood up and pushed his chair into the table. He placed one hand on the table, one on the back of her chair, and caged her in. His determined blue eyes drilled into hers. "You can keep fighting this, Callie, but you and I are going on a date."

The Ping-Pong ball in her throat swelled and the air left the room. He was so close that Callie could see a small scar on his upper lip, taste his sweet, coffee-flavored breath.

"And while I'm here, I might as well tell you that you and I are also going to get naked. At some point, I'm going to make you mine."

Callie was annoyed when tears burned, furious when her heart rate accelerated. "I'm not... I can't... I'm not ready."

Mason's steady expression didn't change. "I didn't say it was going to be today, Callie. But one day you will be ready and—" he lifted his hands to mimic an explosion "—boom."

Boom. Really? Callie blinked away her tears and straightened her spine. "Seriously? Does that work on other women?"

"Dunno, since you're the only one I've ever said it to." Mason bent down to drop a kiss into her hair. "Start getting used to the idea, Cal. Oh, and butt out of your kids' lives. At twenty-eight and older, they can make their own decisions."

Callie scowled at his bare back as he walked away from her. Really! Who was he to tell her how to interact with her children? And how dare he tell her that he was going to take her to bed? Did he really think that he could make a statement like that and she'd roll over and whimper her delight? He was an arrogant know-it-all with the confidence of a Hollywood A-lister.

But he also, she noticed, had a very fine butt. A butt she wouldn't mind feeling under her hands.

Noah...

Noah would've preferred to meet with Paris Barrow at her office—did the multidivorced, once-widowed socialite have an office?—but Paris insisted on meeting for a drink at April, a Charles Street bar. Hopefully, since it was late afternoon, the bar would be quiet and he could pin Paris down to some specifics with regard to the design of her yacht. Engine capacity, size, whether she wanted a monohull or a catamaran. He had to have some place to start. Oh, and getting her to sign a damn contract would be nice—at least he would be getting paid for the work he was doing.

But Paris, he decided after couple of frustrating conversations, had the attention span of a gnat...

Noah pushed his way into the bar. Another slick bar in another rich city; he'd seen many of them over the years. Looking around, he saw that his client had yet to arrive, and after ordering a beer, he slid onto a banquette, dropping his folder on the bench beside him.

It was his second full day back in Boston and, in some ways it felt like he'd never left. After being kicked out of the Brogan house by his favorite pain in the ass, he spent last night on the *Resilience* and his brothers and Levi had each brought a six-pack. They'd steadily made their way through the beers while sitting on the teak deck, their legs dangling off the side of the yacht. No one had mentioned his abrupt departure from the house and he was glad. The last thing he wanted to discuss was Jules and the past.

Noah murmured his thanks when the waitress put his beer in front of him. Taking a sip, he wished he could make the memory of Jules standing in the bathroom, looking dazed and turned on, disappear as easily as he did this beer. He'd heard the door open and turned and there she was, shirtless in the bathroom, a wet dream fantasy in full Technicolor. Her hair was around her shoulders, her slim body curvier than before, her surprisingly plump breasts covered by a pale pink lace bra. He'd immediately noticed the darker pink of her pert nipples and her flushed skin.

Then he'd made the mistake of meeting her eyes.

Noah shifted in his chair, his junk swelling at the memory. Emotions had slid in and out of her eyes; there was surprise and shock, and it was obvious that nobody had told her that he was back in town. But those emotions quickly died and he'd caught the hint of hurt before appreciation—and, yeah, flat-out furious lust—took over. Her eyes had traced his body and he knew exactly what she was thinking, because, God, he'd been thinking it, too.

He wanted her…his hands on her long, slim body, his mouth on her lips, her skin, on her secret, make-her-scream places. Whatever they started with that one kiss so long ago hadn't died. It had been slumbering for the past ten years.

Well, it was back, wide-awake and roaring and clawing…

The impulse to kiss her, to taste her again had been overwhelming, so he had. And it was as good—no, freakin' spectacular—as he thought it could be. He'd thought about dragging her back into the shower, stripping her under the water and taking her up against the tile wall. He still wanted to do that more than he wanted to breathe.

He was so screwed…

"Noah? Noah?"

Noah jerked himself out of his reverie and looked up into Paris's merry blue eyes, her face devoid of lines. Standing up—hoping he wouldn't embarrass himself—he took her outstretched hand. She looked damn good for someone in her sixties, thanks to the marvel of modern plastic surgery.

Paris sat down opposite him and put her designer bag on the table. She ordered a martini, and after the smallest of small talk, she leaned back against the banquette, eyeing him. "So, I understand that you were once engaged to Morgan Blake."

Oh, Jesus. Noah kept his face blank and waited for her to continue. "I told her that you were designing a yacht for me—"

"Well, technically I'm not. Yet," Noah clarified. "You haven't signed the contract, nor have you paid me my deposit, so right now we're still negotiating."

Paris wrinkled her nose before opening her bag and pulling out a leather case. She flipped it open and Noah saw that it was a checkbook. Paris found a pen and lifted her eyebrows. Noah gave her the figure, his heart racing as she wrote out the check. Taking it, he tucked it into his shirt pocket before withdrawing a contract from his folder. Paris signed it with a flourish and tossed her gold pen onto the table. One payment down and he'd receive the bulk of the money when she approved his final design. "Now, can we talk about Morgan?"

"No."

Paris pouted. "Why not?"

"Because we need to talk about hulls and engines and square feet and water displacement. I'm designing the yacht, but I do need some input from you," Noah said, his voice calm but firm.

Paris looked bored. "Just design me a fantastic yacht within the budget I gave you. I hear that you are ridiculously talented and wonderfully creative. Design me a vessel that will make people drool. I don't want to be bothered by the details."

The perfect scenario, Noah thought, pleased. There was nothing better than getting a green light to do what he wanted. He just hoped that Paris wouldn't change her mind down the track and morph into a nitpicking, demanding, micromanaging client. But if she did, he would handle her.

Noah handed Paris her copy of the contract, wincing when she folded it into an uneven square and shoved it into the side pocket of her bag. She drained her martini and signaled the waitress for another. "So, about Morgan."

God. Really? "Paris, I don't feel comfortable discussing this with you. You're my client."

Paris waved his measured words away. "Oh, please! I'm an absolute romantic and a terrible meddler. I nose around in everyone's business. You'll get used to it."

He most definitely would not. "There is no Morgan, Paris. That ended a long, long time ago."

"Oh, I got the impression she'd like to pick up where you left off."

Okay, it was way past time to shut this down. "Yeah, my girlfriend might object to that."

Paris's eyes gleamed with interest. "You have a girlfriend? Who is she?"

He could've mentioned Jenna in Cape Town or Yolande in London, who were both beautiful and accomplished good friends he occasionally slept with. But another name popped out of his mouth, thanks, he was sure, to a hot encounter in a bathroom yesterday morning. "Jules Brogan."

Paris's eyes widened with delight. "I know Jules. She decorated my vacation house in Hyannis Port."

Oh, crap! Crap, crap, crap.

"She was named Boston's Most Exciting Interior Designer a few months back."

She was? Why had he not heard about that? Probably the same reason the family hadn't told Jules about his return. They didn't discuss either of them ever.

"She's your girlfriend?"

"We've known each other for a long time." That, at least, was the truth.

Paris's pink mouth widened into a huge smile. "She can do the interior decoration for my yacht. Aren't you supposed to give me an idea of the interior when you present the final design?"

Oh, hell, he didn't like this. At all. "Yes. But I have my team of decorators I normally work with in London," Noah stated, wondering how this conversation had veered so off track. Oh, right, maybe because he *lied*?

"I want Jules," Paris said, looking stubborn. Her face hardened and Noah caught a glimpse of a woman who always got what she wanted. "Do not make me tear up that contract and ask for my check back, Noah."

Je-sus. Noah rubbed the back of his neck. She would do exactly as she said. Paris wanted what she wanted and expected to get it. *No* did not feature in her vocabulary.

Noah leaned back, sighed and eyed his pain-in-the-ass client. "You're going to be a handful, aren't you?" he asked, resigned.

Paris's expression lightened. "Oh, honey, you have no idea. So, what should I tell Morgan?"

Noah groaned and ordered a double whiskey.

Jules...

Jules heard the muted sound coming from her phone and, without looking at the screen, silenced the alert. Eight thirty in the morning and today was, Jules squinted at the bottom right corner of her computer, Thursday.

The only way to stop thinking about Noah, and his wet, naked, ripped body, and the fact that he was back in her orbit, was to go back to work. Instead of taking the break she needed, she slid right back into sixteen-hour days and creating long and detailed schedules so that nothing slipped through the cracks.

Jules moved her mouse and today's to-do list appeared on her monitor.

The reminder of her 9:00 a.m. meeting with the girls was followed by a list of her appointments with clients, suppliers and craftspeople. Her last appointment was at five thirty, and then she had to hustle to make her appointment with her beautician, Dana, for an eyebrow shape and a bikini wax. She was not going to dwell on the fact that the bikini wax was a last-minute request.

It had nothing to do with looking good for a brown-eyed blond.

You keep telling yourself that, sweet pea.

Jules reached for her cup of now-cold coffee and pulled a face when the icy liquid hit the back of her throat. Yuck. Resisting the urge to wipe her tongue on the sleeve of her white button-down shirt, she pushed back her chair. Her phone released the discreet trill of an incoming call and Jules frowned down at the screen, not recognizing the number. As early as it was, she couldn't ignore the call; too many of her clients and suppliers had this number and she needed to be available to anybody at any time.

"Jules."

She recognized his voice instantly, the way he said her name, the familiar tone sliding over her skin. "Noah."

There had been a time when she'd laugh with excitement to get a call from him, when her heart would swell from just hearing his voice. But those were childish reactions and she was no longer the child who'd hero-worshipped Noah, or the teenager who'd thought the sun rose and set with him. He was no longer her best friend, the person she could say anything to, the one person who seemed to get her on a deeper level than even her twin did.

"What do you want, Lockwood?"

"We need to talk."

"Exactly what I said to you ten years ago," Jules said, wincing at the bitterness in her voice. After their kiss, he'd avoided her, ducked her calls. She hadn't suspected he was leaving until he came by her mom's house one evening to say goodbye. The kiss was never mentioned. When she asked to speak to him privately he'd refused, explaining that he didn't have time, that there was nothing to discuss. He and Morgan were still engaged. He was dropping out of college. He was going sailing. He didn't know how often he would be in contact.

Please don't worry about him. He'd be fine.

She'd been so damn happy to receive his first email, had soaked up his news, happy to know that he was safe and leading the race. He'd spoken about the brilliant sunsets, a pod of southern right whales, a squall they'd encountered that day, the lack of winds the next. Reading his words made her feel like they were connected again, that their relationship could be salvaged…

Then she noticed the email was sent to a group and that her mom, her siblings, his siblings, plus a few of his college buds, received the same message. Jules never received a personalized email, nor did she receive one of his infrequent calls back home. She'd been relegated to the periphery of his life and it stung like a band of fire ants walking over her skin. She still didn't understand how someone who meant everything to her had vanished like he was never part of her life at all.

"There's nothing to say, Noah. Too much water under the hull and all that. We're adults. We can be civil in company, but let's not try and resurrect something that is very definitely over."

"Oh, it's not over, Jules. We're just starting a new chapter of a yet-unwritten book," Noah replied softly. Then his voice strengthened and turned businesslike. "I do need to talk to you—I need to hire you."

Jules dropped her phone, stared at the screen and shook her head. "Yeah, that's not going to happen. Speaking of work, I'm late for a meeting."

"Do not hang up on me, Ju—"

Jules pressed the red phone icon on her screen and tossed the device onto her messy desk. Work with him? Seriously? Not in this lifetime.

The display room of Winston and Brogan doubled as a conference room, and most mornings Jules, Darby and DJ started their day with a touch-base meeting, drinking their coffee as the early-morning Charles Street pedestrians passed by their enormous window. Jules sat down on a porcelain-blue-and-white-striped chair and thought that it was time to redesign their showroom. It was small, but it was the first impression clients received when they walked through the door, and it was time for something new, fresh.

"Creams or blush or jewel colors?" Jules threw the question into the silence before taking a sip of her caramel latte.

Darby didn't look up from her phone. "Jewel colors. Let's make this place pop."

"Whatever you two think is best," DJ replied, as she always did. Jules smiled, her friend was a whiz with money but, unlike her and Darby, she didn't have a creative bone in her body. They made an effective team. Darby designed buildings. Jules decorated them, and DJ managed their money.

The fact that they worked so well together was the main reason their full house design firm was one of the best in the city. Oh, they fought… They'd known each other all of their lives and they knew exactly what buttons to push to get a nuclear reaction. But they never fought dirty and none of them held grudges. Well, she would if they allowed her to, which they never did.

Darby crossed her legs and Jules admired the spiky heel dangling off her foot. The shoe was a perfect shade of nude with a heart-shaped peep toe. So, she'd be borrowing those soon. Hell, they'd shared the same womb, sharing clothes was a given.

"Tina Harper, she was at college with us, is pregnant. Four months." Darby looked up from her cell and Jules noticed that her smile was forced. Her heart contracted, knowing that under that brave face her sister ached for what could not be. When they were teenagers, Darby was told that, thanks to chronic endometriosis, the chances of her conceiving a child were slim to none. Closer to none… It was her greatest wish to be a mama, with or without a man. And the way their love lives were progressing, it would probably be without one.

"Didn't she date Ben?" DJ asked.

Darby shrugged. "God, I don't know. At one point, Ben had a revolving door to his bedroom."

"Ben still has a revolving door to his bedroom," Jules pointed out, thinking of the youngest Lockwood brother. He was probably the best-looking of the three gorgeous Lockwood boys and he was never short of a date or five. She could say the same for her brother, Levi, and Eli and, she assumed, Noah.

Noah. Jules sucked her bottom lip between her teeth. As always, just thinking his name dropped her stomach to the floor, caused her heart to bounce off her rib cage. Remembering their half-naked kiss threatened to stop her heart altogether.

"So, how does it feel having Noah back?" DJ asked.

"He's back in your life, not mine," Jules replied, trying to sound casual.

She'd been interrogated by every member of her family so they could find out what had caused the cold war between her and Noah. Her stock answer, "We just drifted apart," resulted in rolling eyes and disbelieving snorts but she never elaborated. They periodically still asked her for an explanation. She knew Noah was staying mum because a) Noah wasn't the type to dish, and b) if he had, then the news would've spread like wildfire. The Brogan/Lockwood clan was not known for discretion. Or keeping good gossip to themselves.

Sometimes she was tempted to tell them that she and Noah had shared some blisteringly hot kisses just to see the expression on their faces. But then the questions would follow… Why hadn't they explored that attraction? Why couldn't they get past it?

It was a question that, when she allowed it to, kept her up at night. Why hadn't they dealt with the situation, addressed the belly dancing elephant in the room?

Ah, maybe it was because, shortly after kissing her ten years back, Noah flew Morgan to Vegas to, she assumed, celebrate their engagement. Their kiss, him dropping out of college, his engagement, him turning pro… He'd made every decision without asking her opinion. Okay, she understood that he wasn't obliged to check in with her but she had run everything past him and he did talk to her about his dreams, his plans. That Christmas season, Noah had clammed up and it felt like twenty-plus years of friendship had meant nothing to him...

That he and Morgan never married wasn't a surprise, nor was it a consolation. He'd wasted two years of his time, his money and attention on Morgan, but it was his time and money to waste. Still, Jules couldn't help feeling that his engagement was a big "up yours" to their newly discovered attraction. His lack of communication, blasé explanations and his lack of effort to maintain their friendship had severed their connection. Because she would never be able to fully trust him again, they could never be friends again.

And being lovers was out of the question. That required an even deeper level of trust she was incapable of feeling.

"Did you date anyone in California?" Darby asked her, pulling her attention off the past.

She had actually. "Mmm."

"Really? And...?" Darby asked, intrigued.

"Two dates and I called it quits. Since we live on opposite sides of the country, there was no point."

She always gave guys two dates to make an impression before she moved on, thinking that dating was stressful and who got anything right the first date? If they had potential, she extended the period, making sure that hands and mouths stayed out of the equation. Not many made it to twelve weeks and most of those didn't pass her was-he-a-better-kisser-than-Noah? test. Actually, none of them were better kissers, but the two who came close made it into her bed. One lasted another few weeks; the other went back to his ex-girlfriend.

She hadn't had a relationship that went beyond four months since college...and at nearly thirty she'd only had three lovers. How sad was that?

Yet, she continued to date, thinking that one day she'd find someone who made her forget about that nuclear hot kiss on a snowy evening so damn long ago. She had to find someone. There was no way she'd allow her best sexual memory to be of Noah Lockwood…ten years or four days ago.

"Maybe I should go back on Tinder," Jules mused, mostly to herself. But at the thought, her heart backed into the corner of her chest, comprehensively horrified. She didn't blame it, meeting guys on the internet was a crappy way to find love. Or to find a date with a reasonably normal man.

"Oh, come on," DJ retorted, calling her bluff. "Psychos, weirdos and losers. You don't need any of that."

"Says the girl who has sex on a semiregular basis," Jules murmured. Since college, DJ had an on-off relationship with Matt, a human rights lawyer, who dropped in and out of her life. It was all about convenience, DJ blithely informed them, and about great sex with a guy she liked and respected.

Jules wanted one of those.

"Please stay off the net, Jules," Darby begged. "You are a magnet for crazies."

Jules couldn't argue the point. All she wanted was to meet guys like her brother and Eli and Ben. Despite their grasshopper mentality when it came to women, the three of them—even, dammit, Noah—were interesting, smart, driven and successful men. They were honest and trustworthy—well, three out of four were—and she wanted a man like them and her dad. Was she asking too much? Were her brother and her friends the last good men left in Boston? And if she found that elusive man, would she ever be able to trust him not to hurt her long enough for her to fall in love? Or would her fear send her running?

DJ gently kicked her shin with the toe of her shoe and Jules blinked, lifting a shoulder at DJ's scowl. "What?"

"Why don't you take a break from dating for a while, Jules? You've been scraping the barrel lately. Whatever you are looking for, you're not finding."

Darby tipped her head. "What *are* you looking for?"

Jules stared out of the window. *I'm looking for a guy who makes me feel as alive as I do when Noah kisses me. I'm looking for a guy who will make me stop thinking about him, stop missing him, who will fill the hole he left in my life. I'm looking for someone who will make me feel the same way I did during that bold, bright moment the other day. Noah can't be the only man who can make me feel intensely alive... That would be cruel. No, there is someone else out there. There has to be...*

Noah was the only man who made her explore the outer edges of love and despair, attraction and loathing. Kissing Noah made her feel sexy and feminine and powerful beyond measure. But his actions when they were younger made her feel insignificant and irrelevant. He'd hurtled her from nirvana into a hell she hadn't been prepared for.

He'd dismissed her opinions, ignored her counsel, and those actions she could, maybe, forgive. But she'd never forgive him for destroying their friendship, for flicking her out of his life like she was a piece of filthy gum stuck to his shoe.

DJ clapped her hands, signaling that she was moving into work mode. Jules forced herself to think business. She had designs to draw up for a revamp to a historic bed-and-breakfast, craftspeople to meet to finalize the furnishings for a bar in Back Bay. Maybe she should stop dating for a while and immerse herself in work.

They had enough of it to keep them all busy for months, if not years.

"Profit and loss, expense reports… I need your receipts," DJ said, and Jules wrinkled her nose. "I need the cost estimates on the Duncan job."

"Ack," Jules said. She loved designing but hated the paperwork it generated. "Deadline?"

"Yesterday."

"Hard-ass," Jules muttered.

"I am," DJ replied, not at all insulted. "That's why we are in the black, darling. It's all me."

Darby and Jules laughed, knowing that DJ was joking. They were a team and each of them was an essential cog in the wheel. As always, they were stronger together.

Darby looked at her watch and stood up, nearly six feet of tall grace. Jules looked out of the window and lifted her hand to wave at Dani, the personal assistant they shared, Merry, their shop floor assistant and their two interns.

Her smiled faded when she saw who was standing behind them, six feet four inches of muscle wearing chinos, a blue oxford shirt and a darker blue jacket. His wavy hair was cut short and, like always, he was days beyond shaving that dark blond scruff off his face.

Through the display window, his eyes met hers and her stomach contracted, her heart flip-flopped and all the moisture in her mouth disappeared.

It seemed that Noah did indeed intend to talk.

Three

Jules...

Jules shoved her hands under her thighs and tingles ran up and down her spinal column. Darby and DJ turned in their seats to see who'd captured her attention and immediately jumped to their feet, their beautiful faces showing their delight at seeing him. Noah was, always had been, one of their favorite people.

Kisses and hugs were exchanged and while her sisters—one by blood and the other of the heart—and Noah did a quick catch-up, Jules allowed her eyes the rare pleasure to roam. Tall, broad, blond, hot...all the adjectives had been used in various ways to describe him, and Noah was all of those things. But Jules, because she'd once known him so well, could look beneath the hot, sexy veneer.

There were fine lines around those startling eyes and

a tiny frown pulled his thick sandy brows together. He was smiling but it wasn't the open, sunny smile from their childhoods, the one that could knock out nuclear reactors with one blinding flash. The muscles in his neck were tense and under the blond scruff, his jaw was rock hard.

Noah was not a happy camper.

Noah stepped away from Darby and DJ and their eyes met, the power of a thousand unsaid words flowing between them. Noah pushed back his navy jacket and jammed his hands into the pockets of his stone-colored pants, rocking on his feet. His eyes left hers, dropped to her mouth, down to her chest, over her hips and slowly meandered their way back up. Every inch he covered sent heat and lust coursing through her system, reminding her with crystal clear certainty what being held by him, kissed by him was like. Suddenly, she was eighteen again and willing to follow him wherever he led...

The thought annoyed her, so her voice was clipped when she finally remembered how to use her tongue. "What are you doing here, Noah?"

Noah pulled his hands from his pockets to cross his arms and his eyes turned frosty. "Nice to see you, too, Jules."

Darby, sensing trouble, jumped into the conversation. "Do you have time for coffee, Noah?"

Noah shook his head. "Thanks, hon, but no."

Jules linked her shaking hands around one knee. "Why are you here, Noah?"

"Business," Noah replied. He held out his hand and jerked his head to the spiral staircase that led up to the second floor, the boardroom and their personal offices. "You and I need to talk."

Jules didn't trust herself to touch him—he was too big and too male and too damn attractive. She didn't trust herself not to throw herself into his arms and slap her mouth against his, so she ignored his hand and slowly stood up. After taking a moment to brush nonexistent lint off her linen pants, and to get her raging hormones under some sort of order, she darted a look at Darby and then DJ, and they both looked as puzzled as she did. "Okay. I have some time before my conference call in thirty minutes."

She didn't have a call, but if dealing with Noah became too overwhelming, she wanted an out. Walking to the spiral staircase, she gestured for Noah to follow her. As they made their way up the stairs she could smell his subtle, sexy cologne, could feel his heat.

She was two steps ahead of him. If she turned around, right at that moment, they would be the same height and their mouths would be perfectly aligned. She could look straight into those deep, dark eyes and lose herself, feel his mouth soften under hers, find out whether his short beard was as soft as it looked, whether the cords of his neck, revealed by the open collar of his button-down shirt, were as hard as they looked.

She hadn't touched him long enough the other morning, and if she turned around, she wouldn't have to wonder...

Jules gave herself a mental head slap and carried on walking. How could they go from friends who'd never so much as thought of each other in that way to two people who wanted to inhale each other? And, dammit, how could she suddenly be this person who wanted to rip his clothes off and lick him from top to toe?

Jules groaned silently as she hit the top step and turned right to head for her corner office. Giving herself another mental slap, she reminded herself that she would rather die than give Noah the smallest hint that he still affected her, that she'd spent far too much time lately remembering him naked, imagining his hands on either side of her head, lowering himself so that the tip of his...

Oh, dear God, Brogan! Jules curled her arm across her waist and pinched her side, swallowing her hiss of pain. *Get a grip! Now!*

At her office door, Jules sucked in a breath and stepped inside her messy space.

Making a beeline for the chair behind her desk—she needed a barrier of wood and steel between her and Lockwood—she gestured him to take the sole visitor's chair opposite her. Steeling herself, she met his eyes and opened her hands. "So, business. What's up?"

Noah...

Noah sat down in the visitor's chair and placed his ankle on his knee, thinking that Jules's eyes were the color of a perfect early morning breaking over a calm sea. Light, a curious combination of blue and gray and silver. Looking into her eyes took him back to those perfect mornings of possibility, to being on the sea, where freedom was wind in the sails and the sun on his face.

If the dark hair and light eyes combo wasn't enough to have his brain stuttering, then God added a body that was long, slim and perfectly curved and, as he remembered, fragrant and so damn soft to the touch. Being this close to her, inhaling the light floral scent of her perfume, in the messy, colorful space filled with fabric swatches and sketches, magazines and bolts of fabric, Noah's lungs collapsed from a lack of air.

The urge to run was strong, away from her and the memories she yanked to the surface.

A decade ago there had been reasons to distance himself from Jules, including that clause written into his sponsorship deal with Wind and Solar. As a new year bloomed he'd grasped that his friend was no longer a child or a girl but a woman who he was very attracted to. They'd kissed and he knew they could never be lovers because they were such good friends. Two seconds later the thought had hit him that they could never be friends because they had the potential to be amazing lovers.

Walking away from her, shivering, into the falling snow, he knew something fundamental had shifted inside him and that there was only one thing he was sure of: their friendship would never be the same again.

Now and then, whether it was monster waves or his mom's death or Ethan morphing from a loving father into a money-grabbing bastard, Noah faced life head-on with his chin and fists raised. He had the ability to see situations clearly, to not get bogged down in the emotion of a life event. As tempted as he'd been to say to hell with everyone and fall into the romance of the moment—best friends kissing and being blown away by it!—he'd been smart enough to know that decision would come back to bite him in the ass.

Even if he'd been able to push aside his other problems back then—no money for the legal fights and his fake engagement to Morgan—he knew he was standing in a bucket on an angry sea. They couldn't be friends or lovers or anything in between. Her siblings were his and vice versa. They shared two dozen or more mutual friends and her parents were two of his favorite people. He and Levi had been talking about going into business together since they were in their early teens. He and Jules had been—were still—tied together by many silken cords, and if they changed the parameters of their relationship and it went south, those cords would be shredded.

If Jules hurt him, his brothers would jump to his defense despite the fact that they adored Jules; she was their sister from another mother. If he hurt Jules, her family would haul him over the coals… Either way, the dynamic of their blended family would be changed forever and he would not be responsible for that.

He could not relinquish the little that was left of the Lockwood legacy because of one kiss, a fantasy moment. He had to save the boatyard and the marina, and now the estate, if not for him, then for his two brothers. He owed it to his mom to keep Ethan's grubby, money-grabbing paws from what was hers and, morally, theirs.

"Are you just going to sit there in silence, or do I have to guess why you are here?"

Jules's snippy voice pulled him out of the past and Noah blinked before running his hand over his face. Right. He did, actually, have a valid, business-related reason to be there.

"Congratulations on your award as the best designer in the city, Ju," Noah said. Despite his frustration with the situation, he was extraordinarily proud of her. He'd always known she was an incredibly talented designer. But he hadn't expected her and DJ and Darby to create such a successful and dynamic business in so short of a time. People said that his level of success was meteoric, he had nothing on Jules and her friends. From concept to kudos in four years, they were a phenomenal and formidable team.

"Thank you," Jules replied, her voice cool. She rolled her finger, impatient.

Right, time to sink or swim. Noah preferred to, well, sail. "I have a job for you."

Jules's small smile didn't reach her eyes. "Not interested. I'm booked solid for months."

Yeah, he'd expected that. "I'm designing a superyacht,

a bit of a departure from the racing yachts I've developed my reputation on. My client is pretty adamant that she wants you to design the interiors."

"As interesting as that project would be, I can't take on another client, Noah. It's just not possible."

Jules leaned back in her chair and crossed her legs. Her eyes were now a cool gray and Noah knew she was enjoying having him at her mercy, being able to say no. Jules was taking her revenge on him for walking out of her life and, yeah, he got it, he'd hurt her. But the hell of it was that he needed her. He needed her now more than he ever had before.

Ignoring his need to save Lockwood Estate, his reputation depended on him persuading her to say yes. Noah opened his mouth to explain, to tell her how much rested on him gaining her help and cooperation but his phone rang, stopping him in his tracks. Grateful for the reprieve, he pulled his phone out of the inside pocket of his jacket and glanced down at the screen. A once-familiar number popped up on his screen.

The thought that there was no way she'd still have the same phone number as so long ago jumped into his mind. Then he remembered that he'd had the same number all of his life.

But why would Morgan be phoning him? Confused and shocked, he shook his head and tucked his phone, the call unanswered, back into his jacket pocket. He had nothing to say to his ex and never would.

"So, as fun as this nonconversation has been, I need to get back to work," Jules said, standing up and gesturing to the door.

Noah cursed softly and pushed an irritated hand through his hair. "Ju, we need to talk. At least, I need to talk—"

Jules placed both hands on the desk and glared at him, her eyes laser cold. "No, Noah, we really don't! You don't get to walk into my office demanding my time when you walked out of my life years ago, tossing our friendship without a word of explanation. How dare you think you can demand that I work for you when you treated me like I was nothing?"

Jules shook her head, her eyes glistening with unshed tears. "I mourned you. I mourned what we had. You abandoned me, Noah. You walked away from me and our friendship like it was nothing, like I was nothing." Jules circled her desk, headed toward the door and yanked it open. She rested her forehead on the door frame, and for the first time Noah realized how much he'd hurt her. Suddenly, his heart was under the spiky heel of her shoe.

No one knew, nobody had the faintest idea, how hard it was for him to leave Boston. On the surface it had been a pretty sweet deal, he'd been offered the money he needed and he had the opportunity for travel and adventure. He was twenty-three years old and the world was his playground. But underneath the jokes and the quips, his heart wept bloody tears. He was still mourning his mom, feeling helpless and angry at her death. He was gas-fire mad with Ethan for treating her like crap and lying to them.

His stability, everything he knew was in Boston: it was in the kind eyes and solid, unpushy support of Callie and Ray, in Levi and his brothers standing at his side, not talking but being there, a solid wall between him and the world. It had been in DJ's and Darby's hugs, in their upbeat, daily text messages.

It had been everything—her smile, her understanding, her kisses, her laugh—about Jules.

Leaving meant distance, walking away from everything that made sense. It had been frickin' terrifying and, apart from burying his mom, the hardest thing he'd ever done. Sailing that tempestuous, ass-cold Southern Ocean had been child's play compared to leaving Boston. And, because he'd just barely survived leaving once, he knew he couldn't fall back into the life he had before. He wouldn't allow himself to rely on Levi's friendship, Callie's support, his brothers' wall and Jules's ability to make everything both better and brighter. Because he couldn't survive losing any of it again.

Once was ten times too many...

Jules gestured for Noah to leave. "I have a call I need to take. Clients to look after."

Noah stood up and pushed his hands through his hair. Okay, this was salvageable. He would just tell Paris that Jules wasn't available, wouldn't be for some time. This wasn't a train smash. It was business. Paris would understand that. *It was business...*

In fact, it would be better if he and Jules didn't work together. Professional wasn't something he could be around Jules.

At the door, Noah stopped in front of Jules and bent his knees to look into her spectacular eyes. He wanted to explain, to banish some of the pain he saw there. "I never meant to hurt you, Jules."

Jules looked up at him and lifted her chin, her eyes flashing defiance. "But you did, Noah. And you still haven't explained why."

He didn't do explanations. Noah sighed, dropped a quick kiss on her temple—the intoxicating scent of her filling his nose—and before his hands and mouth did something stupid, he walked away.

It was only when he reached the sidewalk that his heart started to beat normally again, when his brain regained full power.

Noah stepped off the sidewalk to hail a cab. It was a good thing Jules have didn't the time—or the inclination—to work for him; she turned his brain to mush.

Jules...

The following Saturday, Jules picked up two breakfast rolls and made her way to the marina, where she knew she could find her brother, Levi. Despite them living in the same house, it had been ages since she'd spent any time with her older brother and she was looking forward to seeing him, but she did, admittedly, have an ulterior motive. She needed him to make a steel frame for a coffee table, and Levi, or rather the newly named Lockwood-Brogan Marina, owned a welding machine.

Along with his business degree, Levi also knew how to weld and the ham-and-egg sandwich was her way to bribe him. If Levi couldn't, or wouldn't, she'd ask Eli or Ben...

All three Lockwood boys and Levi had held part-time and summer jobs at the marina, and they all knew how to use their hands; Noah's grandfather had made sure of that. As a result, she and her sisters rarely had to pay for home repairs.

Besides, the boys had frequently made their lives hell: short-sheeting their beds, hiding their dolls, scaring the crap out of them. Making them work was payback.

Jules, dressed in a pink-and-red-patterned sundress and flip-flops, walked into the blessedly cool reception area of the marina and smiled at Levi's new receptionist, Meredith. The young blonde was talking to a middle-aged couple but she smiled before lifting her chin, silently telling her that Levi was in his office. Jules nodded her thanks, walked behind the counter and down the short passage to the end office, which had a spectacular view of the marina. Levi, dark-haired and blue-eyed, had his feet up on his desk and his tablet on his knees.

"Playing 'Angry Birds'?" Jules asked, tossing his sandwich into his lap.

"You know me too well." Levi placed his tablet on his messy desk and lifted the packet to his nose. He narrowed his eyes at Jules. "Ham and egg... What do you want?"

"A frame to be welded."

Levi unwrapped his sandwich, and after taking a bite, chewing and swallowing, he shook his head. "Eli is better at welding than me. Or, better yet, he can send one of his welders from the shipyard to do it."

"But that will take forever."

Jules perched on the edge of his desk, leaving her sandwich in front of him. If necessary, she'd bribe him with the second sandwich to get her frame welded today. She batted her eyelashes at him, knowing that he loved to be adored. "Please, Lee? You have a welding machine and you're—" she gestured to his tablet "—obviously not busy. The steel bars are already in your workshop at home."

Levi glared at her. "For your information, I was going over our financials."

The note of worry in his voice caught Jules's attention. "Everything okay?"

Levi was slow to respond, but when he did, his face carried no hint of his normal good humor. "Noah and I recently bought a majority share of the marina on the waterfront and are in the process of updating the facilities. We're asset rich and cash flow tight at the moment."

"But you're okay?"

Levi nodded. "I am. The businesses are. I'm not so sure about Noah. He's seriously stressed and I know it's money related. Did you know that he wants to buy the Lockwood Country Club Estate off Ethan?"

Jules frowned, confused. "Buy it? Why would he buy it since the Lockwood Trust owns it?"

"But Ethan owns the Lockwood Trust, not Noah and the guys. Ethan was awarded the estate when the boys took Ethan to court. How do you not know this?"

Because she never talked to or about Noah?

"Did you not wonder why Noah was staying with us, why he's sleeping on the *Resilience* and not at Lockwood House?"

"Well, I did, but—" Jules ended her sentence with a shrug. "I knew Ethan and Noah had a falling-out but not much more than that. So, what happened?"

Levi held up a hand. "Ask Noah. If he wants you to know, he'll tell you."

Jules's mouth dropped open. "You don't know either!"

Levi shrugged. "Noah doesn't talk much. You know that."

She really did. "So, what do you know?" Okay, she was curious, she'd cop to that.

Levi pushed a hand through his dark hair. "The guys need to raise a cracking amount of cash in order to get a mortgage to buy the estate off Ethan. In order to do that Noah needs to finish the design on the yacht he's working on but his client is being difficult."

"Noah always delivers. That's what he's known for, what he does." Noah was exceptionally good at what he did and was reputed to be one of the best racing yacht designers in the world.

"Well, this client wants something that Noah can't deliver and if he doesn't deliver, he won't get paid. If he doesn't get paid, he can't buy Lockwood House and the estate."

My client is pretty adamant that she wants you to design the interiors. Her heart and stomach dropped to the floor as Jules remembered Noah's words in her office. Her firm "no" had put his project, buying his family house and land, in jeopardy. *God, Noah.*

Levi continued to speak. "The client isn't listening and Noah's project is up the creek. Without her cash, he can't buy the estate. Without the estate, he doesn't get Lockwood House. And you know how much the house means to him."

Yeah, she did. All his memories of his mom were tied up in that house, in the country club she managed and the land she loved.

Levi balled his wax paper and threw it into the wastepaper bin across the room. He eyed the second sandwich. "I'll do your welding this afternoon if you hand over that sandwich."

Instead of tossing him the second sandwich, she scooped it up and headed for the door. "Hey! Where are you going with that sandwich?"

At the door, Jules turned. "Is Noah using Grandpa Lockwood's old office and is he there?"

Levi nodded. "Should be. He works longer hours than I do." He sent her his patented I'm-hungry-feed-me look that was difficult to resist. But Jules had other plans for her sandwich, so she left his office and headed for the spiral staircase at the end of the hall, the one that would take her to the conference room and Noah's office.

"I'm not welding your frame without the sandwich!" Levi's words trailed after her.

She didn't care. She had a bigger problem to fix.

Four

Noah...

Noah, dressed in navy cargo shorts and a gray T-shirt under an open denim shirt, turned away from his architect's desk as she walked into his office without knocking. Standing in the doorway, she noticed his look of complete surprise before his face settled back into its inscrutable can't-faze-me expression.

"Jules. Good morning."

To hell with being polite, they were so far past that. "Why didn't you tell me that your project was in jeopardy?"

Noah lifted his broad shoulders in a weary shrug. "You're busy. I can't expect you to drop your other projects just because I asked. I thought my client was being unreasonable and that I could persuade her to consider other designers."

"Did you manage to do that?"

Noah tossed his pencil onto the desk and rubbed his fingers into his eye sockets. "Nope."

"So I'm it or you lose the project?"

Noah twisted his lips and finally nodded. "Basically." He lifted a hand. "Don't worry about it, Jules. I have other clients who have been begging me to design racing yachts. It's not a big deal."

Jules leaned her shoulder into the door frame. "But if you lose this project, you lose all your work and also the ability to buy back Lockwood House and everything else."

"Levi and his big mouth. I'll make a plan. If I don't buy it this time around, I'll wait until it comes back on the market and buy it then. For the first time since 1870 it'll leave Lockwood hands, but I'll get it back."

Jules saw the determination in his eyes. He would eventually take back his family's legacy but at what price? God, he'd already lost his mom and his home, was it fair that he lose this opportunity, too? Who knew when he'd get the chance to purchase Lockwood Estate again, if ever?

A management company ran the country club and estate but Jules couldn't bear the thought of another family owning and living in Beth's beloved and historic house; they might add on, rip it down, change it. No, a Lockwood deserved to live there or at the very least, the house should remain empty until one of the brothers decided he was going to move back in.

She hadn't recognized the consequences of her decision, because Noah hadn't told her, and she could kick him for that. If she'd known, she wouldn't have hesitated. This affected not only Noah but Eli and Ben, and her refusal to help felt like she was letting Bethann and her sons down. Yes, she was busy, but she could delegate work to her assistants and carve out some time for the project.

Jules walked into his office, dumped her bag onto his chair and placed the sandwich on his mostly empty desk. She couldn't eat; this was too important. But he might be hungry.

"Eat up, and when you're done, we'll go over the design brief."

Noah sent her a hard stare. "You're going to take the job?"

Jules rolled her eyes so hard that she was sure she could see her butt. "Of course I am."

"Why?" Noah demanded, his eyes wary.

"Because, as annoying as you are, you and that house are a part of my family, and family steps up when there's a problem. You need this job to be able to buy that house, and to raise the money to do that, you need me. There's no way that I am going to be responsible for the estate passing out of Lockwood hands. Bethann might start haunting me."

"It's a strong possibility and something I'm also worried about."

Noah looked down and, judging by the way his shoulders dropped, Jules knew he was trying to hide his relief. He hated anyone to see that he was worried, to think that he was weak. He liked the world to think that he was a tough-guy sailor, one who took enormous risks with aplomb, conquered high waves with a whoop and a yell, and he liked them to think that he did it with ease. Jules was the only person, apart from maybe her parents, who'd glimpsed the turmoil roiling inside of him.

But Jules, as always, saw more than she should and, standing in his office, in front of this delicious-looking man, she sensed the tension seeping from him, could taste his relief. And suddenly, weirdly, she wanted to put her arms around his waist, lay her head on his chest and tell him that it would be all right. That they would be all right. But, as much as she wanted to do that, she couldn't.

She'd trusted Noah once, trusted him with her deepest fears and feelings, her innermost thoughts. But he'd dismissed her, abandoned their friendship and ignored her.

No, she couldn't allow herself to be seduced by memories, to fall back into that space where the world was a brighter, better place with Noah in it. He was her client, sort of, and she had a job to do. This would be business and only business. She could never regain what was lost.

She'd work with Noah, give him her best effort but she'd never ever trust him again.

"Thanks, Jules. But before you accept, there's something else you should know."

That didn't sound good… Noah pulled in a deep breath before dropping his conversational grenade. "My client thinks that we're dating."

"Sorry?"

"She thinks you are my girlfriend, lover… Call it what you will."

Jules stared at him, her insides feeling like they were on a roller-coaster ride. His girlfriend? Why would his client think that? And why did the idea of being with Noah, tall, built and ripped, send shivers of…well, lust, up and back down her spine? What was wrong with her?

And, oh, Lord, being alone with him was an exercise in restraint. Yeah, she was still angry that he'd walked out on her, that he ignored her for years—no, she wasn't angry, she was hurt—but, worse than that, she was on fire, inside and out. Jules licked her lips and then swallowed, trying to get some moisture back into her mouth. Between her legs, an ancient drumbeat thrummed and her nipples pushed against the fabric of her pretty lace bra.

Just because Noah mentioned that someone thought that they were lovers. Ridiculous to the nth degree.

Jules dropped her eyes from his chest, allowed them to bounce off his muscled thighs before staring at the black and brown slate tiles that covered his office floor. She shouldn't be thinking about how attractive she found him. She had bigger problems than that to deal with. Like the fact that his client thought they were dating.

Uh…why would their client think they were dating?

Jules's eyes darted up to meet his, her eyebrows rising. "Want to explain how I went from being your designer to your girlfriend?"

Noah looked equally frustrated. "She was trying to set me up with…someone, so I said that I have a girlfriend. She asked who she was, your name was the first name that popped into my head."

Really? Surely he had a dozen names he could've thrown at his client. Noah was a good-looking, sexy, moderately famous and very successful guy. He had to have an encyclopedia-size black book of eligible candidates suitable to be his arm candy, so why did her name leave his lips?

"Because this is Boston, which is in some ways a ludicrously small town, she recognized your name and got all excited, insisting that she knew you and your work and that she wanted no one else to design her interiors."

Well, she'd made an impression on someone. A rich someone who had the money to buy a phenomenally expensive yacht. "As long as your client isn't Paris Barrow. I'm prepared to work with anyone but her."

Noah closed his eyes and Jules groaned her dismay. No! Why was the universe torturing her? She not only had to work with her oldest friend who now made all her hormones jump, but she also had to work with the client from hell? Paris wasn't mean but she found it hard to make a decision and stick to it. One day it was pastels, the next earth tones, a week later it was the colors of the Mediterranean. Wood, then steel, then ceramic, then a combination of all three.

Paris lived in her own world, surrounded by people whose mission in life was to make her happy. What Paris wanted, Paris got. Even if that meant changing her mind a hundred times.

She was a deliciously sweet, generous nightmare of epic proportions.

And, worse than that, she was incredibly nosy and horribly romantic. Married multiple times, widowed once, each and every one of her husbands was the love of her life. She was, so Jules heard, on the lookout for husband number six. Paris wouldn't be content with the idea of her and Noah just dating. Before she could blink twice, Paris would have them engaged and booking a church.

Jules tossed up her hands. "Uh-uh, no way. Not Paris Barrow, you're on your own."

Noah smiled, flashing white teeth. "Chicken," he murmured.

Jules hopped off her stool and slapped her hands on her hips. "She's like a walking, talking dating show! Everyone around her drops like flies when she comes into their lives."

Noah lifted an eyebrow. "Dead?"

Jules waved her hands to dismiss his words. "No! They fall in love, get married, get engaged. She's, again, a walking, talking bottle of fairy dust! And you told her that we're dating?"

"No, I told her that you were my girlfriend. One step up," Noah replied, very unhelpfully.

"Oh, God. She's going to harass us about the fact that we're not engaged, not married. Paris is a staunch proponent of buying the cow before you drink the milk."

Noah's low laugh danced over her skin. "I think you're making too big a deal about this, Ju. We pretend to be lovers, she harasses us a little, we resist. It's all good."

Jules sent him a dark look. "You have no idea what you're dealing with."

Noah folded his arms and his biceps pulled the fabric of his shirt tighter. Jules sighed, he had the sexiest arms she'd ever seen. Bar none. Noah's brown eyes turned serious. "Is our dating going to be a problem for you?"

For some reason Jules wanted to reassure him that there wasn't anybody in her life who caught her interest. Except him. Since he'd walked back into her office, into her life, she couldn't stop thinking about him, wondering how he tasted, whether his strength would be a counter to her softness, whether they'd be the perfect fit she imagined.

More than the physical attraction, there was a part of her that wished she could go back, to reexplore their closeness, to plumb his mind. She'd enjoyed the way he thought, his analytical brain, the tenderness beneath the suit of armor he wore. The combination of attraction and friendship was lethal. It could lead to more than she was ready for, for much more than she could deal with. No, she could not go back to what they had; it was dead. She couldn't risk having Noah in her life again and losing him.

It had nearly broken her once. There was no way she'd give him the power to do that again.

As for her attraction to him? She was a normal woman in her late twenties with needs, sexual needs, that had been long neglected. Noah was a gorgeous specimen and very capable of assuaging those needs. Her attraction to him was a simple combination of horniness and nostalgia and curiosity. It didn't mean anything; it couldn't mean anything.

He was a family friend, no more, no less.

A family friend with sexy arms, muscled shoulders and strong, strong legs. And a face that he could've inherited from a fallen angel.

Crap.

"Jules? Is your dating going to pose a problem to us working together? To acting like my other half around Paris?"

Jules blinked and shook her head, pulling her attention back to his question. "No, not at all. I'm not in a relationship with anyone."

"Okay, good. To keep things simple, I suggest that we never meet with Paris together, that one or the other deals with her, you on the interiors, me on the design."

Jules thought that he was onto something. There was no point in giving Paris any ammunition. And this way, Paris couldn't comment on their relationship. Or nonrelationship. Or, to put it another way, lie.

"That sounds like a plan," Jules agreed. "When does she want to meet with me?"

"As soon as possible, this week if we can arrange a time. Paris has a habit of forgetting meetings and darting off to Madrid or Mexico."

Yeah, she was familiar with the socialite's modus operandi. When Jules had designed her house, she'd have workmen waiting to start, waiting for Paris's final approval only to find that the blasted woman was at a spa in Monte Carlo.

One step at a time, Jules thought. "Let's start with what you imagine the interior of the yacht to look like."

"You don't want to get a brief from the client?" Noah asked, surprised.

"Normally I would, but Paris changes her mind on a minute-by-minute basis. Trust me, she's easier to handle if you don't give her the whole box of crayons to play with."

Jules walked over to her tote bag and bent over the side of the chair to pull a sketchbook from its depths and thought she heard a low groan from behind her. When she whipped her head around, she saw Noah staring at the floor, his clenched fist resting on his thigh. "You okay?" she asked, heading back toward his desk.

Noah's eyes flew up and Jules almost took a step back at the leashed power in his gaze. He rose, slowly and deliberately, and the air in the room disappeared. That power she saw on his face, in his eyes, was pure, undiluted desire. For her.

Holy hell.

The sketchbook slipped from her fingers as Noah's hands gripped her hips, as his masculine, fresh scent hit her nostrils and her chest banged against his. She couldn't stop her body's instinctive move to push her breasts into his chest, her hips aligned with his and… Yeah. There it was. Long. And hard. All for her.

Using her last few remaining brain cells, Jules slapped her hand against his chest, trying but failing to push him away.

"If you're going to be my fake girlfriend, I want one real kiss."

"Not a good idea, Noah."

"Screw good ideas," Noah whispered, his mouth descending to hers. His words whispered over her lips, and his eyes bored into hers. "Every time I've seen you since I came back, I've wanted to kiss you. It's bizarre but I keep wanting to check whether I imagined the power in our kiss. I don't sail much anymore, Ju, and kissing you is the closest I've come for months to feeling that same adrenaline."

God, how was she supposed to resist? He was all man, so sexy, and in his arms she was the woman she'd always wanted to be. Strong, sexy, powerful, feminine. But they shouldn't be doing this, it so wasn't a good idea...

Noah's mouth on hers kicked that thought away and all Jules could think about, take in, was that Noah was kissing her. He kissed like a man in his prime should, a man who was fully confident with who he was and how to make a woman feel incredible. He took and devoured, and just when she thought she might dissolve into a heap of pure pleasure, he toned it down, went soft and sexy, tender. He built her up, eased off, built her up again.

Sexually frustrating but soul-tinglingly wonderful. This...*this* was what she'd been missing from every other man who'd held her, kissed her. None of them made her core throb, her heart liquefy. No man before him made her feel intensely feminine, indescribably powerful yet, simultaneously, willing to be sheltered and protected. He made her feel everything she should.

Everything that she shouldn't.

She should step away and if he'd been demanding or insistent Jules might've done that, but Noah's hands didn't move from her hips, he didn't push his erection into her, didn't bump or grind. He just used his tongue and lips and, yeah, his teeth to maximum effect. Man, he was good.

Jules had no reservations about touching him, freely allowing her hands to sneak up under his shirt, exploring the thick muscles of his back, the ridges of his stomach, his flat, masculine nipples, the trail of hair that led down, down. She avoided his shaft, knowing that if she touched him there, if he touched her breast or between her legs, they would be making love in front of a clear window looking out to a busy marina.

But, damn, she was tempted...

Noah groaned deep in his throat, his mouth eased off hers and then his forehead was against hers, his eyes closed. "Crap," he muttered.

Crap indeed. Jules knew what he was thinking, he didn't need to voice the words. Like her, a part of him kept hoping that the attraction that had flared to life so long ago would dissipate at some point but... No.

It was still there. Hotter and brighter than before.

Noah's fingers dug into her hips. "Being your boyfriend and not being able to have the benefits of the title is going to be harder than I thought."

Because she was on the point of saying "To hell with it, let's get naked," Jules forced herself to step back and pushed her hand into her hair. "That shouldn't have happened. Nothing is going to happen, Noah."

Maybe if she kept saying it often enough the thought would sink into their stubborn heads.

Noah used one finger to push a curl off her cheek. "It just did, Ju. We can't deny that there's something bubbling here."

"I wasn't going to deny that. But we're not going there, Noah," Jules said, feeling that familiar wave of stubbornness sweep over her.

"Why not? We're adults. It doesn't have to mean anything."

Jules nailed him to the floor with a hard look. "Sex might not mean anything to you, Noah, but it does to me. It's not a way to scratch an itch, a way to pass some time." She shrugged. "I only share my body with men

I can trust, Noah. And, unfortunately, you're not that man anymore."

Jules ignored the flash of emotion she saw in his eyes, determined to ignore her inner voice that insisted that she'd hurt him, and bent down to pick her sketchbook off the floor. Holding it against her chest, she rocked on her heels. "I think we need some time to wrap our heads around the events of this morning."

She needed some distance from him, from the passion still swirling between them. "I'm going to go, but if you can send me the yacht's blueprints, I can put something together and we can thrash out a proposal to present to Paris."

Noah rubbed the back of his head and nodded. "Sounds like a plan."

Jules was grateful he didn't argue. "And when we meet again, it will be as professionals, Noah. This can't happen again."

It was Noah's turn to look stubborn. And frustrated. Jules could relate. "I can't just act like I'm not attracted to you, Jules, nor can I forget that you were once my best friend. I can't treat you like just a colleague."

Jules pulled her bag over her shoulder as sadness wrapped its cold self around her heart. "When you chose to walk out on us, on our friendship, you made anything deeper impossible, Noah. You neither gave our attraction, nor our friendship, a chance. I tried to salvage what we had, you didn't even meet me halfway. It was your choice, Noah, and you have to live with the consequences."

Jules, feeling sick and sad and, dammit, totally sexually frustrated, walked to the door. "I'll call you when I have something to show you."

Jules forced her feet to walk out the door, down the hallway. She just managed to throw a cheerful "'bye" to Levi and wave to Meredith. It was only when she passed through the access control gate and pulled her sunglasses over her eyes that she allowed a few annoying tears to escape.

She thought she was done crying over Lockwood, dammit.

Darby pushed her shoulder into the doorjamb and Jules met her eyes in the long freestanding mirror. Her sister was dislodging strands of hair from her messy bun every time her head moved. Dressed in low-slung sweats and a tank top, Darby shouldn't have looked so damn gorgeous, but she did. Her fraternal twin could wear a burlap sack and make it look like haute couture.

"So, another date?" Darby asked, her wide smile in place but her eyes showing concern.

"Nothing serious. Robert has been bugging me to have dinner with him for a while so I called him up and told him I was free tonight." She'd dated Robert the year before Noah left. He'd always been far more invested in their relationship than she was and Jules had hurt him when she'd finally called it quits. He was a nice guy, a kind, gentle man who'd been her first real boyfriend and her first lover.

"I thought you said you weren't going to go to dinner with him, that you didn't want him to think that there was any chance of you hooking up again."

That was before Noah returned and placed her heart, mind and body on a Tilt-A-Whirl. Jules refused to meet Darby's eyes. Hell, she was having trouble meeting her own. The only reason she called Rob was because she wanted to feel back in control, on firm footing and, because she was hoping for a miracle, a little part of her prayed that she'd look at him and magically fall in love with him. She knew Rob, knew how to handle him, what to expect. With Rob she'd be in control. He was safe and predictable...

Everything that Noah Lockwood wasn't. God, she was so pathetic.

Embarrassed at her behavior and her lack of maturity, Jules didn't answer her twin. She had to pull herself together, dammit!

Darby walked into Jules's bedroom and sat down on the end of her king-size bed, covered in blindingly white linen. Darby pulled her legs up and wrapped her arms around her knees, her slate-gray eyes curious.

"Where did you disappear to today?"

"I just needed some alone time."

After leaving Noah's office, Jules had needed to walk and then to run. Because she always kept a fresh set of gym clothes in a bag in the trunk of her car, she'd decided to head out of town to the Blue Hills Reservation to work out her frustration on a long trail run. After doing eight miles, she'd spent the rest of the afternoon sitting on the bank of the pond.

She'd kissed Noah. And she'd more than liked it. Holding her pencil in her hand, her sketchbook on her lap, she'd stared at the scenery, not seeing much beyond the blue sky and the forest. She was more interested in the movie playing in her head...his masculine, fresh-tasting mouth doing crazy things to hers, his strong body pressed up against hers, his warm male skin under her fingertips, the sounds of approval and desire he made deep in his throat. She hadn't been able to stop thinking about what they did, his hard body and what it all meant.

And when she couldn't think about that anymore, when those thoughts became too overwhelming, she allowed herself to wander back in time, to sitting on her parents' roof with Noah, talking about anything and everything. The goofy text messages they exchanged, the way their eyes would cut to each other as they shared a joke no one else was privy to. She was extremely close to Darby and to DJ but Noah understood her on a fundamental level they didn't.

What could these kisses, the intense attraction between them mean? Where was this going, what were they trying to be? Jules looked at her twin, unable to tell her sister—the person she shared everything with—how close she'd come to begging Noah to do wild and wicked things to her on the floor of his office. How she was both horrified and thrilled by the let's-get-naked-immediately thoughts that bombarded her whenever Noah stepped into a room.

"Jules, talk to me."

She couldn't, not today. Her feelings for Noah, her need and her resistance were too overwhelming to be discussed. But, because she was obligated to inform Darby of any developments in the business, and because it was a good way to change the subject, she could tell her about Paris. "I took on a new client today."

Darby looked surprised. "You don't have time for a new client."

So true. "It's Noah. His new client wants me to design the interiors of her yacht, is insisting upon it. My involvement has become a deal breaker so I said yes."

"I didn't think Noah could be pushed around."

So only Levi knew about the turmoil between Ethan and his stepsons? Jules wanted to explain the situation to Darby but it wasn't her tale to tell. She'd always kept

Noah's secrets—the few he shared with her—and always would. "This project is important to him."

Darby shrugged. "It's your call, Jules, but be careful of burning yourself out. You are working extremely long hours as it is."

Jules knew Darby was mentally measuring her stress levels, whether she'd lost or gained weight, whether she was as healthy as Darby wanted her to be. A college basketball player and a sports fanatic—she'd moved on from triathlons and was now into CrossFit—Darby was a health nut. Her twin no longer ate processed food and most carbs or drank coffee. She'd also stopped eating chocolate! Chocolate, for God's sake!

Jules didn't know how she got through the day.

"Blow Robert off, Jules, and come to The Tavern with us."

"That would be rude." And being in The Tavern would make her think of all the fun nights she'd spent there with Noah. Plus there was a good chance that Levi or his brothers would drag him to the bar tonight and she'd spend the evening trying not to beg him to take her to bed. The day had been long and hard enough as it was.

"May I point out that you only ever run away when you don't want to talk, and the only time you don't want to talk is when you are confused? And the only time I've seen you confused about a man is with Noah. So, did he kiss you or what?"

In the mirror, Jules watched herself turn a bright shade of tomato red. *Ah, crap.* How could she lie now?

Darby approached her from behind and wrapped her arms around her waist. Bending down, Darby rested her chin on Jules's shoulder. In the mirror, gray eyes met pure silver. Darby shook her head, a small smile touching her lips.

Darby was looking inside her and reading all her unspoken thoughts. "It's just an attraction, twin."

Darby squeezed her gently. "I'd believe that if there wasn't a whole lot of substance beneath the sexy. And you both have it in spades."

Five

Noah...

Being back in The Tavern was like revisiting his youth. Nothing about the upmarket bar had changed in the years Noah had been gone. The staff still wore white shirts, black pants and red aprons, there were still the same elegant black-and-white photographs of Italy from the '50s and '60s on the wall, and Dom, the head bartender, was still behind the bar, a little grayer, a little fatter, just as attentive. Noah recognized a few of the patrons and knew that, as Bethann's son, most recognized him. Grandpa Lockwood might've conceived the idea of the country club, but his mom had developed the estate's facilities and she built and designed the two restaurants, this bar, the gym and the handful of shops to serve the estate which now, cleverly, included a coffee shop serving light meals.

Being back at The Tavern with his brothers, Levi, DJ

and Darby was so normal and, damn, it was good to feel normal again, to be wearing faded blue jeans instead of designer pants, flat-heeled boots and a T-shirt instead of an expensive button-down and loafers. The bar inside the club had a stricter dress code—business casual—but this was a place for the residents to relax, to blow off steam. In here he wasn't the professional sailor or the yacht designer; there was no one he needed to impress.

Everything he enjoyed most—the cold beers, good music, easy laughter and companionship of people he'd known all his life—was in this room.

Well, except for Jules.

Noah took a sip of his beer and looked across the room, idly watching Dom pour red wine into a glass. He wanted to go back in time, to when Dom was younger, to before he understood Ethan was more concerned about money than his stepsons. He wanted to rewind to when Jules looked at him like he was a superhero, when he was young and blissfully unaware of the crap storm coming his way.

While it felt wrong for Jules not to be there, a part of him was grateful. Since kissing her this morning he'd been unable to concentrate, to focus. He'd tried to distract himself by having lunch with Eli and Ben, and Ben's latest blonde. He'd exchanged eye rolls with Eli at her baby-girl voice and take-care-of-me-big-boy attitude. Because they were in company, they avoided talking business and it was a relief to delay telling his brothers he was working with Jules. There would've been questions: Are you friends again? What happened to cause the great rift? Did you behave like a dick? What did you do to piss her off?

He'd have to have a conversation with them about Jules at some point. He might only be in Boston for a short period but none of them—because the Lockwoods were one of Boston's founding families and because Callie and Ray had been most A-listy of A-list couples—were low profile. Before one of them heard the red-hot gossip that he and Jules were dating, he needed to give them a heads-up and, at the very least, some sort of explanation.

Hell, they wouldn't have to wait to hear the gossip, put him and Jules within ten feet of each other and sparks flew. And that would raise more questions and speculation…

The best way to douse those sparks would be to avoid her, but that was impossible. Apart from the so-called fact that they were "dating," they were also now working together; he'd sent Paris an email confirming Jules's commitment to the project. While he was in Boston the next month or two, and because his friends and family were hers, they were going to be living in each other's pockets. And trying to keep his hands and mouth off her was something he didn't seem to be able to master. Kissing her wasn't nearly enough… Limiting himself to a few kisses was like giving a drunk the smallest sip of whiskey, waving the glass in front of his nose while keeping his hands bound to his sides.

Having Jules, kissing Jules and not being able to take it to its natural conclusion was a cruel and unusual punishment.

Speaking of punishments…he'd never grasped how much he'd hurt Jules, how much his departure had affected her. He'd been so caught up in his own grief, misery and, yeah, homesickness that he couldn't think about those he left behind. Apart from the odd email and phone call back home, he focused all his attention on the present, on winning his races, being the best damn sailor he could be. Emotional distance, the ability to step away from a situation and focus, became a habit. Those traits, and the need to keep busy, kept him winning races, as many as possible as soon as possible.

Winning, disconnecting, moving forward was an entrenched habit, but here in Boston he was battling to connect with his cool, rational, thinking side. He had Jules to thank for that.

Levi jammed the end of a pool cue into his side. "Can you, at the very least, acknowledge that I'm kicking your ass?"

Noah looked at the pool table and cursed. Only a few balls remained, and if Levi sunk those, he'd be handing over some cash. He was out of practice.

Levi bent over the pool table, eyeing his shot. Noah was surprised when he lifted his eyes to lock with his. "Anything I need to know about? You seem distracted."

He could lie but this was Levi. He could justify not telling his brothers—they were younger than him and this was none of their business—but Levi was Jules's brother. And a protective one at that. If he was going to open this can of worms, it had might as well be now.

"Just the past smacking me in the face." Noah lifted his beer bottle to his lips. "This life is very different from the one I've been leading."

"High-end clients and cocktails," Levi said after taking his shot, the five ball rolling into the far right pocket. Damn.

"Pretty much," Noah agreed. "This, a simple evening playing pool with my mates, is something I haven't done in years."

"Your fault, not ours," Levi said with his characteristic bluntness. "We were here."

He couldn't argue with that. Noah put his beer bottle onto the high table and rested his hands on the top of the cue. He needed to say this, had to get it out. "Lee, Jules and I—"

Levi held up a hand and his face turned dark. "Oh, hell, no! I don't want to know."

And he didn't want to spit the words out but he had to give Levi a heads-up, he owed him that much. But how to gently tell him that he wanted his sister with a ferocity that terrified him was turning out to be harder than he thought. He mentally tested a few phrases but none of them sounded right and all of them would end up with him sporting a broken nose. So he settled for simple. "Paris Barrow thinks we are dating—long story—but I should tell you that something is cooking between us."

Levi rolled his eyes. "That's the best you can do?"

"I'm trying to avoid a trip to the emergency room," Noah admitted. "So, yeah, that's all I can say."

Levi stared at him while he made sense of that statement. When he did, his expression darkened. "I need brain bleach." Levi bent over his cue again, stood up to speak and bent down again, frustration radiating off him in waves.

He stood up, tossed the cue on the table, dislodging the few remaining balls. "Crap, Noah! She's my sister and you are my oldest friend. I should punch you just for looking at her, but then you might piss off again and we might not see you for another decade!"

Underneath the frustration he heard anger and, worse, hurt. His absence hadn't only affected Jules, it had touched Levi, as well. And, he surmised, Eli and Ben and, to a lesser extent, DJ and Darby.

He didn't even want to know what Callie thought about his time away...

Levi's punch to his shoulder packed restrained power and rocked Noah back onto his heels. "Don't mess this up,

Noah. You hurt her and we'll have words. We're partners and that will make for a tough atmosphere. Be very, very careful, because one wrong move will have consequences."

He knew that. God, he wasn't an idiot.

"Thanks for spoiling the game and my mood, dude," Levi said and stomped off toward the bar.

Crap. *Good job, Lockwood.* His phone vibrated and when he pulled it out of his pocket, he read the name on his screen. Morgan. Dammit.

Hi. Where are you? Would you like to get together for a drink for old times' sake?

It took Noah two seconds to type out a solid, in caps NO. After pressing Send, he shut his phone down and slipped it back into the pocket of his jeans. Not now. Not ever.

He'd rather chew his wrists off than allow her back into his life. The fact that she was spectacularly beautiful and amazingly good at sex had confused his twenty-three-year-old brain and he'd stayed with her far longer than he should have. Jules had detested her from the moment they met and the feeling had been mutual. Trying to juggle his best friend and girlfriend had been a pain in his ass. But as time went on, the sex became wilder and Morgan became clingier, and Jules more disparaging about their relationship.

Fresh air wafted toward him and Noah turned to look at the open door. All rational thought evaporated as he took in Jules's teeny-tiny dress and ice-pick heels that made her legs look longer than should be legal. Black material skimmed her curves and fell from a round neck over perfect breasts, leaving those creamy shoulders and toned arms bare.

Not knowing whether he could take much more, Noah lifted his eyes to her perfectly made-up face, her extraordinary eyes dominating the rest of her features. Her mouth, frequently ignored because her eyes were so startling, was covered in a light gloss and he wanted to pull that plump bottom lip between his teeth. She'd subdued her hair into some wispy, complicated roll, and diamond studs glinted in her earlobes.

Mine, his body shouted. *Mine! Mine! Mine!*

Calm the hell down, caveman, his brain replied. *You don't believe in love, or commitment.* And, as he'd learned from his mom and Ethan, love made people act foolishly and lose control. He had no intention of following in their footsteps. He was more than happy to learn from the mistakes of others.

So, instead of walking over to her, throwing her over his shoulder and kissing her until she screamed with pleasure, he turned at the sound of amused female laughter and looked into DJ's lovely face.

DJ grinned. "Watching you two has always been one of my favorite forms of entertainment."

Jules...

Jules stepped into the always busy bar and instinctively made her way to the back right-hand corner, where the gang always made themselves at home. Yep, they were all there. Darby was leaning across a pool table, about to make an impossible shot, Eli was looking resigned at losing some more money to her, and Levi and DJ had their backs to the wall, beer in their hands. Ben was wedged between two blondes at the bar and he didn't look like he wanted, or needed, rescuing.

Same old, same old...

Jules wove her way between the tables, greeted a few regulars and smiled at Dom behind the bar. Then she looked back to the billiards area and her heart belly flopped when she noticed Noah standing in the shadows, looking hot. He was the reason she'd rushed through her dinner with the still-pleasant Rob, the reason she'd kept checking her watch. Noah was the reason she steered her car here instead of heading home. She was a pigeon and he was her homing device.

Because that thought annoyed and irritated her, Jules indulged her inner toddler and ignored Noah, pretending not to notice the way his broad shoulders filled out that designer T-shirt, the way his jeans clung to his muscular thighs and outlined his impressive package perfectly. Before Noah, her eyes had never dropped below a guy's belt. Jules's cheeks heated and she closed her eyes, mortified.

Only Noah could make her feel so out-of-control crazy.

As if he could feel her eyes on him, Noah swiveled his head and their gazes collided, a million unspoken thoughts arcing between them. Jules, because she could read him so well, managed to decipher a few heading her way. *I want you. I missed you. God, you're hot. This is complicated.*

Did he still have the ability to read her eyes? Would he be able to discern that she was terrified of what him returning to Boston meant, scared that he would hurt her again? Would he see her wishes that they could go back, that he would kiss her again, that he would show her how spectacular sex could be?

The flash of awareness in Noah's eyes told her that he received her this-is-crazy-and-we-should-stop messages.

They really should. Jules watched Noah approach her and desperately wanted to thread her fingers into that

thick hair, feel that blond stubble against her lips, feel
him rock himself against her core.

What they should do and what they were going to do
were two vastly different things.

Noah...

Noah handed Jules a G&T, heard her quiet thank-you
and leaned his shoulder into the same wall Jules had
her back against. She smelled fantastic, but beneath her
smoky eyes and expertly applied makeup, she looked
frazzled. And exhausted.

Like him, she was working long hours and if she was
going home to lie awake fantasizing about how they
would burn up the sheets, he could sympathize. When
he finally fell asleep on those long nights, he often woke
up with a hard-on from hell, his mind full of her, throbbing with need.

God, he was so tired of solo sex.

"Darby looks like she's cleaning up," Noah said, trying to distract himself from images of Jules naked, under
and on top of him. "When did she get so good at pool?"

Jules smiled and he saw the kid she used to be, fun
loving and so damn naughty. "Darby dated a pool player
in college and she spent hours being coached by him. She
said it was the only way she could get any of his attention. As a result, she got really good at it. And Deej and
I are really grateful for her skill."

There was more to this story. "Okay. Why?"

"Throughout college Darby hustled guys who assumed
she was just a pretty face and her winnings always funded
our bar bill. Some of her bigger bets also paid for a few
beach and skiing weekends away." Jules took a sip of her
drink and smiled. "As you know, Mom and Dad put us

on a budget. If we wanted money to party and play, we had to work for it."

For all their worth, and it had been considerable, Ray and Callie believed in making their kids work for their money. His mom learned that from them, too; he and his brothers were expected to work at the club as golf caddies or, while he was alive, for Grandpa Lockwood at the marina. At the time he'd resented putting in the effort, but those long summers spent busting his butt taught him the value of hard work. He couldn't have achieved his sailing and financial success without knowing how to put his head down and graft. Jules wouldn't have built a business without it either.

If he ever had kids, it would be a lesson he'd pass on.

Except having kids, getting married—or getting married and having kids—wasn't part of his plan. Designing Paris's yacht, buying back this estate and leaving Boston was. Jules wasn't part of the plan either. Noah looked at his watch and saw that it was nearly midnight. He hadn't planned on staying this late and had work he wanted to complete tonight, but when Jules arrived, he knew he wasn't going anywhere. Standing next to her, breathing in her scent, was where he most wanted to be.

And staying later meant more drinks and he was pretty sure that he was close to the limit. Damn, he wouldn't be driving himself home tonight and that meant either asking one of his brothers for a lift. Except that Eli had left Darby to talk to a redhead in the corner and Ben was… Well, Ben was gone—so that meant he would be catching a cab.

Noah pulled his phone out of his back pocket and powered it up. After he plugged in his code, his phone lit up like a Roman candle on the Fourth of July.

"You're a popular guy," Jules said, and he heard the

snark in her voice. The possibility of her being jealous gave him an unexpected thrill.

Noah stifled a smile and scrolled through his messages. One from Paris, a few from his team back in London and four, five, seven from Morgan. "Crap on a cracker," Noah muttered, scowling.

"Problem?" Jules asked, lifting her finely arched eyebrow.

Having nothing to hide, he held up his phone so that she could see his screen and the various missed calls and notifications from his ex.

"Wow," Jules said, eyes widening.

"Yeah, did I tell you that the reason I named you as my girlfriend was because Morgan has put it out there that she wants us to get back together?"

Jules dropped her head and ran her finger around the rim of her glass. "Is that a possibility?" she asked quietly.

"I'd rather get smacked repeatedly in the teeth by a flying boom," Noah stated flatly.

There was that small smile, the one he'd been looking for. Jules lifted her head and he saw the relief in her eyes, and a hint of humor at his quick response. "So why does she think that's a possibility?"

"Because she's deluded?"

Jules smacked him on the arm. She thought he was being sarcastic or, worse, rude about Morgan's issues. He rubbed the back of his neck. "I wasn't joking. She actually is bipolar and she also has some other mental health problems. Her dad described her to me as being 'emotionally fragile.'"

He'd been thinking about calling it off when Morgan had had her first proper meltdown, staying in bed for two weeks, not eating or drinking or, God, bathing. She'd bounced back from that episode and he'd decided to give her some time to recover before he broke up with her.

But every time he distanced himself, she went into a decline and he genuinely worried for her. When she was healthy, she was a fun partner and, well, yeah, the *sex*. Her skill between the sheets was partly to blame—along with too much whiskey—for him agreeing to even entertain the idea of commitment.

Her father had worked fast, offering him exactly what he needed when he most needed it. Two years passed and when he was released from his sponsorship deal with Wind and Solar, the first thing he did was visit Morgan and formally end their engagement. Why he bothered, he didn't know since they were both leading very separate lives. But he did the deed and a week later Ivan sent him a brief text message stating that Morgan was in the hospital and that they both blamed him for her nervous breakdown.

He'd tried to let her down gently. He'd seen Morgan a handful of times over those two years they were supposed to be engaged and, within a month of him leaving Boston, their twice-a-week phone calls fizzled to once a month and then to one every couple of months.

He sent her the same emails he sent everyone else and Ivan paid for her to visit him in various ports as he raced, but those visits became, thank God, rarer and rarer. The cash kept coming in from Wind and Solar and he kept the few liaisons he had time for very low-key and trouble-free.

Amazing that, ten years later, when he was supposed to be so much wiser and mature, he was in another fake relationship, but this time with Jules. Maybe life was finally realizing a fake relationship was all he was capable of.

Jules, as he expected her to, looked shocked. "Wow. That's… Wow." It took a moment but then her natural curiosity and frankness reasserted itself. "I still don't understand why you became engaged to her. I know you didn't love her—" Jules's eyes dropped from his and he saw her swallow "—like that."

He'd never loved a woman, not like that. And he never wanted to. What could be worse than thinking someone loved you, lived and would die for you, only to find out that you'd been played for a fool and what you thought was love was something else? The concept of love was too nebulous, too open to interpretation.

Jules looked like she was waiting for an answer and Noah wasn't sure how to respond. Reticence was a habit he couldn't break, not even with Jules. Besides, his fake engagement to Morgan wasn't exactly something he was proud of but it had been the best choice at the time. "There were reasons, Jules. Can we leave it at that?"

Jules's chest rose and fell, and when she finally lifted her face to look at him, he saw profound sadness in her eyes. She opened her mouth to speak but then shook her head and remained silent. He shouldn't ask but the words left his mouth despite his best intentions. "What were you about to say, Ju?"

Jules scraped the last of the gloss off her bottom lip with her teeth. Then she bobbed one shoulder. "I was just thinking that we used to tell each other everything but then I realized that wasn't true. I used to tell you everything but you didn't reciprocate. You were very selective with what you wanted me to know and, as an adult, I can recognize that now. But it still makes me sad."

God, didn't she realize that he told her more than most, that she, at one time, knew him better than anyone else? "I did talk to you, Jules. As much as I could," he quickly added as a qualifier. "Besides, talking about boyfriends and how mean or unreasonable our parents were wasn't exactly life-and-death stuff."

"It was more than that and you know it," Jules protested.

Yeah, it had been but he couldn't think about that now. Because remembering made him want to go back to when his life was uncomplicated, to that time when his mom was alive, his father loved him and life was golden. His biggest worries were what amateur race to enter next, getting his assignments in on time, dating that cute blonde in his marine systems class.

"Whatever it was, we can't go back, Jules. We have to deal with the here and now," Noah said. God, he was tired and, yeah, sad. This was the downside to being back in Boston, hanging out with his family and people who knew him well. He couldn't insulate himself from emotion, distance himself when conversation turned personal.

It wasn't easy to do when he was talking to someone who'd lived across the road for most of his life. He'd desired other women, of course he had—he was in his thirties and had always enjoyed a healthy sex life—but there had never been anyone whom he thought about constantly, whom he, let's call it what it was, *obsessed* over. Even in his teens he'd never spent this amount of emotional energy thinking about a girl.

He was so completely and utterly screwed. And because he was on the point of saying to hell with it and throwing caution to the wind—and his obsession at her feet—he thought that it might be a good idea if he took his ass back to his boat.

Yep, Eli was on his way out with that redhead, so his only options were a taxi or to sleep on the couch at Jules's house. Not that he would sleep knowing that Jules was upstairs, in that comfortable bed…

An expensive cab ride it was, then.

Super.

Six

Jules...

Jules sat in Noah's visitor's chair and propped her bare feet up on his cluttered desk. Leaving her sketch pad on her knees, she dropped her thick pencil on top of the pristine paper and lifted her arms to gather her hair and twist it into a knot. She picked up a lime-green pencil from the small table next to her elbow and jammed it into her hair, working the pencil in to keep it all up.

She darted a look at Noah sitting at his high desk, black-framed glasses resting on the bridge of his nose. His brow furrowed in concentration as his hand flew between his notepad and a desktop calculator. Every now and again, he scribbled something on the plans spread out in front of him.

Hot damn, sailor. Or a hot sailor, damn. Both worked in Noah's case.

Seeing that Noah was concentrating on his blueprints, Jules pushed her hands under the large sketch pad and pulled her tight skirt up her thighs so that she didn't feel like she was sitting in a fabric tube. An improvement, she thought. Jeans or jammies would be miles better but she'd left the Brogan and Winston offices earlier that day to meet Noah and Paris at Joelle, a see-and-be-seen cocktail bar that was housed in one of the chicest boutique hotels in Back Bay. Possibly in the city. They'd thought that it would be better for Jules to meet Paris on her own but their client had declared them a unit and insisted on a "Team Paris" meeting. Her words, not theirs.

While Paris downed margarita after margarita, she and Noah tried to nail down Paris's wishes, expectations and desires for her yacht and its interior.

Two hours and four margaritas later, none of which had, sadly, passed their lips, they still had nothing. They were, however, handed a glossy invitation to a soiree Paris was planning at the end of the month. "Just a few friends, darling. Casual chic, be there by seven."

Through experience Jules knew *casual chic* could mean anything from ball gowns to beachwear, and seven actually meant later—much, much later. Everybody knew to add an hour or two onto Paris's stated time.

Jules tapped the point of her pencil against the white paper, leaving tiny dots on the surface. "She wants it to feel open but also cozy. Sophisticated but relaxed. But mostly, it has to look like it cost a fortune."

Noah lifted his head to look at her. Or rather, he looked at her after he eyed quite a bit of her exposed thigh. Jules thought about tugging her skirt down but then Noah would know that she noticed him checking out her legs, and he might also realize that she liked him looking at her legs. *Aargh!*

Noah straightened and lifted his arms in the air to stretch, pulling his button-down shirt across his ridged stomach and wide chest. Through the white cotton she could, if she stared hard enough, see his flat brown nipples. Jules couldn't stop her eyes from skating over his stomach, over his pleasing, and promising, package to look at his thighs covered by his gray suit pants. They'd be tanned and, as they'd been since he was fourteen, corded with muscle. Pleasantly furry.

Man, her old friend/new colleague was seriously *hawt.* As in smokin'.

And…none of this was helping her with her other problem, her real problem of not knowing what the hell Paris wanted.

Jules dropped her head back and groaned. "I need inspiration."

Noah stood and rested his hands on his hips. "How can I help?"

Jules lifted her head up and rubbed the back of her neck. "Did Paris say anything to you about the interiors when you first spoke to her about designing the yacht? Was there anything in those conversations that could steer me in the right direction?"

Noah thought for a minute. "Not really. She told me to design something that would make her friends drool. Gave me the budgeted figure and said to come back to her when I had some thoughts. I've managed to pin her down to some specifics—what she wants the boat for, cruising the Caribbean and possibly the Med, and for entertaining, which means big reception and deck areas. Her eyes glazed over when I mentioned anything to do with engineering or design." Noah frowned. "'Design a boat, here's a small deposit to get you started, make it spectacular.'

"I don't think she's very interested in sailing."

Jules laughed at his deadpan comment. "What makes you think that?" she quipped. "So, tell me about the boat."

Noah walked around the desk to her and perched his butt on the corner of his desk. "I sent you the blueprints. All the specs are in there."

"Yeah, but I have no idea what the boat actually looks like. Maybe I can take some inspiration from your design…"

"I didn't send you the concept drawings of the yacht?" Noah asked, sounding shocked by his inefficiency.

"Nope."

Noah frowned again before walking back to his drafting table and pulling a folder out from underneath his blueprints. Flipping it open, he removed a sheaf of papers and returned to his spot on the desk. Stretching out his long legs, he handed Jules the sheaf of papers, a hint of nervousness in his eyes. It almost seemed like Noah was seeking her approval, that he wanted her to like his work.

Strange, since Noah was the most self-assured man she knew.

Jules looked down and her breath hitched. Despite the roughness of the sketch she could see the fluid, almost-feminine lines of the yacht, the gentle curves, the sensuous bow. Moving on to the paper below, Jules tipped her head to the side. Noah took his rough design to his computer and the color printout in her hand looked like a real, already built yacht, just ten times more beautiful than the concept drawing.

Sleek, elegant, feminine…spectacularly well designed.

"Oh, my goodness, Noah, it's…" Jules couldn't think of an adjective that adequately contained how wonderful she thought his design was. She sighed, slumped back in her chair and looked into Noah's intensely masculine face. "It's… Wow."

"You like it?"

"Are you kidding me? It's gobsmackingly, shockingly beautiful. I have no words."

Pride flashed in Noah's eyes. "I like it."

"You should." Jules tapped her nail on the glossy paper. "You've put so much thought into the design, you know exactly what you want the interior to look like."

Noah nodded, so Jules picked up her sketch pad, found a clean page and picked up a bright pink pencil, prepared to make a list.

"I thought about echoing the fluidity of its lines with a feminine interior," Noah said, "but by *feminine*, I mean sleek and sexy as opposed to frilly and fancy."

Yeah, she understood. Long lines, gentle curves, no harsh edges.

"I'd like comfortable white furniture with pops of color. Bold pinks or oranges or reds, feminine colors but strong tones. There are a lot of windows to show off incredible views so we have to consider the sea an accessory."

Noah tossed more suggestions at her and Jules wrote quickly, struggling to keep up with him. Interesting textures, hidden flat screens, storage space. He'd thought about it all. He eventually ran out of ideas—thank goodness because her hand was starting to cramp—and gripped the edge of his desk with both hands, his intense eyes locking with hers. "Make it feminine, sexy but soft. Accessible but with a hint of mystery. Look inside."

Her head jerked up at his last sentence and the air between them turned thick and warm. "What do you mean by that?" she asked, unable to disguise the rasp in her voice.

Noah's intensity ratcheted up a notch and... *Zzzz...* She was sure that was the sound of her underwear melting. "I look at the yacht and I see you. Sexy, slim, so damn feminine."

"Noah." Jules pulled his name out into three, maybe four, syllables. It was a plea but she wasn't sure what she was asking for. *Please kiss me* or *please don't? Please stoke the fires and make me burn* or *please hose me down?*

"What do you want, Jules?"

Nothing. Something. *Everything.*

Jules was unable to answer him, and when a minute or two passed—or ten seconds, who knew because time was irrelevant—Noah surged to his feet. Tossing her sketch pad to the floor, he gripped her biceps, lifted her up, and up again, so that her mouth was aligned with his. Still holding her, his mouth touched hers...sweet and hot and sexy and... *Dear Lord.*

Jules wasn't sure how his arms came to be around her waist and how her skirt got high enough to allow her legs to wind around his hips. All she knew was that her core was pressed against his impossibly hard erection, her nipples were pushed into his chest and his mouth was turning her brain to slush.

She didn't want to be anywhere else.

For years she'd been kissing guys who made her feel something between mild revulsion and "mmm, this is okay" but nobody turned her into a nuclear reactor like Noah did. Nobody had ever made her feel she'd choose making love to him over dodging a missile strike or a tunnel collapse. If she got to touch and be touched by Noah, she'd take her chances.

Oh, man, she was in so much trouble.

Noah's hand ran up the back of her thigh, over the bare skin of her butt. "A thong. Nice."

It would be so much nicer if he got rid of that tiny scrap of material that called itself underwear. "Take it off." Jules spoke the words against his lips, dipping her hands into the space between his pants and his lower back, wanting to go lower, to feel his butt cheek under the palm of her hand.

Noah pulled back, his eyes intensely focused. On her, on making her his. She wanted that, to belong to him again, if only for this moment in time. "Jules…"

She knew what he was about to say and she didn't want to hear it. Yes, it was a bad idea. Yes, they'd only just reconnected. Yes, there was a lifetime behind them and they had no idea how to navigate the future. But she wanted this, wanted to know Noah before they reestablished their friendship. Because the yacht project had them spending so much time together, she couldn't keep him at arm's length, even if she wanted to. Which she didn't. She wanted Noah back in her life, the hole in her heart was finally closing. They were on their way back to being friends.

God, she hoped he knew there couldn't be more between them, that this night and a burgeoning friendship was all they could have. They'd make love, get it out of their systems and accept that they could never go beyond a casual friendship.

Because, as nice as it was to have Noah back in her life, she was never going to open up to him again in the way that she did when she was a child, then a teen. She'd trusted him once and he'd abused that trust when he left her, stayed away without so much as an explanation for an entire decade.

Noah was going to leave again; it was what he did, and this time she wasn't allowing her heart to leave with him.

But sex, pleasure—yeah, she trusted him with her body. If she wanted to know passion, and she did, then it had to be now, today. Tomorrow could take care of itself.

"I want this, Noah. I want you."

He opened his mouth to argue but Jules didn't give him a chance, she just molded her lips against his and slipped her tongue inside his mouth to slide against his. She heard his deep, feral growl, felt his fingertips push into the skin of her butt. When the thin cord of her thong snapped, she knew she'd won the small argument.

Or that Noah had let her win. She didn't care.

"One time," Noah muttered, pulling away from her mouth to push his lips against her neck. "One time and we get over this."

Jules nodded her agreement and briefly wondered if Noah knew she would agree to selling her kidney on the black market if it meant making love to him. She was under his spell...

Or for the first time ever she was finally experiencing the joy of really, really good foreplay. And if foreplay was this intense, sex itself was going to be fan-damn-tastic.

Suddenly she couldn't wait. She put a little distance between their bodies and attacked his shirt buttons, needing to see him, feel him. Whoops, button gone. Oh, well, tit for tat since her tattered thong was lying at their feet. Her thong was forgotten as Noah's hand ran up the inside of her leg, skating past her core, making her squirm.

Jules spread his shirt apart and placed an openmouthed kiss against the skin above his heart. Noah. God, she was making love to Noah. Suddenly scared, she rested her forehead against his chest, her hands on his belt buckle but making no attempt to divest him of his pants.

Was this a mistake? She was sure it was…

Noah's hand stilled. "Second thoughts?"

"Yes? No… I don't know."

"If you want to stop, we can pretend this never happened. Or we can carry on and pretend this never happened. Either way, in the morning this can all be a wonderful dream or a fantastic memory."

"Do you want to stop?"

Noah's strangled chuckle rumbled across her hair. "Honey, I have a sexy woman in my arms, the one I've fantasized about since I first tasted her luscious mouth a decade ago. That kiss changed everything and I've been wanting to kiss you, taste you there and everywhere, since then. Hell, no, I don't want to stop."

Jules looked up at him. "You thought about me?"

Noah used one finger to push her hair off her forehead and out of her eyes. "More than I should've. I imagined you naked and responsive and the reality is a million times better than the dream."

"How can one kiss change us?"

"God knows," Noah said, lifting his hand to pull her silk T-shirt out of the band of her skirt. His hand trailed over her rib cage before covering her breast, his thumb pulling the lace of her bra over her already aching nipple.

"Stop or carry on, Jules? Tell me now."

She wanted this. It was just one time and they'd forget it happened in the morning. Or was she deluding herself? When dawn broke, forgetting anything wouldn't be easy to do but she was willing to find any excuse, clutch any straw to be with Noah. To know him intimately.

Thinking that actions would say more than words, Jules gripped the edges of her T-shirt and slowly pulled the fabric up her torso, revealing her lacy white bra. She heard Noah's intake of air, and when she looked at him, his eyes were on her breasts. Using one finger, he gently rubbed one nipple before transferring his attention to the next.

"I guess that's a yes."

"A huge fat gaudy yes," Jules responded huskily.

Jules gasped when Noah grabbed her hand and pulled her across the room and into a space between the wall and his drafting table. Pushing her into the corner, he placed her back to the wall and undid the front clasp of her bra. Then both her breasts were in his hands and she groaned. "As much as I like that, want to explain why we are in this corner?"

"Windows. Marina. Can't see us here," Noah muttered, bending to suck her nipple. A hot stream of lust hit her core and Jules moaned. Noah couldn't use long sentences and she couldn't speak at all.

Lord, they were in a world of trouble.

To hell with it. Nothing was hurting now. And she wanted more. She wanted it all.

Jules reached for Noah's pants, undid his belt buckle and managed, somehow, through luck rather than skill, to flip open the button to his pants. Jules was very conscious of his erection under her hand and she couldn't resist running her fingers over his length, imagining him pushing into her body, slowly and, oh, so deliciously. She slid the zipper down and then pushed his pants over his hips, wrapping her hand around his shaft and skating her thumb across its tip.

Noah cried a curse and lifted her skirt to bunch it around her waist. They were half-undressed but they didn't care, nothing was more important than having him fill her, stretch her, make her scream.

"Condom," Noah muttered.

Protection. Yeah, that was important. Noah reached

behind him and patted the desk, grunting when his hands
closed around his wallet. Pulling it to him, he flipped it
open, digging beneath the folds. Eventually, he pulled out
a battered foil packet that Jules eyed warily.

"That looks old."

Noah ripped open the packet and allowed the foil to
float to the floor. "It'll do the job."

That was all she cared about. Jules tried to help him
roll the latex down his length but Noah batted her hands
away. Covered, his hand slid between her legs and Jules
shuddered. *Oh, God, yes. There. Just like that.*

"Do you like that, sweetheart?"

"So good." Jules spiraled on a band of pure, undiluted
pleasure and lifted her head, looking for Noah's mouth.
He kissed her, hard and demanding. Noah lifted her thigh
over his hips and plunged inside her. Feeling both protected and ravished, Jules had the sensation of coming
apart and being put back together as Noah worked his
way inside her, as if she were spun sugar and liable to
break.

"Noah," Jules murmured, her face in his neck, trying
to hold on. In another dimension, Jules heard the vibrant
ring of his phone. Focused on what Noah was doing to
her, making her feel—she'd never believed it could be this
magical, this intense—Jules ignored the demands of the
outside world, but when the phone rang again she tensed.

Noah clasped her face in one hand, using his thumb to
lift her jaw so that their eyes clashed and held. "You and
me, Jules. The rest of the world can go to hell."

Jules nodded as he pushed a little deeper, a little further and she whimpered. She wanted more, she needed
every bit of him. "So good, No. You feel amazing."

"It's going to get better, Ju. Hold on."

"Can't. Need to let go... Oh, God."

Noah stopped moving. Jules whimpered and ground down on him, wanting to set the pace. Jules thought she heard Noah's small chuckle but then he was moving, sliding in and out of her, the bottom of his penis rubbing her clit and she was done. The world was ending and it was...

Stars and candy and electricity and fun and...

Mind-blowing. And emotional. Tears pricked her eyes and she ducked her head so that Noah didn't see the emotion she knew was on her face. This was only supposed to be about good sex, great sex, but here she was, trying to ignore that insistent voice deep inside claiming this was more, that it always had been, that she was a fool if she thought they could be bed buddies and brush this off.

This is Noah, that voice said, *your best friend, your hottest fantasy. He's not just some random guy who gave you the best orgasm of your life. He's the beat of your heart—*

No! No, he wasn't.

Those feel-good hormones were working overtime, her serotonin levels were making her far too mushy. She could not allow herself to allow the lines between sex and love to blur, to mix it up with friendship and good memories to make one confusing stew. Sex was sex; friendship and love had nothing to do with this.

She wouldn't allow thoughts of love and forever to mess with her mind. She was smarter than that.

Noah...

Sex against the wall with his onetime best friend. He was not proud. Noah ran a hand over his face, listening as water hit the basin in the bathroom adjacent to his office. He hadn't intended that to happen...

Liar, liar...

He hadn't been able to think of much else than touching Jules—tasting her, sliding into her warm, wonder-ful heat—since he'd returned to Boston. And since he was being honest, he could admit, reluctantly, that he'd told her the truth when he'd said that he'd often thought about doing that and more since their decade-old kiss. He'd sailed many oceans and had spent many long nights, waves rolling under the hull, imagining doing just that.

But not up against a wall. Not for their first time… That was all types of wrong.

Noah tucked his shirt back into his suit pants and ran his hands through his hair. He dropped to his haunches and picked up Jules's sketch pad, smiling a little at her girlie, swirly handwriting. He closed the book, picked up the colored pencils that had rolled off the table and placed them on his desk. What now? Where did they go from here?

Noah looked at the closed door and wondered what was going through Jules's smart head. Hell, what was going through his? Not much since he was still trying to reboot his system. All he was really sure of was that sex with Jules was the best he'd ever had and, yeah, he'd had his fair share. He'd been single all of his adult life and sex wasn't that difficult to find.

But that had been a physical release, some fun, some-thing he enjoyed while he was in the moment but rarely thought about again. Jules, sex with Jules, was not some-thing he was going to be able to dismiss as easily. Or at all.

Yeah, it happened at the speed of light—something else he wasn't proud of—but he had a thousand images burned into his brain. Her eyes turned to blue the wetter she became, her brows pulled together as she teetered on the edge. The scar on the top of her hand, the perfect row of beauty spots behind her ear. Her mouth, the com-bination of spice and heat, feisty just like she was. Her scent—he'd never be able to smell an orange again without becoming mast hard. She'd ruined citrus for him… or made it ten times sexier.

And, God, how was he supposed to work twelve inches from where he'd had the best orgasm of his life? Unless he moved his desk, his concentration would be forever shot. In the morning he'd move his desk to the opposite corner. There wasn't as much light and the view was crappy but he'd manage to get some work done.

Or maybe he was kidding himself. Just having Jules back in his life was a distraction he didn't need.

He needed her to complete this project… She was red-hot at the moment and was in the position to pick and choose her clients. Paris wanted her and only her.

Once Jules produced her portfolio of design ideas for Paris to look at—hopefully she'd fall in love with one of the proposals, and quickly!—Paris would sign off on the design and a hefty pile of cash would hit his bank account. He'd use that money for the down payment on the house. He already had a preapproved mortgage in place to tide him over until he sold his apartment in Wimbledon and George paid him out for his share in their yacht rental business in Italy.

Ridiculous that he had many millions in assets but, thanks to the timing of other investments, he was experiencing a temporary cash flow problem.

Up until fifteen minutes ago he was also experiencing a sex flow problem.

His phone vibrated on his desk, and Noah picked up the device, wishing the damn things had never been invented. He saw the missed call from earlier, frowned at the unfamiliar Boston number and saw that his caller had left a message. Dialing into his voice mail service, he lifted the phone to his ear, keeping one eye on the bathroom door.

"I cannot believe that you would embarrass me this way! Paris Barrow told me that you are seeing Jules Brogan! How dare you, Noah? Her of all people! Why didn't you just take out a banner ad stating that I meant nothing to you?"

Noah looked at the screen, cut the call and shook his head. Getting harassed by your ex was a very good way to chase away any lingering fuzzies. It was also a great way to kill the mood.

Crap. Ignoring Morgan, leaving her long text messages unread and not confronting her directly was not getting his point across. It didn't matter whether he was in a fake relationship with Jules or neck-deep in love with her or anyone else, what he did and who he did it with was nobody's business but his own. He was going to have to meet with his ex and explain to her, in language a five-year-old could understand, that his love life was firmly and forever off-limits.

Noah rubbed the back of his neck. Obviously his return to Boston had flipped Morgan's switch.

The door to the bathroom opened and Noah saw the resigned but determined look on Jules's face. Nothing had changed.

Having sex up against the wall—hell, having sex—was going to be a onetime thing.

Damn. Crap. Hell.

Jules rubbed her hands on her thighs before folding her arms, causing her breasts to rise. And, yep, his IQ just dropped sixty points back to caveman mentality. "So, that happened," Jules said, darting a glance at the corner. Judging by her trepidation, he expected to see that the wall had caught alight.

And how was he supposed to respond to that? Yeah, it happened. He wanted it to happen again... Next time in a bed.

"Not one of our smartest moves, Lockwood."

And here came regrets, the we-can't-do-this-agains. Jules lifted her tote bag off the floor and brushed past him to pick up her sketch pad and pencils. As he pulled in a breath, he smelled that alluring combination of sex and citrus, soap and shampoo. All girlie, feminine Jules in one delightful sniff. His junk stirred.

"I'm going to head home. It's been a long day."

It had but, thank baby Jesus, it ended with a bang. Noah gave himself a mental kick to the temple for the thought. It was asinine, even for him. He frowned, wondering when she was going to spit out what she was actually thinking...

This isn't a good idea. This can't happen again. Let's pretend I didn't get nailed against a wall and that it wasn't the most head-exploding, soul-touching sex of my life.

Jules half smiled as she held the sketch pad against her chest. "Let me work with what you gave me and hopefully I'll have a couple of sketches, sample materials for you in a couple of days. Will that work for you?"

What was she rambling on about?

He'd left stubble burns on her neck, her blouse was incorrectly buttoned up. Noah wanted to undress her, take her on the desk and then, when he was done, he'd dress her again. Properly this time.

Or maybe he'd just hide her clothes and keep her naked.

"Noah?"

Jules looked at him as if expecting an answer. What the hell did she say?

"Oh, God, you're getting weird. I didn't want us to act weird," Jules muttered, shifting from foot to foot. "Are you waiting for the other shoe to drop, the sky to fall down? Relax, I'm not going to ask what this means, whether we can do it again. I'm fully aware of your bam-wham policy."

Bam-wham... *What?*

"What are you talking about?" Noah was impressed that he managed to construct a sentence that had the words in the right order.

Jules patted his chest, much like his mom had to placate him when he was ten. "It's all good. No. That was something that had been building to a head for ten years and it needed to erupt. Now we can go back to doing what we do best."

"And that is?" And why did he sound like he had a dozen frogs in his throat?

Jules's smile was just a shade off sunny. "Being friends." Jules patted his arm this time and it took Noah everything he had to not react. "I'm out of here. I'll talk to you in a day or two, okay?"

Noah watched her walk out of his office and two minutes later, heard her run down the metal stairs to the ground floor of the building. Hayden, the marina's night manager, would make sure she got to her car safely so he could stay here and try and work out what the sodding hell just happened.

And, no, it most definitely was not okay.

Jules...

Ladies and gentlemen, the award for Best Actress goes to Jules Brogan.

Oh, why couldn't sex with Noah have been meh and

blah? Why did it have to be skin-on-fire, want-more wonderful? It had taken a herculean effort for Jules to turn her back on Noah and leave the office. Now at the bottom of the stairs leading to the reception area of the marina's office, she ignored the burning urge to retrace her steps.

She and Noah didn't have a future. They never had. He was only in town long enough to complete this project and within a few weeks, maybe a month or two, he'd be gone again. If she didn't keep her distance she would be staying behind, holding her bleeding heart in her hands. This time she wouldn't only be mourning the loss of her friend but also her lover.

She'd cried enough tears over Noah, thank you very much.

As more tears threatened to spill, Jules could only pray that Noah wouldn't follow her in order to continue their going-nowhere conversation. And situation.

She couldn't allow history to repeat itself; that was just stupid. They needed to keep their relationship perfunctory and professional. Two words that weren't associated with sex.

What had she been thinking... Had she been thinking at all? Their kiss so long ago had knocked them out of the friends-only zone and had, admittedly, rocked her world. How could she possibly have thought she could handle sleeping with him?

Then again, when Noah touched her, when his eyes darkened to that shade a fraction off black, her brain exited the room and left her libido in charge. Her libido that hadn't seen much action and couldn't be trusted to make grown-up decisions.

Jules waved off the night manager, who offered to walk her to her car, and stepped into the warm night.

Pulling in a deep breath, she waited for the night air to clear her head. Walking down the marina, reason and sanity returned.

Use that brain, Brogan.

She wasn't living in Victorian times; this wasn't a catastrophe. She was fully entitled to have sex with and enjoy a man, his skills and his equipment. This didn't have to mean anything more than it was: a moment in time where they did what healthy adults did. It was sex, nothing more or nothing less.

A fun time was had by all up against the wall.

She wasn't a poet, nor was she a liar... Jules sighed. Despite her brave words to Noah and her insouciant attitude, sex did mean something to her, sharing her body was a curiously intimate act. She never slept with men unless the relationship was going somewhere...and, because there hadn't been many contenders to feature in her happily-ever-after life, she was a shade off being celibate.

Sleeping with Noah had been an aberration, an anomaly, a strange occurrence.

Jules pushed through the access gate to the marina, turned to look back at the double-story office building and blew out a long, frustrated breath.

She couldn't sleep with him again. It was out of the question. He'd hurt her, disappointed her, and she couldn't trust him not to do that again. Erecting a wall between them was the smart, sensible course of action. It was what she had to do.

So why, then, did it take her five minutes to open her car door and another ten to start the car and drive home?

Seven

Callie...

Callie hugged DJ and Darby, and then pulled Jules into her arms, keeping her there for an extra beat, wishing she could ask Jules to stay behind, to demand that Jules tell her why she'd spent most of breakfast staring out of the window of the coffee shop, her thoughts a million miles away.

"Are you okay, baby girl?" Callie whispered in her ear.

Like she did when she was a little girl, Jules rested her forehead on Callie's collarbone. "I'm fine, Mom."

No, she wasn't, but this wasn't the time to push and pry. Not when there were so many ears flapping, Darby's, DJ's and also, dammit, Mason's. She'd introduced him to her daughters and he'd been courteous but professional, thank God. Points to him that he kept his flirting between them.

Enough of him, this was her time with her daughters and she wasn't going to waste a minute of it thinking about Mason. Callie's eyes flicked across the restaurant, saw that Mason was looking at her, and she shook her head. Distracting man! He wasn't, in any way that counted, her type. Too young, too good-looking, too… poor?

God, she was such a snob! She had enough money to last several lifetimes and it wasn't like Mason was penniless. He had a good business, looked financially liquid. She'd never judged men, or anyone, by their bank balance. Why was she doing it with him?

Because she was looking for any excuse, poor as it was, to keep her distance.

It didn't matter, nothing was ever going to happen between them! Irritated with herself, Callie stepped back and framed Jules's face with her hands, sighing at the confusion she saw in her eyes.

There was only one thing she could say, just one phrase that she knew Jules needed to hear. "Just keep standing, honey. Keep your balance until it all makes sense."

It had been Ray's favorite piece of advice, one he'd used his whole life. And, except for him dying when he was supposed to be retiring, it mostly held true.

"I needed to hear that, Mom." Jules managed a small smile. Then the smile evaporated and pain filled her eyes. "I miss him, Mom."

"I do, too, honey," Callie said, touching Jules's cheek with her fingers.

Callie walked her to the door, holding her hand. At the door she hugged her girls again and caught Mason's gaze over Jules's shoulder. His blue eyes were on her, a curious mixture of tenderness and heat. Damn that lick of heat spreading through her!

Jules stepped back and when she smiled, mischief danced in her eyes. "He's really good-looking, Mom."

That point had crossed her mind a time or two. Callie opened the door and ushered her brood outside. Shaking her head, she retraced her steps to her table, sat down and pulled her notebook out of her bag. Flipping it open to the first page, her eyes ran down her bucket list.

She'd moved to a new house in a different section of the estate so she could tick the first item off her list. She squinted at number two. Seeing tigers in the wild meant planning a trip. Was that still what she wanted to do?

"Learn a new skill? Bungee jump? Have phone sex?"

Callie heard the voice in her ear and when she whipped her head around, she found Mason's face a breath away, his sexy mouth hovering near hers. Callie wanted to scream at him for reading her private list but her tongue wouldn't cooperate. Then she felt his thumb stroking her back, while his other hand was on the table, caging her between his arm and his chest.

So close, close enough to kiss.

"Do you know how much I want to taste you right now?" Mason murmured.

"Y-you read… It was private," Callie stuttered, mortified. Her cheeks were definitely on fire. She'd mentioned sex! On her list! Now Mason knew she wanted some… Callie looked around the coffee shop, convinced that a million eyes—people she played bridge and tennis with—were all watching them, somehow knowing that she wanted to kiss Mason more than she wanted to breathe.

God, she was losing her mind.

"I'll tell you what's on my bucket list if it makes you feel any better," Mason replied, his hand moving up her back to cup her neck, the heat of his hand burning into her skin.

"You're probably just going to steal my ideas and call them yours," Callie muttered.

Mason's eyes flicked down to the list and Callie slammed her hand down on the page to cover her writing.

"I've traveled, thrown myself off a bridge on a rope, don't need another job. Wouldn't mind another trip some-where." He smiled and Callie's stomach flipped over. "I have had one-night stands, wouldn't recommend it."

Callie placed her face in her hands and groaned. "What are you, some sort of mutant speed-reader?"

Mason's laugh raised goose bumps on her skin. "Only a few items are on my list, Callie."

Callie scowled at him. "Do I even want to know?" She placed a hand on his shoulder to push him away but got distracted by the muscles bunching underneath his polo shirt. *Nice...*

Seeing that she was stroking him like he was expen-sive velvet, she yanked her hand away and, yes, dammit, blushed again. "Back up!"

Mason flashed her a smile and jerked her pen from her hand before picking up her notebook. Flipping to a new page, he pulled off the cap of her pen with his teeth and started writing.

He flipped the page back to her list, wrote some more and handed the book back to her. Callie looked down, no-ticing that he'd placed asterisks next to her "have a one-night stand" and "have phone sex" bullet points, drawing a line from both to what had to be his phone number.

Her face turned so hot she was sure that her skin was about to reach meltdown temperature. Mason skated his fingertips down her cheek before sending her a slow smile and turning away.

After a few minutes of resisting the urge to peek—she was embarrassed enough as it was—Callie turned the page and saw Mason's so-called bucket list. It was comprised of just three bullet points and a sentence.

Take Callie on a date.
Make her laugh.
Kiss her good-night.
See previous page for additional suggestions.

Clever, sexy man. A very dangerous combination.

Jules...

Since arriving at Whip, an exclusive cocktail bar situated in a boutique hotel on Charles Street, Noah had looked on edge. His jaw was tight and his eyes were a flat deep brown, suggesting that he was beyond pissed. But why? What had happened? What had she done?

"Are you okay?" she asked, jabbing her elbow into his side.

"Fine," Noah said through gritted teeth.

Jules sighed. Since their conversation the other night at The Tavern, Jules now saw their past a little clearer and remembered having to badger Noah to open up, to tell her anything. He was one of those rare individuals who internalized everything, preferring to rely on himself and his own judgment to solve his problems.

Unlike the rest of the clan, Noah had refused to openly discuss girls, college, his problems. The best way to get Noah to talk had been to join him on the back roof of Lockwood House and refuse to budge until he'd opened up. That was how she found out that his tenth grade girlfriend had dumped him, that he was going to study yacht design, how he was dealing with news that his mom had been diagnosed with pancreatic cancer.

But if she'd struggled to make him speak up on a thirty-foot-high roof back when they were friends, there was no chance of him opening up to her in a crowded room heaving with people who considered eavesdropping an art form.

Jules accepted Noah's offer to get her a drink from the bar and, standing by a high table, looked around Whip. She took in the deep orange walls, the black chandeliers, the harlequin floors. The decor was upmarket and vibrant… She approved. Just like Darby studied and commented on buildings, critiquing decor was an occupational habit for Jules.

Jules looked at Noah's broad back, saw that he would be waiting at the bar for a while and, feeling anxious, tapped her tiny black clutch bag on the table. By mutual, unspoken agreement, they'd given each other some space this past week, hoping to put some distance between them and their hot, up-against-his-office-wall encounter. She hadn't thought about him a lot, only when she woke up, ten million times during the day and when she went to sleep at night.

Jules sighed. Despite her busy days and her insane workload, the urge to touch base with Noah was at times overwhelming. A random thought would pop into her head and the only person she wanted to share it with was Noah. She'd be out and about, see an innovative light fixture or an interesting face and she'd reached for her phone, wanting to tell Noah about what she'd heard, done or seen.

A part of her thought she was sliding back into the habits of her younger self, to when she'd been in constant contact with Noah, but this was something more, something deeper. Every time she forced herself to cut the call, to erase the already typed message, she felt like she was stabbing a piece of her soul, like she was fighting against the laws of nature.

Not being connected to Noah was wrong. But her instinct for self-preservation was stronger than her romantic self, so she kept her distance.

But, God, her heart leaped when she opened the door to him tonight. It threatened to jump out of her chest when he placed a hand on her lower back to escort her to the classic luxury car he'd kept locked up in the underground garage at Eli's apartment. She'd gripped the door handle to keep from leaning sideways and touching her lips to his, from threading her fingers into his hair.

Jules tossed another glance at Noah's back. She really needed that drink and the soothing effects of alcohol, though a swift kick in the rear might be equally effective.

Noah was off-limits. Today, tomorrow, always. She rather liked having her heart caged by her ribs and not walking around in someone else's hand.

"Jules Brogan?"

Jules turned and smiled when a still-fit-looking older man with shrewd green eyes and silver hair held out his hand to her. Jules tipped her head, not recognizing his face.

"Ivan Blake."

Okay, the name sounded familiar but she couldn't place him. The connection would, she hoped, come to her in a minute or two. "I hear that you are Paris's interior designer."

"For her yacht, yes."

"And I understand that you and Noah are seeing each other?"

Now, what did that have to do with him? Since she wasn't prepared to answer him, she just kept quiet and looked around the room. "You don't know who I am, do you?"

"Should I?" Jules asked him, her voice three degrees cooler than frosty.

"I'm Morgan's father."

And a million pennies dropped. "Ah." What else could she say? I never liked your daughter, and I think she played Noah like a violin? "Is Morgan here?"

Because her presence would really make this evening extra interesting. And by *interesting* she meant freaking awful.

"She wasn't feeling well so she decided to stay home."

Thank God and all his angels, archangels and cherubs.

"She's been trying to reconnect with Noah and she feels like you are standing in her way," Ivan said.

Jules nodded to Noah, who was standing a head and sometimes shoulders above many men at the bar. "He's a big guy, Mr. Blake, I couldn't stand in his way."

"You're missing my point, Miss Brogan."

Jules allowed her irritation to creep into her voice. "You're missing mine. Noah is a successful, smart, determined man. If he wanted to reconnect with Morgan, I wouldn't be able to stop him. And tell me, Mr. Blake, when is Morgan going to stop having her daddy fight her battles?"

"Morgan is fragile."

Jules wanted to tell him that Morgan was also manipulative, but she kept silent. Wanting to walk away but hemmed in by the crowd, she had to stand there and keep her expression civil.

"Would you be interested in doing some work for me?"

Jules's eyes snapped up at the change of subject. Say what? "Are you kidding me? Morgan would disembowel you if you hired me."

"Not if you distanced yourself from Noah to give her a chance to win him back," Ivan said, his voice both low and as hard as nails.

"I don't need the work, Mr. Blake."

"But your sister does. She's been looking for a breakthrough project for a while, a way to put her name out there, to allow her to work on bigger and more exciting projects. She needs a chance and you could give that to her.

"I'm on the board of a very well funded foundation dedicated to promoting the art and artists of this city. The foundation has acquired a building not far from the Institute of Contemporary Art which we intend to demolish and replace with another smaller art gallery and museum. We're looking for an architect to design the space," Ivan continued.

Dear Lord, that was so up Darby's street.

"Walk away from him, just like he walked away from you, and I'll put in a good word."

Wow.

Jules frowned at him, feeling like she was part of a badly written soap opera. "You're kidding, right? People don't do this in the real world."

"Oh, they do it far more often than you think," Ivan said, a ruthless smile accompanying his words. "Just think about my offer. I'm prepared to give Darby a fair chance, maybe throw some design work your way."

"If I break up with Noah," Jules clarified, trying to stifle the bubble of laughter crawling up her throat. This was both too funny and too bizarre for words. He was offering Darby a huge project, a project that would catapult her career to the next level if Jules broke up with her fake boyfriend.

Again… Wow.

A part of her wanted to say yes; this man was offering her sister an opportunity of a lifetime. An art gallery and museum... Was he kidding? Darby would sell her soul to work on a project like that! Jules hesitated, conscious that she had yet to say no, that she *should* say no.

"Turning me down would be a bad business decision, Ms. Brogan. I can promote you and your sister, but the pendulum swings both ways."

And that meant what? He'd blackball and bad-mouth them? Jules tipped her head to the side and was surprised at the resignation she saw in his eyes. He didn't want to do this, act this way. The man was tired, emotionally drained.

"Why are you letting her push you like this?" Jules asked softly.

Ivan pulled in a deep breath, and sorrow and anger and fear mingled in his eyes. Ivan stared at her and was silent for so long that Jules didn't think he was going to answer or acknowledge her question. "Because," Ivan said, speaking so softly that Jules had to strain to hear his voice, "I'm scared that if I don't she's going to go a step too far."

Ivan ran his hand over his jaw and stepped back. "Let me know your decision, Ms. Brogan."

Before she could reply, tell him that she wasn't interested, Ivan Blake faded into the crowd, leaving Jules alone and wondering if she'd imagined the bizarre conversation.

"Have you seen Morgan?" Noah asked through clenched teeth.

Jules turned at Noah's voice and, not for the first, and probably not the last, time that night, noticed how good he looked in his black suit, slate-green-and-black-checked shirt and perfectly knotted black tie. Jules followed his eyes and saw that he was looking at Ivan Blake, his expression as dark as thunder.

He handed her an icy margarita and Jules took a sip. "She's not here, No. You can relax." His expression immediately lightened and his shoulders dropped from around his ears.

So his bad mood was due to his fear of running into Morgan. Now that made sense and it was something she could fully relate to.

"Thank God. And how do you know?" Noah replied, his hand wrapped around a tumbler of whiskey.

"Her father told me," Jules said.

"He spoke to you? What did he want?" Noah released a bitter laugh. "Oh, wait, let me guess. He wants you to break up with me."

No flies on her big guy. "Yep. How did you guess?"

"Because his daughter has been bombarding me with text and voice mail messages, begging to meet, to give her another chance."

Jules reached out, grabbed the lapel of his jacket and twisted the fabric in her fist. "You do that and I swear, I will drown you in the bay."

A small smile touched Noah's mouth and he removed his jacket from her fingers and smoothed down the fabric. "I'm not stupid. I got stuck in that web once. I'm not moronic enough to do that again."

"If she's hassling you, you need to tell her that, Noah."

Noah scowled. "I've been trying! I've asked her to meet. I even popped by their house but apparently no one was home. But I did catch movement behind the drapes of what was always Morgan's room."

"You know where her room was?"

Noah shrugged. "Sex." Ew. Jules shuddered but Noah

didn't notice. "She's been trying to get my attention for three weeks and now she won't talk to me, answer the door?"

"Of course she won't. She knows you're going to tell her something she doesn't want to hear. Instead, she sent her father to try and manipulate the situation."

He wore his normal inscrutable expression but Jules saw the worry in his eyes. "Would he be able to manipulate you?"

The urge to thump him was strong. "I'm going to pretend that you didn't ask me that."

"Sorry, but Ivan Blake has the ability to discern what people want or need and then push the right buttons to obtain his—or in this case, Morgan's—goal."

There was a story there and she'd ask him to explain, but first she wanted to go back a few steps, to get him to clarify an earlier point. Actually, thinking about it, it was still related to the topic at hand. "What did you mean when said you got caught in his web? As I said the other night, *you* stayed engaged to the girl long enough that she couldn't have been all bad."

"The sex was fantastic," Noah said, and Jules narrowed her eyes. He lifted up his hands in apology. "I was young and she was talented. But she was hard work."

"Again…you were together for nearly two and a half years! Why?" Jules demanded, knowing there was something she didn't understand, a huge puzzle piece she was missing.

Noah took a sip from his glass, his eyes never wavering from hers. "I never proposed to Morgan." What? Well, that was unexpected. Still, it didn't explain the long engagement.

Noah ran a hand through his hair and Jules noticed his agitation. Good, he should be agitated since he'd allowed whatever he had with Morgan—the supposedly fantastic sex, ugh—to get so out of hand.

"That Christmas Eve we had a discussion about commitment, but I was drunk and exhausted and don't remember much of it. I woke up the next morning, sporting a hangover from hell, to this wave of good wishes on our engagement," Noah said, pitching his voice at a level only she could hear. "Getting married was the last thing on my mind.

"Then, now and anytime since," Noah added, his words coated with conviction.

His statement was an emotional slap followed by a knife strike up and under her ribs, twisting as it headed for her heart. She shouldn't be feeling this, there was nothing between them but a long-ago friendship, a few kisses and hot sex. Still, something died inside of her and in that moment, standing in a crowd of the best-dressed and wealthiest Bostonians, she felt indescribably sad and utterly forlorn.

She'd never imagined that Noah would live his life alone. Like his mom, he had an enormous capacity for love, provided he thought you were worth the effort. Once, a long time ago, she had been worth the effort. But that boy, the one who'd trusted her in his own non-communicative way, had loved her, of that she was sure.

This adult version of Noah, tough, stoic, determined, didn't. And he would never allow himself to. The thought popped into her head that if he wasn't going to marry, then neither was she, but Jules dismissed it as quickly as it formed. His decision had no impact on her future plans...

She hoped.

Annoyed with herself, Jules opened her mouth to bring

them back to the ever so delightful topic of his engagement to Morgan. "So why stay engaged, No? Fess up."

Noah rubbed his hand over his jaw, and Jules wondered if he'd tell her the truth or fob her off. "So, there I was on Christmas morning, nursing a hangover from hell, and before I could make sense of what I was hearing, Ivan handed me a massive sponsorship deal. It was three times bigger than any offers I'd received before, included a new yacht, an experienced crew."

Jules struggled to make sense of his words. "But you were sponsored by Wind and Solar."

"Which he has a controlling but little-known interest in," Noah explained. "He made me an offer I couldn't refuse."

"To drop out of college, to run away?"

Noah's jaw tensed. "That's your perception, not mine."

"You left me with barely a word and definitely without an explanation. You abandoned me and our friendship. You also broke your promise to your mom to look after your brothers and to finish college," Jules hissed.

The color drained from Noah's face and Jules wished she could take her words back. It wasn't like Noah left his brothers alone and defenseless when he went away ten years ago; Eli was already in college and Ben was about to start his freshman year. They both had a solid support system in her mom and dad and Levi, and could turn to any of them if they needed help or guidance.

His brothers had been fine but he did leave them. As for finishing his education, his lack of a degree hadn't hurt his career at all, so who was she to judge? But it was just another promise he'd made that he'd broken...

We'll always be friends, Ju. There will never be a time that we don't talk. I'll always be there for you, Ju. You can rely on me...

She could and she had...until she couldn't. And didn't.

Noah drained his glass of whiskey. "Just to clarify... I finished my education. I didn't break that promise. I did my best to look after Eli and Ben. That was part of the reason I had to leave, why I had no choice but to take the—" Noah jerked his head in Ivan's direction "—as-shat's offer. I'm sorry I wasn't around, Jules, sorry that I missed your dad's funeral, that I couldn't hold your hand. But, Jesus, I was doing what I needed to do!"

"You're not telling me everything, Noah."

Noah stepped closer to her, trapping Jules between the wall and his hot, masculine frame. Her traitorous body immediately responded to his nearness, and her nipples puckered and all the moisture in her mouth and throat dried up. He was using their attraction as a distraction from their conversation but Jules didn't care. Her need to be kissed was the only thought occupying her shrunken brain.

She shouldn't kiss him, because kissing was one small step from sleeping with him again, thereby narrowing that emotional distance she needed to keep between them. Jules placed her hand on his chest to push him away but her actions had all the effect of a ladybug's.

"We're supposed to be lovers, Jules. Can you damn well act like it?" Noah muttered, dropping his head so that his mouth was a hairbreadth from hers. Jules sighed, forcing her body to relax.

"You drive me crazy, Noah."

"Ditto, babe."

Noah's mouth skated across hers in a leisurely slide, his lips testing hers. Jules wound her arms around his neck, her fingers playing with the surprisingly soft hair at the back of his head, wishing that she could run her hand down his back, over his butt.

Noah tore his mouth off hers and pulled back, lifting his hand to her face. Holding her cheek in his hand, the pad of his thumb glided across her bottom lips and she shuddered, the sensation almost too much to bear. "Yeah, I far prefer soft and sexy Jules to spitting and snarling Jules."

Jules opened her mouth to blast him but Noah spoke before she could, resting his forehead on hers. "Wind and Solar offered me a hell of a deal but it came with a huge price... I was caught between a rock and a hard place."

Oh, she wasn't going to like what she was about to hear.

"After Mom's death, I needed a lot of money very quickly. Blake offered me more than I needed, but the catch was that I had to stay engaged to Morgan for two years, enough time to get her mentally healthy."

Well, hell. Jules was trying to make sense of his words, this new information, when she saw their client, a champagne glass in one hand and delight in her eyes, approaching them. "I'm here! Let the party begin. Come, come, there are people I want you to meet! Oh, Julia, you look delightful! Come, come..."

Eight

Noah...

Jules—why did people assume her full name was Julia?—looked sensational, and that was a huge, irritating problem since Noah had this uncontrollable desire to pull her from the room, find a private space and rip that very delightful, extremely frivolous dress from her amazing body.

He didn't know if her blush-pink-and-black lace dress was designer or not—he so didn't care—but it suited her perfectly, being both quirky and sophisticated. She'd pulled her hair up into a sleek ponytail high on the back of her head and her makeup was flawless, with her face looking like she wasn't wearing any at all.

His childhood friend, gangly and gawky, was gone and the sexy woman she'd morphed into made all his blood run south. Grown-up Jules was sunshine and hurricane, calm seas and storm surges, the beauty of a tropical sunset and the tumult of the Arctic Ocean.

Like the many seas he'd sailed, she was both captivating and fascinating, with the power to both soothe his soul and rip it in two. Excitement pumped through his body and he felt alive. Rediscovering Jules was like setting off across the Atlantic Ocean, not sure what type of sea or weather conditions he'd encounter but damn excited to find out.

Noah allowed himself the delight of watching Jules, long legged and sexy, as she followed in Paris's wake. He hadn't seen her since she left his office ten days ago and it was nine days, twenty-three hours and thirty minutes too long. He'd spent most of that time with half his mind on his work and the rest dreaming, lost in memories of how she felt, tasted, smelled.

There was action in his pants and Noah thought it would be a very good idea if he stopped imagining her naked so he didn't embarrass himself. He knew of a quick way to deflate his junk, so he scanned the room, looking for Blake. He needed to speak to Morgan's father, make it very clear to him, so that he could explain it to his daughter, that he'd rather swim in shark-infested waters than hook up with Morgan again. He was sorry that she was a little rocky, slightly unstable, but she was no longer his problem.

Jules smiled and his heart flip-flopped. Damn Paris and her ill-timed interruption.

What was going through Jules's head? Did she hear and understand that he'd needed the money, that he hadn't had another option? That he did what he needed to do because he was between the devil and the Bermuda Triangle? But if she did think that he was a money-grabbing moron, then it was no one's fault but his own.

He wasn't good at opening up, exposing his underbelly. Communicating wasn't his strong point; he preferred action to words. Even his brothers didn't know the extent of Ethan's treachery. They didn't know about his many affairs, the incredible amounts of money he spent on girls just hitting their twenties.

He'd kept that from them, thinking that they didn't need to be burdened with that knowledge. In hindsight, he should've gone to Callie and Ray, asked for their help, their advice.

But looking back, he hadn't asked for help, shared what was going on because if he had, they would've seen how hurt he was, how out of control and messed up he'd felt. And if he'd fallen apart back then, he didn't think he would have recovered. And maybe that was another reason why he'd been prepared to accept Ivan's offer, since it had given him the option to run away, to put some distance between him and his mom's death, Ethan's betrayal, the need kissing Jules had evoked.

When he was sailing, he had to be fully present—his crew's safety was his responsibility—and he had to compartmentalize. Standing back from the situation, from the emotions, had allowed him to function and had become an ingrained habit.

He was finding that difficult to do with Jules now. She was constantly on his mind and not always in a sexual way. He found himself wondering about the weirdest things—did she still make her own granola, refuse to eat olives, make those face masks with oatmeal and honey?—and fought the impulse to connect with her during the day, just to hear her voice, see her smile.

And he wanted her back in his arms, naked and glorious, more than he needed his heart to pump blood through his body.

Noah rubbed the space between the collar of his shirt and his hair and caught Jules's concerned frown, the "Are you okay?" flashing in her eyes. She was worried about him, and her thoughtful expression suggested that she was still mulling over their conversation. There was no way Jules would leave that subject alone; she wouldn't be satisfied with the little he'd told her. She'd have questions…lots of questions.

He was still debating whether to answer them or not. He wanted to, for the first time in, well, forever, he wanted someone else's perspective, another opinion. No, hell…

He wanted Jules's perspective, her opinion. Wanted it but didn't want to want it…

This was why globe hopping, dropping in and out of people's lives was so much easier. Noah did up his jacket button, pushed his shoulders back and centered himself. Introspection could wait for later, right now he needed to socialize, to earn his crust of bread. And that meant discussing boats and sailing, recounting the highlights of his career and listening to amateur sailors as they tried to sound like they knew what they were doing.

Noah had played the game long enough. He understood the value of networking; it was extremely likely that a number of Paris's friends might have a spare fifty million for a new boat and he wanted them to think of him to design their vessel. Yeah, okay, designing an expensive yacht had been more fun than he'd expected. Building and designing boats, all types of boats, was his passion and rubbing elbows with potential clients was crucial for his business.

So get your head in the game, Lockwood.

Noah squared his shoulders, looked around the room to find Jules and saw her staring at the back of a silver-haired man, her eyes wide with distress. Noah instinctively made his way across the room, determined to reach her. Keeping his eyes on her, he was nearly at her side when a low voice calling his name halted him in his tracks.

No wonder Jules looked distraught. He didn't even need to look at the man's face, he knew exactly who'd caused his heart to stop, his blood to freeze. What the hell was his stepfather doing back in Boston? Just before leaving Cape Town, he'd checked to see where Ethan was and had been told that he was in Cannes. That he intended to remain there for the foreseeable future.

His stepfather, because he was a contrary ass, was exactly where Noah didn't want him to be: in Boston, breathing the same air he was.

Noah's fists clenched and he searched for and then connected with Jules's sympathetic gaze. She didn't know how or why he was at odds with Ethan but her loyalty was first and foremost to him. Her support was a hit of smooth, warm brandy after a freezing day on the water.

"Keep cool," Jules mouthed, holding out her hand. Noah gripped her fingers and nodded, grounding himself before turning around to face his stepfather.

"Ethan."

It seemed to Noah that the whole room was holding its breath, waiting to see how this encounter played out. Then he remembered that no one outside of his brothers knew of his war with Ethan. Noah was used to keeping his own counsel and Ethan wouldn't tell anyone that his stepson had instituted legal proceedings against him. The world only saw what Ethan allowed them to see, and that was the veneer of a charming, rich man-about-town.

His hid his snake oil salesman persona well.

"Hello, son."

Noah gritted his teeth. He'd once loved Ethan calling him son, loved the fact that blood and genes didn't matter to him so the *son* felt like a hit of acid. Funny how having his and his brothers' inheritance stolen tended to sour the adoration.

It took everything Noah had to shake Ethan's hand, to pull his mouth into something that vaguely resembled a smile.

"I thought you were in the South of France."

Ethan whipped a glass off a passing tray and smiled, his blue eyes the color of frost on a winter's morning. "I've been back for a month or so." Ethan sipped at his drink, not breaking eye contact with Noah. "As you know, I've put Lockwood Estate on the market."

Noah tightened his grip on Jules's hand. It was the only thing keeping him from planting his fist into his stepdad's face. "And as you know, I'm enforcing the clause that you have to offer it to us first, less twenty percent of the market value."

"My lawyer informed me. I find it tiresome having to wait." Ethan smiled the smile he stole from a shark. "If you don't manage to buy it within the prescribed time period, I'll still sell it to you."

"What's the catch?" Because there would be one, there always was.

"The marina. Give me the marina and twenty million and you can have the estate and all your mother's crap."

His mother's crap being the Lockwood furniture, the paintings, the silver. God, he wondered if there was anything left. Her jewelry, her collection of Meissen figurines?

He was going to kill him, he really was. While the house had sentimental value, the marina was a valuable asset and one that could easily be sold. And that was why

Ethan wanted it. Yes, the estate was bigger and more valuable, but it would be harder to unload. Ethan was doing what he did best, making life easier for himself. Jerk.

Ethan was exploiting Noah's love for Lockwood land and his family's legacy. It was a deal he could never, would never, agree to. Partly because he was done being exploited by his stepfather but also because Levi was now a full partner in the marina and wouldn't allow such a half-ass arrangement.

"Out of the question," Noah replied.

"Pity. I'd rather go broke than let you have the estate."

"Please, you're far too materialistic and vain for that," Noah replied, his harsh growl coming from deep within his throat. Red mist was forming in front of his eyes, and he was moments from losing it.

Punching Ethan would so be worth the assault charge...

"I have a plan B and if my life turns out the way I'm planning it to, I might take the estate off the market anyway. No matter what happens, I refuse to put another cent toward your mother's house. I'd rather watch it fall apart, board by board."

It was an empty threat, one that was verbalized purely to needle him since Noah knew the maintenance of the Lockwood house was paid for out of the profits from the country club and its facilities. There was no way the management company would allow the magnificent home to fall apart on the grounds of such an exclusive estate.

Noah tensed but Jules squeezing his hand kept his inscrutable expression in place. But, damn, it was hard.

Pulling her hand from his, Jules stepped between him and Ethan and smiled. Noah's protective instinct wanted her behind him but the quick shake of her head kept him from moving. She smiled but her eyes were deep-freeze cold. When she spoke, her voice held an edge he'd never heard before. Tough, compelling, hard-ass. "Uncle Ethan, it's been a long time."

Ethan's smile turned oily; the old man loved the attention of a pretty woman. The younger the better. That love of attention emptied his bank accounts faster than water ran from a tap. "I know that I should remember you, but forgive me, pretty lady—" *Pretty lady? Gag.* "—I don't… Wait! Jules Brogan?"

Jules nodded. "Hello."

Ethan flushed and ran a finger around the collar of his shirt. "I'm sorry about your dad."

"Not sorry enough to come to his funeral, though."

Ethan pouted. "Noah wasn't there either."

Typical Ethan, always trying to flip the tables and shift blame. "Noah was, if I recall, crossing the Indian Ocean at the time. What was your excuse for not being there for my mom, to support her when she lost the man who was your neighbor and friend for more than twenty years? The same woman who cooked for you and your boys for months before and after Bethann died, who took in your boys when they were on school breaks, who was more their parent than you were?"

"Uh…"

Noah wanted to smile at Ethan's red face, at the hunted look in his eyes. He saw Jules open her mouth to blast him again but seeing Paris approaching them, he gripped the back of her neck. Jules looked up at him and he shook his head, gently inclining his head in Paris's direction. Their hostess and client held a PhD in gossip and he didn't want them to star in her melodramatic account of their run-in with Ethan.

Noah's eyebrows flew up when Paris wound her arms around Ethan's neck before dropping a kiss on his temple. She grinned. "Surprise! My sweetie told me he hadn't spoken to you for a while, that you'd had a tiny falling-out so I thought this would be a perfect occasion for you two to kiss and make up!" Paris's eyes sparkled with excitement. "Ethan told me that he taught you to sail, Noah, and he's kindly offered to guide me through the process of designing and buying a yacht."

Noah's heart plummeted to the floor and nausea climbed up in his throat. Noah looked at Ethan and saw the malice in his eyes, revenge-filled amusement touching his mouth.

"Darling!" Paris said, dropping a kiss on Ethan's lips. "There is music so we must dance."

Ethan raised his glass to Noah and invisible fingers encircled Noah's neck and started to squeeze. "We'll speak soon…son."

Noah hauled in shallow breaths as they walked away, dimly hearing Jules's calling his name.

When he finally pulled his eyes to her face, he clocked her distress and concern. "Noah, are you okay?"

Noah shook his head. "Nope. Basically, what I am is screwed."

Jules…

Jules was still reeling from the unexpected encounter with Ethan—and she could only imagine how Noah felt. They'd left the soiree as soon as they could and the drive back to Lockwood was silent. Without a word, Noah opened her car door, escorted her to her front door and, in the dim shadows on the porch, stared down at her with enigmatic eyes.

She had a million questions for him, a need to dig and delve, to understand the past, but it was late and clarity wasn't what she most wanted from Noah right now. No, this wasn't about what she wanted but what she needed to give him...

A couple of times at Whip she'd looked his way and while he seemed to be talking, having a good time, she'd sensed that it was all one damn good performance. He played the game well but she could tell that Noah was played out, mentally and emotionally. For the first time she appreciated how hard it was for him to return to Boston and to face his past.

Jules glanced across the road to Lockwood House, looking hard and menacing under the cloudy sky. He'd come home to buy his inheritance back but dealing with his past had to be harder than he imagined. She'd assumed that his spat with Ethan had been just that, a spat, an old bull, young bull thing, something that would blow over. She hadn't really noticed that Eli and Ben didn't speak about their stepfather much; he was always out of the country, and because he was a sailor and yachtsman, she'd assumed that Noah had more contact with Ethan than they did.

That was a mistake. Noah loathed Ethan, and Ethan returned his antipathy.

Something fundamentally destructive had occurred to cause such unhappiness...

Noah placed a hand on the door above her head and looked down at her, his face as hard as the house over the road. "It's been a long and crappy evening, Ju, I don't want to talk about it or answer any questions."

"Fair enough," Jules replied, placing her hands flat against the wooden front door behind her. Arching her chest, she looked up at him, deliberately lowering her eyes. She knew what Noah wanted and it was the one thing she could give him, what she wanted—no, needed—as much as he did. To step out of their complicated lives and feel.

Warm skin, wet lips, heat...

Noah's voice was low but rough. "I want you. But you know that already."

"I do." Jules nodded, hooking her hand around the back of his neck. "And I want you, too. Take me to bed, No. Take me away to a place where our passion is the only truth."

"Nothing changes, Jules. As soon as I buy Lockwood, I'm still leaving," Noah stated quietly, still looming over her.

His blunt statement hurt, of course it did, but it didn't distract her from wanting what they both craved. "Kiss me, Noah."

Judging by his hard eyes and tense body, Jules expected to be hurtled to mindlessness by hard and fast sex. So his soft kiss, the tenderness in his touch, surprised her.

Noah bent his knees, placed an arm beneath her bottom and lifted her so that her mouth was aligned with his. Her feet dangled off the floor, but it didn't matter because Noah was holding her, exploring her mouth, seemingly desperate to taste her. Her breasts pushed into his chest and she shifted her knee, brushing against his erection.

Yum...

Noah allowed Jules to slide to the floor, silently demanding the key to the door. She licked her lips and shook her head, her brain stuttering. Noah released a frustrated sigh, reached for her clutch bag and flipped it open. His fingers delved inside and he withdrew the key, handing the bag back to her and stabbing the lock all in one fluid movement.

Impressive, since she wasn't sure how to spell her name. "How can you think, act? All I can think about is how wonderful you make me feel."

Noah gripped her wrist and jerked her inside. "I'm motivated. I've been imagining ripping that dress off you all evening."

Okay, that statement pierced the fog. But…no. As much as she wanted to get naked, this dress was too expensive to be a casualty. She slapped her hand on Noah's chest. "Do not harm this dress, Lockwood."

When he just smiled at her, Jules slapped him again to make her point. "Seriously, Noah. Don't do anything to this dress."

Noah held up his hands before his expression turned, and she saw determination, tenderness and a great deal of fascination in his face. He touched her cheek and his fingers trailed over her jaw. "You are so damn beautiful, Jules."

Jules touched her tongue to her top lip. When he spoke in that reverent voice, his confidence and cockiness gone, she saw Noah at a deeper level, stripped bare. She liked the softness beneath the bad-boy layer, the tenderness beneath his alpha facade.

She liked him. She loved him. And in ways she shouldn't.

Determined not to go there, not to think about that now, Jules closed the front door and linking her fingers with Noah's, led him up the stairs. She smiled as they both instinctively avoided the steps that creaked, staying to the side of the hallway to muffle their footsteps. They were adults but they were acting like her parents still occupied the master suite down the hall.

Jules led Noah into her bedroom, shut the door and kicked off her heels. Turning around, she looked at her man, taking a moment to watch him watch her. Deciding that her dress needed to go—because she didn't fully trust that wild look in Noah's eye—she reached under her arm and found the tab to the hidden zip, slowly pulling it down her side. The dress fell apart and Jules, enjoying this striptease more than she thought she would, slowly stepped out of it, draping it over the back of her chair. In the corner of her eye she caught her reflection in her freestanding mirror, saw her strapless, blush-colored bra and matching high-cut panties. Her underwear covered as much as her bathing suit normally did but she looked wanton, like a woman anticipating her lover.

And, dammit, she was.

Who would make the first move? Jules didn't know, so she just stood there as the tension in the room ratcheted upward.

Noah lifted one eyebrow, his face hard in the light of the bedside lamp she'd left burning. "You sure about this?" he asked quietly, his lashes dark against his cheek. "Because if we start, I'm not sure that I'll be able to stop."

"I'm sure."

"Then I'm damn grateful."

Noah shrugged out of his jacket, pulled down his tie and tossed both onto the chair, covering her dress with his clothing. Flipping open the button on his collar, he stepped toward her, the pads of his fingers skimming the column of her neck. Her collarbone, the slope of her breast. His gentle touch gave permission for the butterflies in her stomach to lift off. Him taking it slow was more erotic than deep, hot kisses and on-fire hands.

He was such a tough man, so self-contained, but his tenderness was a surprise, his need to draw out their lovemaking astonishing. But he'd speed up in a minute, and they'd go from zero to ballistic. There was too much chemistry between them to allow for a long, slow burn.

Noah held her head in both hands and his thumbs drifted over her eyebrows, down her temples and across her cheekbones.

"Kiss me, No."

Noah half smiled. "Shh. Don't think, don't rush, just feel. Enjoy me loving you. There is no hurry."

Noah didn't wait for or expect a reply, he just lowered his head and his mouth finally—finally!—skimmed hers. As they kissed along slow, heated paths of pleasure, she touched him where she could. She tried to open his shirt with hesitant, shaking fingers, and it seemed like eons passed before she managed to separate the sides of his shirt, allowing her hands to skate across his chest. She pulled her fingers through his chest hair, across his flat nipples, over his rib cage. She dragged her nails over his stomach muscles, feeling like a superhero when he trembled under her touch.

Through the fabric of his pants, she stroked the pad of her finger along his erection, from base to tip, and was rewarded by the sound of a low curse.

Needing more, Jules flipped open the snap on his pants, pulled down his zipper and released his straining erection. Using both hands to cage him, she arched her neck as Noah's mouth headed south, nipping the cords of her neck, sucking on the skin covering the ball of her shoulder.

Without warning, Noah spun her around, ordering her to put her hands on the wall. Following his lead, she gasped when his mouth touched every bump on her spine, barely noticing when her bra fell to the floor at her feet. Stepping close to her, his hands covered her breasts, his thumbs teasing her nipples into hard points.

"I want you," he said, dipping his head to her neck, sucking on that patch of skin where her neck and shoulder met.

Noah hooked his thumbs into her lacy panties and slid them down her legs. Then Noah's hands were on her butt, his fingers sliding between her legs, finding her most sensitive spot with ruthless efficiency. Jules lifted her arms above her head, rested her forehead on her wrists and began to pant.

One finger entered her, then another, and she climbed...reaching, teetering, desperate.

Noah chuckled, pulled his hand away to tease her breasts, slid his fingers across her flat stomach.

"Noah..."

Noah's chest pressed into her back, his erection flirting with her butt. "Yeah?"

"I need—"

"What, babe?"

Jules turned her head and torso and lifted her face, prepared to beg. His eyes, sparking with gold flecks, met hers and then his mouth was over hers, possessive and demanding. Wriggling so that she faced him, Jules hooked a leg over his hip and groaned when his erection brushed her curls, finding her sweet spot.

Pulling her backward, Noah half lifted and half dragged her to her bed, sitting and pulling her down so that her legs fell on either side of his thighs, as close as they could be without him slipping inside.

Noah pushed her hair off her face. "Babe, I need a condom and to get my clothes off. I'm not making love to you half-naked."

Jules moved against him, sliding her core up him. She smiled when Noah's eyes rolled upward. "Okay, in a minute."

Noah gripped her hips and lifted her off him, the muscles in his stomach and arms contracting. *Wow, hot.* Noah stood up, picked up his jacket and found the inside pocket. He pulled out a strip of three condoms, which he tossed onto the bed next to her hip. Jules flopped back on the bed and watched Noah strip, boldly inspecting him from the top of his now-messy hair to his big feet still encased in his shoes. He had a tattoo just above his hip and Jules sat up to take a closer look. After he removed his socks and shoes, she reached for him, allowing her fingers to skate over his ink, a nautical rope.

The knot of the bowline rested on his hip while the rope traveled across the very top of his thigh and onto his lower stomach. Jules appreciated the artist's work, the battered quality suggesting the rope was well used. "Do you miss sailing, No?"

Noah's fingers tunneled into her hair. "Not as much as I missed you."

Not sure how to respond, Jules stared up at him with wide eyes.

Noah pinned her with his gaze, his big body looming over hers. Her legs fell open and his erection nudged her opening. "I need you, Jules. I need to be inside you. To feel... Jesus, Jules."

Jules silently finished his sentence for him: *to feel complete.*

Jules wound her arms around his neck as he slid inside her, just once, skin on skin. Like him, she craved this contact, just for a brief second or maybe a minute, with no emotional or physical barriers. Then Noah pulled out, rolled a condom on and returned to loving her.

Which he did, as he did most things, extremely well.

Nine

Jules...

The next morning, when Jules stepped into her mom's sunny kitchen—Levi's kitchen because it was his house now—Darby grabbed her hand and hopped on one foot.

"Juju! News!"

Jules eyed the full coffeepot. Since Noah spent most of last night doing wonderful things to her that might be illegal in certain countries, she was exhausted. Her brain was fried and her energy levels were low. Speaking of, where was the man of the hour, of the past several hours? Her bed was empty, he wasn't in the bathroom and he wasn't helping Levi make breakfast.

Maybe he wanted to avoid facing her family first thing in the morning. God knew she did. But it turned out that she needed coffee more than she needed to avoid conversation.

"Guess who had a date last night?" Darby asked, hopping from one foot to the other.

Okay, she and Darby had the twin thing going on, but Darby could *not* know that she'd slept with Noah. No way. Turning her back on her sister, Jules ignored Levi's greeting and grabbed a mug from the cupboard above the coffeepot. Pouring some of the brew into her cup, she took her time turning around, hoping that they wouldn't notice the stubble burn on her jaw and her many-orgasms glow.

"Isn't there a rule in the Bible about talking about this stuff on a Sunday?" Jules asked.

Levi, who was melting butter for—thank you, God— eggs Benedict, glared at Darby. "Don't think so but I wish there was." Levi frowned at her. "Are we talking about you?"

"Me?" Jules slapped her hand on her heart. "Why me?"

She waited for Levi to say that he'd seen Noah walking out of her bedroom but Levi just shook his head and returned to his task of making breakfast.

Dammit. There was nothing to feel embarrassed about. She and Noah were consenting adults, but she didn't feel comfortable with the idea of her brother knowing that she and Noah… Jules shuddered. Too much to handle on little sleep and with no caffeine in her system.

Darby cocked her head. "You look exhausted, Jules. How much sleep did you get last night?"

Not much since she'd spent most of the night exploring the land of Noah. "It's been a long, long week and last night was difficult. Ethan was at Paris's cocktail party and he is going to be the liaison between Paris and Noah, helping her to make decisions about the yacht."

"Dammit," Levi grumbled.

"Why is that a problem?" Darby reached for an apple

before jumping up on the kitchen counter, her long legs swinging. "Ethan knows yachts. He taught Noah to sail."

Levi shook his head and turned back to the stove. Jules touched his arm and waited until he looked at her. "How much do you know about their falling-out?"

"Not that much. You know Noah. He's not great at communicating. I've gathered bits and pieces from Eli and Ben, stuff they've said over the years, but I don't know what happened, *exactly*." Levi shook his head. "And I'm not telling you, Jules. It's his story to tell."

His reticence wasn't a surprise. Levi wasn't a gossip.

"I have no idea what's going on," Darby complained, between bites of her apple.

"I'll tell you what I can when I can, Darbs," Jules replied. Wanting to get off the subject of Noah and his past—he'd hate to know they were discussing him—Jules tossed her a smile. "So, what's the big news?"

"Oh, God, gossip." Levi groaned. "Can this wait until later?"

"No." Darby pointed a finger at Levi. "It concerns our mother."

Levi stepped away from the stove and frowned at her. "What's wrong with Mom? Is she hurt? Why aren't you telling me anything?"

Levi went from zero to protective in two seconds flat. Sipping her coffee, Jules eyed her siblings over the rim of her cup.

"She's fine," Darby replied before a sly smile crossed her face. "In fact she's more than fine. I heard that she had a hot date last night. Dancing was involved."

Jules hoped it was with the coffee shop owner. Apart from the fact that he was sexy in an older guy/action hero–type of way, her mom hooking up with him would ensure a decent supply of coffee for a long time to come.

Yeah, it wasn't pretty but Jules was willing to encourage this relationship to feed her coffee addiction.

"She went clubbing?" Levi demanded, his expression turning dark.

Go, Mom.

"Where? What? With who?"

Levi looked like he was ready to blow. How could he not know that Darby was winding him up? "Darbs…" she warned.

"Okay, not clubbing. But she did go dancing at a salsa club and she was looking fine."

"How do you know all this?" Levi said, sounding skeptical. Jules shook her head. Darby had friends everywhere and she encouraged those friends to talk, okay, report back to her. She was like the human version of social media.

"A friend of a friend. She also had a dinner date the night before last."

Two guys? Way to go, Mom! Jules grinned but Levi looked like he wanted to rip someone's head off. "Who is he? Where does he work? What does he do? Do we know him? Seriously, I'm going to go over to her house and—"

Jules lifted an eyebrow, waiting to hear what he would do to their mother.

"—give her a stern talking to!" he finished.

Jules giggled. "Calm down, Rambo. She's allowed to have some fun."

"Fun is bowling or golf, not salsa and dinner dates!" Levi picked up some scallions and started chopping the hell out of them.

"Mom is allowed a life. She's been alone a long time. If she wants to get it on, good for her. At least one of us is getting some."

Levi dropped the knife and slapped his hands over his ears. "Shaddup, Darby. Seriously!"

Darby laughed, enjoying Levi's discomfort and her eyes met Jules's, inviting her to share the joke. *Mom's not the only one who is getting lucky...*

Darby heard her silent words and her smile faded, her eyes widening. Jules bit her bottom lip. She normally told Darby everything but she wasn't ready to discuss Noah with her and she wasn't ready to articulate what she was feeling. Mostly because she didn't know what she was feeling, except confused.

Darby glanced at Levi and, seeing that his concentration was back on the scallions, lifted her eyebrows. "Noah?" she mouthed.

Who else? Jules nodded and shook her head. She held up her hand, silently begging her sister to let it go.

Darby pouted before slumping back in her chair, defeated. *We will talk about this.*

I know. Just not yet.

Are you okay?

Yep. Just confused.

Darby waggled her eyebrows. *Tell me this, at the very least. Was he good?*

Jules placed her hand on her heart. *He was amazing.*

"What's going on?"

Jules turned to see DJ standing in the doorway, her eyes bouncing from face to face.

"My mother is salsa dancing and dating two guys. I'm freaking out, and Jules hasn't had any sleep." Levi looked up from his task and pointed his knife at Jules, then Darby. "And Jules and Darby are doing their weird twin, silent communication thing."

DJ placed her hands on her hips, eyed Jules and her sister before turning her attention back to Levi. "Your mom deserves to have some fun, and Jules also, if I'm not mistaken, got herself some last night and that's what they were discussing."

Okay, so it might not just be a twin thing; it might be an I've-known-you-since-you-were-six thing. DJ moved to stand behind Levi's back and pointed her finger to the ceiling.

Noah?

Again, who else?

Was it good?

Why were they so concerned about Noah's prowess in the sack? Seriously?

"I can feel the air moving behind me, DJ," Levi growled. "Enough already with the sex talk. I don't want to know who is having sex, when. *Ever*," Levi said before sending Jules a hard look. "Do I need to beat someone up for you?"

Jules quickly shook her head. "No! I'm good." Seeing the concern on Levi's face, she scrambled to find some words since Levi didn't do the silent communication thing. "I'm good. We're good. Everything is good."

Levi folded his massive arms across his chest. "Good."

Jules frowned at his sarcastic repetition of her word.

"Because I would hate to have to kick my best friend's ass. Speaking of, can you find him and tell him that breakfast will be ready in fifteen?"

Maybe Levi was better at the silent communication thing than she thought.

As she had a hundred times before but not for a long time, Jules climbed up the ivy-covered trellis that led up to what used to be Noah's bedroom within Lockwood House and wondered what she was doing. She wasn't ten or fourteen or even eighteen anymore.

A month after Bethann's death, Ethan had closed up the house and moved to the apartment they kept in the city. She remembered hearing her father and mother discussing his abhorrent behavior, his lack of respect, but being young and self-involved, she hadn't paid much attention to their hushed conversations. All she knew was that Noah was hurting and that their family, which had seemed to be rock solid, detonated with Bethann's passing and the reading of the will. Within three months of her death, Noah had left Boston and dropped out of her life.

Why hadn't she pushed and probed, demanded more information? In hindsight, it was easy to see how much Noah was suffering, to see how unhappy he'd been with Morgan, to discern that she wasn't given him the emotional support he needed. Sex with Morgan might've temporarily dulled the pain but sex wouldn't have dulled his grief, his fear.

But Jules knew why she hadn't dug deeper with Noah. She had been upset with him about his involvement with Morgan—jealous, maybe?—and frustrated when he pulled back into his noncommunicative shell. She'd been dealing with her own grief and frustration at not being able to connect with her friend, betrayed by the announcement of his engagement and devastated by his kiss.

Devastated, confused, emotionally battered.

But that was in their past and she had to deal with Noah as he was today, with the adults they both were. He wasn't a young man anymore and she wasn't a teen. They could, presumably, separate attraction from sex, love from friendship, curtail their wild imaginings…

She was a successful businesswoman, a confident woman…

Who was, technically, trespassing. Jules raised the sash window and flung her leg over the windowsill. Actually, there were no technicalities involved, she was definitely trespassing.

Jules dropped her feet to the floor and wasn't surprised to see Noah in his room, dressed in a pair of old, well-fitting jeans and a long-sleeved gray shirt, the sleeves pushed up to his elbows. Thanks to his recent shower, his blond hair looked a shade darker. She inhaled the dust and mustiness of a closed room but also soap and toothpaste and his special Noah-only scent.

Jules stood up straight, slapped her hands on her butt and looked at Noah. "Levi says breakfast is nearly ready."

Noah sat on the edge of what used to be his bed and frowned at her. "Not that hungry, actually."

Jules wanted to go to him, to drape her arms around his neck and snuggle in, but the expression on his face was remote, his body tense. Knowing that he wouldn't open up without some prodding—if he opened up at all—Jules sat on the edge of the sill and stretched out her legs. "Why did you break into your dad's house, No?"

"Ethan's house," Noah corrected her, his mouth tightening. "He stopped being my dad a decade ago."

"What happened, Noah?"

Noah stared at his feet, his hand draped between his bent knees. "My mom's will wasn't clear and there was room to maneuver. Ethan essentially tried to screw us out of our inheritance. When he was faced with the choice of inheriting millions or keeping his kids, he chose the cash." Noah stared at the hard, glossy wooden floor. He cleared his throat and when he continued speaking, Jules heard his voice crack with emotion. "He raised us. We called him Dad. Eli and Ben were toddlers when he came into our lives and he spent twenty-plus years being our dad. He was at every sport match he could make, at every play, prize giving. I thought he loved my mom with every fiber of his being.

"Two weeks after her death, I called him at the city apartment and a woman answered his phone, a very young-sounding woman. He was in the shower and she told me that she intended to keep him busy for the rest of the night, if I understood what she meant."

Jules fought the urge to go to him, but if she did he'd clam up and stop talking. She gripped the sill to keep herself in place.

"I confronted Ethan the next day and he laughed in my face. He told me to grow up, that the woman I talked to wasn't the first nor would she be the last. It was what men did, he said."

No, it wasn't. Her dad never cheated on her mom.

Noah's knee bounced up and down. "He then went on to tell me that he'd done his job—he'd raised us as Mom wanted him to do, and he was cashing in. The businesses, the house, the bank accounts, it was payment for being incarcerated in his marriage, his life, for the past twenty years."

Jules bit her lip at Noah's bleak tone. "If I behaved, let him take, well, everything, he'd continue paying for our education, if not, we could waft in the wind."

"Oh, Noah."

"I couldn't let him do that, not without a fight. I needed money to hire lawyers and Ivan gave me more than I needed, provided I stayed engaged to Morgan for two years. After a lot of legal wrangling, the judge gave us the marina and boatyard. Ethan got the cash and the estate. I needed to keep sailing to keep generating the cash to upgrade the marina and boatyard so that they could become profitable again."

"But you did it, Noah. You saved your grandfather's businesses."

Noah lifted his head to look at her. "The price was enormous, Jules. When I finally broke it off with Morgan she had a nervous breakdown and was admitted to some psychiatric facility. They blamed me, despite the fact that our relationship hadn't been anything more than a few calls and emails for months."

"They needed someone to blame, No, and you were handy."

"Maybe." Noah stood up and walked over to his desk, looking at the medals hanging on the wall, the sailing trophies still on the shelf. "Most people think that the opportunity to sail for Wind and Solar was a dream come true."

"Wasn't it?"

She could see the tension in his back in the way he held his neck. But when he turned around and looked at her, Jules saw the devastation on his face. "Leaving Boston was a freaking nightmare. Oh, the sailing was fun, visiting new places was interesting, but when I stepped onto that plane at Logan, I left everything behind. My mom was gone and I was still mourning her, trying to come to terms with her early, brutally unfair death. I lost my dad, too. I didn't recognize the man standing in front of me, taking us to court for *his paycheck.* I had to leave my brothers and hope like hell that they were sensible enough to stay out of trouble, and if not, to run to your folks if they found themselves in a sticky situation. I left my friends, not only Levi, but other friends of both sexes. I left you, the person who knew me best, and I left this weird thing between us, an attraction that blew in from nowhere and was left unexplored. I felt like I had my entire life ripped from me…"

"Which you did." Jules waited a beat before speaking

again. "You could've told me this, Noah, at any time. I would've understood because, dammit, I needed to understand."

Noah shrugged. "Time passed and as it did, the words grew harder to say."

Noah pushed his thumbs into his eyes and Jules wondered if it was because he didn't want her to see the tears there. Hers were about to overflow.

Noah folded his arms, looked up at the ceiling and, a long time later, looked back. The grief was gone and determination was back on his face. "There is no way I am going back there, Jules, back to that place where I felt lost and scared and alone. I've learned how to live on my own, be on my own—I can't do this happy-family thing..."

She didn't recall asking him to but...okay.

Noah looked around the room, his face hard. "This is just a house, these are just things. This is just land. My mom isn't here and by buying it I won't change the past, change what he did, the choices I made. Mom doesn't care whether it stays in the family or not—she's not here!"

Jules winced at the muted roar. "I'm killing myself, and for what? To design a boat for a woman who doesn't seem to care what I come up with or not? So that I can raise the money to buy a property I'm not sure I even want in a town that holds nothing but bad memories for me?"

Well, that stung.

"I could forget about buying the house and the estate. I could walk away. I have a client begging me to meet him on the Costa Smeralda, another in Hawaii, both wanting designs I could do in my sleep. I don't need to be here, Jules! I don't need this crap in my life! Sun, sailing and sex...with none of the drama!"

Jules nodded, pain punching tiny holes in her stom-

ach lining and her heart. He didn't want a life in Boston
and he didn't want her. He needed his freedom, she knew
this… She'd always known this. So why did it hurt so
much? Jules pushed her hair off her face and forced herself to look him in the eye, to confront her feelings. "I'm
sorry you feel like that, No. I'm sorry that you think a
life in Boston can't give you what you need."

"You don't know what I need, Jules!"

Yeah, she did, but getting him to realize that was an
impossibility. But she'd try. At least once… "You need
us, Noah, and you need *me*. You need to wake up with
someone who loves you, who gets you, understands your
past and who will always be on your side. You need to
spend your days with your brothers and play pool with
them in The Tavern and golf outside your front door.
You need to have coffee and dinner with my mom and
talk about your mom. You need to buy this house and
you need to *stay*."

Noah frowned at her and she could see hope and frustration and fear going to war in his eyes. "Why do you
say that?"

Because she loved him. She'd loved him every day
of her life and she'd fallen in love with him again when
she saw him standing naked in her shower. Her brain had
just needed a little time to come to terms with what her
heart always knew.

"Because if you walk away from this house, from
Boston, from me, you're going to regret it every day for
the rest of your life. You belong here, Noah. You belong
with me."

Jules held up her hand, knowing he was about to make
a hard rebuttal. "I get it, Noah. I understand how much
it must have hurt leaving because I felt it, too. Not having you in my life was horrendous and I was determined

that I wouldn't give you another chance to hurt me. But here I am, doing it again. Love is scary, Noah, but it's the one thing that should be scary! We shouldn't just be able to jump into love without thought. I know if you walk away again I'll be in a world of pain, *again*, but I can't divorce myself from what I feel because loving you is an essential part of who I am."

Jules stood up and made herself smile as she placed one leg over the windowsill. "If you leave, if you don't fight for this house, fight for your life, fight for me, you'll be an old man living with regret, unable to look yourself in the eye."

"I don't love you, Jules."

Such impetuous, defiant words. Jules closed her eyes, trying to hold back the pain. "Of course you love me, Noah. You always have. Just as I've always loved you. You're just too damn scared to admit it and even more terrified to do something about it."

Callie...

There was no way that Mason would hear that she'd been on two dates in the past week. While many of her friends frequented his coffee shop, she doubted that he made it a habit to quiz the elderly about their love lives.

And if he did, he shouldn't.

Her friends, the few who knew she was dating, wouldn't think to tell him. To them Mason was part of the service industry, not someone to gossip with. The thought made her feel ugly, petty and ashamed. She shouldn't even be coming here but she was as addicted to his gorgeous face as she was to his coffee blend.

Oh, who was she kidding? He could serve strychnine-flavored java and she'd be coming back for more. It was

official: she was pathetic. Callie pushed open the door to
the coffeehouse and cursed when her eyes flew around
the room, instinctively seeking out the man she'd come
to see. She'd blown off a round of golf this morning with
Patrick and an invite to lunch with John. Her dates thought
that their evenings had gone well but, apart from the salsa
dancing, she'd been as bored as hell—and Mason was to
blame.

Patrick and John were perfectly nice, urbane, successful men in their early sixties. Accomplished, successful
and courteous, they were appropriate men for a woman
of her age to date.

They were also deeply, fundamentally, jaw-breakingly
boring. And they seemed, dammit, old.

"Stop frowning. You're going to get wrinkles," Mason
murmured.

Callie turned her head to see him standing behind
her, dressed in khaki shorts and an untucked, white button-down shirt with the cuffs rolled back. He was car-
rying a cup of coffee and a slice of carrot cake, and her
mouth watered—at the sight of him and the dessert. She
couldn't indulge; she had to try and keep her muffin top
under some sort of control. Though she suspected that
horse had bolted a long, long time ago…

"I already have wrinkles," Callie told him, sitting
down at the nearest table and glaring at him.

"Hardly any," Mason replied, his eyes wandering over
her face and down her neck. "In fact, you have the most
gorgeous skin. Want some coffee?"

*No, I want to stop thinking about you. I want to stop
imagining what your hands feel like on my skin, your
tongue in my mouth. I want to be able to date and not
feel like I am cheating on my dead husband and you.*

Callie sighed. "S'pose."

Mason delivered the coffee and carrot cake to a nearby table before returning to her side. He held her chin and lifted her head, blue eyes assessing. "Who pissed on your battery?"

He was so damn irreverent. "Don't be crude."

Mason's thumb skimmed her bottom lip. "Stop acting like you are 103. Spit it out, woman."

She should object to him calling her "woman," should tell him to go to hell. But his rough voice and the tenderness in his eyes just warmed her from the inside out.

Or more accurately, from that space between her legs and up.

Callie gestured for him to take the other seat. "Don't call me 'woman,' and don't loom over me. Sit if you want to but don't…*hover*."

Mason frowned, slid into the chair opposite her and rested his arms on the table. He didn't speak. He just looked at her with assessing eyes. Callie drummed her fingers on the table between them, wondering what to say. She couldn't tell him that she'd missed him, that she'd wanted to be with him, that eating out with another man seemed wrong.

"Cal? Talk to me."

"Jules, my daughter, is going through a rough time. She and the man she loves, who I think also loves her, can't find a way to be together."

Mason remained silent for a moment. "As a parent, I fully understand that you are worried but that's not why you are upset. Tell me the truth, the full truth." Mason stopped one of his passing waitresses, ordered a latte and turned his attention back to her.

"I wanted an espresso," Callie muttered.

"No, you didn't, and aren't I supposed to be the child in this nonrelationship?" Mason asked, his voice sounding tougher than she'd ever heard it. Callie flushed, sat back and tried to get her anger under control. None of this was his fault and her acting like an angry teenager wasn't helping.

"One of the reasons I like you, Callie, is that you appear to be a straight shooter. So, last chance, speak or shut up," Mason said, his eyes flat and his jaw hard.

Callie ran her thumbnail across the wooden table. "I went on two dates this past week."

Mason immediately stiffened. "Why are you telling me this?"

"Because they were very nice, very successful men of a certain age and they were—"

"I think I'm going to throw up," Mason interjected.

"—as boring as hell. I spent most of that time wishing they were you," Callie continued, ignoring him.

Mason's eyes lightened, darkened and lightened again. Callie fell into all that interest and emotion and, yeah, desire. "What are you saying, Callie?"

"I'm saying that I am a fifty-four-year-old woman who is not only just coming out of mourning, but menopause, too. I am a cocktail of hormones, insecurity and confusion. I am both terrified of having sex and equally terrified of not ever having it again. I've been a wife, am still sort of a mommy, but I've forgotten how to be a woman."

Mason ran his hand over his jaw, visibly shocked by her blunt speech.

"I want you but I don't want to want you. I don't want to disappoint you but I don't want to disappoint myself. I'm never getting married again—Ray was the only husband I'll ever have."

"Jesus."

If she stopped now, she'd never start again. "If you keep asking me, I might say yes to a date. I might even get up enough courage to put my overweight, very un-sexy body in your hands and I might let you kiss me."

"*Might?* Screw that."

Mason pulled her to her feet and led her through the crowded tables toward the counter on the far side of the room. Callie tried to tug her hand away but he was too strong and, yeah, this was the most excitement she'd had since she and Ray made love in the hot tub—

The slap of Mason's hand on a swinging door dragged her from that memory—from the guilt rising in her—and she found herself in a tiny kitchen. Mason hauled her across the room and, keeping his hand around her wrist, flipped the dead bolt on the back door. Hot, humid air swirled around her as Mason guided her down the steps and, the next moment, her back was against the rough brick wall. Mason stared down at her, his eyes boring into her.

"Tell me now you don't want this and I'll back off."

Callie placed her hands on his chest and lifted her face up. "I do but I shouldn't—"

"Again, screw that."

Mason's hands captured her face and his mouth covered hers and plundered, sliding over hers like he owned it, his tongue twisting hers into submission.

This wasn't a boy's kiss but a man's, a man who knew what he wanted and how he intended to get it. There was no hesitation because Mason listened to her body language, saw the desire in her eyes. Impatient and determined, he wasn't the type to waste time, to hang around waiting for her to be 100 percent ready.

Turned out that he was right, she was ready. Her tongue knew what to do, her hands ran up his strong back, down his hard butt, skirted around to feel his flat, hard stomach. Since she was touching him, Mason ob-

viously thought that a little quid pro quo was in order
and his broad hand sneaked between them and covered
her breast, immediately finding her nipple and rubbing
it into a hard, tight point.

It felt natural to tilt her pelvis, to push against that
long, hard erection…

His erection. His…

Erection.

God, she was kissing a man who wasn't her husband,
who was so much younger than her, in the alley behind
his coffeehouse. *Whoa, brakes on, Brogan.*

Mason, feeling her resistance, rested his forehead on
hers. "Please don't regret this, Callie. You didn't do anything wrong."

Callie's hands fell to her sides as Ray's face flashed on
the big screen in her mind. What would he think? What
would her kids think? Her friends? Callie stepped away
from Mason, who looked flushed and, oh, so frustrated.

"Then why do I feel like I have?"

"This again." Mason shoved his hands into his hair.
"He's dead, Callie, and you're alive, still here, still sexy,
still a woman. You didn't die with him."

"A part of me did, Mason!" Callie cried. "And the part
of me that is waking up is still coming to terms with all
of this!"

Mason's eyes flashed with irritation. "I'm not going to
beg, Callie. Or run after you. Or wait forever."

Callie narrowed her eyes, suddenly furious. "That's
such a man thing to say! Because it's not going your
way, you issue a threat? Guess what, Mason? I'm not
young enough or stupid enough or insecure enough to
fall for that BS!

"This goes at my pace or it doesn't go at all," Callie
added, furious.

Callie saw the regret in his eyes, the apology hovering on his lips. It had been a spur-of-the-moment statement, something she instinctively knew he regretted, but it gave her a damn good excuse to walk away, to put a whole lot of daylight and space between her and this man who'd dropped into her life and flipped it upside down.

"I'm not going to come back here for a while. I need time to think," Callie told him.

Mason nodded, clearly still frustrated but back in control. He gestured at the still-open door. "I'll follow you in shortly. I need some time."

"For what?" Callie asked the question without thinking and frowned at his raised eyebrows. Then Mason shocked her by grabbing her hand and placing her palm on his very hard penis. Through his shorts she could feel his strength, the sheer masculinity under her palm. She leaned forward, wanting to kiss him but Mason pulled back and dropped her hand.

He turned away, and when he spoke his voice sounded rough. And a little sad. "Go inside, Callie. I'll see you when and if I see you."

Walk away, Brogan. It was the right thing to do. She didn't want to, but Callie forced herself to pull open the door to the coffee shop, to step back into the cool kitchen.

Back to reality, where it was safe. But where it was also so damn lonely.

And brutally unexciting.

Ten

Noah...

Of course you love me, Noah, you always have. Just as I've always loved you. You're just too damn scared to admit it and even more terrified to do something about it.

Jules's words rolled around Noah's head as they had every minute for the past three weeks. He wanted to dismiss them, to shrug them off as a figment of her overactive imagination, but they ran across his mind on a never-ending ticker tape.

He wanted her, of course he did, she was everything he wanted, but he was too damn scared, comprehensively terrified of what it meant to go all in with Jules. Noah thought that he had just cause to be. He'd had everything at one point in his life; he'd had the world at his feet. A solid family structure, parents who adored him, pain-in-the-ass brothers who'd charge hell if he needed them to. Friends—good, close friends.

Then, like a cheap car slamming into the back of a heavy rig at high speed, his life had crumpled and crashed around him and his world as he knew it ended. Everything he knew, relied upon, was no longer there. The people he thought he knew morphed into strangers. His dad became his enemy, his girlfriend a means to an end, his friendship with Jules suddenly colored by a shocking dose of lust. Leaving his life behind hadn't been a choice. But walking away still hurt like the hot, sour bite of hell.

He didn't think he could cope with loving something—a person, his life, normality—and having it ripped from him again. But nor could he live a life that didn't have Jules in it. And he didn't want her as his friend…

Rock and hard place, meet the devil and the deep blue sea.

He loved her, of course he did. He'd loved the ten-year-old Jules who caught frogs and climbed trees, the fourteen-year-old with braces, the young woman he'd watched evolve into an adult woman. Then he kissed her and he saw a thousand galaxies in her eyes, felt the power of the universe in her touch. That hadn't changed: Jules was still, and always would be, the person who made his world turn.

Tides changed, the moon waxed and waned, and seas dipped and rose but Jules was his sextant, his North Star, his GPS.

Wherever she was, was where he wanted to be. But fear, cold and hard, still gripped his heart. God, he'd much rather be fighting a squall in the Southern Ocean than be caught in this emotional maelstrom.

Noah looked up at the rap on his door frame, happy for any distraction coming his way. Levi stood in the doorway, dressed in board shorts and dock shoes, his red T-shirt faded by sunlight. Noah noticed the six-pack in his hand, the bottles dripping with condensation. Hell, yes, he could do with one or three of those.

Levi walked into his office, tossed him a beer and sat down on his chair, his long legs stretched out in front of him. Noah cracked the top, took a long sip and rested the cold bottle on his aching head. "So, you need to make a formal offer on the Lockwood Trust in two days or the estate will go on the market," Levi said bluntly.

He was aware. "There's no chance Paris will sign the final design by then. Ethan won't let her."

"Has Jules completed her designs?"

Noah glanced at the folder holding Jules's sketches, the fabric samples, the wonderful mock-ups of the yacht's interiors. They'd been communicating via email for weeks but Jules still managed to do a stunning job and Paris, and anyone with taste, would love her designs. "She's done. So am I. Paris just needs to approve the designs."

"So when are you meeting her?"

"I haven't made an appointment to see her yet." Levi pulled a face and Noah shook his head at his friend's disapproval. "I know I should but I keep wondering what's the point? Ethan will shoot down everything I say, he'll demand a redesign and time will run out. I've been working on other projects but my fees won't earn anywhere near as much as what Paris cane pay me. Basically, I'm screwed."

Levi frowned before pointing the top of his bottle in Noah's direction. "Sorry, who are you and what have you done with Noah Lockwood?"

Noah sent him a blank look, wondering if Levi had had a few more beers before ending up in his office.

"Noah, one of the things that set you apart from other

sailors was your utter belief in yourself and the course you were on. You backed yourself a hundred percent and you never ever gave up. Where's that dude?"

Noah opened his mouth to blast Levi, to defend himself, but Levi spoke over him. "You always raced until the bitter end, sometimes you went across the finish line without realizing that you were done, that you had won the race, because you were so damn focused, because you fought, right up until the end. You still have a couple of days. Why the hell aren't you still fighting?"

"I...uh..." Crap, he didn't have an answer for that.

"My sister—the miserable one living in my house—and your future are deserving of all your effort, Noah, all your competitive spirit and every last bit of determination," Levi said, emotion bleeding through his tough words. He leaned forward, his intense gaze nailing Noah to his chair. "It's the Rolex Sydney Hobart Yacht Race, you and your closest competitor are in the Bass Strait and it's neck and neck. Are you going to alter course, or are you going to hold your nerve, and your course, and fight for the win?"

Adrenaline pumped through his system. He could taste the drops of seawater on his lips, the wind blowing in his hair. Wind catching his sails, he could hear the whoop of his teammates as his yacht sailed forward.

Keeping his eyes on Levi's, he drained his beer and reached for his phone. "I'm going to hold my course."

Levi nodded and the fire of frustration in his eyes died. "Thank God, I wasn't looking forward to kicking your ass."

For the first time in days, Noah smiled. "As if you could. Now, get lost. I've got a house to buy and a meeting to set up."

Levi ambled to his feet, snagging the plastic cage holding the beers. "And a girl to win?"

"Yeah. And a girl to win."

Levi looked concerned. "And if you lose?"

Noah lifted one shoulder and held his friend's eye. "I never lose, Levi. But there's a first time for everything and if that happens, I'll do what I always do…"

"And that is?"

"Stand in the storm, ride it out and keep adjusting my sails."

Jules…

I am not going to cry. That will not happen. This is business. Paris is a client and Noah is a colleague. You can do this. You have to do this.

Woman up, Brogan.

Jules placed her hand on the wall next to the elevator in the lobby of Paris's building and stared at the expensive marble flooring. Dammit, this hurt. Every cell in her body ached, her eyes were red rimmed from crying too many tears and from nights without sleep. She felt sick from the tips of her toes to her ears. God, even her hair hurt. She was fundamentally, utterly miserable.

Her fault, so her fault. She told herself not to fall for Noah again, she knew a broken heart was a possibility. Heartbreak, such small words for such a life-altering condition. Jules wished she could go back to her childhood, when skinned knees and broken arms hurt and were inconvenient but they healed, dammit. This…this gut-ripping, soul-mincing pain was going to be with her for a long, long time. And she knew she'd never be the same person again, she was irrevocably changed. Quieter, harder, a lot more lost and very alone.

This was now her life.

Jules looked down at the screen on her phone and glared at the prosaic, to-the-point message on her screen. Five o'clock meeting with Paris. Be there.

Noah's terse instructions were followed by Paris's address.

Jules hadn't spoken to Noah since leaving him in his childhood bedroom nearly a month ago. He didn't come back to the house for breakfast, and when he didn't contact her on Monday, or on any day that following week, she assumed that history was repeating itself and Noah was retreating from her bed and her life. She spent every moment she had working on her designs for the yacht—the sooner she finished with them, the sooner this would all be over—and couriered the finished designs and the sketches to Noah's office two weeks ago.

She'd yet to hear whether he approved, what he thought. She could be going into a presentation showing Paris sketches and designs Noah hated. Because she still had her pride, and that meant that she had a reputation to maintain, a job to complete and that meant—*grrr*—obeying his text message order. She'd never bailed on a project and didn't intend to now. No matter how difficult it would be to see Noah again, knowing he chose his fear over her, she would get into this damn elevator and finish the job.

If she didn't, she would never be able to look herself in the eye again. *Time to be brave, Brogan.* An hour, maybe more, and she'd be done. She could go home, pull a blanket over her head and shut out the world. And release all the tears that were gathering in her throat.

Jules left the elevator and walked down the long hallway, telling herself that this was it, this was the last time she would be seeing Noah for God knew how long.

Standing outside Paris's door, she worked her fist into her sternum, mentally tossing water on the fire in her stomach.

An hour, Brogan. You can do this. You have no choice!

Wishing she was anywhere else—she was exhausted and stressed and *sad*, dammit—Jules knocked on Paris's door and jumped when the door swung open. Noah stood there, strong and confident in his gray suit, white shirt and scarlet power tie. His hair was brushed off his forehead and he looked like he could stroll into any business meeting anywhere in the world and take control.

Jules met his eyes and frowned at the tenderness she saw within those brown depths, the flicker of amusement. He thought this was funny? His inheritance was on the line and her heart was hemorrhaging, and he was amused? Jules welcomed the surge of anger and clenched her fists, the urge to smack him almost overwhelming.

She hauled in a breath, then another, knowing that her face reflected all her suppressed rage. She was going to kill him, slowly and right there. A sympathetic female judge would understand, she was sure of it.

"You look like you are about to blow a gasket."

A gasket, an engine, input the codes to set off a nuclear strike. How dare he stand there looking rested and relaxed? Did he have any idea of the strolls she'd taken through hell lately?

"I— You— I'm… God!" Jules rubbed her fingers across her forehead. She couldn't do this, there was no chance. She was leaving, going home and crawling into bed before she fell apart completely. She wasn't brave and she definitely wasn't strong.

"I've got to go." Jules managed to whisper the words

and turned to leave. Noah's hand on her arm pulled her back to face him, and then his hands were on her hips and drawing her slowly and deliberately toward himself. When not even an ant could crawl between them, he brushed his mouth across hers, his tongue tracing the seam of her lips, before lifting his head.

Why was he doing this? Was he trying to torture her?

No more. She was done with this. Jules slid her fingers under his open suit jacket, grabbed the skin at his waist and gave it a hard twist.

Noah's eyes widened and she heard his pained gasp. "Ow. For what?"

"Do you know how much it hurts to kiss you, knowing that I might never be able to do that again?" Jules hissed, furious at the tears that clouded her vision. "That's not fair, Noah, and worse than that, it's cruel."

Noah rubbed the back of his neck, looking shocked and a little embarrassed. "Jules, babe, just hang on."

"For what, Noah? No, I'm done! I can't do this anymore. It hurts too damn much!"

Noah touched her cheek with his knuckle. "I'm asking you, one more time, to trust me. Please, Jules."

Jules shook her head, willing away the tears in her eyes. "I don't think I can, Noah. You've drained me of the little strength I had left."

"Dammit, Jules—"

"Julia? Oh, is Julia here?" Paris trilled from somewhere in the cavernous apartment behind them. "Noah! Is that Julia? If it is, tell her to come and have a glass of champagne and to show me her pretty, pretty work."

Jules closed her eyes, twisted her lips and, refusing to look at the man she wanted the most but couldn't have, turned on her heel and forced herself to walk into Paris's luxurious apartment.

Noah...

Noah was regarded as one of the best sailors of his generation, one of the top money earners in the sport. He was a decent businessman, successful and wealthy. A good brother and friend. None of that meant anything, everything was stripped away, and he was now just the man who'd made Jules cry.

Never again. He was done with that. From this moment on, Jules and her happiness were his highest priority, making sure that she'd never have cause to doubt him again, his lifetime goal. And, because he didn't want her to suffer longer than she had to, Noah injected steel into his spine and followed his woman into the overly decorated lounge of Paris's apartment.

Ethan was at the meeting, just as he'd expected and banked on him to be. Noah had given their encounter a lot of thought so he had a plan. Taking control of the presentation—knowing that Jules needed something to anchor her—he suggested a virtual tour of the yacht. He quickly connected his laptop to Paris's big-screen TV and, thanks to some very high-tech computer software, showed Paris what he and Jules envisaged for the yacht, inside and out. Pity their client couldn't feel the waves rolling under the hull, taste the salt on her lips, but that being said, it was still kick-ass tech.

As he'd requested, Paris and Ethan kept their comments until the end, allowing him and Jules to complete their presentation before they were bombarded with questions.

"It's beautiful." Paris sighed and clasped her hands. "Utterly marvelous. What shall I call her?"

"Whatever you like." Noah smiled but it faded when he darted a glance at Jules and saw her blank face.

"Before your rhapsodizing gets out of control, my dear, I should like to point out that there are some very crucial design flaws in what Noah has presented," Ethan said, his voice pitched low. No, there weren't. How could Paris not hear the malice in his voice, see the spite in his eyes?

And so it started.

Placing his ankle on his knee, Noah cocked his head. Ethan met his eyes, not for one minute believing that Noah would rake up the past. It was a fair conclusion for him to reach; generally, Noah would rather bleed to death before asking for a bandage, help or even a plaster. Well, not this time. There was too much at stake.

"There are no flaws in the design," Noah said, his voice calm. "Ethan is just saying that to irritate me."

Paris frowned. "Nonsense! He's your stepfather. He raised you. And he's just trying to make your design better and to look after my interests."

Noah shook his head, conscious of Jules's eyes on his face. "Ethan never looks after anyone's interests but his own, Paris. He doesn't want you to sign off on the design, because if you do that, then he has to sell Lockwood Estate to me, at twenty percent below the market price. He'd lose twenty million if that happens."

"That's not true," Ethan bit out, turning an alarming shade of red.

Noah dropped his leg, leaned forward and opened a folder, pulling out a copy of the judgment. He pushed it across the table in Paris's direction. "Proof." Noah reached across the table and took Paris's hand in his. Damn, he didn't want to hurt her but when it came to choosing between her happiness and Jules's, between saving his inheritance and kicking Ethan out of his life forever, he would. Besides, she and Ethan had only been together a few weeks; she was as much a victim of his machinations as he was.

"Paris, I like you. You're a pain in the ass to work for, but you have a warm heart, a romantic heart. I think you are wonderfully charming and witty but you *are* a woman of a certain age."

Paris narrowed her eyes at that statement and Noah ignored her, along with Ethan's growls of disapproval. Noah forced himself to articulate the words. "Ethan doesn't date woman your age, in fact he rarely dates anyone over the age of twenty-five." *Dammit, just spit it out!* "The only reason he's dating you is because you are rich and he's broke."

"I am not! This is slander! How dare you?"

"Noah—"

Noah ignored Jules's quiet warning and flicked a quick glance at Ethan, looking apoplectic with rage. He pulled out another stack of papers and put them in front of Paris. "Photos of his last ten girlfriends, copies of his credit report—he owes money all around town."

Paris looked down, flicked through the papers and when she lifted her head again, her eyes were flint hard. *Gotcha, you bastard.*

"Those are bogus—you can't prove anything. Paris, it's not true. He's been lying to you, too... He and Jules aren't romantically involved, he just said it to appeal to your softer side," Ethan shouted.

Noah cursed when doubt flew into Paris's eyes. Deliberately not looking at Jules, he held Paris's gaze and waited for the question. If she didn't believe him, he was sunk. He'd lose the house, his time and the money.

He could live with losing all three but, God, if he lost Jules...

"Are you and Jules not romantically involved?"

Noah had to answer her honestly, knowing that nothing else but the truth would get him through this quagmire. "There's nothing romantic about Jules and I," he replied, sighing when he heard the harsh note in his own voice and Jules's gasp.

Okay, not off to a good start. He rubbed his hand over his head, ordering his tongue to cooperate. "*Romance* implies something ephemeral, wishy-washy, fleeting. Jules and I have known each other too long and too well to settle for such a weak description of our relationship."

Paris tipped her head to the side. "So how would you characterize it?"

Well, hell, he was going to have to say it after all. And with an audience. Okay, then. Noah shifted his gaze from Paris's face to Jules's, her light eyes surprised and, yes, terrified.

Join the freakin' club.

"She's been my best friend all my life, my rock, my true north. She's the reason the moon pulls the tide, why the earth spins, the reason my sun sets and falls.

"Yes, we started off by faking something that we thought wasn't there, not knowing that it was, that it has always been a part of me, of us."

Jules clasped her hands together, her face devoid of color, her eyes begging for more. Something to banish the last of her fear, something that would restore her trust. Noah kept his eyes on her face but directed his words at Paris. "Sign off on the yacht or don't, Paris. Yeah, a part of me will be sad at missing out on reclaiming the house and land that's been in my family for generations, but I'll live with it. What I can't live without, what I refuse to live without, is Jules. I'd live in a freakin' cardboard box if it meant being with her. She's my..." His voice broke when he saw the tears in Jules's eyes. He swallowed and bit the flesh on the inside of his cheek to keep it together. Were her tears a good sign? Bad? He couldn't tell.

He forced himself to speak again, this time speaking to Jules directly. "You're...everything, Jules. You always will be, I promise."

Jules lifted her fist to her mouth, the tears now running down her face. What did they mean? Did he still have a chance? God, he hoped so. When they were alone he'd drag more out of her. Things like "Yes, let's give us a chance" or "Okay, we can go out on a date." He was intelligent enough to know that he'd hurt her—again—and that she'd take her time forgiving him, that she'd have to learn to trust him all over again.

He could live with that. After all, he wasn't going anywhere for a while and when he did he was coming straight back to Boston.

Paris cleared her throat, pushed the stack of papers incriminating Ethan away from her. "Out."

Noah thought she was talking to him but then realized that she was looking at Ethan. "You have a minute to leave my home. If you do not do so in that time, I will not only have you ostracized from polite society, I will tell every rich young lady I come across that you have impotence issues."

Noah turned to smile at Jules and his breath hitched at the flicker of hope he saw in her eyes. He pushed his chair back, intending to go to her, to pull her into his arms, when Paris gripped his wrist. Her fingernails pushed into his skin. "Oh, no, you don't. You are going to keep your hands off her until we've gone through your design in detail. Then I'll sign off on the design and write you a check."

Noah groaned, Jules whimpered and Paris looked from him to Jules and back to him, resignation in her eyes.

"Oh, all right, then! Contract signing and check but I'll expect you both back here tomorrow to talk about my beautiful, beautiful yacht. Will you two have sorted yourselves out by then?"

Noah, still unsure, darted a glance at Jules, who had yet to speak. "Hopefully."

Jules pulled a tissue out of her bag, wiped her eyes and hauled in a breath. Then her eyes focused and she nodded at the folder in front of him. "Let's get this done, Noah."

So, what did that mean? And where the hell did he stand?

Jules...

Noah decided that the closest place they could find privacy was on the *Resilience*, and unlike what happened in movies, they didn't run down the sidewalks of Boston, pushing past people to get to the marina. Silently, they took the elevator to the ground floor, where they caught a taxi to the marina. At the access gate, Noah plugged in his code, escorted Jules through the turnstile and to the far quay where his magnificent J-class yacht was berthed, her tall mast making her easily recognizable.

It felt like she was having an out-of-body experience— had Noah really told her, in front of people, that he loved her? It was so surreal, like it was the best dream ever. God, she really hoped she never woke up. Jules slipped off her shoes, sighing when her bare feet hit the teak deck. She headed to the bow, where she sank down and dangled her feet off the edge of the yacht.

Jules lifted her head and saw Noah looming over her, looking unsure. She patted the space next to her and Noah shrugged out of his jacket, pulled off his tie and dropped them to the warm deck, immediately lifting his face to the sun.

"Did you mean it?" Jules asked quietly, searching his eyes for the truth.

Because he knew her so well, he didn't need clarification on exactly what she was asking. He nodded. "Absolutely." Noah flipped open the cuffs on his shirt and started to roll them up. "You were right, you know. About me loving you, that I always have."

She could barely hear his precious words over the sound of her own heartbeat... Dare she believe this was really happening?

Noah managed a smile, his eyes intense as he tucked a strand of hair behind her ear. Immediately the wind blew it across her mouth again.

"Do you...love me? Back at Lockwood House, you told me you did but that could've changed in the last three weeks."

She saw his fear of being rejected and her heart lurched. This was Noah as she'd never seen him before: humbled, vulnerable, uncertain. *This mattered, she mattered.*

Jules touched his cheek, ran her hands over his thin lips. "My first memory was you picking me up when I fell. I think Darby pushed me off the swing. You helped me up and I looked at you and I felt...whole. My three-year-old heart recognized you... I'm not putting this well." Jules stumbled over her words. "I've spent the last ten years looking for something I always had, something that I only feel when I'm with you. You are what I need in my life, No, the only thing I need. It's more than love. It's..."

Noah finally smiled at her. "Right."

Yeah, it was. Being with Noah was where she was supposed to be, being his was what she was meant to do. They had their careers and their interests and their friends, but they were destined to be a unit. She and Darby might've shared a womb but she was convinced she and Noah shared a heart.

Noah's mouth skimmed hers but he pulled back when desire flared. "Can we do this? Be together?"

"We can do anything, No. Yeah, your work is mostly overseas but we can work around that." It would be hard but he was worth it. He was worth *everything*.

"My client consults are overseas. My work doesn't have to be. Technology pretty much allows me to work anywhere, and most of my correspondence with my free-lance staff is done online. I'd still have to travel but I could easily make my base here in Boston."

"Is this where you want to be?" Jules asked him, unable to disguise the tremor and hope in her voice.

"Jules, you are where I want to be," Noah replied, sounding confident again. "Your business is here, your clients are here. If I want to be with you, and I do, then Boston is where I'll be." He held up his hand when she opened her mouth to speak. "And, yeah, of course I'm moving here to be with you but, as you pointed out, my brothers are here, Levi, my businesses. Added bonuses."

The sun was shining, the air was fresh but her lungs felt constricted; she couldn't breathe. This was her fantasy, the best news she could get and she was on the verge of passing out. The cliché about being careful what you wish for drifted through her head.

Jules sucked in some air, waited for her head to clear, before using both hands to hold back her hair. She wanted to look at Noah, see his eyes when she asked him her next question, the one she had to have an answer for.

"Can I trust you? Will you promise not to wander off with my heart again?"

Noah scooted closer to her, his hand covering the side

of her face. "My heart is yours, babe. It always has been. You know that."

"As mine is yours," Jules said.

Noah pushed a curl behind her ear. "I need to go to Costa Smeralda to meet with an oil sheikh who wants me to design a state-of-the-art yacht. No longer content to have oil wells and hotels and race horses, he now wants to sail competitively. I thought you could come with me and we could have a preengagement honeymoon."

Jules's mouth curved. "So, we are getting married?"

Noah's mouth slid across hers in a kiss that promised her forever. "Damn right we are. But right now you need to kiss me."

So Jules did. In fact, they kissed for so long and with so much abandon that numerous complaints were laid at the receptionist's desk against the couple who were, as one elderly sailor stated, "oblivious to the world."

It took a minute of Levi calling their names and one shrill whistle to pull them apart.

"Get a room!" Levi told them, looking up at them when they peered over the hull of the boat. Their dopey, radiant faces told him everything he needed to know.

"Lee, we've decided to get married!" Jules shouted, incandescently happy.

Levi placed his hands on his hips and smiled. "Honey, that decision was made for you twenty-plus years ago by Mom and Bethann. You've just taken your time to get with the program."

Jules and Noah exchanged broad smiles. It was probably true but neither of them minded.

"Congrats, guys. But enough public displays of affection, okay?" Levi asked. *"Please?"*

Jules laughed, shook her head and looked at Noah as

Levi turned away. "Love you, Noah." She couldn't say
it enough, she had ten years of lost time to make up for.

"I love you more, babe. So, do you want to go be-
lowdecks?" Noah said as he stood up, holding out his
hand.

Jules placed her hand in his and allowed him to pull her
up and into his chest. Yes, of course she did. On land or
sea, being with him was the only place she wanted to be.

Epilogue

Callie...

One down, four to go, Callie thought, thinking of the call she'd received from Jules an hour earlier. She stood in front of the front door to Mason's coffee shop, frowning at the closed sign. It was after five; Mason closed at four thirty and he'd already be on his way home.

It was better that he was gone, she wasn't even sure why she was there. Callie rested her hand on the cool glass and remembered feeling and sounding as giddy as Jules did when she and Ray announced that they were in love, that they were getting married. It was all so new; she'd been a virgin, he'd only had one other lover. They were each other's first loves, their *only* loves. She didn't know how to love anyone but Ray and didn't think she could.

He'd been a wonderful husband, a considerate lover, an excellent father. They'd traveled, raised their kids, socialized. And she still loved him with every breath she took. He'd been her world, still was. Oh, she'd been to grief counseling and knew she could be idealizing Ray and their relationship, it was what everyone did. But they'd had fun, dammit, and it was as good as she remembered.

Her attraction to Mason, the crazy, heat-filled dreams, her fantasies of his broad hands on her skin, touching her in the places that only Ray knew, filled her with guilt and she felt like she was cheating on her husband. Her lust for this younger, *hotter* guy was tearing her in two.

And the affection she was feeling, the connection that arced between them, burned a hole in her stomach. She had no right to feel this way, to be both terrified and excited at seeing Mason…as well as annoyed and irritated and turned on. Even in those early days with Ray their attraction hadn't burned so brightly. It had been a steady flame instead of a bonfire.

She loved her husband, she *did*. So why, when she was supposed to be so happy for her daughter, so excited for her future, couldn't she stop thinking about this denim-blue-eyed man? Why could she still taste him in her mouth, feel his hand on her breast? Why did she ache between her legs?

And, this made her blood run cold, what compelled her to run to him, oh, so desperately wanting to share her wonderful news? Why was he the first person she wanted to tell?

It couldn't work, it would never work. She was Callie Brogan, still in love with her husband and Mason was the coffee shop guy.

The door under her hand moved and Callie lifted up her tear-soaked face, her eyes colliding with his. His hand encircled her wrist and he gently pulled her into the empty shop, chairs on tables, a mop and bucket in the center of the floor. He wiped away her tears with his thumb before gently pulling her into his arms, his hand holding the back of her head.

"Hey, honey, what's the matter, huh? What can I do?"

"Nothing. Uh…my daughter is in love and getting married." Callie managed to hiccup through her tears and, burying her nose in his flannel shirt, she sank into him. "I'm so happy, and I just wanted to tell you."

Stroking her back, Mason buried his face in her hair and, somehow, knew what she needed him to do.

He just held her.

* * * * *

ON TEMPORARY TERMS

JANICE MAYNARD

For everyone whose childhood
was not storybook perfect.
For everyone whose parents were
embarrassing or hurtful or not present at all.
May you find love and acceptance in other
relationships and know that you are not
defined by the difficulties and struggles
of the past. God bless…

One

Abby Hartmann liked her job most days. Being a small-town lawyer included more good weeks than bad. But on this particular Saturday morning—the dreaded once-a-month half day—things were definitely looking up. With her palms damp and her heartbeat fluttering, she smoothed her skirt and waved a hand toward the wingbacked chair opposite her large cherry desk. "Have a seat, Mr. Stewart."

She straightened a few papers and folders, and took a deep breath. The man whose sheer presence shrank the square footage of her office was a commanding figure. Close-cropped dark brown hair. Deep chocolate eyes. A lean, athletic body. And a stillness about him. An intensity. As if at any moment he could leap across the small space separating them, grab her up and kiss her witless. He seemed almost dangerous, which made no sense at all. Maybe it was the quivering physical awareness making her restless.

Her reaction was disconcerting. Just because the guy had a sexy Scottish accent and a seriously hot body was no reason to lose her composure. Besides, no matter how attractive, the Scotsman embodied the rich, entitled male arrogance that set her teeth on edge. She'd met dozens like him, albeit not Scottish. Men who took what they wanted and didn't mind who they left behind in the dust.

Duncan Stewart seemed uncomfortable as well, but perhaps for a different reason. "I'm not sure why I'm here," he said. "My grandmother likes to be mysterious at times."

Abby managed a smile, though she was entirely off her game. "Isobel Stewart is an original, that's for sure. It's no big secret. She's updated her will and wanted me to go over it with you. Do you mind my asking why you've decided to relocate from Scotland to North Carolina?"

He raised an eyebrow. "I'd have thought that was obvious. Granny is well past ninety. Grandda has been gone almost a year now. You know my brother, Brody, has a new wife and baby, and they've moved back to Skye."

"I had heard that. Your sister-in-law owned the bookstore down the street, Dog-Eared Pages—right?"

"Aye. Since none of us have been successful in persuading Granny to sell out and leave Candlewick, *somebody* has to be here to look after her."

"That's astonishingly generous on your part, Mr. Stewart. Not many men I know, young or old, would put their lives on hold for their grandmothers."

Duncan couldn't decide if the odd note in the lawyer's voice was admiration or sarcasm. "I didn't really have a choice," he said. His reluctance to play a part in this drama shamed him. Still, he was going to do the right thing. It didn't mean he was comfortable with the lawyer's praise. The woman sitting across the desk from him seemed harmless, but he would be in no rush to trust her. He didn't have a very high opinion of solicitors in general, or of the entire legal profession for that matter. He'd seen too much nastiness during his parents' divorce.

Abby Hartmann stared at him. "*Everyone* has choices,

Mr. Stewart. In some instances, I might think you were in it for the money, but your grandmother has told me more than I ever needed to know about you and your brother. I'm aware that you're extremely comfortable financially with or without your share in Stewart Properties."

Duncan winced. "I'm guessing she also told you our father isn't getting a dime, and she made it sound like a big deal."

Abby gave him a small smile and nodded. "She might have mentioned it in passing. I Googled him. Your dad has a dozen thriving art galleries all over Great Britain, right? I doubt he cares about his mother's money."

"He and Granny have a complicated relationship. It works best when they both live on different continents."

The lawyer grimaced, her face shadowed for a moment. "I can certainly understand that."

Though Duncan had not wanted to come here today, he found himself willing to prolong the conversation for no other reason than to enjoy the lawyer's company. He'd been expecting a middle-aged woman in a gray suit and glasses with precise opinions and tightly controlled behaviors. What he'd found instead was a barely five-foot-three curvy bombshell.

Maybe he had formed too many opinions of female solicitors from television and movies, but Abby Hartmann broke the mold. According to the diplomas on the wall behind her head, she appeared to be in her late twenties. She was warm and appealing, and nothing about her was rigid. Her hair was chin length and wildly curly, neither red nor blond, but an appealing amalgam of both.

She wore a black knee-length pencil skirt that showcased a rounded ass and beautiful legs that were now hidden beneath her desk. The buttons on her red shirt struggled to contain her stellar breasts. In fact, Duncan had a difficult time keeping his eyes off that tantalizing sight.

He wasn't a Neanderthal. He respected women. Still, holy hell. Abby Hartmann was stacked. Her attire was not provocative. She had left only the first two buttons of her top undone. A tiny gold cross dangled at the upper slopes of her breasts. But that cleavage…

Moving restlessly, he cleared his throat and wished he hadn't declined the bottle of water she had offered him earlier. "I love my grandmother, Ms. Hartmann. She and my grandfather built Stewart Properties from the ground up. In her eyes, it keeps him alive."

"Call me Abby, please. She told me your grandfather chose to change his surname to her maiden name in order to keep the Stewart clan name going. That's pretty extraordinary, don't you think? Particularly for a man of his generation?"

Duncan shrugged. "They had a grand love affair, one of those you read about in books. He adored her and vice versa. From his point of view, she gave up everything for him—her family, her homeland. I suppose it was his way of saying he wanted her to have something in return."

"I think it's lovely."

"But?"

"I didn't say but…"

Duncan grinned. "I'm pretty sure I heard a *but* coming."

Abby flushed. "I don't mean to discount your grandparents' devotion, but I doubt things like that happen anymore. The passionate love affairs. The epic gestures. The decades-long marriages."

"You're awfully young for such pessimism, aren't you?"

"And you don't know me well enough to make that judgment," she snapped.

He blinked. The lawyer had a temper. "My apologies. We should get on with the will. I don't want to take up too much of your time."

Abby groaned audibly. "Sorry. Hot-button issue. Perhaps

we could back up a step or two. And yes, we'll go over the will, but first, one more question. If your grandmother left Scotland to settle here with your grandfather, how did you wind up a Scotsman?"

"My grandparents had only one child, my father. Dad was always fascinated with his Scottish roots. As soon as he was an adult, he moved to the Highlands and never looked back. Scotland is the only home Brody and I have ever known, except for the occasional visits here to Candlewick."

"I know about your brother's boating business in Skye. What did you do there?"

"I was his CFO." He stopped and sighed. "Still am, I guess. We don't know how long this hiatus will be. I've urged him to replace me permanently. It's not fair for the business to limp along indefinitely."

"I'm sorry. This must be a very challenging time for you."

The genuine kindness in her soft gray eyes warmed him. For the first time in days, he believed he might survive this sea change in his life. "Not as hard as losing Grandda. That shook all of us. He was an amazing man."

"Yes, he was. I didn't know him well, but his reputation in Candlewick is impressive. People around here would do most anything for your grandmother. She is beloved, you know."

"I do know. That's one reason none of us had the heart to insist she leave. That and the fact that we would have had to pick her up bodily and carry her onto a plane kicking and screaming."

"Boggles the mind, doesn't it?"

"You don't know the half of it. When a cantankerous old Scotswoman sets her mind to something, there's no choice but to get out of her way."

"I don't envy you the task of keeping her in line." Abby smiled, her eyes alight with humor.

Duncan tried not to notice the way her breasts moved when she shifted in her chair. "Would you have dinner with me one evening?" he asked impulsively.

The lawyer stilled. The air in the room hushed. Even Duncan was momentarily abashed. He was not at all an impulsive kind of man.

Abby gnawed her lip. "I'm not sure that would be ethical."

Duncan seized on the weakness in her argument and the fact that she hadn't given him an unequivocal no. "You're not *my* lawyer," he said.

"Perhaps I should have been more clear from the beginning," she replied, looking rattled and mildly alarmed. "My colleague, Mr. Chester, has been your grandparents' lawyer for a very long time. But he's on medical leave at the moment following serious heart surgery. I've been charged with handling your grandmother's affairs in the short term. We have a client who is very interested in purchasing Stewart Properties. It's a cash offer."

Duncan's cynicism kicked in, laced with a big dose of disappointment. Lawyers were snakes, every single one of them. "Not interested."

Abby's gaze narrowed. "It's a very fair offer."

"I don't care. I don't want to hear about it. Granny doesn't want to sell."

"I thought you were looking out for her best interests," the lawyer said, a bite in her voice.

"I definitely am. So it raises a big red flag for me when her lawyers try to force her to sell a company she loves."

"Mr. Chester cares about your grandmother's well-being. We all do."

"How touching."

"Are you being intentionally rude and cynical, or does it come naturally to you? I resent having my professional ethics called into question."

"And I resent people who try to take advantage of an old woman."

"How does making her extremely wealthy take advantage of her?"

"Granny doesn't need more money. She has plenty."

"No one *ever* has enough money, Mr. Stewart. Trust me."

Duncan heard something in that remark…something wounded and weary. But he chose not to pursue it at the moment. Despite his entirely logical antipathy toward lawyers and the inescapable notion that he should stay far away from this woman, he circled back to his original proposal. "Have dinner with me," he said.

"No."

Duncan frowned. "Think of it as community service. I'm lonely. I don't know a single person in town other than my ancient grandmother and you. Have pity on me, Abby Hartmann. And call me Duncan. I feel as if we know each other already."

"Don't lay it on too thick, *Duncan*. I'll think about it. But don't push me. Besides, why would you want to have dinner with a snake-in-the-grass lawyer? I'm getting very mixed signals from you."

Duncan held up his hands. "I'll no' mention it again. At least not for a few days. And you have a fair point. Now how about that will?"

Abby seemed relieved at the change of subject. Duncan entertained himself by watching her shift back into lawyer mode. She clicked a button on her computer, consulted a notepad, and opened a legal-size folder, muttering to herself charmingly as she did so.

He'd always been attracted to smart women. Something about their unwillingness to put up with crap from men challenged his masculinity and brought out his fighting instincts. Abby was no pushover. Though he was well aware that his arousal was not one-sided, he was not foolish enough to assume that meant an easy conquest.

If he wanted the lushly rounded lawyer in his bed, she would make him work for it. He liked that. A lot...

At last, she slid a second folder across the desk to him and opened it. "Here you go. You've seen an earlier version of this. One significant addition is an *escape* clause, if you will. After twenty-four months, if you're unhappy and still want to go home, your grandmother has agreed to sell Stewart Properties and accompany you back to Scotland. I've flagged the changes and the spots where you'll add your name. Your brother and grandmother have already signed."

Duncan frowned. "They have?"

"Yes. Brody needed to do it before he left. Your grandmother came with him."

"Why did no one tell me?" Duncan had a bad feeling in his gut.

"I'm telling you now."

Duncan scanned the paragraphs of legal-speak, searching for the alterations that necessitated this visit. His heart pounded. The tiny pink "flags" denoting spots requiring his signature mocked him. Surely he wasn't reading the document correctly. "I don't understand," he said slowly. "Granny told us she was leaving her company to Brody and me fifty-fifty."

"In light of recent developments—Brody's marriage, your relocation to America—your grandmother and your brother thought it would be only fair to change the split to eighty-twenty. You've given up your career and your life in Scotland. They want to make sure you don't suffer for that decision."

"I made the choice willingly," he insisted. "I didn't ask for anything in return. This is preposterous. I won't sign it."

"Have you *met* your grandmother?" Abby asked jokingly, her expression sympathetic. "I can assure you she won't be moved on this point. Besides, you're not getting a free ride by any means. You'll earn your money. The company is enormous and complex. I'm told that one of the two managers is moving to the West Coast any day now to be closer to family. Your grandmother wants to be involved, but she is no longer physically capable of an intensive workday. The future success or failure of Stewart Properties will rest on your shoulders."

"Thanks for the pep talk."

"We have a saying in this country, Duncan. *The buck stops here.* Your decision to move to Candlewick and look after your grandmother is not going to be easy. Dealing with elderly people never is. But you'll have the added stress of running a multimillion-dollar company, give or take a few zeroes."

"Again, you suck at this."

She grinned. "My job is to clarify the gray areas."

"Consider them clarified." Duncan felt mildly ill. "I have a strong urge to leave it all to Brody."

"I don't think he would take it."

"Great. Just great."

"Think of it as an adventure."

He signed the requisite spots and shoved the folder away. "There. It's done. I hope I can count on you in the weeks and months to come."

Abby's soft pink lips, lightly coated in gloss, opened and shut. "For legal advice?"

Duncan sat back in his chair and smiled at her, letting her see, for the very first time, the extent of his male interest. "For everything."

Abby went through the rest of her workday in a daze. She fluctuated between excitement that Duncan Stewart had asked her out on a date and the absolute certainty that he had been joking.

Fortunately, she had dinner plans with her best friend, Lara Finch. The two of them met at Abby's house and rode together the twenty miles to Claremont. There were places to eat in Candlewick, charming mom-and-pop establishments, plus the usual pizza joints, but for privacy and a change of scenery, it was nice to make the extra effort.

Over chicken crepes, Lara quizzed her. "Something's up, Abby girl. Your face is all red, and you've barely said a word since we got here."

"I talked in the car."

"Correction," Lara said. "*I* talked in the car. You did a lot of listening."

"You're the designated driver. I've had a glass of wine. That's why my neck is hot, and I'm flushed."

"Abby!" Lara gave her a look that said she wasn't going to be put off.

"Oh, fine. If you must know, I met a guy today."

Lara put down her fork, leaned back in her chair and stared. Speechless.

Abby winced. "It's not *that* unusual, is it?"

"The last time you mentioned a man to me was sometime around the turn of the century."

"We didn't even know each other at the turn of the century," Abby pointed out dryly.

Lara picked up her fork again and waved it in the air. "I was using poetic license to make a point. This mystery man must be something special. Please tell me he has a brother. I'm currently in a bit of a dry spell myself."

"He does," Abby said. "But unfortunately for you, he's already married."

"Bummer."

"Yeah." Abby debated how much to say. If she admitted the full extent of how meeting Duncan Stewart had affected her, Lara would never let it go. "Do you know Isobel Stewart?"

"Of course. Everyone knows Miss Izzy. She has several accounts at the bank."

Lara was a loan officer at the local financial institution, a position with a great deal of responsibility and authority in a small town. She, like Abby, found Candlewick's pool of eligible men to be lamentably small. Not only that, but a lot of guys were put off by Lara's cool demeanor and elegant looks. Abby's friend had the proverbial heart of gold, but she had been known to freeze a man in his tracks if he stepped over an invisible line.

"Well, this was Miss Izzy's grandson."

"Brody?"

"No. He's the one who just got married."

"To the bookstore lady…"

"Right."

"So there's a brother number two?"

"Oh, yeah."

"It's the accent, isn't it? I'll bet even if he had two heads and warts, women would fall all over him."

"Are you saying I'm shallow?"

"Don't be defensive. Tell me why he's so adorable and irresistible that my dearest friend is in a dither."

"I don't even know what that means."

"A dither. A state of flustered excitement or fear."

Well, poop. That was Abby's exact state. "There was something about him, Lara. An intensity. Or maybe an air of danger. I'm not sure I can explain it. He was very *masculine*."

Lara's eyes rounded. She fanned herself with her napkin and took a sip of water. "So what are we going to do to make sure this very dangerously masculine man notices you?"

Abby tried not to smirk. "Not really an issue. He's already asked me out."

Her friend with the runway-model body and the ash-blond hair and the sapphire eyes goggled. "Seriously? It was the boobs, wasn't it? Lord, what I wouldn't give to have those boobs for twenty-four hours. They're guy magnets."

"I don't think he was even serious," Abby admitted, voicing her worst fears. "He's lonely, and by his own admission, he doesn't know anybody in town."

"There must have been more to it than that or you wouldn't be acting so jittery."

Abby's cheeks flamed hotter. "He flirted with me almost from the beginning, and then he asked me out. But he also insulted my profession and questioned my motives. I didn't know what to say."

"So what *did* you say?"

"I told him I had to think about it."

"Ah. That's good. Make him work for it."

"Lara! That's not what I meant. I'm not sure my dating him is ethical. I've worked too hard to get where I am in my career…to make sure everyone knows that I'm not like my father."

"Oh, good grief. You're not representing him in a court of law. Besides, isn't Miss Izzy technically your *boss's* client?"

"Yes, but—"

Lara interrupted with a triumphant grin. "Problem solved. Now for the important question. Do you have any good undies, and what are you going to wear when you finally put him out of his misery?"

TWO

Abby chose to wait a week before contacting Duncan Stewart. That would give her time to decide if she really wanted to go out with him. If she realized in the interim that he had only been playing with her, then she wouldn't have embarrassed herself for nothing.

She planned to call him the following Saturday morning. The Friday night before, Lara was at her house for a battle-of-the-Chrises movie night. It was an old game they played. Tonight would be Chris Pine versus Chris Hemsworth.

While they popped popcorn in the kitchen, Lara rummaged in the fridge. "Has your dad harassed you lately?" she asked, popping the tab on a soda and taking a sip before hopping up on the butcher block countertop and dangling her legs.

Abby grimaced. "No, thank God. He's been suspiciously quiet. Almost too quiet. Makes me nervous."

"Mom wanted me to make sure you know you're invited to our place for Thanksgiving."

"That's a long time from now," Abby said, her throat tight.

"Not all that long. My mom loves you. Our whole family loves you. It's not your fault that your father has gone off the deep end."

Abby dumped the popcorn into two bowls and sighed. "It feels like my fault. Maybe I should have tried harder to get him medical help. I don't know if he has diagnosable medical issues or if he's just a deeply disturbed jerk."

"I shouldn't have brought it up," Lara said, her expression rueful. "But I can't bear to see you go through the holidays again like you did last year. That was hell. You're like my sister, Abbs. And you deserve better." She hopped down and grabbed a bowl. "Enough gloomy talk. Let's eat. Don't forget the cheesecake I brought."

"Do cheesecake and popcorn really go together?"

"Cheesecake goes with everything," Lara said.

An hour and a half later, when the first movie credits rolled, Abby was already yawning. "Sorry," she muttered. "I didn't sleep much last night."

Lara kicked her foot. "Dreaming about the luscious Scotsman?"

"Not exactly. He hasn't contacted me, you know."

"If I'm not mistaken, you told him to give you time to think about it."

"I did."

"So what's the problem?"

"I don't know if I want to go out with him."

"Liar."

"Excuse me!" Abby said, affronted.

"Of course you *want* to go out with him. But you're scared."

"Oh." That much was true. "I'm fifteen pounds overweight, Lara."

"Not every guy wants a stick figure. He liked what he saw. And besides, you're a beautiful woman, whether you believe it or not."

Easy for Lara to say. She was the epitome of the perfect

female. If she weren't so wonderful, Abby would be compelled to hate her on sight. "Well, it's a moot point, because he hasn't gotten back to me, and I honestly don't think I have the guts to call him."

"Let's look at this objectively, honey. How often do new men wander into town?"

"Almost never."

"And when they do, how often are they young, hot and available?"

"Almost never."

"And when one of them is young, hot and available, how often is he the decent type who loves his grandma and is willing to sacrifice his own happiness for hers?"

"You're making him sound like a cross between Robin Hood and James Bond. I'm pretty sure Duncan Stewart just wants to get laid."

"That's what all men want. It wouldn't hurt you either."

"Lara!"

"You're staring down the barrel at thirty. Then it'll be thirty-five and forty. All the good men will be gone. You've got a live one on the hook, Abby. Don't toss him back."

"That's the most sexually regressive, ridiculous speech I've ever heard."

"You know I'm right."

"I don't see you *fishing*."

"Maybe if I had a charming Scotsman asking me out, I would be."

"I don't know. He's arrogant and rich and snarky. Probably hasn't had to work for anything in his life."

"Text him. Right now. Tell him yes."

"You're bullying me."

"Correction. I'm *encouraging* you. There's a difference."

Abby picked up her cell phone, her stomach churning. "I don't know what to say."

"Do it, Abby."

Without warning, her cell phone dinged. She was so startled, she almost dropped it. The words on the screen left no doubt about the sender.

Have I given ye enough time, lass? Dinner Tuesday? Pick you up at 6?

"It's him, Lara." She held out the phone. "He must have been serious."

Lara read the text and beamed. "Of course he was serious. The man has good taste. Text him back. Hurry."

Hands shaking, Abby pecked out a reply...

Two conditions. We don't call it a date. And you let me tell you about the offer on your grandmother's business...

She hit Send and sighed. "I'm not finishing the rest of that dessert. Do you think I can lose ten pounds by Tuesday?"

Lara handed her a fork. "Eat the damn cheesecake. You're perfect just the way you are. If Duncan Stewart doesn't agree, he's an idiot."

Duncan had fallen into a routine of sorts. It wasn't familiar, and it wasn't home, but for the moment, it was workable. His grandmother liked to sleep later in her old age. Since Duncan was up early every day, he headed into town and opened up the office before anyone else arrived. He liked having a chance to look over things unobserved.

He was definitely the new kid on the block. All the staff had been cordial and helpful, but he guessed they were wondering if anyone would be getting the ax. That wasn't his plan at all. Stewart Properties appeared to be thriving. It was up to him to make sure that success continued.

The company comprised two equally profitable arms—

mountain cabin construction and mountain cabin rentals. Isobel and Geoffrey had capitalized on a tourist market in its infancy decades ago, and had built their reputation bit by bit. The main office had been located in Candlewick since the beginning, but satellite offices operated in Asheville and several other spots within a hundred-mile radius.

In a little over a week's time, Duncan had learned the basics of daily operations. He had already spotted the invaluable employees and the ones who might be potential problems. Because his training and degrees were in finance, he wasn't concerned about the accounting practices. Where he would have to pay attention was in the actual design and building modules.

Because his grandmother was determined to maintain her involvement in the day-to-day operations, he went back up the mountain each morning around eleven and picked her up at the palatial wood-and-stone home she and her husband had built for themselves. It was far too big for an elderly widow. It was even too big with Duncan in the house. But Isobel wanted to stay, so the status quo remained.

After a shared lunch in town, Duncan deferred to Isobel's decisions and insights about the various company decisions. Her mind was as sharp as it ever had been. Her stamina, however, was less reliable. Some days, she made it until closing time at five. Other times, someone was drafted to take her home at three.

This particular Tuesday was a good day. Duncan and Isobel had spent several hours going over potential new architectural plans for a series of cabins to be built on land they had recently acquired. Other, somewhat dated, house plans were being culled.

At last, Isobel closed the final folder and tapped it with a gnarled finger. "These new ones are going to be very popular. You mark my words."

Duncan scrubbed his hands across his scalp and yawned,

standing up when she did. "I believe you, Granny. You're the boss."

Isobel reached for his hand and pressed it to her cheek. "Thank you, my boy. Thank you for everything you've done for an old woman. It means more to me than you'll ever know."

He hugged her, glad she couldn't see how much he had struggled with the decision to uproot his life. "I love you, Granny. You looked after Brody and me when we were lost boys after Mom and Dad divorced. I owe you for that, even if for nothing else. Besides, I'm enjoying myself."

And it was true. He was. He hadn't expected to, not at all, so the rush of adrenaline in the midst of new challenges was a bonus.

When they released each other and stepped back, he grinned. "I suppose I should tell you. I have a date tonight. Don't wait up for me."

The old woman's eyes sparkled, and she chortled with glee. "Do tell, boy. Anybody I know?"

"Abby Hartmann? She's at the law firm where you sent me to sign the new will."

"Ah, yes. Abby." Isobel's brows narrowed. "Abby is a nice young woman."

"Why do I get the impression you don't approve?"

"Abby hasn't had an easy life. She deserves to be treated well."

"I wasna' planning on beating her, Granny."

"Don't be sassy, boy. You know what I mean. I'd not want you to trifle with her affections."

"She strikes me as an extremely savvy young woman. I think she can handle herself."

"Maybe so. Will you bring her by the house so I can say hello?"

"Next time perhaps. Let's see how tonight goes."

Isobel's eyes gleamed. "So you're not entirely sure of yourself. That's a good thing."

"Whose side are you on?" he complained.

"I'll always be in your corner, Duncan, but we women have to stick together."

Several hours later, Duncan parked in front of Abby's neat, bungalow-style white frame house and studied the property. She lived on a quiet side street only two blocks off the town square. Her handkerchief-sized yard was neatly manicured, and her windows gleamed in the early evening sun.

Since the moment Abby accepted his invitation Friday night, they had texted back and forth a time or two. He found himself eager to see her again, surprisingly so. Perhaps he needed a break from work or a distraction from his complicated new life. Or maybe he simply wanted to determine if the gut-level attraction he experienced in her office was still there.

Her conditions for accepting his invitation had angered him at first. But after some consideration, he decided, what the hell? Abby could talk about this mystery buyer all she wanted. It wasn't going to change the bottom line.

When she opened the door at his knock, he caught his breath. Her smile was tentative, but everything else about her was no-holds-barred. The glorious hair. Her long-sleeved hunter green silk dress that hugged her hourglass figure from shoulders to knees. Black stiletto heels that gave her an additional few inches of height.

"You look beautiful," he said gruffly. "I'm very glad you decided to say yes."

"Me, too. Let me grab my purse."

They chatted about inconsequential topics on the drive to Claremont, both of them on their best behavior. The drive was just long enough to break the ice. Duncan had chosen an upscale special-occasion restaurant that specialized in French cuisine.

When he helped Abby out of the car, his hand beneath her elbow, the punch of desire left him breathless. He'd been celibate out of necessity during this transition from Scotland to North Carolina, but whatever he felt for the petite lawyer was more than a sexual dry spell. She fascinated him.

Over dinner, he quizzed her about her life. "So tell me about your childhood. Did you always want to be a lawyer? I thought most girls went the princess route at first."

Abby laughed as he had wanted her to. Her long-lashed eyes reminded him of a kitten he'd had as a boy. He'd named her Smoke, and she had followed him everywhere.

The waiter interrupted momentarily. Afterward, Abby answered his question. "To be honest, I was obsessed with the idea of international studies. I wanted to go to college abroad, anything to get away from my hometown. But I was pragmatic, even as a kid. I knew we didn't have the finances to swing that. My mom died when I was three, so my dad raised me on his own. Money was always tight."

"Law school isn't cheap."

"No. I was very lucky. Mr. Chester Sr., who was your grandparents' original lawyer, had a long-standing tradition of mentoring students at the local high school. When he died, his son continued the program. I was fortunate enough to get an internship at the law firm during my senior year in high school. I realized that I liked the work. After four years at a state university, Mr. Chester helped me with law school applications, and I was accepted at Wake Forest. When I finished, they offered me a job here in Candlewick."

"Didn't you have aspirations to head for the big city and make your mark?"

Abby's smile slipped. He couldn't quite read her expression. "I think we all imagine what it would be like to start over someplace new. For me, the pluses of staying put outweighed any negatives. I haven't regretted my decisions. How about you, Duncan? What was your life like back in Scotland?"

He shrugged, even now feeling the bittersweet pull of all he had left behind. "Ye've heard of the Isle of Skye, I suppose. It's truly as beautiful as they say. Water and sky and everything in between."

"You miss it. I hear it in your voice."

"Aye. But I'm a grown man. I can handle a bit of disappointment."

"How did you wind up working with your brother?"

"Brody started the boating business, both commercial fishing and tourist craft, when he was in his twenties. When I finished university, he begged me to join him and handle the financial stuff. We've had a good partnership over the years."

"You told me that day in my office that he's holding the job for you."

"He wants to. I don't think it makes sense. Granny is healthy as a horse. She could live for another decade. And I hope she does."

He was shocked when Abby smiled at him and reached across the table to take one of his hands in hers. Her fingers were soft and warm. "I think you're a very sweet man, Duncan Stewart."

"I'm *not* sweet." He bristled.

She stroked her thumb across his knuckles. "It's a compliment."

"Didn't sound like one." He lifted his free hand, the one Abby wasn't holding, and summoned the waitress. "May we see a dessert menu, please?"

"Oh, not for me," Abby said, her smile dimming.

"They're famous for their bread pudding. I read about it on Yelp."

"You'll have to eat it. I'm too full."

"Nonsense. You only had a salad and a tiny chicken breast. I can't eat dessert alone."

Now Abby looked genuinely upset. She let go of his hand, leaving him bereft. "No dessert," she said firmly. "I'm dieting."

He ordered one for himself anyway and frowned. "Why in God's name are you dieting, lass? You're perfect."

Abby stared at him, waiting for the punch line... searching for the calculation in his eyes, the attempt to butter her up with compliments to lure her into bed. She saw none of that. Instead, Duncan seemed genuinely baffled and irritated by her insistence on refusing dessert.

She tried again. "You're tall and lean, Duncan. For women like me who are short and chu—"

He reached across the table and put his hand over her mouth. "Don't you dare say it. My God, girl. Are the men in this country blind and stupid? I've spent every minute of this evening wondering how long it will be until I get to see your naked curvy body pressed up against mine. And you're worried about dessert?"

The waitress arrived with a decadent bread pudding topped off with real whipped cream. She set the plate on the table with fresh napkins and two spoons and walked away. In the ensuing silence, Abby felt her face turn red. Embarrassment mixed with sexual tension.

Duncan, his expression inscrutable, picked up a spoon and scooped out a bite of caramel-laced, whipped-cream-topped perfection. "Open your mouth, lass. I've an urge to feed you, since I can't do anything else at the moment."

Abby's lips parted even as her knees pressed together.

The way Duncan Stewart was looking at her ought to be illegal.

He lifted the spoon to her mouth. "Wider," he said hoarsely.

She obeyed and moaned when he spooned the dessert between her lips. The flavors exploded onto her tongue. She chewed and swallowed, light-headed. Duncan watched her like a hungry hawk studying a mouse. "Do you like it?" he asked. His voice was sandpaper, the accent almost buried beneath rough desire.

"Yes." The word stuck in her throat. "Do you want some?"

"Only if you feed it to me."

Abby recognized the sexual challenge for what it was. Never in her life had she found herself in such a position. Duncan Stewart had turned a simple meal into sexual foreplay, and now he demanded an equal partner.

"I don't sleep with a man on the first date," she said desperately, reminding herself of all the reasons she made that rule.

"Understood. Besides, this isn't a date—remember?" He growled his response, restless, agitated. "I'll settle for dessert. Now, lass. Before it gets cold."

The way Abby felt, she was never going to be cold again. With trembling fingers, she retrieved the spoon and scooped a bite for Duncan. He watched her intently.

"Stop that," she complained.

"Stop what?" His complacent smile was suspect.

"Stop imagining me naked."

"Is that what I was doing? I didn't know you were a mind reader."

"Open your mouth, Duncan."

"Yes, ma'am."

Why had she never realized how erotic it could be to feed a man dessert? When Duncan's sharp white teeth barely missed her finger as he snagged the pudding, she shuddered. "Is that enough?" She sat back in her chair and took a hasty drink of water, almost choking.

The man laughed at her, damn him.

"I'm still hungry," he said.

"Feed yourself."

"If you're not going to sleep with me tonight, I thought we could at least sublimate."

"Do they teach you that line in wicked, sexy Scotsman school?"

Three

Duncan chuckled, though his sex was hard as stone and he wanted to howl at the notion he couldn't have her tonight. "I have no idea. I've no' been particularly successful with the ladies over the years. Too busy with work, I suppose."

"Oh, please."

"'Tis true," he insisted. "There haven't been as many women as you might think. Brody was always the one with the easy banter and the sunny personality. I spent a lot of time alone. I liked walking the moors and tinkering with boat engines and whatnot. Women were complicated and sometimes, frankly, too much work."

"So why me?"

At first he thought she was flirting, begging for a compliment. But on second glance, he saw the uncertainty beneath the question, and it squeezed his heart. "Ah, heavens, Abby, ye're poetry wrapped in a woman's body. I walked into your office and it was like being punched in the chest. I could have taken you then and there. I can't explain it. Perhaps you think I'm daft."

She stared at him, eyes huge. She gnawed her bottom lip. "It's not natural for a man your age to have to live with his grandmother. You're a long way from where you belong. I think you're probably homesick and horny. It's skewed your thinking. I've never driven *anyone* sexually insane."

"Surely you've heard of chemistry, sweet lass."

The doubt on her face made him determined to tamp down his own lust until he could convince her of his sincerity.

"Is that what this is?" she asked.

"Maybe. Or a bit of fairy magic. We Scots are staunch believers in fairies, you know."

Abby smiled wryly. "Here's the thing, Duncan. I like you. Mostly. And let's be honest. You're a very sexy, appealing man. But this sounds like a really bad idea."

"Why is that?"

"If we end up in bed together, I risk becoming the latest gossipy tidbit in Candlewick. I've worked too hard to prove myself in a career that's extremely important to me."

"So we'll fly under the radar. Secret love affairs can be very hot."

"I think you're missing the point," she sputtered, mortification painting her cheeks crimson.

"I know what I want, Abby. If you're honest, I think you want it, too." Her resistance made him push all the harder. "But if I'm wrong, all you have to do is say no, and I'll leave you alone."

The long silence that followed made him regret his noble pronouncement.

At last, Abby spoke, her expression troubled. "If we do this, you and I would definitely be temporary. Short and secret would be the name of the game. I don't want the whole world to know when it's over. So if they never know when it starts, we dodge that issue."

Some of his jubilant mood faded. "I've never gone into a relationship already planning its demise," he groused.

"Lawyers are all about endings and beginnings. It's what we do. Life flows more smoothly when expectations are clear and everyone signs on the dotted line, metaphorically speaking, of course."

He pretended to wipe his brow. "Whew. I thought you were about to make me sign a contract before I undress you."

"I thought about it," she said.

"You're joking." He raised an eyebrow, searching her features for the truth.

Abby's grimace was self-mocking. "You know...lights out. Nothing too kinky at first."

"Define *at first*."

He was delighted when her choked laughter told him she understood his naughty question.

Abby glanced at her watch. "This has been lovely, but I *do* have work tomorrow."

"Of course." He paid the check, and they made their way to the car. Though it was only early September, in the mountains, the nights cooled rapidly after the sun went down.

His companion was quiet...too quiet. He would give a lot to know what she was thinking. She hadn't once mentioned the prospective buyer for Stewart Properties. He was relieved, but the omission worried him. He hated secrets. Did the sexy lawyer have some wicked plan in mind to wait until he was weak with wanting and then try to coerce him into selling? He didn't know her well enough to trust her.

It wasn't hubris on his part to believe he could coax her into bed tonight if he pressed the issue. Sexual arousal hummed between them like a breathless, tangible force, incubated and nourished by circumstance. The faint scent of feminine perfume in the air. Her slightly off-key humming to the songs on the radio. The pair of sexy high heels that tumbled to the floor of the car when Abby kicked them off and curled her legs beneath her for the ride back to Candlewick.

Duncan gripped the steering wheel, white-knuckled. The road home was strewn with dark, convenient pull-offs where a man could drag a woman against him and undress her and dive deep to slake his hunger.

He wanted Abby with a wild, urgent passion that rattled him and made him restless. His own reckless urges gave him pause. She asked for time. Time would be his friend. All he had to do was cultivate a modicum of patience.

God help him, perhaps he could do it.

On Abby's front porch, he curled an arm around her waist and eased her into the shadows for a good-night kiss. She made no pretense of protest.

As kisses went, it was world-class. They jumped straight over *getting to know you* and ploughed into *where have you been all my life?* Abby was short and he was tall, so the logistics were tricky. Abby solved their dilemma by hopping up onto the door stoop.

Now he could run his hands from her shoulders to her narrow waist to the sensational curves of her bottom. The thin fabric of her green silky dress was no barrier at all. "Ye're a stunning woman, Abby Hartmann," he muttered. "I'm glad we met." He nipped the side of her neck with his teeth and grinned when she made a little squeak in the back of her throat and nuzzled closer.

"Me, too," she said. "Thank you for dinner."

"So polite," he teased.

"It's what we do here in the South. But don't mistake nice manners for being a pushover."

"Understood." He had never felt such an odd mixture of lust and tenderness toward a woman. "I'll feed you again tomorrow night," he said. "Six still work?"

Abby pulled back and ran her hands through her hair, visibly flustered, even in the semidarkness. Her porch light was off, but the streetlight out at the road gave them a hint of illumination. "I have book club tomorrow night," she said. She rummaged in her small purse, extracted a key and unlocked the door.

"Thursday?"

"Dinner with friends."

He ground his teeth until his jaw ached. "Friday?"

She turned, linked her arms around his neck and kissed him square on the mouth, her magnificent breasts pressed firmly against his chest. "Friday would be perfect. But only if you take me by the house to see your grandmother beforehand and let me tell her about the buyer Mr. Chester has in the wings."

Duncan lost it for a good ninety seconds, maybe a full two minutes. He forgot where he was. He forgot he had decided to be a gentleman. He even forgot he was in a semi-public setting.

He was angry and aroused, a dangerous combo. Abby's lips were addictive. She looked so charming and innocent in person, but she tasted like sin. He wanted to strip her bare and take her up against the front door. Her hands played restlessly with his belt at the back of his waist. His erection was buried in the softness of her stomach. There was no hiding the state of his body. She had to know.

But she didn't back away, and she didn't seem to mind.

At last, and to his eternal embarrassment, Abby was the one to drag them back from the edge. "I have to go inside, Duncan."

She said it apologetically, stroking his cheek with one hand as if she could pacify the raging beast inside him.

He shuddered and dragged in a great lungful of air in an attempt to find control. "Of course." He stole one last, hurried kiss. At least he meant it to be hurried. In the end, he lingered, coaxing her lips apart with the tip of his tongue and stroking the inside of her mouth until they both breathed raggedly.

Finally, he cupped her face in his hands and kissed her nose. "Stop seducing me, woman."

"I'm not," she protested.

He dared to cup one of her breasts through two layers of smooth cloth. The weight of her firm, rounded flesh nestled in his palm. The pert, firm nipple begged for the touch of his thumb. "Aye, lass," he said. "Aye, ye are."

Abby escaped into the house with her virtue intact, but it was a close call. She slammed the door, locked it and peered through the curtains to make sure the tall, handsome Scotsman made his way back to his car.

Her knees trembled and her mouth was dry. She was such a fraud. From the beginning, she had known that going out with Duncan Stewart was a bad idea. She had rationalized to herself that getting on good terms with him could mean an opportunity to press the case for selling his grandmother's business.

And yet as the evening unfolded, Abby had let herself be sidetracked by the warmth of the Scotsman's wicked smile. This was exactly the kind of thing that made mixing business with pleasure problematic. She was supposed to be initiating contact with Duncan's grandmother and explaining why selling Stewart Properties could be in Miss Isobel's best interests. Instead, Abby had forgotten her mission, endangered her stellar reputation in the law office and danced perilously close to becoming Duncan's temporary fling.

The following day on her lunch hour, she and Lara munched apples and did their customary two-mile walk. Lara, being Lara, didn't bother to hide her eagerness for details. "Spill it, Abby. Give me every juicy tidbit. My vicarious love life is all I have at the moment."

Abby swallowed the last bite of fruit and tossed the core in a public trash receptacle as they rounded the corner and headed away from downtown. "I had fun."

"That's it?"

"He's interesting…well traveled, well-read. A gentleman."

"Well, that sounds boring as hell."

"No, it doesn't. You're just being mean. It was nice to spend time with a man who can carry on a conversation." She didn't mention the whole dessert thing. Even now she couldn't think about the bread pudding incident without getting aroused and flustered.

"So no sex?" Lara eyed her with an expression that was equal parts resignation and disappointment.

They finished the third circuit of the block and turned back toward their respective places of employment. "You know me, Lara. I'm not impulsive, especially when it comes to intimacy."

"You went out with a client. That's a start."

Abby stopped in the middle of the sidewalk, her heart pumping, and stared at her friend. "I thought you said my dating him was okay?"

Lara's smile was smug. "It's not up to me, now is it? At least tell me he kissed you good night."

Abby shoved her hands in the pockets of her black dress pants and started walking again. "Yes. So?"

"Are we talking a polite peck on the cheek?"

"Not exactly."

"You're such a tease."

Lara grabbed her arm, but Abby evaded the hold and kept walking. "I have an appointment in fifteen minutes. Gotta get back."

"Well, shoot." Lara glanced at her watch and realized what time it was. "This conversation isn't over." She raised her voice to be heard as Abby headed in the opposite direction.

Abby gave her a wave over the shoulder. "See you tonight."

Fortunately for Abby, Lara was more circumspect during their once-a-month book club meeting that evening. The dozen women in the group ranged in age from Lara and

Abby's twenty-something to eighty-one. This week, they were meeting in a back room at the pizza shop.

Over cheesy slices of thick-crust pepperoni, the conversation zipped and zinged from one topic to the next before settling on the plot of the novel they were supposed to have read. Abby had finished most of it. The heroine died of a terrible disease two chapters from the end, so she had lost interest.

Lara loved stirring up controversy and discussion. While Abby's friend debated whether or not the hero's character was supposed to symbolize lost dreams, Abby surreptitiously fished her cell phone from her purse and checked for messages. She hadn't heard a peep from Duncan since he left her last night. Maybe her insistence on talking to Miss Izzy had scared him off.

He seemed pretty mad when she suggested it, but then again, not so mad that he hadn't kissed her until her toes curled and her limbs turned to water. The man knew how to kiss.

If he'd changed his mind about the second date, it was probably a good thing.

When the waitress came to do drink refills, Lara lowered her voice and leaned in. "Whatcha doin', kiddo? This is supposed to be a work-free zone."

"It's not work," Abby said. "I was only checking to see if I had a text from Duncan. He asked me out again for Friday night, but I made him mad, so he may be done with me."

"What did you do that was so terrible?"

"I told him I would only go out with him a second time if he would take me to see Miss Izzy beforehand and let me tell her about the offer we have for her property."

Lara sat back in her seat and pursed her lips. The conversation ebbed and flowed around them. "I'm impressed. Playing hardball."

"It's not that," Abby whispered. "But Mr. Chester asked

me to take care of *one* thing while he's on leave, one simple thing. All I need to do is tell Miss Izzy about the offer. If she's really dead set against selling, all she has to do is say no. I will have fulfilled my obligation, and that will be the end of it. I don't know why Duncan is making such a big deal about it."

"I'll bet *I* do."

"How could you possibly know what that Scotsman is thinking?"

"He didn't really want to move here, right?"

"Correct."

"And if Miss Izzy accepts the offer being brokered by your law firm, Stewart Properties changes hands and Duncan is off the hook. The poor man probably feels guilty, because deep down, he *wants* you to convince his grandmother to sell out. But that makes him a bad person, so it's easier to keep you away from her."

"Well, it's a moot point because I don't think his dinner invitation is still on the table."

Lara reached for a breadstick and dunked it in homemade marinara sauce. "The man wants you, Abby. He'll figure out a way to have you and appease his conscience at the same time. You wait and see."

Four

By Thursday evening, Abby's spirits hit rock bottom, and her opinion of Lara's romantic advice fell lower still. Forty-eight hours had passed and not a single word from Duncan Stewart. The man kissed her as if she had been the only oasis in a trackless desert, and then he had simply walked away.

She almost opted out of dinner with friends. It was difficult to fake a good mood when all she wanted to do was watch romantic comedies and mope around her small house. In the end, she went, but only because the outing took her mind off Duncan and the affair that never was.

No matter how many times she told herself it was for the best—that it was completely inappropriate for her to date the grandson of one of Mr. Chester's influential clients—she didn't believe it in her heart. How long had it been since a man was really interested her? Almost never?

Duncan Stewart might ruin her for other men, but that was a risk she was prepared to take. Even knowing he would be in Candlewick a limited amount of time, maybe only two years (and that their affair would likely be far shorter than that), was not a negative.

He fascinated her. For once in her neatly planned life, she wanted to make the rash, dangerous choice. She wanted Duncan.

When dinner wound to an end, she decided to leave her car at the restaurant and walk the relatively short distance home. She'd had several glasses of wine, so she didn't want to take any chances that she might not be in full control. The night was crisp with a hint of autumn, but not cold. Other people were out and about on the streets even at this hour.

Crime was virtually nonexistent in Candlewick. Some people compared their little town to the fictional Mayberry. In many cases, that description wasn't far off.

By the time she made it to her street and up the block to her own sidewalk, it was late. Sleepy, and still caught up in wondering about Duncan, she didn't spot the intruder at first. Then something moved in the shadows, and she sucked in a sharp breath.

Frozen with fear and in quick succession disgust, she called out to the shadowy figure. "What are you doing here, Daddy?" She stayed where she was out at the road, not wanting him to follow her into the house.

The large hulking shadow turned into an old man under the harsh glare of the streetlight. Once upon a time her father had been handsome and dapper. Even now—when he wanted to—he could clean himself up, get a haircut and present to the world a reasonable facsimile of a sophisticated adult.

Unfortunately, his demons—both mental and pharmaceutical—now controlled him to such a degree that most days he was a broken-down shamble of a man.

"I wanted to see my baby, but I couldn't get in the house," he said. The words were slurred. When he moved closer, she smelled alcohol on his breath.

Abby clutched her purse more tightly in her arms. "Well,

you've seen me. I need to get to bed. It's late." She took a breath. "The reason you couldn't get in is because I changed all my locks."

He held out his hand, his expression half cagey, half pitiful. "You're doin' mighty well in that lawyer job of yours. How 'bout giving your old man a loan? I'm running a little short this month."

Don't engage. Don't engage. Don't engage. The mantra had preserved her emotional health and sanity on more than one occasion. "I have to go," she said. No matter how unfounded, waves of guilt battered her self-esteem. It was not even the middle of the month. He received several pension checks, one from the government and a couple of others from his few stable periods of employment. There was no reason in the world for him to be out of money.

Even if he was, it wasn't her responsibility. She turned her back on him and took a step. But Howard Lander was not giving up.

He scuttled up beside her. "A hundred, Abby girl. That's all. And I'll pay you back, I swear."

Fury rose inside her chest in a choking cloud. Good parents provided a loving, nurturing environment for their children to succeed. Not only did Abby's father not support her as a teen and young adult, he had actually harmed her and nearly derailed her academic successes.

"If you don't stay away from me," she said, her throat raw with tears, "I'm going to take out a restraining order against you."

The old man stumbled and gaped, genuine puzzlement in his half-vacant expression. "Why would you say that?"

Abby laughed, though she wanted to sob. "Every time you come inside my house, you steal from me, Dad. Money, jewelry, prescription drugs. Did you somehow think I never noticed?"

Even in his addled state, he didn't bother to deny her accusation. "I've had a few hard times. No reason for a man's daughter to be cold and cruel."

"I can't do this anymore, Daddy. If you won't leave me alone, I swear I'll move to the other side of the country. It's embarrassing enough that the whole town knows what kind of man you are."

He'd been a door-to-door salesman back when that was still a thing. A combination of charm and dogged persistence had given him moderate success. In between bouts of selling encyclopedias and household items, he'd chased one get-rich-quick scheme after another, always convinced that his fortune was just around the next corner.

By the time Abby was eight, Howard Lander stopped *wasting* his money on babysitters, instead choosing to leave her at home alone after school and on the weekends. Fortunately, she had been mature for her age and not prone to wild stunts that might have endangered her life or burned down their home.

For Abby, high school graduation brought a moment of release, of freedom. College and grad school had been some of the happiest years of her life. Coming home to Candlewick and working for the Chesters' law firm, on the other hand, had been a mixed blessing.

Her father stood, shoulders hunched, staring at the ground. "I never meant to harm anyone. I've made my share of mistakes, but I had good intentions."

Sadly, that part was probably true. There was no malice in the old man. Only unfounded optimism, a total misunderstanding of finances and an ability to con people out of their money one way or another.

"Good night." Abby made herself walk away, but her father was in one of his more stubborn moods, fueled by alcoholic courage.

"You owe me," he shouted. "I could have given you up for adoption when your mother died, but I didn't. That's worth something. Wouldn't look too good for you if I start telling everyone how badly you treat the only parent you've ever known."

The callous, calculating threat put another crack in her shattered heart. She had paid for her meal that night with cash. The change was in her pocket. Seven dollars and thirty-two cents. She fished it out and shoved it at him. "Take it and go. I don't want to see you here ever again."

She ran up the walk and into the house, slamming the door and bolting it behind her. The tears came in earnest, blurring her vision and knotting her stomach. The bedroom was too far. She fell onto the sofa, buried her face in the cushions and cried until her bones ached.

Every time she tangled with her father now, she felt dirty. She had worked so hard to make something of herself...to lead a decent, normal life. Yet always, her past hung over her head, reminding her that she might forever be tainted by his dishonesty.

At ten, she dragged herself down the hall to take a shower. Looking in the mirror was a mistake. Her eyes were bloodshot and puffy, and smeared mascara made her resemble a rabid panda. It was a good thing Duncan Stewart couldn't see her now.

As if she had summoned him somehow with her thoughts, her phone dinged. She picked it up and read the text.

We never made a plan for tomorrow night, did we?

They hadn't. She had agreed to see him again only if she could speak with Miss Izzy first about the prospective buyer. She gripped the phone, torn about how to answer. She knew that dating Duncan Stewart was a dead end and a bad idea. Ethics aside, they had nothing in common. He was wealthy and had lived a life of relative ease.

She was sure he'd never had to worry about having the

electricity or the water turned off because the bills hadn't been paid in three months. And she was equally positive he had never been forced to eat boxed macaroni and cheese five nights in a row because it was the only thing in the pantry a kid could microwave easily. Or the only food available, period.

Wistfully, she did the grown-up thing.

I don't think it's a good idea for us to see each other socially, Duncan. Too many layers of complications.

Thirty seconds passed. Then sixty. At last, the phone dinged.

What about that kiss?

Despite her low mood, she smiled.

What about it?

Don't be coy, Abby. We're both adults. I want you. You want me.

She tried to be incensed by his careless arrogance, but damn it, the man was right.

Not all itches have to be scratched.

You don't know me very well yet, but here's the thing, lass. I rarely take no for an answer.

Neither do I! She threw in a few emojis for good measure.

Fine. I'll take you to see Granny before dinner. But don't be surprised when she says no to your buyer.

And if she says yes????

Abby could almost *feel* the frustrated male silence on the other end. Maybe Lara was right. Maybe Duncan was conflicted about letting Abby get to his grandmother, because if the offer was good enough, he'd be off the hook and headed home to Scotland.

At last, he answered. I'll pick you up at five thirty. We'll have hors d'oeuvres with her, and you can make your pitch. But no bullying or hard-sell tactics. If she says no, you drop the subject. Period.

You're an arrogant ass, Duncan Stewart.

Aye, but you like me anyway...

She turned off the phone and tossed it in a drawer, as if it had the power to regenerate and bite her.

Duncan was dangerous to her peace of mind for many reasons. Clearly, he knew women well enough to recognize mutual interest when he witnessed it. Abby could protest 'til the cows came home that this relationship was a terrible idea. All Duncan had to do was kiss her until she forgot the many reasons why she should stay away from him.

Friday was an exercise in torture for Duncan. Every time he saw his granny's smiling face, he felt guilty. Tonight, he was going to let a lawyer with her own nest-feathering agenda get close to his grandmother, just so he could find his way into that lawyer's bed.

Any way you sliced it, that made him scum.

In the moments when he wasn't thinking about Abby, he pondered the escape clause in the will. He had come here to America, fully expecting his grandmother to live for another decade or more. It was possible. The women in her genealogy had all closed in on the centennial mark, several of them passing it. Granny Isobel could very well celebrate her hundredth birthday here in Candlewick. She was in good health and of sound mind.

To hear that his indenture had an escape clause troubled him. Without it, he had no choice but to dive headfirst into Stewart Properties and make a new life for himself. But knowing there was a carrot dangling out there—the chance to go home to Scotland in two years—meant that he would always be marking time. In many ways, the possibility of reprieve made things worse.

In a difficult situation, a man needed to hunker down and make the best of his fate. How effective would Duncan be if he were always looking wistfully over his shoulder from whence he had come?

Somehow, he made it through the day. Granny Isobel was beside herself at the prospect of company. She had ordered a trio of fancy appetizers from a local caterer, along with a selection of wines to have on hand for Abby's visit.

One of the receptionists took Isobel home at three so she could nap in preparation for her visitor. Duncan stayed at the office until the very last minute, going over spreadsheets and trying his damnedest to wrap his head around the ambitious construction schedule planned for the upcoming two quarters.

The business's forward motion had slowed in the year since his grandfather's death. First Brody, and now Duncan, had helped Isobel get the company back on track. It relieved Duncan more than a little to know that auditors would be coming in soon. If there were any problems, he wanted to know about them.

At five, he called his grandmother to see if she needed anything else to go with the food. She professed to have it all under control. He grinned to himself. In his grandparents' heyday, they had thrown wildly lavish parties up on top of the mountain. Invitations to the big house were highly coveted. He'd heard more than one story about dancing until dawn and draining multiple cases of champagne and good Scottish whisky.

At five twenty, he locked up the office and headed out to pick up Abby.

When he bounded up her steps and knocked, she answered the door wearing a smile, black dress pants and a soft berry-pink cashmere sweater that clung to her ample curves. He scooped her up and kissed her, careful not to smudge her rosy lip gloss.

Abby was stiff in his embrace at first, but then she sighed and kissed him back. "You're an outrageous man. I don't know why I don't smack you."

He pulled back and grinned at her. "I'm guessing you have to be on your best behavior until you accomplish your damned objective. But I warn you, it's a fool's errand. Granny won't sell."

"If you're really so worried about me talking to her, I could take *you* to meet the prospective buyer one day next week. You wouldn't have to tell Isobel right away."

"Oh, no," he said, grimacing. "I don't do secrets. They never end well. If we're doing this, we'll be upfront about your agenda."

"Mr. Chester asked me to present the offer. I'm not responsible for the outcome."

"If you say so." He kept an arm around her waist as they walked out to the car. "Granny is beside herself with excitement that you're coming. I suppose I hadn't realized how much she has missed Brody and Cate and the baby since they left. With just me around, the house has been too quiet."

"Maybe I could have lunch with her one day."

He gave her a sideways frown. "Are you suggesting that idea as a lawyer or as a decent human being?"

"The two aren't mutually exclusive," Abby said, glaring at him.

He helped her into the car and closed her door. Even when she was mad at him, he felt a sexual pull. That reality didn't bode well for his peace of mind.

When he was behind the wheel with the engine running, he apologized. "I'm sorry. No more cheap shots about your profession today, I promise."

She grinned wryly. "Only today?"

He shrugged, feeling lighthearted and pumped about the evening to come. "I'll take the rest of the calendar under consideration, I swear."

The trip up the mountain was quick. When they arrived, Abby stepped out of the car and stared at his grandparents' house in admiration. "I'd forgotten how beautiful it is up here. I've never been inside, though."

"Some of the exterior upkeep has been let go. Brody and I put a lot of sweat equity into cutting back bushes and fixing gutters…things like that. For a long time after Grandda died, Granny couldn't bring herself to stay here with him gone. But now that she's back, she's happy again. This house was something they built together, just like the business."

After unlocking the front door, he stood aside for Abby to enter. He tossed his keys into a carved wooden bowl on a table in the foyer and motioned for Abby to follow him. Raising his voice, he called out. "Granny. We're here."

He'd half expected his grandmother to be hovering by the front door, ready to greet her guest. "She's probably in the kitchen."

"I love all the artwork," Abby said. "Everything is warm and welcoming, but so very unique."

"Aye," Duncan replied, half-distracted. "They collected paintings and sculptures from all over the world. *Granny*. Where are you?" He rounded the corner into the kitchen, and his heart stopped. A small figure lay crumpled in the center of the floor.

"Granny!" He fell to his knees, his heart pounding. "God, Granny. Call 9-1-1," he yelled, though Abby was at his elbow, her eyes wide, her expression aghast.

While Abby fumbled with her cell phone and punched in the numbers, Duncan took his grandmother's hands and chafed them. "Talk to me, Granny. Open your eyes." Abby finished her brief conversation. "Get me a wet cloth," he said. "The drawer by the sink."

Moments later, she crouched at his side and handed him a damp square of cotton. Duncan placed it on his grandmother's forehead. Her lips were blue. His heart slugged in his chest. CPR. He needed to do CPR. He'd had the training. Instinct kicked in. He began the sequence of compressions and breaths. Counting. Pushing. Praying.

Abby took one of Isobel's frails wrists and held it.

Duncan shot her a wild-eyed glance. "Anything?"

"No." Tears welled in Abby's eyes but didn't fall.

"Damn it." He repeated the CPR sequence again. And again. Until his chest ached and his arms ached and his heart was broken. "I just talked to her half an hour ago." This couldn't be happening. It wasn't real.

Abby put her arms around him from behind and laid her cheek against his. "I think she's dead, Duncan," she whispered. "I'm sorry. I'm so very sorry."

Five

Abby hadn't realized she could hurt so badly for a man she had known for such a short time. The two hours that followed were nothing less than a nightmare. A parade passed through the house… EMTs and ambulance drivers and Isobel's personal physician and eventually a representative from the local funeral home. At long last, the elderly woman's tiny, cold body was zipped into a dreadful black bag and loaded into the back of a hearse.

If she'd had a choice, Abby wouldn't have chosen to witness that last part, but Duncan wouldn't leave his grandmother and Abby wouldn't leave Duncan. Somewhere along the way, he had withdrawn inside himself. He spoke when necessary. He thanked everyone who helped. He made decisions. He signed papers. But the man who had picked her up at her home earlier that evening was gone.

At last, they were alone. The sprawling house echoed with silence and tragedy.

"You should eat something," Abby said quietly. "Let me fix you a plate."

He didn't respond. She wasn't even sure he heard her.

They had been standing at the front of the house watching as the vehicle bearing his grandmother's body drove away. Quietly, Abby closed and locked the door and took Duncan's arm. "Let's go to the kitchen," she said. "I'll make us some coffee."

As soon as they entered the room, she winced. It was impossible not to remember seeing the small, sad body lying forlorn and alone in the middle of the floor. The doctor believed Isobel likely suffered a massive cardiac event and had died instantly without suffering.

Abby had searched Duncan's face to see if this news brought him comfort. Nothing in his anguished expression told her that was the case.

Now, as Duncan stood irresolute, she eased him toward a chair. "Sit," she said firmly, as she would with a child. She bustled about the unfamiliar kitchen, finding plates and cups and silverware. By the time the coffee brewed, she had scooped out small portions of the appetizers that were to have been Isobel's contribution to the evening's social hour. Baked Brie with raspberry jam. Fresh minced tomato and mozzarella on bruschetta. Mushrooms stuffed with sausage and ricotta.

She put a plate in front of Duncan and laid her hand on his shoulder. "Try to eat something," she said. He stared at the food, but he didn't see it. That was painfully obvious.

Her heart breaking for him, she poured two cups of steaming coffee, carried them to the table and sat down beside him. She took his hand in both of hers, worried that his long fingers were cold. "Talk to me, Duncan," she said quietly. "Talk to me."

He blinked as if waking from a dream. "She was with me at the office this afternoon. She was fine. I talked to her on the phone after five. She was fine. How could this happen?"

"Miss Izzy was an old woman. I guess her heart gave out."

"I should have been here."

She heard the reproach in his voice. She understood it.

But it stung, even so. Duncan was hurting, and he needed a place to direct his pain.

"You heard the doctor. He thinks she died instantly."

Duncan's eyes flashed. "But she shouldn't have died alone."

There was nothing to say to that.

Abby picked up a fork and forced down a few bites of food, though she didn't really feel like eating at all. She was hoping that Duncan would follow her example by rote. After a few moments, he did. He cleared half of what was on his plate, drank one whole cup of coffee and poured himself a second one. Then he paced the kitchen, his agitation increasing by the moment.

Abby was at a loss. "Should we call your brother and your father?" she asked.

He glanced at his watch. "They'll all be asleep by now. No need to wake them. Granny was very specific about her funeral arrangements. The entire family came en masse for Grandda's services. She was honored and glad to have us here. But she insisted that when her time came, no one was to come back to the States. She wanted to be cremated and have her ashes spread on top of the mountain."

Suddenly, Duncan walked out of the kitchen. She followed him. His mood was volatile, so she was worried. Down the hall, he opened the door to his grandmother's bedroom and stood there. Not entering. Only looking. Her bed was neatly made. The novel she had been reading earlier, perhaps before napping, lay facedown on the mattress.

Abby slipped an arm around his waist, trying without words to offer comfort where there was none. A minute passed. Then another.

Duncan was immovable, a statue in a house that had become a mausoleum. When he finally spoke, his words were barely audible. "Do you think she knew how reluctant I was to come here and stay? That I didn't really want to learn the business? That my heart wasn't in it?"

The guilt-ridden questions came from the depths of his grief.

Abby leaned her cheek against his arm and sighed. "Your grandmother adored you, Duncan. The fact that you were willing to give up everything to move here and help her run Stewart Properties made her happier than she had been since your grandfather died. She didn't see your doubts, Duncan. All she saw was a grandson's devotion."

"I hope so."

Abby juggled her own share of guilt. She mourned Isobel's passing for the family's sake. But for Abby, this sudden change meant that Duncan would not be staying in Candlewick. The idea of an affair with the wealthy, charismatic Scotsman had never been realistic from the beginning. Now, though, all the delicious *might-have-beens* were gone for good.

Duncan's posture was rigid. Grief was hard for a man, especially one as masculine and dominant as a Stewart clansman. Abby feared for his mental well-being. The blow of this untimely death so soon after the trauma of uprooting his life and relocating to the States had clearly shaken him to the foundations.

She stroked his arm. He was in shock, whether he realized it or not. His thinking was muddled, his emotions on overload. "Come to the den," she said softly. "Sit and rest. We could watch a movie. Or talk."

Duncan shook his head as if trying to wake up from a dream. "I should take you home," he said, his tone oddly formal. "Let me get my keys."

Abby got in front of him and made him look her in the eyes. "I'm not leaving you alone tonight, Duncan. There are half a dozen bedrooms. I can sleep anywhere. But I won't walk away and let you rattle around this big old house by yourself."

"I'm not a child." His gaze was slightly unfocused, his voice rough, as though normal speech was difficult.

She went up on her tiptoes and kissed his cheek. "I know that. But you're hurting, and no one should have to bear this alone."

In the end, she wasn't much help at all. Though she managed to get him into the den, he merely stared at the TV screen blankly for hours, unseeing. She might as well have shown him old Bugs Bunny cartoons or sitcom reruns. He would never have known the difference.

At eleven, she powered down the electronics and began turning off lights. She touched his arm. "Why don't you go take a shower, Duncan? It might make you feel better. In the morning, I'll help you with whatever decisions you have to make. Tonight, though, you need sleep."

He nodded and stood, but his compliance seemed illusory at best.

When Duncan was safely in his bedroom, Abby wandered through the house, checking doors and windows. There was an alarm system, but she had no idea how to arm it. Maybe for one night it wouldn't matter.

Finding a guest room was not difficult. Isobel Stewart and her late husband had entertained out-of-town company often. The suite Abby picked at random was decorated beautifully, though a tad formally for her tastes, in deep burgundy and navy. The bathroom had been updated in recent years. All of the necessary amenities were available in drawers and cabinets, including the kind of shower cap hotels offered.

She took a shower, brushed her teeth and put her same clothes back on. Tomorrow, Lara would bring her a small bag of essentials. Earlier, she had sent a brief text to let her friend know what had happened. Lara's rapid, heartfelt response was one small note of sunshine in a horribly gloomy experience.

At last, she folded back the covers on the large, opulent bed and slipped between the sheets. Sleep should have come easily. Adrenaline and emotional exhaustion had left her feeling wrung out. Even so, she couldn't settle. Her ears strained to hear any sound from Duncan's bedroom. He was almost directly across the hall from her. She had left her door open a crack so she would know if he stirred.

Her premonitions were on target. At 1:00 a.m., she awoke to the sound of someone prowling about in the hallway. In the distance, the kitchen lights came on. Various rustling noises told her Duncan might be getting a snack. He must be hungry. What he had eaten earlier was hardly enough to keep a grown man going for very long.

She debated joining him. Scrambled eggs could be considered comfort food at this hour. She could fix him a light breakfast. But soon, the lights were out again, and she heard him go back to his room.

The disruption of her slumber, coupled with her concern for Duncan, made going *back* to sleep almost impossible. Frustrated, she got up and used the bathroom. Then she stood in the center of the bedroom in the dark and pondered what to do. Was he sleeping? Had he slept at all?

Tomorrow would be another long, difficult day. In this situation, even strong adults sometimes needed help from a doctor in the form of a sleep aid. Not that Duncan would take kindly to that suggestion.

When she heard his door open a second time, she stepped into the hall without second-guessing herself. Duncan jerked backward, startled. "Why are you up?" he growled.

Abby wrapped her arms around her waist and shrugged. "I heard you. I was worried."

"I'm sorry I woke you. You should have gone home."

She wouldn't let his harsh words hurt her. She couldn't. He was lashing out because he didn't know what to do with the emotions tearing at him. "Have you slept at all, Duncan?"

"On and off."

They stood there in the narrow hallway. Duncan wore nothing but a pair of flannel sleep pants that hung low on his hips. His broad chest was bare. His hair stood on end. Though there was not enough light to see for sure, Abby knew his jaw was covered with stubble. The scent of his skin, warm from his bed, wafted in the air between them.

"Duncan, I—"

He held up a hand, cutting her off. "Don't bother. I've said it all to myself, and nothing helps. She was old. Old people die. I get it. But I wasn't ready. And I didn't know it would feel like this." He dropped his head and stared at the floor, dejection and sorrow in every angle of his big, masculine frame.

Abby's heart clenched and ached. He was so very much alone and so very far from home. She took his hand before she could change her mind. "I'm going to lie down with you," she said firmly. "On top of the covers. That way you won't be alone. It helps, I think, to have someone close when you face a loss."

It was a mark of his utter desolation that he didn't protest. Nor did he make some silly male comment about her climbing into bed with him. If anything, the vibe she got from him was gratitude, not that he actually expressed it in so many words.

His bed was a king. The covers were rumpled as if he had fought with them for hours. Together they straightened the sheets and comforter. Without asking, Duncan fetched an extra blanket from the closet. Then he climbed into bed. The light in the bathroom was still on with the door pulled almost completely closed. Abby didn't mention it. Whether an oversight or not, that tiny beam of light was comforting in this dark, dark night.

When Duncan was settled, Abby lay down on top of the covers on the opposite side of the bed and pulled the spare blanket around herself.

Duncan reached out a hand and turned off the lamp. "Thank you, Abby."

The tone in his voice made her want to cry. "You're welcome," she whispered.

The next time she surfaced, it was still dark outside. Confused and disoriented, she blinked and moved restlessly until her memory came crashing back. She was in Duncan's bedroom…in his bed. A noise had awakened her.

She froze for a moment. Was it an intruder? Had her failure to set the alarm left them vulnerable?

For long seconds, she listened. And then it came again. A keening, terrible sound. The sound of a man in the throes of a nightmare.

Duncan flung an arm over his head and cried out. She could *feel* the agony of his dream.

Throwing her blanket aside, she scooted across the mattress and approached him carefully, not wanting to make things worse…certainly not wanting to embarrass him. She put her hand on his arm and spoke his name. "Duncan. Wake up, Duncan. It's me, Abby."

It took several tries, but finally he shuddered and opened his eyes. His face was damp. "Did I dream it?" he asked hoarsely. "Is it true?"

Abby's throat hurt. "I don't know what you dreamed. But if you're asking me about your grandmother, then yes. She's gone."

"Bloody hell." His voice broke on the second word.

Abby couldn't help herself. She scooted beneath the covers and wrapped her arms around him. He buried his face in her neck, shaking. She stroked his hair. "Ssshhh," she said. "It's okay, Duncan. It's going to be okay."

For the first time, she saw him as something other than the wealthy grandson of a wealthy family for whom everything in life had come easily.

He was just a man.

The clock on the bedside table marked the passage of time. Abby drifted in and out of sleep. Duncan slept, as well. She heard his heavy breathing. She felt the weight of his limbs. And with every hour that passed, she knew her own personal grief—grief for the relationship that would wither on the vine before it had a chance to take root.

For whatever reason, Duncan Stewart spoke to something deep in her heart, some vulnerable, fragile, hopeful spot that wanted a man with a voice like warm honey and a deep streak of honor and a strength that would care for a woman and yet respect her ability to care for him, also.

None of it mattered. He wasn't hers to keep.

When her arm went numb, she tried to ease it out from under him. His bare chest radiated heat. Since she was fully dressed, she was too hot. When she tried to push the covers aside, Duncan muttered and rolled toward her, one powerful leg trapping both of hers against the mattress.

In a single stark second, she felt the press of his aroused sex against her hip. *Oh, Lordy.* Her stomach flip-flopped. Duncan was asleep. She knew that. A man's body had certain predictable reactions in compromising situations.

Was this *her* fault? Had she subconsciously wanted this?

No. Heck, no. She might be a sex-starved single woman with few prospects, but she wasn't that desperate. She had wanted to help Duncan through the night. That was all. Besides, she was fully dressed. Nothing could happen.

He mumbled something unintelligible and slid a hand underneath her sweater.

Abby froze, her breath catching in her throat. When

Duncan cupped her breast and stroked her nipple through her thin, satiny bra, her brain shut down. It felt so damned good she wanted to groan out loud. But that might wake him up, and how would she explain the current situation?

Duncan murmured a word, a Gaelic word. It sounded like sunshine and warm breezes and a man's intent. Abby melted inside, her good intentions winnowing away like sand castles at high tide.

She tried, she really did. "Duncan," she whispered. "I don't think you want to do this." She cupped his face in her hands, feeling the rough growth of a day's beard. Her lips brushed his cheek, the bridge of his nose. "Wake up, Duncan. Please."

"I'm awake," he muttered. Now he pushed the bra to her armpits and found her bare breasts. He palmed one. Then the other. "Gorgeous," he said. "So beautiful."

Abby forgot to breathe. Her entire body went liquid with pleasure. His fingers teased the tips of her breasts. Tugging, twisting. Then he bent and tasted her, scraping his teeth against her sensitive flesh and biting gently.

When she cried out, he ripped at her sweater, dragging it and her bra over her head in short order, tangling her hair and leaving her naked from the waist up. Now her remaining clothing frustrated him.

Abby knew they were careening down a dangerous slope. "Duncan, please."

He froze, his chest heaving. He reared up on one elbow. His free hand was at her waistband, struggling with the fastening on her pants.

His eyes were open. In the faint illumination from the bathroom light, they glittered with intent. "Are ye asking me to stop, lass?"

It was up to her. She could stand up and walk away, and nothing would happen. The hushed silence after his question seemed to last forever, though it was probably only seconds that passed.

She was defeated by his misery and his raw need and her own yearning. Everything inside her wanted to give him peace and release. She wanted that and more for herself. She wasn't going to have Duncan Stewart for any kind of happily-ever-after. But she could have tonight. She *would* have it.

"No." She swallowed hard, trying to find her breath, her courage. "Don't stop."

Six

Under the circumstances, she expected Duncan to rush madly toward the finish line. He was sleep-deprived and grief stricken and a man at the end of his emotional and physical reserves.

Duncan had other ideas.

As she lay trembling and aghast that she hadn't been smart enough to stop this madness, he unbuttoned and unzipped her pants, dragged them down her legs and tossed them aside. Now she wore nothing but a pair of fairly ordinary bikini panties.

Duncan pressed two fingertips to the damp fabric covering her sex. She was glad it was dark. Suddenly, she was conscious of her convex tummy and her rounded thighs. He stroked her through the fabric, making her squirm. "I've no' ever seen a more beautifully feminine woman, Abby Hartmann. Ye're like a feast for my hands and my eyes. I want to gobble you up, and I don't know where to start."

"You could just get on with it," she muttered. She hadn't expected him to linger over the first course.

He stood up long enough to remove his pajama pants but came back to her immediately, dragging her into his embrace and burying his face in her hair. "I wanted you the first moment I saw you, Abby." He kissed the shell of her ear, his breath hot on her neck. "I don't think you have a clue what you do to a man. You're soft and warm and curvy, all the things I'm not. Women are special creatures, beautiful and rare."

If any American man of her acquaintance had uttered those words, she might have laughed. Duncan's sleep-roughened voice and rolling accent made everything he said plausible.

Then he lapsed into Gaelic and Abby lost her head completely. "Duncan…" she whispered his name, arching her back as he kissed his way from her nose to her chin to her throat and then paused to enjoy her cleavage.

For a hazy moment, she wondered if she were dreaming. The line between fact and fiction had been blurred tonight. She slid her hands into his hair, winnowing her fingers through the thick, healthy strands…feeling the strong bones of his skull.

His naked body touched hers everywhere, it seemed. She felt the damp warmth of his skin, tasted the salt of his sweat, heard the harshness of his breathing as his arousal mounted and her own raced to meet and match it. Despite her self-consciousness, for one wild instant, she wanted to turn on every light in the room and feast her eyes on the work of art that was Duncan Stewart.

He smelled like a man in the best possible way, and in his utter dominance, her femininity unfurled, reveling in the absolute freedom to take what she wanted and demand what she needed.

When her fingernails raked his back, Duncan choked out a laugh. "Have a care, little cat. You'll leave a scar. Is that what you want?"

It was a joke, a lighthearted sexual tease. Her own response stunned her. If marking a man was a primal instinct, then yes. The thought of any other woman having Duncan made her heart weep.

She soothed the scratches with gentle touches. "My apologies, Mr. Stewart. It's your own fault. You make me a little crazy."

"Only a little? I'll have to try harder." He kissed her unexpectedly, his tongue stroking deeply into the recesses of her mouth and stealing every bit of oxygen from her lungs. It was a kiss that lasted forever and yet ended far too soon—in turns sweet and coaxing, then forceful and demanding.

He moved on top of her now, spreading her legs with his hips, but not joining their bodies. Abby felt faint, half-asleep, wholly dizzy with drugged arousal. She wound her arms around his neck, clinging to the only anchor in the room. Everything else spun dizzily.

Duncan reached between their bodies and fingered her gently. She was so slick and ready it was almost embarrassing. With an exclamation that might have been a Gaelic curse, he centered the head of his erection at her entrance and pushed steadily.

Duncan had never been very good at self-deception. He knew what he was doing, and he knew there would be repercussions. But he couldn't have walked away from Abby even to save his own life. In that moment, she was everything to him.

Her body gloved him in warm, clenching heat. His life was a shit-storm of pain and regret at the moment. Abby offered absolution and escape. He chose the latter without shame or regret. He had wanted her before today. Now he needed her, as well.

"Am I hurting you?" he groaned. She was tight and so small in his big bed. His height topped hers by at least a dozen inches.

Abby shook her head. "No." She toyed with the hair at

his nape, sending lightning bolts of heat down his spine to join the conflagration elsewhere.

"God, you're sweet," he groaned. "I could keep you in this bed for days." Reality tried to intrude. He ruthlessly pushed it away.

She canted her hips, forcing him deeper. "I won't break," she said, the words shaky. "You don't have to be so careful with me."

"I don't want to hurt you," he said roughly, still moving in her as if he could take her like this again and again until dawn. For hours, he had slammed every door that kept his emotions in check. Now Abby's very softness and transparent caring made his self-protective instincts for naught. He knew she was here to comfort him. He knew, and he took her anyway. What kind of man did that make him?

Abby sensed his distress and cradled his face in her hands. "Don't think, Duncan. Only feel. You and me. In this bed. Maybe we're dreaming, right? Maybe this is as good as it gets. Show me everything, you big stubborn Scotsman. Make me fly."

He lost his head after that. His body took over, recklessly chasing a wicked, shocking release that was destined to destroy him so completely he would never be himself again. He felt the press of her bosom against his chest. He smelled the faint scent of her hair and her perfume.

Her body cradled his perfectly, welcoming his wild lust and transmuting it into something far more unexpected and dangerous. He plunged into her again and again, thrusting himself against the head of her womb until she cried out and shuddered in his arms.

He waited for her orgasm to take its course. Then he released the almost-superhuman hold he had kept on his own body and groaned her name as he emptied himself into her keeping.

* * *

When he woke up, sunlight filled the room, and Abby was gone. Duncan's head throbbed, though he had consumed no alcohol. Memories swam in his brain with disturbing, drunken chaos. His grandmother's still, cold shape on the floor. The doctor's sympathetic gaze. Abby's warm, naked body in his bed.

God, what had he done?

To give himself time to steady his careening emotions, he took a shower, shaved and then sat down in a chair beside the bed with his cell phone. Staring at it, he prepared a speech for his brother and his father. This was tough news to deliver over the phone, particularly from such a distance.

It hurt to think about Abby right now. His relationship with her, such as it was, represented every bit of guilt he felt about his grandmother. Had he made a huge mistake? Was Abby the enemy in this situation? Did she have a secret agenda? Or were her compassion and gentle caring sincere?

Because he didn't know the answer to any of those questions, he shoved them aside and dialed his brother's number. Today was going to be long and difficult. He might as well get started.

Abby left Duncan's bed just before dawn, slipping from his embrace with every care not to wake him. She needn't have worried. He slept deeply, sprawled on his back, his body completely relaxed.

It wouldn't last. She knew that. But at least she had given him a few hours of peace and oblivion. Perhaps that would sustain him through the ordeal to follow.

She went back to her own room and dozed until eight thirty. Then she freshened up and made a plan with Lara via text. When that was done, she scrounged in the kitchen for something to eat. Duncan's bedroom door was closed. She would not intrude.

After eating a banana and a cup of yogurt that she didn't really taste, she went back to her bedroom and called in to work, requesting a few days of vacation. It was a bad time with Mr. Chester out, but he would understand. Isobel Stewart had been a client for decades. Her family certainly deserved an extra measure of attention and care under the circumstances.

At ten, Duncan still had not appeared. It seemed foolish to worry about a grown man. But Abby began to second-guess herself. Was he hoping she would go away so they wouldn't have to face each other?

When Lara arrived, Abby hurried to the front of the house to meet her friend outside. She didn't want to disturb Duncan's privacy.

The morning was crisp and cool. At these altitudes, the first frost would soon dust the rhododendron thickets with white. Lara jumped out of the car and hugged her friend tightly. "Are you okay, honey? This must have been a terrible shock."

Abby hadn't realized she was so close to the edge. Lara's concern broke down her defenses, and she burst into tears, tears born of stress and lack of sleep and uncertainty about the days to come.

Lara let her cry, patting her back and holding her close. At last, Abby pulled away and wiped her nose. "I'm sorry. I didn't know that was going to happen."

"You look like hell, darlin'. No offense."

"None taken." Abby shook her head. "I've never seen a dead person before, Lara…at least not one that hasn't been all prettied up in a casket. It was awful. Poor Miss Izzy. Duncan is drowning in guilt that she died alone, and I can't say that I blame him. I feel pretty awful about it, too. She was excited about me coming by to see her. I've worried that it was too much."

Lara took her by the shoulders and gave her a little

shake. "Don't be a goose. Most elderly people I know would think this kind of death was a great blessing. No lingering illness. No nursing home. No loss of independence. Miss Izzy died happy. Her grandson moved here to run the company with her. She had everything to live for. I guess her heart gave out. And now she's with Mr. Stewart, the love of her life."

"I hope Duncan will find comfort in that thought. He's very upset. It was so sudden. She was at work with him yesterday. They had talked on the phone right before he picked me up. Then we got here, and she was on the floor..." Abby put her fist to her mouth, reliving those awful moments.

Lara curled an arm around her again. "There are worse things in life than death. Duncan will make peace with this. But it will take some time, perhaps."

"I want to help him," Abby said. "With all he has to do. Is that weird?"

Lara pursed her lips. "Well, I don't know. Is he going to let you?"

It was a good question. And one Abby couldn't answer. She pointed to the back seat. "Is that my suitcase?"

Lara nodded and lifted it out. "I packed in a hurry, but I think you've got enough for a couple of days. Plus, it's not like you don't live close. If you think you'll need your car, let me know, and I'll figure out a way to get it up here to you."

Abby shook her head in bemusement. "You have the best heart of anyone I know, Lara. I don't know why you have to pretend all the time that you're a hard-ass."

The other woman held up a hand, her expression alarmed. "You keep those wretched opinions to yourself, you hear?"

"Understood." Abby hesitated, feeling her neck heat. "There's one more thing."

Lara nodded. "Anything for you, cupcake. Name it."

"My father came by the house the other evening. I've changed the locks on all the doors. And I didn't let him in. Will you please drive by occasionally and see if everything looks okay?"

"Damn it, Abby. Get a restraining order."

"That would be public and embarrassing."

"You went to court and legally changed your last name to your mother's maiden name to distance yourself from him. What's the big deal about one more step? One more piece of paper? You shouldn't have to live in fear."

"He's not dangerous. I don't think."

Lara scowled. "He's dangerous to your peace of mind. That's enough for me to want him gone for good. So, yes. I'll check on the house. Anything else?"

Abby's eyes welled with tears, her emotions too near the surface. "Thank you, Lara. You're the best."

"Well, of course I am."

The other woman leaned into the front of the car and extracted a large picnic basket. "Mama and I got up early and started cooking. I know it's just Duncan, and you of course, so we didn't go overboard. But there's fried chicken and green beans and corn. Plus, rolls and baked apples and pecan pie. Should be enough there for two or three meals if you don't want to leave the house. Call me if there's anything in particular he needs. Folks in town want to help, but they don't know him very well. I promised I'd stay in touch with you."

Abby nodded. Small communities like Candlewick were known for their generous support in times of crisis. The Stewart heir would receive many kindnesses, even if he didn't expect anything to come his way.

She rested the suitcase on the wooden settee on the porch and picked up the picnic basket. "I should go inside and check on Duncan. I haven't seen him yet this morning."

"He was probably up most of the night after a shock like that. I'm sure I would have been if it were me."

Abby bit her lip and swallowed the need to blurt out the truth. Some stories were far too personal to share, even with a beloved girlfriend. "Thanks for everything, Lara. I'll call you later today when I know something."

She waved as her friend drove away, and then turned to set the suitcase just inside the front door. After that she picked up the heavy woven basket, closed the door with her hip and carried the food to the kitchen. Lara's mom had written out careful instructions for how to refrigerate and reheat each item.

When Abby rounded the corner and entered the room, Duncan was standing there, staring at the floor. He seemed calm, but she couldn't read his expression. She cleared her throat. "My friend Lara brought lunch," she said. "I just need to put a few things away."

His head jerked up, and he flushed. He pulled the basket out of her grip and set it aside. Then he took her by the waist and set her up on the counter. His gaze was clear and direct and troubled. "I'm sorry, Abby. About last night. It never should have happened. I've been trying to figure out how to apologize."

There was no warning, no preparation for this confrontation. Her heart shredded and her stomach shrank. He was too close. She felt raw. Exposed. "No apology needed," she croaked. "It was a difficult few hours."

He brushed the back of his hand over her cheek. "You saved my life last night, and you don't even know it. But I let it go too far."

"There were two of us in that bed," she snapped. "Don't play the noble hero. It was no big deal."

His eyes narrowed. "You're angry."

Maybe so, but not for the reasons he thought. She scrambled for composure. These next few days would depend on her ability to keep things light. "Neither of us meant for anything to happen last night, Duncan. Let's call it extenuating circumstances. You didn't take advantage of me. I don't want your apologies. Still, my firm will be handling your grandmother's probate, so it's probably a good idea for us to establish some boundaries."

"I agree." His tone was formal, his gaze frosty. "On another note, we didn't use protection. You should know that I'm in good health."

Abby's face flamed. Never in a million years had she imagined herself in the midst of such a conversation. "As am I," she said. "It was an unfortunate lapse, but I'm on the Pill for other reasons, so pregnancy isn't a worry."

"That's good."

"Yes."

Despite the negative tenor of their conversation, he still stood in the vee of her outspread knees. Though he wasn't touching her, they breathed the same oxygen. He ran a hand through his hair, betraying possible frustration. "I've spoken to my family."

"How did that go?"

"They were shocked, of course. And sad. No one is ever prepared for the fact that goodbyes are sometimes not an option."

"What happens next?" She hopped down from the counter, forcing him to step back. Without waiting for permission, she began putting away the food Lara had brought.

"I have a problem," Duncan said. "I don't know what to do."

She closed the refrigerator door and stared at him. "What's wrong?"

"I told you Granny wanted to be cremated."

"Yes."

"But it doesn't make sense. Grandda is buried in the cemetery in town. There's a plot beside him. People want to pay their respects at a funeral, both former and current employees. Some of them worked for my grandparents for decades. Why wouldn't I have a traditional funeral so her friends could say goodbye?"

"Do you have any idea why she mentioned cremation? Was there some significance to having her ashes scattered on top of the mountain?"

"I don't think so. If I had to guess, I'd say she wanted to make things easier for our family. No funeral, no problem. Or maybe she was simply trying to be economical."

"Old people get that way sometimes, even when they have nothing to worry about financially."

"Yes. They do."

"Well, at the risk of seeming disrespectful, I'd say what matters is the choice that feels right to *you*. She's gone. You're here. If you think a traditional funeral is the way to go, then do it."

He nodded slowly. "I will." His expression lightened. "Thanks, Abby. I hadn't expected all these decisions. It's a lot. I don't want to make a mistake. I want to honor her memory…hers *and* Grandda's." Before she could stop him, he reached out and pulled her into a bear hug. "Thank you for being here with me."

Seven

Duncan used his gratitude shamelessly as an excuse to touch her again. Abby was right. They couldn't carry on an affair under the circumstances. But God, he wanted to feel her in his arms again.

He stroked her hair, but other than that, behaved himself.

Last night had taken him to the depths and then at the last moment, thrown him a life raft in the form of sexy, curvaceous, kindhearted Abby Hartmann. Even now, the memories made him hard. He released her reluctantly. "I have to go to the funeral home at one o'clock to view the body. I picked out a casket online this morning, and the dress shop in town sent over a fall suit that Granny would have liked. I wanted her to have something new. But there are a few other things that require my attention. Come with me. Please."

"Of course." She wrapped her arms around her waist, visibly uncomfortable. "I've taken a week off from work, Duncan. I want to help you any way I can."

"But not sleep with me."

"Of course not!"

He smiled wryly. "Just making sure." Tormenting Abby

was one of the few pleasures he had left. Besides, he still wasn't sure if she was an angel come to save him or a cagey lawyer with her own reasons for hanging around. He wanted to believe she was innocent and pure, but he could swear she was keeping secrets from him, and that raised all sorts of red flags. "I'm starving," he said. "Let's see what your friend brought us."

Over a home-cooked meal that was better than anything he had tasted in his entire life, Abby grilled him.

"What will you do with the house?" she asked.

He took a sip of water and grabbed another chicken leg. "I don't know. But whether I sell it tomorrow or a year from now, it has to be cleaned out. My grandparents weren't hoarders, but they were married for a long, long time. There are closets and cabinets and drawers…" He shook his head, shuddering. "Brody and Cate helped Granny get started with some of it, but they barely scratched the surface. It's going to be a mess."

"Do you feel like you have to deal with it personally? For sentimental reasons?"

"Oh, no. Not at all. A few months ago, Granny gave Brody and me some mementos of our grandfather. Beyond that, we're guys. We don't care about dishes and such. I think the best thing is to take all the clothing and linens to charity and then have a big estate sale."

"I could help with emptying the drawers and closets and bagging up the things to give away."

"And I'll have to do Grandda's office myself."

"Is a week enough time?"

"I think it will have to be."

Abby didn't press about the business, and he was glad. By every standard, he should be relieved that he could sell and walk away. But somehow, now that his grandmother was gone so suddenly, it didn't seem that easy.

When the meal was done, they cleaned up the kitchen in

silence and put the food away. He touched her arm. "The funeral is going to be tomorrow afternoon at two. I didn't see any reason to wait. Sunday afternoon is a time most people are free."

"Makes sense."

He played with a strand of her hair, unable to keep away from her despite his best judgment. "When it's done, let's go to Asheville overnight. To that big, fancy hotel I've heard about. We'll have a nice dinner, relax and come home on Monday to tackle all this."

She looked up at him, her eyes huge. "You're asking me to go away to a hotel with you?"

"We could reserve two rooms." But he didn't want to…

"I'm getting very mixed signals from you, Duncan."

He grimaced. "I know."

"Funerals are grueling. You'll need a break afterward."

"Is that a yes?"

Her gaze searched his face as if looking for answers he couldn't give her. The whole situation was screwed up. It made no sense at all to get further involved with Abby. The only reason he had come to Candlewick in the first place was for his grandmother. Now, that reason was gone. Complicating matters further was the reality that Abby's legal firm would push the idea of selling the business immediately. Duncan needed time to process what he had lost.

Abby sighed, leaning into his chest for a brief moment before stepping away self-consciously and puttering at the sink. "Lara brought me a suitcase of clothes and other necessities. I think I'll shower and change. I'll be ready whenever you want to leave."

She escaped, leaving Duncan to realize that she had never actually said yes to the Asheville idea.

Viewing his grandmother's body turned out to be much more heart-wrenching than he had expected. She seemed even smaller in death. Abby stayed at his shoulder the entire time—at one point, slipping her hand into his.

He squeezed it. "She was a formidable lady. She and Grandda let Brody and me stay with them for several months when our parents divorced. She gave us sympathy and support, but she didn't coddle us. That was the Scots in her. She knew we had to be tough in a tough world."

He turned suddenly and looked down at Abby. "I'm sorry. This must bring back memories of losing your mother."

She shook her head. "No. I was too young. But I *will* admit to having a distaste for funeral homes. Something about the smells and the creaky floors and the guys in suits. Maybe we should do the whole Norse funeral-pyre thing and put our loved ones on flaming boats and send them out to sea."

"You do realize that Candlewick is in the mountains."

"It's a metaphor," she said, resting her head on his shoulder for a brief moment. "Work with me, Duncan."

He bent and kissed his grandmother's cheek. "I love you, Granny. Godspeed. Give Grandda a big hug from Brody and me."

The funeral home employee stood several feet away, discreetly waiting for his cue to close the casket.

Duncan hesitated. Watching that lid go down was not something he wanted to witness. He gave the man an apologetic glance. "We'll step outside if you don't mind."

In the hallway, he felt oddly dizzy. He hadn't signed on for this. Running Stewart Properties was one thing. What did he know about giving his grandmother a proper send-off? What if he did something wrong?

Abby dragged him to a nearby chair. "Sit." She handed him a bottle of water. "It's going to be okay, Duncan."

"Aye." He took a long swig, draining half the container. "I suppose it is. But when?"

Afterward, there was more to be done. All of the paperwork had to be finalized, the flowers ordered, a brief obituary written for the online listing, the Presbyterian minister nailed down for the words of committal and the burial scheduled for immediately after the brief service.

When they finally walked out of the funeral home into the bright autumn sunshine, Duncan felt as if he had gone three rounds with the old bully from his school back home. That huge, blustering kid was the one who taught Duncan to be light on his feet and how to take a blow to the face and keep going.

Looking back, those days were sweet and simple compared to this.

He barely remembered driving up the mountain.

Now, each time he had to return to his grandmother's house was going to be painful. The echoing silence. The memories.

Abby dropped her purse on a chair in the foyer and eyed him with an assessing gaze. "What do you want to do? Get to work? Take a nap? Channel surf in front of the TV?"

He rolled his shoulders. What he really wanted to do was take Abby to bed. His hands trembled with the need to touch her and feel her warm curves against him. "If you're up for it, we could climb the mountain. I haven't been up to the top since Grandda died."

"I love that idea. I went there once with a date a million years ago. We were both in high school. He wanted to impress me. We climbed a fence and ended up in poison ivy. You can imagine the rest."

Duncan laughed, as she had meant him to... "Hopefully, today will be more uneventful."

They changed clothes, grabbed a couple of water bottles and set out. The sun hung low in the sky, but they had plenty of time to get back to the house before dark. Years ago, Geoffrey and Isobel had built a trail all the way to the top of the mountain. They owned several hundred acres of pristine forest. When Duncan sold everything, what would happen to this peaceful wilderness?

The thought troubled him, though it wasn't really his problem.

Abby was in great physical shape, but he had to adjust his stride to accommodate her vertically challenged legs. She wore khaki shorts, a white cotton shirt tied at her waist and tiny leather hiking boots that made her look like a very sexy mountain climber.

He tried not to fixate on her legs. Or on the peeks of her stomach where her shorts and her top separated. The day was hot. She started out with only two buttons undone on her shirt. By the time they made it to the summit, a third one was loose. He liked his odds. Especially when tiny droplets of sweat rolled down between her breasts. He could almost imagine tasting each one.

They found the old weathered bench that had been there forever and flopped down, breathing hard. In front of them, a swath of treetops had been cut out, framing a postcard vista of the town of Candlewick far below.

Abby drained half of her water and wiped her mouth. "I'd forgotten how stunning the view is up here."

The view was definitely stunning, but it was closer to home. The woman beside him far outshone the scenery. Duncan found himself hot and horny and desperately conflicted. He was going back to Scotland very soon. Before—when he'd known he was here in North Carolina for at least two years—he had entertained the possibility of a relationship with the smart, sexy lawyer. The attraction was definitely mutual, and Abby was unattached.

But how fair was it for him to use her sympathy and her

generous heart and her gorgeous body to help him through a bad time and then walk away?

When Abby stood to shoot a few photographs with her smartphone, Duncan stayed where he was and brooded. If Abby's boss had his way, Duncan would exit this experience a very wealthy man. He could take a share of his money back to Scotland and invest in Brody's company, perhaps become a full partner. Is that what he wanted?

Abby turned back to him and smiled. "Say cheese." He frowned, but she took the shot anyway. "Something to remember you by," she said lightly.

Had she said it on purpose? To let him know that she knew? They might have blistering chemistry, but their timing sucked. Not to mention the possibly/probably unethical fact that Abby's boss was going to oversee the disbursement of Isobel Stewart's estate.

When she sat down again at his side, he flinched and put another few inches between them. His mood was volatile. Her nearness was a provocation he couldn't handle in his current mental state.

Abby sighed. "This isn't going to work, is it?"

"I don't know what you mean," he lied with a straight face.

She leapt to her feet and paced. "You're all alone, Duncan. You have a gargantuan task ahead of you, even if you only consider the house and not the business. Your brother has a brand-new wife and an even newer baby. He's in no position to help you with this. From what you've told me of your father, he's far too self-absorbed to drop everything and support his younger son or deal with actual *work*."

He cocked his head. "What are you trying to say, Abby?"

With her hands on her hips, she faced him, cheeks flushed, rose-gold curls tumbling in the breeze. "I'm the only friend you have at the moment. You need me. And I want to help you. But we have this *thing* between us. It's awkward."

"You told me pretty clearly to keep my hands to myself."

"I may have been wrong about that," she said, her expression hard to read. "Or at least unrealistic. Before your grandmother died——when you and I were flirting with the idea of a temporary fling—you were going to be a resident. I was worried about my career. About gossip. But you're leaving Candlewick now…or at least you will be soon. As long as we're discrete, I can't see that anything we do or don't do is anyone's business but ours."

Again, he got the impression she wasn't telling him the whole truth. What was she hiding? What was her endgame?

"I've never been a man who *uses* a woman for sex."

"What do you call it if the woman is using you in return?"

His head snapped back in shock. "Excuse me?"

Abby gazed at him with a wry, self-mocking smile. "I'm not writing a fairy tale here, Duncan. I live in a small town with an extremely limited dating pool. It might be nice for me to enjoy a liaison without worrying about repercussions when it's over. You're like a yummy homemade dessert from a local bakery…with a definite expiration date stamped on the box. You'll be going back to Scotland sooner rather than later. In the meantime, we could fool around."

He gaped at her. "You're propositioning me?"

"I'm sorry if that offends your alpha male sensibilities."

To be honest, it kind of did. He had wanted to pursue her…to convince her. "I'll have to think about it," he said, sounding stiff and pedantic even to his own ears.

"Fine," Abby said. "You do that." Her eyes flashed fire, and her face turned beet red. "I'm going back to the house."

She set off down the trail at a breakneck pace. He was so shocked by her offer and his own stupid response that it took him several minutes to jump up and follow her.

The woman was fast. He'd give her that. They were almost back at the house before he caught up with her, and that was only because a branch had gotten tangled in her hair. She was cursing and pulling and—if he wasn't mistaken—about to cry.

"Steady, lass," he said, sliding his arms around her from behind and stilling her flailing arms. "You're making it worse."

She froze. He held the branch steady with one hand and used the other to separate her hair from its prison, one strand at a time. Then he cupped her face in his hands. "I'm sorry, sweet Abby. You took me by surprise."

She couldn't quite meet his eyes. "It's no big deal. I misread the situation. I'm going home now. You can let me know when and if you need assistance loading boxes and filling garbage bags."

He kissed her forehead. "Don't be mad."

"You don't want me," she said quietly. "I'm not mad. I'm embarrassed."

"Quit being a bloody fool," he shouted. "Of course I want you." A tension headache wrapped his skull in a painful vise.

She looked up at him, blinking, her expression stormy and wounded. "It didn't sound like it. I tend to forget that men don't like pushy women. I'm accustomed to problem solving. I guess I overstepped my bounds. I apologize."

He released her, took a step backward and jammed his hands in his pockets to keep from shaking her. "For the life of me," he growled, "I dinna ken how a woman can be a selfless angel one minute and a contrary mule the next."

Clearly, she didn't like *that* remark. "Go to hell, Duncan. I changed my mind. I wouldn't sleep with you if every last man in Candlewick vanished tomorrow."

She took a step in his direction and thumped a finger into his chest. "You're arrogant and entitled and you think men rule the world. Well, I have news for you, *Mr.* Stewart. That may work in Scotland, but here in America we're—"

He snatched her up and kissed her ruthlessly, not giving any quarter until the fight left her, and she groaned low in her throat and every hair on the back of his neck stood at attention.

Now that he had regained control of the situation—for the moment—he decided to enjoy his advantage. Keeping one arm around her, he used his free hand to unbutton her shirt. "I love your bosom, lass. Have I told you so?"

"You might have mentioned it," she mumbled. "And FYI, nobody here calls it that."

He was debating the logistics of baring her lovely body when he realized her bra had a front closure. "Sweet heaven," he muttered. With one quick flick of his wrist, her heavy, pink-tipped breasts spilled into view. He released her so he could fill his palms with the pleasing weight of them. "Don't tell me I don't want you. It's the daftest thing you've ever said to me."

"I know this is wrong," Abby whispered, her expression equal parts troubled and yearning. "Wrong time. Wrong place. Wrong man. Wrong woman. But I don't care."

He scooped her into his arms and strode toward the house. "I care," he said, breathing heavily, not from his burden, but from the urgent need to put an end to this dance. "No more discussion," he said firmly. "We're on the same page. And if we want to keep it a secret between us, that's our right. Small towns are the same the world over. Gossip is the breath of life. I won't have you tormented when I'm gone."

"I agree," Abby said. "Need-to-know only."

"Put your hand in my pocket. Get the key."

When Abby giggled, his neck heated. "That was a serious request, lass. I find I don't want to put you down. I'm afraid you'll run away when I'm not looking."

Abby located the key quickly, and soon he had her inside with the door closed and locked behind them. "Now what?" she asked, her smoke-gray eyes darker today…filled with secrets.

"I have a really large, fancy shower in my bathroom. Why don't we see if we'll both fit?"

Eight

Abby couldn't decide which was worse: breaking half a dozen ethical codes of conduct or taking advantage of a man who was at a low point in his life. The more frightening thing was…she didn't really care. Some hitherto dormant part of her personality had wrested control from her careful, always-cautious self and decided that this was the year Abby Hartmann was going to have a wild and glorious affair.

Duncan hadn't been kidding about his bathroom. It was a decadent homage to marble and glass. And mirrors. Way too many mirrors. She sucked in her tummy and concentrated on the important things. Like watching her Scots lover undress. He stripped off his clothes with an economy of movement that was elegant and yet deeply masculine. No self-consciousness there.

She already knew that his chest and arms were golden brown from his days spent on the water. Clearly, not all of his responsibilities involved a boring desk job. Though he was as fair-skinned as she was, he had a light, seemingly permanent tan except for a strip of white around his hips and upper thighs. The dusting of hair on his muscled body had been gilded by the sun.

His erection reared against his belly, long and thick and hard.

Some unknown force sucked all the oxygen out of the bathroom. Spots danced in front of her eyes, and her limbs froze.

Duncan's smile was gentle but knowing. "Don't get shy on me now, Abby. I liked the warrior woman up on the mountain."

Locking gazes with him was too intimate…like staring straight into the sun. She propped her foot on a stool and bent to unlace her boot. "I'm not shy," she muttered. Out of the corner of her eye, she watched him, but he didn't move. When she had removed her sock and shoe, she swapped feet and repeated the process.

Because Duncan had unbuttoned her shirt and unfastened her bra, her breasts bounced when she bent over. It seemed stupid to hide them away again when she was about to get in the shower.

With her feet now bare, she straightened slowly.

Duncan's gaze narrowed. Slashes of red colored his cheekbones. "Take off your clothes," he said. "I want to watch."

A deeply flawed part of her personality refused to let her resist a dare. Duncan's sexual demands challenged her to match his confidence. She lifted one shoulder and let it fall. "No one's stopping you."

She slipped off her shirt and bra and tossed them aside. Shoulders back, chin up, she let him look his fill. When the muscles in his throat worked and his Adam's apple bobbed up and down, she surmised that he was not quite as relaxed as he appeared.

"Now the rest," he said hoarsely.

The shorts had a zipper, one that could be lowered very slowly while a man watched. When the zipper opened as far as it would go, she shimmied the khaki shorts down her hips all the way to her ankles, stepped free, and kicked them aside.

Every wild, rushing impulse in her brain screamed at her to cover herself with her hands. She had never felt more naked or more vulnerable. But then again, she had never been as aroused.

Duncan nodded slowly. He turned and started the water flowing in the shower, adjusting the temperature and testing it with his hand. He faced her again. "Can your hair get wet?"

"I was hoping you might wash it for me."

His erection jerked and bobbed visibly as if her words had been an actual, physical touch. "I could do that. Come here, Abby."

It wasn't far. Five steps. Six at the most. The journey took forever, because her world had skidded into slow motion.

He put his hands at her hips and slid her underwear down her legs. When he knelt at her feet and tapped her ankle, she stepped out of the panties automatically, afraid of what he might do next and equally afraid that he might not.

But nothing happened. Duncan straightened. He pulled her into the shower enclosure, joined her and closed the glass door. The water was warm, but not hot enough to produce an obscuring cloud of steam. Good move on his part. They were drenched in moments.

He reached for a travel-sized bottle of shampoo and squirted it into his hands. "Turn around," he said gruffly.

Given long enough, Abby might have melted like hot wax and slipped down the drain. Having Duncan massage her scalp and neck was one of the most erotic, pleasurable experiences of her life. She felt him behind her, large and tall. Her head fell back against his chest. "Forget sex," she mumbled. "This is amazing."

Chuckling, he turned her to face him and aimed the showerhead to rinse her hair. "I hope you're joking." He took the washcloth and dried her face. "You look about sixteen right now. I didn't realize you had freckles. Just a few." He touched the bridge of her nose. "They're tiny. And cute. Like you."

"I was a mess when I was sixteen. Acne. Braces. Zero confidence. Trust me. It wasn't my best moment."

The water sluiced over his broad shoulders. She wanted to touch him, but despite her bold request on the mountaintop, she found—in this intimate situation—she was regrettably out of her depth.

Duncan's eyes, always dark brown, glittered with hunger. "Touch me, lass. Please."

How could she refuse? How could she let her bold show of feminine courage amount to nothing but words?

Without speaking, she reached for the bar of soap and the second washcloth. When the cotton was wet enough for her liking, she lathered the soap, set the bar aside and took Duncan's hard erection in her palm, wrapping it in the slightly rough fabric of the washcloth.

His breath hissed out in a gasp. At his hips, his hands fisted. His eyes squeezed shut. Carefully, gently, she washed him. First his sex. Then his chest and his neck, and at last his back.

Duncan's entire body was rigid. Neither of them had done a complete head-to-toe. But they had both been under the water long enough to take care of the immediate sweat and dirt from their hike.

When she released him, he stayed where he was, eyes still closed. Clumsily, Abby did a quick swipe of other, more personal areas of her own body. She had spent one night in Duncan's bed, but she didn't feel comfortable enough with him yet to let him wash her in a way that might lead to more than she had bargained for.

Before he could stop her, she opened the glass door. "I'm all clean now. I think I'll dry my hair while you finish up."

As an extra measure of safety, she didn't even remain in Duncan's bathroom. She darted across the hall to her own and began the arduous process of taming her naturally curly hair.

She'd half expected Duncan to follow her after a moment or two. When he didn't, she was disappointed. She finished drying her hair and smoothed the bouncy waves behind her ears.

Grabbing her silky, thigh-length robe out of her suitcase, she slipped her arms into the sleeves and tied the sash. At the last minute, she scooted back to the bathroom and added a spritz of her favorite perfume.

Then she hovered in the middle of the bedroom and lost her nerve. Biting the edge of her fingernail, she thought of all the reasons she shouldn't have sex with Duncan Stewart. Without him at her side, it was far easier to be sensible. But then again, she was tired of being sensible.

She crossed the carpet, reached for the doorknob and screeched when the door swung inward, the bottom edge catching her bare toes. "Ouch. That hurt."

Duncan, wearing nothing but a strategically placed damp towel, had entered just as she was prepared to go in search of him. "Sorry. I thought you'd gotten cold feet."

"More like bloody," she groused.

He scooped her up in his arms and carried her back to his bedroom. "It's your own fault. If you hadn't been such a chicken, we'd be in bed by now."

She punched his shoulder. "I'm *not* a chicken. I needed to use my hair dryer."

"I *have* one in this bathroom, too, you know. Be honest. You got scared in the shower."

His chest was warm and hard beneath her cheek. He held her with disarming ease, not even breathing heavily.

"Maybe a little," she admitted. "But that doesn't mean I don't want you."

"That's verra good," he said, looking down at her with a feral masculine grin that curled her aching toes. He dropped her on the mattress. "Don't move. I'll get supplies."

She held up her foot, loathe to get blood on the very nice comforter. "It's not really so bad. More of a scrape than a cut."

Duncan returned and sat down on the bed, lifting her leg across his lap. "Let me take a look." He dabbed at the blood with an alcohol wipe. "I think two tiny Band-Aids will do it."

Abby screeched. "That stings."

"Quit bein' such a wee bairn. Hold still." He spread anti-biotic ointment across the two toes with the worst abrasions and covered them. "All done." His thumb pressed the arch of her foot. "Do you hurt anywhere else, lass?"

Abby fell back on her elbows. Unfortunately, that made the sides of her robe gape. "My lips could use a kiss," she whispered. "You know. 'Cause they went numb when I was looking at this huge, gorgeous, naked man a little while ago."

Duncan's gaze locked on to her breasts. His pupils dilated. "I understand." Lazily, as if he had all the time in the world, he tossed the towel aside, flipped back the covers and dragged Abby between the sheets with him.

The cool cotton made her shiver.

They rolled together in a delicious tangle of arms and legs and fractured breaths. "Duncan," she said, suddenly fixating on the one question she had never asked. "Is there a woman back in Skye who might have a problem with what's happening between us?"

He had been about to kiss her, but now he froze and reared back, a frown creasing his noble brow. "No. And if there *had* been anyone like that, I'd have ended it before I left. Would no' have been fair to ask a lass to wait for me when I thought I was coming here to stay."

"I suppose that's true."

"Do you always talk this much during sex?" he asked, grinning to let her know he was teasing.

Abby sniffed. "If you'd kissed me already, I wouldn't have been able to talk, now would I?"

Duncan was more than a little infatuated with his sharp-tongued, quick-witted Abby. She was fierce and caring, and now that he had her naked again, he was done with conversation for the moment.

He took her chin in one hand, tilted it up and captured her mouth roughly, nipping her bottom lip with sharp teeth. She tasted like sweet honey and feminine temptation.

Taking his time with her, he gave her every nuance he'd been too obliterated the night before to offer. Coaxing, persuading, insisting. She met him taste for taste, ragged sigh for ragged sigh. When had merely kissing a woman ever made his entire body ache with need?

He had let her keep the sexy robe for a moment, but now he wanted it gone so he could taste and touch and torment her lush, beautiful breasts. With his teeth and his tongue and his fingertips, he played and cajoled and teased. Her nipples were pert, rigid raspberries. Her curves were a man's playground, warm and full and sensitive to his touch.

But other delights awaited.

Before Abby could think to protest, he slipped the narrow sash from her robe and anchored her wrists at the spindled headboard. Her eyes widened. "What are you doing, Duncan?"

"Dinna fash yerself, lass. I've a mind to play. But you can stop me anytime. Do you understand?" He gazed at her for long seconds, letting her see the full extent of his hunger, but also telling her with more than mere words that he would keep her safe.

Whatever she saw in his eyes must have reassured her. "I understand, Duncan. You're the boss."

She said the last three words deliberately. Nothing in their relationship to date had been about Abby taking a subservient role. She was a smart, well-educated woman who was the equal of any man. Her sly comment indicated that she was willing to play his game.

Hearing those three words in the context of this sexual encounter snapped the tight control he had kept on his libido. Abby was naked and willing in his bed. Tonight, he would not let her go.

He slid a bit lower on the mattress and deliberately parted her legs. The scent of damp female skin and shower soap filled his lungs. He traced the crease where her leg joined her body. "Sometimes a man likes dessert *before* his dinner."

Abby actually cried out when he tasted her intimately. Her thighs tightened around him, but he kept her legs spread. The sight of her moist folds, ready for him, sent his arousal up a thousand fold. He ran his tongue over her sex lazily, hitting the most sensitive spot and then bit her inner thigh when she climaxed wildly. "Untie me," she cried.

He rested his cheek on her trembling thigh as she came down from the top. "I dinna think I will. Unless you really mean that. Do you want me to stop, Abby?"

Her chest rose and fell rapidly. Her entire body was one pink blush. Her gaze couldn't quite meet his. He had never seen a more erotic, sensual tableau of abandon.

She swallowed visibly. "No, Duncan. Don't stop."

He went a little crazy after that. He made her come twice more in a similar fashion until he allowed her to recover and catch her breath. It seemed best to take a linear approach next so he shoved *all* the covers back and nibbled her perfectly pink-polished toes.

Abby was ticklish at first. But when he took her toes one at a time and suckled them, she didn't seem to mind.

After that, he kissed his way up her shapely calves, pausing to nip the insides of her knees, before returning to her female secrets.

Again, she tried to close her legs. He gripped her ankles firmly. "Don't try to thwart me, Abby. You said I'm the boss. I know very well what you want. It's the same thing I want. Do I need to tie your feet apart to make you behave?"

"No," she said quickly, her breath coming in sharp pants. "Don't do that. I'll behave. I promise."

He nodded slowly. "Excellent." Her faux submissive dialogue went straight to his gut and kept him on a slow boil.

Abby watched him with trepidation in her wide-eyed gaze. He wanted to laugh, but he was having too much fun and he didn't want to ruin the mood.

When he stood up, she dug her heels into the mattress, alarm on her face. "Why are you leaving?"

"Nothing so dreadful, sweet Abby. Close your eyes and rest."

"Fat chance," she muttered.

He was gone less than two minutes. When he returned, Abby's eyes were closed, but her body was rigid. He stroked her hair. "This next bit will go easier if you can't see what I'm doing."

At his matter-of-fact words, Abby struggled wildly. But the knots at her wrists held firm. Her robe was made of a thin fabric that was almost transparent…almost, but not quite. Artfully, he arranged it over the top of her face, taking care not to cover her nose.

He tapped her chin. "Is it dark in there, lass?"

She nodded her head slowly.

"Do you want me to stop?"

Her silence lasted eons, it seemed. He'd given her multiple orgasms. His own erection ached like the devil, but he was not anywhere close to being done with Abby Hartmann. He waited impatiently for her answer.

"No," she whispered. "I don't want you to stop."

"Good girl." The words were gruff with arousal and pleasure and a rush of affection for this woman who had given him so much in such a short time. "You won't regret your answer, I swear."

Nine

Abby had unwittingly unleashed a monster. Duncan Stewart was the most sexually uninhibited man she had ever encountered. When she said as much, he scoffed. "It's not me, lass, it's you. I've been corrupted by a wicked American siren."

Since she was momentarily blind, she couldn't see his face, but she could hear the smirk in his voice. It was when he got quiet that she really worried.

For several long moments, she was aware that he had left the bedroom again. But this time, he hadn't gone far. She could hear water running and the sound of drawers opening and closing in the bathroom.

At last, she felt the mattress give as he joined her. Without realizing she was doing it, she jerked at her bonds. Duncan only laughed, damn his hide. "Patience, my little Venus. I won't make you wait much longer."

Abby wasn't sure what she had expected him to do next. After all, there were only a finite number of ways a man and a woman could make love...right?

And even a Scotsman descended from a long line of occasionally barbaric Highlanders would be completely civilized *now*. Even so, her skin was covered in gooseflesh, and her heart pounded so hard in her chest she could barely breathe. The waiting was excruciating.

Duncan smoothed her hair, toying with the shell of her ear. "Why are you so tense, sweet Abby?"

"You know why," she said tartly. "You're tormenting me deliberately."

"Shall I stop?"

His question was bland. Conversational in tone.

She ground her jaw. Despite the recent orgasms, her body was wound so tightly she craved his touch like a drug. "Just do it," she said desperately. "Do whatever it is you're going to do."

When he touched her hip bone, she jerked and cried out.

Duncan murmured something she didn't quite catch. "Poor Abby. You're imagining the worst, aren't you?"

"Maybe that's because I don't really know you at all." It was a fact. That one inescapable truth should have bothered her more than it did.

He laughed softly. "You know me well enough, I'd say. As well as I know you. We see something in each other, lass. Maybe something that no one else sees. And we're curious."

She licked her dry lips. He wasn't wrong. "I trust you for some odd reason. And I don't know why."

"Mystical connections defy explanation. We Scots don't have a problem with that. Life offers rare gifts sometimes, even when we least expect them."

He ran a finger from her chin, down her throat, between her breasts and all the way to her navel where he played lazily. "I want to devour you, Abby. It gives me pause, to be sure. I've no' been quite so consumed with lust since I was teenager."

The words poured over her like fire that heated from the inside out. She wanted to hold him and cling to him and force him to take her, but she had committed to playing this game, so she took a deep breath and braced for what was to come. "I'm all yours," she whispered.

There was silence for a moment. Perhaps her honesty stunned him. He whispered a phrase in Gaelic again. She *really* needed to learn a few of those words. And then he touched her breast.

She had expected something. She didn't know what. But this wasn't it. Earlier, he had used his teeth on the sensitive tips of her breasts to bring her to the brink of release.

This seduction was different. She felt his fingers massaging her nipples. But there was an added sensation... "Duncan?"

"Relax, lass. It's only honey. Nothing so terrible." He moved to the other breast. "I told you. Sometimes a man likes dessert first. I saw a hummingbird when we were up on the mountain. That made me think of nectar and that made me think of you. Yield to me, sweet Abby, while I enjoy my treat."

She lost herself. There was no other way to describe what happened next. Time and place drifted away until her world was filled with Duncan and only Duncan. He suckled at her breasts, groaning and shuddering as if *he* were the one being tortured, and not the other way around. The feel of his rough, insistent tongue on her aching flesh made her writhe and cry out his name again and again.

The act of helpless surrender fed her need for him to a frightening degree. She couldn't see. She could barely move. All she could do was arch and twist and lift toward him as his hot breath cooled her damp skin and he savored her honey-tipped breasts.

When she could find her voice, she pleaded. "I want to touch you, Duncan. Please. No more games."

He stopped instantly. Fumbling and cursing, he worked to free her hands. In her struggles, the slick fabric knots had tightened. It took him long, frustrating moments. Almost as an afterthought it seemed, he tugged the robe away from her face.

Their eyes met. Duncan was flushed, his expression both exultant and wary...as if he expected her to berate him.

She rotated her wrists, feeling the painful rush of blood returning fully to her chilled fingers. Lifting her aching arms, she took his face in her hands, staring deeply into his beautiful eyes. "You are a wicked, wicked man," she whispered, her throat tight with emotions that were new and terrifying. "At the risk of feeding your already considerable ego, I have to tell you I'm very, very glad you came to my office that first day. I consider you mine now. As long as your feet are on American soil."

His lips quirked in a half smile. "The bargain goes both ways, lass. You'll warm my bed and no other."

She kissed him softly, drunk with wonder that such a man had fallen into her lap. "Do we need legal paperwork?" she teased.

"No. I dinna think so. We've honesty between us, and that's all that matters."

She hesitated. He knew everything about her that was important. "I agree."

What had begun as fury and urgency and grappling for position out on the mountain now shifted seamlessly to something far sweeter and infinitely more alluring. Duncan left the bed only a moment to take care of protection and then he was back.

He kissed the side of her neck. "I can't wait any longer, Abby. I'll go mad if I don't have you now."

"I can't have that on my conscience." She didn't want Duncan to see her insecurity, so she let him take the lead. Though she had been bold in claiming him verbally, the mechanics of sexual variation were less familiar to her.

Duncan had no such handicap. Though she didn't want

to think about the other women who might have shared encounters with him, it was definitely to her benefit that he had enough experience for both of them.

Oddly, Duncan appeared to have exhausted his need for *kink*, as it were. He moved between her legs, spread them wide with his powerful hips and used his hand to guide the head of his erection to her ready sex. With one firm thrust, he lodged deep. With a second, he went all the way.

"Look at me, lass. Don't close your eyes," he said.

The intimacy was painful. Her gaze clung to his. She was mute. Fearful he would realize how fast she was falling, how far, how irreversibly plunged into infatuation. Not love. Love came with time.

His jaw clenched. His brow was damp. "Ye're a wonder, Abby Hartmann. A wee, magical sprite of a woman." He flexed his hips. "Hold on, lass. I've waited too long."

He cursed in Gaelic and moved in her wildly, filling her, pummeling her, claiming her. It was insanity and exhilaration and at the end, another shattering climax. His release came fast on the heels of hers.

Collapsing on top of her, he gave her his full weight, pinning her to the bed in a deeply blissful capture.

Abby didn't mind.

"I canna feel my legs," he said. "Is that normal, do you think?"

She smiled, stroking his hair lazily. "I think we passed *normal* several stops back. Don't worry, Duncan. I'm here for you. Take as long as you need."

Duncan felt exhaustion roll over him like a seductive tide. He couldn't succumb. There was too much to do. Soon enough, he would have time to devote to Abby. But not until a grandson discharged his duty.

He recognized the danger in his current situation. Being with Abby anesthetized him, helped him to forget for a few sweet moments the weight of grief and obligation. He rolled to his side. "I suppose we should eat something."

She ran a hand lazily down his back, threatening to rekindle his interest. "Yes...." Her stomach growled on cue.

Their shared laughter was enough to propel them out of the bed. Duncan caught her close as she walked by him to go to her room. "Wear one of my shirts," he said. "I want you naked underneath." He rummaged in the closet and handed her one. The solid navy cotton was a perfect foil for her vibrant hair.

Abby took the shirt with a raised eyebrow. "Do I have permission to go to my own bathroom, sir?" She gave him a mock salute.

"You're a brat. And yes. But only because if I get you in my shower again, we'll be in trouble."

"Smart man."

He cleaned up and put on old jeans and a flannel shirt. Leaving his feet bare, he prowled the hall until she joined him. "Did you follow the rules?" he asked. The shirttail hit her just above her knees. He caught her close and ran his hands over her bottom. "Good girl."

"I'm gonna get cold."

"I'll turn up the heat."

They made their way to the kitchen, holding hands. Abby's friend and her mother had cooked so much food that Duncan and Abby were able to eat a second meal and still have some left over.

He devoured his portions. "I've always heard about the cuisine in the American South. Clearly, the stories are true. This is amazing."

"Not everyone is a great cook, though. I'm decent, but not in Lara's league. I've learned a few tricks over the years."

"Maybe you could show me a few of those tricks later," he said, stealing a kiss flavored with cinnamon and apples.

"I was talking about food, not sex."

"We could improvise."

Suddenly, Abby blushed from her toes to her hairline, obviously remembering his honey assault. "Stop," she said, her expression mortified. "I can't talk about this at the dinner table."

He manufactured an innocent expression. "Shall we go back to bed then?"

"Duncan Stewart. Behave. We have to be sensible."

She was right. He knew it. But he didn't have to like it. "Fine," he said. He stood with a sigh and began putting things away. "But you're no fun."

When the kitchen was back to rights, she grimaced and touched his shoulder. "At the risk of spoiling your mood, I need to go to my house and get something to wear for the funeral. Lara did a great job packing, but she wouldn't have known what to bring for something like that. I could borrow your car if you don't mind. I won't be gone long."

The notion of her leaving him alone in this huge house put lead in his stomach. "What if I go with you? Is that okay? I'd like to see where you live."

Abby shrugged. "Of course it's okay. I thought you might have things to do here."

"I need to clear my head. A drive will be nice."

Unfortunately for Duncan, the current plan meant that Abby actually had to get dressed. He much preferred keeping her locked away in his castle on the hill.

The drive into town was a familiar one now. Passing the building where Stewart Properties was housed gave him mixed emotions. Guilt. Pride. Consternation. He needed to sell the company in such a way that people wouldn't lose their jobs. Was that even possible?

When he pulled up in front of Abby's neat frame bungalow, he smiled. "I've decided this house looks like you. It's perfect."

"You wouldn't say that when the roof leaks every third time it rains and the wiring is sputtering on its last legs."

They walked up the front path side by side. "So you're reminding me that an old house takes lots of repairs. I live in the Scottish Highlands, lass. *Everything* is old, give or take."

"True." She laughed, unlocking the front door. "But I'm also telling you that repairs are expensive. I have to budget and prioritize them. It's an ongoing process."

She waved him toward the small living room. "Make yourself at home. I won't be long."

He caught her close and kissed the top of her head. "I was serious about going to Asheville tomorrow night. When the funeral is done. Will you come with me?"

"Don't we need to get started on cleaning out your grandmother's house? It's a huge job, Duncan. Even if you call in professionals."

"I understand that. I do. Which is why we'll take a break first…catch our breath after the funeral. I need a buffer between tomorrow and everything else that's to come. Will you go with me? Please?"

She nodded. "Of course."

"Bring something fancy to wear. A long dress. Make it colorful, not gloomy. Granny would want me to honor her by living life to the fullest. We'll have a glass of champagne in her memory."

Abby wrapped her arms around his waist and hugged him. "I think that's a lovely idea. Give me twenty minutes. I'll grab what I need, and we can head back."

When she disappeared down the hallway, he snooped unashamedly. Her house was small and cozy. Hardwood floors gleamed. The pleasant scent of lemon furniture polish lingered in the air. The furniture was stylish and functional, but not expensive. Oddly, there were no framed pictures anywhere. Most people had family photos on display.

Abby's neat-as-a-pin house was warm—not imper-
sonal—but it also revealed very little about her life. The
most information he was able to glean about her in the
short time he was alone to investigate was that she liked
romantic suspense novels, and she had saved a number of
her textbooks from law school.

He was perusing those titles when Abby returned, car-
rying a long garment bag.

"I'm done," she said.

"Your house is charming, lass."

"Thank you. Signing the mortgage for this property was
one of the proudest days of my life. I worked hard to get to
a place where I could support myself."

"You take your independence very seriously."

She cocked her head. "Is that a criticism?"

He returned a book to its assigned spot and shook his
head. "Not at all. You must have matured early. I don't think
I had your drive when I was in school."

His praise seemed to make her uncomfortable. "Sometimes circumstances don't give a person much wiggle room."

He wanted to question that odd statement, but Abby
glanced out the front window and muttered an impreca-
tion, one that seemed completely unlike her. "Come into
the kitchen. Hurry."

"What's wrong?" He followed her immediately, but he
couldn't fathom her mood.

Suddenly, the doorbell rang. Abby paled, her expression
haunted. "I'm not going to answer that. He'll go away."

"He who?" Duncan frowned. "Is someone bothering
you?" His mind jumped immediately to jilted suitors and
scary stalker clients.

"No. Nothing like that." She peeked around the corner
cautiously. "It's my father. We don't get along."

Duncan's stomach tightened. Abby's entire demeanor
had changed. Instead of the playful, confident woman he

had come to know, now she was visibly tense and upset. "I'd be happy to go out there and tell him to go the hell away if you want me to…"

Her eyes rounded in horror. "Absolutely not. All we have to do is wait a minute. He'll give up and leave."

"Your car is parked out front," Duncan said, stating the obvious.

Abby winced. Clearly, she had forgotten that detail. "I often go out with friends. Someone might have picked me up. He'll take the hint."

Ten

Abby wanted to cry. Maybe Lara was right. Maybe a restraining order was the only way to keep her father at bay.

Everyone in Candlewick knew her family history. It wasn't something she could run away from. But no way in hell did she want Duncan to cross paths with the man who had made her life a misery.

Duncan's family might not be perfect, but they were not criminals. Abby's father knew nothing about honor and self-reliance. He had spent so much of his life dodging the law and juggling the consequences of his many slick schemes, he was an embarrassment to her.

She took one last furtive glimpse and was rewarded with a view of her father's dilapidated car driving away down the street. Thank God.

Managing a cheerful smile, though it felt like a clown mask stretching her face, she turned to Duncan, not quite able to meet his eyes. He had chosen one of her kitchen chairs and was seated, leaning the chair back on two legs. "We can go now," she said.

He took one of her hands in his. His male fingers were warm and strong. Hers were icy, trembling. Duncan brushed a hair from her cheek. "I don't like to see you like this, Abby. You're doing so much for me that I want to return the favor. Will you talk to me about him?"

Her stomach hurt. "There's nothing to tell...and nothing you or anybody can do. I hope the two of you never meet. It's for the best. You have to believe me on this one."

Duncan pulled her close in an embrace that was not at all sexual. His unspoken comfort was immeasurably wonderful. She wanted to bawl like a baby, but if she let go even the tiniest bit, she would fall to pieces. That was a humiliation she couldn't bear.

Gradually, her shaking subsided and her breathing returned to normal. She pulled back and rubbed her hands over her face. "Sorry I made such a big deal about it."

He dragged her close a second time. With her standing and Duncan seated, it was much easier for him to give her a searching stare. "You can trust me, lass. Surely you know that."

She wanted to. Badly. How wonderful it would be to hand over to Duncan every bit of her worry and despair and discomfort and know that someone else would intercede on her behalf.

Even so, she didn't want him witnessing the bloodlines she had come from. Her father's deceit made it doubly important for Abby not to let her parentage besmirch her personal honor. Duncan said he didn't like secrets, but the truth about Abby's family life was better left in the dark.

Besides, this thing with Duncan was temporary. There was no need for him to invest emotional support when he and Abby were never going to be anything more than two people having fun between the sheets.

"I know that," she said slowly. "And I do trust you. Maybe someday, when you're back in Scotland and I'm no more than a distant memory, I'll write you a long letter and tell you all about my father. Then, when you're done reading it, you can toss it into the fire."

"And how does that help you now?" he asked, his eyes shadowed and his brows narrowed in a frown.

She swallowed. "Being with you makes me happy, Duncan."

"I'm glad, but that doesn't really answer my question."

"Let's go back up the mountain. You have enough sadness in your life at the moment without worrying about mine."

In the hours that followed, Abby made a concerted effort to shake off the cloud of depression and anxiety that always followed in her father's wake. Duncan needed her. Her own issues could and should take a back seat right now.

Duncan spent some time on the phone with family. The sound of his voice carried around the house. While he was otherwise occupied, Abby pondered her role in the upcoming funeral. She had brought two dresses with her for the somber occasion. One was a black, long-sleeved, lightweight wool, perfectly plain. She had worn it to her law school graduation, because she had finished midyear. The December commencement had been snowy and cold.

It was definitely suitable for a funeral, but tomorrow's weather was supposed to be sunny and warm. That was the problem with the advent of autumn in the South. You never knew what to expect.

She tried on the dress and stood in front of the bathroom mirror. It was nice. Expensive. Classy. But the funeral was going to be stressful. The church would be crowded. Stifling. Surely this was a bad choice.

The other option was also black, but far more casual. The crepe tank dress skimmed her body flatteringly and stopped just above the knee. The matching jacket was short and had three-quarter length sleeves. With the jewelry she had brought, it should do nicely.

If the church was extremely hot, she could always shed the jacket, though that would be a last resort.

When her decision was made, she went in search of Duncan and found him in the den. He wasn't watching TV. Instead, he had tuned the satellite radio to a classical channel. The Beethoven sonata playing was mournful, almost painful under the circumstances.

Duncan glanced up when she entered the room, but his expression was closed. It was no secret to her that he was using sexual intimacy to avoid thinking about what had happened in his life. In his place, she might have done the same. But she also knew that deferring all the guilt and pain and confusion was only a temporary solution.

She paused to kiss the top of his head. Then she curled up in a chair facing him. "Did you talk to Brody again?"

"Aye. He was checking up on me...making sure I was okay."

"And are you?"

Duncan's jaw tensed. "I want everything to go well at the funeral. I need to know that I've honored my grandmother's memory appropriately. Things are different here. Customs. Expectations."

"You've done all you can, Duncan. And you'll see...the town will turn out en masse tomorrow to pay their respects and to greet you. I'll play whatever role you want me to... I can keep my distance, or I can stand at your elbow and introduce you to the people I know."

"I'd be glad of your help."

It was an oddly formal statement from a man who had made passionate love to her a few hours before. Something about him was different, though she couldn't pinpoint the change.

"Is your brother second-guessing his decision not to come?"

"Not at all." Duncan jumped to his feet and prowled the room. "He did have some very definitive ideas, though."

"Oh?"

Duncan stood at the fireplace and stared into the empty hearth, his forearm propped on the mantel. "He and Cate want me to return to Scotland as soon as the funeral is over. Brody suggested putting one of Granny's senior managers in charge at the office. Then, in a couple of months when the baby is older and Brody can arrange for his business affairs to be covered, the three of them will come back to Candlewick with me and stay for six or eight weeks while we liquidate Stewart Properties and sell the house."

Abby's heart fell to her knees. "I see."

"It *would* be easier than doing it alone. Brody hasn't replaced me yet as CFO. My job and my office are waiting for me. There are a lot of big decisions to be made regarding the estate. Perhaps it makes sense to take things slowly."

"Is that what you want to do?" She could barely speak past the knot of hurt and dismay in her throat. She'd been under no illusions about the permanency of her relationship with Duncan Stewart. But she surely hadn't expected it to end so soon.

Duncan continued to prowl. His body language was indicative of his mental turmoil. At one point, he paused in front of the radio and jabbed the power button, filling the room with silence.

He spun to face Abby. "I don't know *what* I want," he said, the words low and taut with emotion. "When I thought my coming here was a years-long sentence, I felt trapped. Now that I'm suddenly free, it all seems different. *Sad. Final.* Grandda and Granny spent their lives building this business and this home. Who am I to toss it all away?"

"Miss Izzy wouldn't have expected you to stay once she was gone."

He ran his hands through his hair. He was pale beneath his tan. "You don't know that. *I* don't know that. Maybe she was hoping I would become emotionally invested and keep Stewart Properties in the family."

"Even if that were true, it doesn't matter, Duncan. She lived a full and wonderful life. She *had* her dreams fulfilled. You aren't bound by anything, either legally or emotionally. As far as her will is concerned, you—and to a lesser extent Brody—have the power to call the shots. There's nothing unethical or immoral about selling out and returning to Scotland."

His gaze narrowed. "Are you being helpful and saying what you think I want to hear, or is this speech about the buyer you and your firm have waiting in the wings like a vulture?"

The sudden attack caught her off guard.

It hurt. A lot.

She lifted her chin. "You're upset. I'm going to pretend like you didn't say that." Tears threatened. "Good night, Duncan. I'll see you in the morning."

Turning her back on him, she walked away, her vision blinded by the hot rush of emotion.

She was almost out of the room when he grabbed her arm and whirled her around. "I'm sorry, damn it. I shouldn't have said that." He cupped her face in his big, warm palms and bent to look her in the eyes. "Don't cry, lass. I can't bear it. I'm a beast, I know. My head's awhirl with all manner of dreadful thoughts. Don't walk away from me. You're the only anchor in my storm."

Though Duncan did his best to make up for his appalling behavior, he knew he had hurt Abby badly. She pretended that his apology had sufficed to set things right between them, but the atmosphere in the house was definitely strained.

They watched a movie together. He had assumed Abby would spend the night in his bed. Now, he was not so sure.

At eleven, she excused herself, pleading fatigue. He wanted to follow her, but a gaping crevasse had opened up between them. Undeniably his fault.

He wanted the clock to fast-forward. He wanted the funeral to be over. He wanted to be alone with Abby at a romantic hotel tomorrow night.

Instead, he had dark, lonely hours to fill.

When it was clear that Abby was not going to change her mind and pick up where they had left off after their provocative afternoon of lovemaking, Duncan showered and climbed into bed. As soon as he turned out the lights, all his doubts and worries tripled.

Maybe Brody was right. Scotland was home. It was familiar. Perhaps a couple of months would be enough time to heal from grief and to prepare for the huge task of dismantling his grandparents' legacy.

At 2:00 a.m., sleep still eluded him. He wandered through the silent house, feeling more alone than if Abby had returned to her own place. Knowing that she was near but out of reach made his gut tight with regret. And what about his plan to escape after the funeral tomorrow? Had his outburst derailed that, as well?

Maybe he had provoked an argument, because deep down, he still mistrusted Abby's motives for staying by his side and in his bed.

He wouldn't be the first man to be manipulated by sex. Abby was ambitious. Nothing wrong with that. She worked hard, and she had a bright future ahead of her at the law firm. Pulling off the sale of Stewart Properties for her boss would be a coup for Abby.

Was that why she was making herself indispensable to Isobel's heir?

Duncan wished like hell that he knew the truth.

His body was exhausted, but his brain ran at high speed. So many things to consider. If he gave in to Brody's urging and returned to Skye immediately, there would be no future at all for Duncan and Abby. Period. Was he ready for that?

And if he stayed, was it fair to keep seeing Abby, knowing that he had no intention of asking for anything permanent? The *only* reason to spend more time in Candlewick was to clean out the house and dispose of all the property. Abby had offered to help him. He could linger two weeks. Would that be long enough or too long?

Sometime after three, he stumbled back to his room and fell into bed. Though he did sleep after that, his dreams were unsettled.

When his alarm went off at eight, he threw an arm over his eyes and groaned. Unfortunately, though his body still craved sleep, he was wide awake now. Maybe he could get a jump-start on cleaning out his grandfather's office. He had to do *something* to pass the hours between now and the funeral.

Abby's bedroom door was closed. When he dressed and made his way to the kitchen, he found that she had made coffee. The American staple had become a crutch in these difficult days. He filled a cup, added some milk and went in search of his houseguest.

He found her outside on the front porch, perched on a wooden bench, enjoying the frosty morning.

She looked up when he joined her and gave him a small smile. "Did you sleep?"

"Not as well as I would have if you'd been in my bed."

He tossed it out there deliberately, hoping to gauge her mood.

She gave him a long stare and then buried her face in her cup again. Finally, she sighed. "I think your brother is probably right. I checked flights for this evening. If you head to Asheville as soon as the service is over, you can fly out and make your connection in Atlanta. You could be home by morning."

"Are you trying to get rid of me?" He propped his hip against the porch rail and scowled.

Abby nodded slowly. "If that's what you want to call it. You need some time, Duncan. Time to get your feet back under you. Having Isobel die so suddenly was a terrible shock. You don't really know *what* you want. Guilt and grief are clouding your judgment."

"So now you're a lawyer *and* a shrink?" He didn't like being psychoanalyzed any more than the next guy.

"I'm only trying to help."

"If you wanted to help me, you'd be naked right now."

Her face turned pink. "I think you're using sex to avoid your problems."

"What's wrong with that?" He was half-serious.

Abby set her cup aside, stood and stretched. The tiny glimpse he got of her smooth belly gave him ideas. She sighed. "Why don't you show me a couple of the other guest rooms? We have a few hours to kill. I'd like to know what I'll be in for if I end up helping you."

Clearly, Abby wasn't prepared to forgive him yet. At least not enough to climb back into bed. That was okay. He could wait. Maybe.

"Fine," he said, feeling grumpy and sleep-deprived. "If you want to be overwhelmed and depressed *before* we even get to the funeral, by all means."

Fortunately, Abby seemed willing to overlook his ill humor. He led the way to one of the three guest rooms not currently in use. "We'll start with this one. Everything needs to go. Draperies, bedding." He threw open a closet. "And look at this. We've got several decades of clothing hanging here. Some of it may be rotting away, it's so old."

"Do you want to try and sell it to a vintage shop some-where?"

"I do not. My plan is to get rid of everything that won't

be worth including in an estate sale. All of it goes to charity. Or the rubbish bin, if necessary."

Abby nodded, rifling through the hangers. "But I might point out that old people have a tendency to stash stuff everywhere. Checking for valuables in pockets and drawers and everything in between will slow things down considerably."

"I suppose." The subject couldn't hold his attention. Not with Abby right in front of him.

He was close enough to indulge his impulses. Lifting a lock of her hair, he rubbed it between his fingers. "I appreciate your efforts on my behalf, Abby, but I'm not going to fly back to Scotland tonight. You promised to go away with me and celebrate Granny Isobel's life."

"That's what a funeral is for."

The words were snippy, but he took heart in the fact that she didn't step away. "Please, lass." He brushed a kiss over the back of her nape, smiling inwardly when she shivered. She might be mad at him, but she wasn't indifferent. "You and me," he coaxed. "Dinner. Dancing. A big, comfortable bed with soft sheets and breakfast in bed."

"You told me I could have my own room."

He nipped the shell of her ear with his teeth. "I lied."

She turned and held him at bay with a hand planted in the middle of his chest. Big, beautiful gray eyes looked up at him searchingly. "You're giving me emotional whiplash, Duncan."

He winced. Her complaint was spot-on. He was acting like a lunatic. Amorous one minute, angry and discontent the next. "In my defense, I'm not usually so volatile. My mates call me stodgy on occasion."

Abby shook her head disbelievingly. "I doubt that. Before Miss Izzy died, you struck me as extremely grounded. Unsure of this transatlantic move, perhaps, but definitely your own man."

"You're not going to have sex with me this morning, are you?" He said it with some resignation, recognizing that *he* had been the one to cause disharmony between them.

"No," she said firmly. "I'm not. We have several hours until we have to leave for the funeral. I think it would be best if we each tackle separate rooms."

He rubbed his thumb over her cheekbone. "And after the funeral? Are you still willing to go away with me?"

She chewed her bottom lip. "For one night only. We come home Monday evening. Agreed? You have decisions to make, possibly even travel arrangements."

"Fine," he said, wishing he had bartered for two nights from the beginning. Abby had the end of their relationship in view, and he didn't want to admit she might be right. He didn't want to let her go. "One night. I'll make it count." The sick feeling in the pit of his stomach told him this temporary affair was going to be far shorter than he had ever imagined.

Eleven

Later that day, Abby fetched a cup of water and as unobtrusively as possible, handed it to Duncan. He accepted the drink with a grateful, intimate smile, downed it quickly, and turned back to his duties in the receiving line with almost no interruption. He'd been on his feet doing this for an hour already, yet the line was still out the door and down the sidewalk.

He was dressed simply but elegantly in a hand-tailored black suit that fit his tall, athletic frame perfectly. The only note of color about his appearance was a jaunty red bow tie. He had insisted that his grandmother wouldn't have wanted everything today to be doom and gloom, so he had worn the pop of crimson in her honor.

Abby leaned in and whispered quietly. "The next couple is the mayor and his wife. She owns the local diner."

Duncan didn't miss a beat. He greeted the man and woman with a warm smile and words of thanks for their presence. Abby didn't know if it was the Scottish accent, or the combo of tall, dark and handsome, or simply the fact that curiosity had won out, but it seemed that everyone in town had come to pay their respects to Isobel Stewart and to extend condolences to her extraordinarily charismatic grandson.

Duncan had decided on an open casket. Miss Isobel looked sweet and serene as people filed past her with tears and smiles. Abby suspected that the spirited old woman would have been mightily pleased.

Geoffrey and Isobel had been longtime members of the First Presbyterian Church of Candlewick. The church was small. Well-worn wooden pews provided seating for eighty worshippers, maybe a hundred if folks squeezed together.

The turnout for today's funeral service was well over twice that number. Mourners were being seated in the choir loft and in a series of folding metal chairs rapidly produced from some other area of the church.

Fortunately, the building did not have ornate stained glass windows. The smaller, tinted-glass panes opened outward to catch the afternoon breeze. Even so, the sanctuary was sweltering. Though the obituary had requested donations be made to charity in lieu of flowers, the entire staff of Stewart Properties had pitched in together for an enormous arrangement of bronze and golden-yellow mums, Miss Izzy's favorite flowers.

The service was slated to begin in less than thirty minutes. Soon, the funeral home staff would begin courteously but firmly cutting off the line so that Duncan could take his place for the service. Abby did not feel entirely comfortable about the prospect of being seated in the front row beside him.

Her position at his elbow had elicited stares and hushed, gossipy whispers. She bore the scrutiny with as much grace as she could. Today was about Duncan and his comfort and well-being. Abby's reputation could handle the fallout.

When there were only a handful of people still waiting to speak to Isobel's grandson, she made a mad dash for the restroom. On her way out, she ran into Lara.

Her friend gave her a hug. "Well," she said, pulling back to gaze at Abby's face. "Is it bad form to say you look sexy in that dress?"

Abby tugged her toward a back hallway. "Ssshhh. Don't give the biddies more fodder. Talking to poor Duncan is the most excitement they've had in months."

"Well, at least since his brother, Brody, knocked up the bookstore lady and married her."

"Those Stewart boys *do* know how to make an impression."

Abby spoke lightly, but Lara knew her too well to be fooled. Her eyes rounded. "You're sleeping with him, aren't you!"

"For heaven's sake, keep your voice down."

"I don't know whether to be proud or jealous. One of you is a fast worker."

Abby shrugged with a wry smile. "I may have taken *cheering him up* a little too far."

"Abby Hartmann. You're a bad girl. Who knew? I don't know what to say."

"Very funny. It just happened. Neither of us planned it."

Lara sobered. "He's not going to stay now, is he? Now that Isobel is dead?"

"Probably not." Abby made herself say the words out loud. "I've offered to help him tackle cleaning out the house…or at least the preparations before a team of professionals comes in."

"Why?"

Lara's blunt question exposed the weaknesses in Abby's self-destructive rationalizations. "I feel sorry for him," she muttered.

"The man is a millionaire several times over. I'm pretty sure he can hire whoever he needs."

"That's cold even for you, Lara. Show some compassion. His grandmother just died."

"And yet he's already coaxed you into his bed."

"It wasn't like that." Abby stopped, suddenly unwilling to justify her behavior. She didn't want to talk about Duncan's grief on the night they found Izzy. What had happened between Duncan and Abby was natural and organic. She wouldn't let that memory be sullied by Lara's understandable cynicism. "I have to go," she said. "It's time for the service."

Lara hugged her again, her expression contrite. "You're a good person. I hope Duncan knows how lucky he is to have you."

Lara's words played again and again in Abby's head during the lengthy service. She didn't think Duncan meant for it to be so long, but he had made the choice to open up the eulogy time for anyone who wanted to say a few words about Isobel. There were many who seized the opportunity to speak about a woman who had done so much and left such a lasting impression.

At last, after a soloist sang one more song, Duncan stepped forward to conclude the remarks.

He cleared his throat. "My grandparents were part of a generation who believed in hard work and family. They raised my father to be self-reliant, and when Brody and I came along, they extended those lessons to us, as well. This town and this community meant the world to them. Candlewick will always be part of the Stewart legacy. Thank you for coming here today. On behalf of all my family, I appreciate the honor you have shown my grandmother."

And then it was over.

The crowd filed out one cluster at a time. After the minister spoke to Duncan briefly, there were a few more well-wishers waiting for his attention.

Abby slipped away to stand beside the casket. "Godspeed, Miss Izzy," she whispered. "He did well, didn't he?" Duncan's words had left no room for misinterpretation. He was saying *thank you* and *goodbye*. When he talked about Candlewick *always* being part of the Stewart legacy, there had been a note of finality in his voice.

Duncan might be conflicted about his inheritance, but it was painfully clear to Abby that his presence in North Carolina was brief, at best.

When the crowd finally dispersed, Duncan took Abby's hand and gripped it tightly. They walked out the back of the church to the small cemetery where Isobel's spot beside her husband had been prepared. Duncan stood straight and tall, but she could read the strain on his face.

The minister read a scripture and said a prayer. Abby and Duncan put two flowers on the casket. Then the little woman was lowered to her final resting place.

Duncan sighed deeply and put an arm around Abby's waist. "Was it okay?" he asked, his expression sober.

"It was perfect."

He nodded. "Good."

The minister shook Duncan's hand. "The ladies of the church want to prepare a meal for you this coming Tuesday. They weren't sure of your plans, so they've asked me to make sure that's a convenient time."

"Of course. Please tell them thank you. I appreciate their kindness."

"I'll drop it by your house around noon."

When the older man disappeared, Duncan rotated his neck. "I'm exhausted," he muttered.

"Are you sure you still want to go to Asheville?"

"I don't want to go alone," he said.

Abby straightened his bow tie for an excuse to touch him. "I'll go with you. You knew I would."

"On the contrary," he said. "I'm not sure of anything about you, Abby. But I'm willing to learn."

* * *

Duncan was so tired his eyeballs hurt. The last hours had been an endurance test. His face hurt from smiling and pretending to be *okay*, whatever that meant. Deeper still was the unexpectedly sharp sting of grief. Seeing the raw earth accept his grandmother's casket had shaken him.

Maybe taking Abby to a luxurious hotel for an overnight getaway was a bloody stupid idea, but he clung to it like a life raft. If he could get her there and get her naked and in his arms, he might be able to sleep tonight.

They arrived at the Gloucester Park Inn at six. The stately four-story building was a local landmark. He barely remembered the drive. Abby had been quiet beside him, and he had concentrated on the directions from his phone. He handed the valet his keys and went to check in.

When he returned, Abby stood beside their two small suitcases. "I told the bellman we didn't need help," she said. "I didn't think you would mind."

"Of course not." He was running on adrenaline, and his nerves were jumpy. Having a third person around, even momentarily, would not help the situation. Abby's mood was impossible to read. "Let's go upstairs," he said.

Their room, actually a suite, was on the top floor of the hotel. Duncan had paid extra for a view of the mountains and a welcome basket of champagne and cheese and strawberries.

Abby kicked off her heels immediately and went to the bay window. "This is gorgeous," she said. She looked over her shoulder at him and smiled. "I've always heard about this place."

He joined her and slid his arms around her from behind. "I like this western part of North Carolina. It reminds me a little bit of home."

"Except no water."

"Aye. That's true." He nuzzled her ear. "Did you bring the fancy dress?"

"I did."

"Then go change and we'll open that champagne. Our dinner reservations are at seven, so we don't have too much time to spare."

"I'm not high maintenance," Abby said, slipping out of his embrace. "It won't take me long."

The beautifully decorated suite was spacious. In addition to the sitting room where they had first entered that included multiple sofas and love seats, there was an enormous bedroom and bathroom. Perhaps in deference to family groups who might book the facilities, there was a smaller nook with a full bath in one corner of the living area.

Duncan could hear the shower running in the other room, so he knew Abby was freshening up. Suddenly, that sounded like a fantastic idea. He took his suitcase into the miniature bathroom and followed her example.

He'd brought an entire change of clothes for tonight. Not only was he hot and rumpled, but he wanted to symbolically shed his funeral attire. Life was made up of beginnings and endings. Today had been one.

Was tonight a beginning? Or simply another ending?

The thought tormented him, so he pushed it away.

When Abby walked out of the bedroom at twenty 'til seven, she took his breath away. Her gorgeous hair fluffed out in a sexy halo around her head. Her makeup was more dramatic than usual, smoky eyes and pouty lips.

But it was the dress that made his mouth dry and his heart pound. Her curvaceous body was showcased in fire-engine red sequins that caught the light when she walked. Tiny spaghetti straps bared white shoulders.

The bodice plunged dramatically, making it clear that his pragmatic Abby had dispensed with a bra. Her curvy hips begged for a man's touch.

"My God," he said reverently. "You look like a film star."

"You're not so bad yourself." She went up on her tiptoes and kissed his cheek. "And you smell yummy."

"I showered, too. We should have done it together and saved water."

"Not a chance, Duncan. I know where that would have ended up. You promised me dinner and dancing."

He grinned at her, feeling some of the weight in his chest ease. "Aye, I did." He reached for the champagne and popped the cork. Carefully, he filled two flutes and handed one to Abby. "A toast tonight. To Isobel Stewart, my stubborn, feisty grandmother. May she and her Geoffrey be together always."

Abby touched her glass to his with a wistful smile. "A lovely thought." She took a sip of the bubbly and sneezed.

Duncan laughed and drained his glass. "That's damned fine champagne."

While he stared, Abby sipped hers slowly. "Don't," she said.

"Don't what?"

"Don't look at me like you're the big bad wolf and I'm dinner."

"I can't help it," he said. It was the truth. "I can't take my eyes off of you."

She set her empty glass aside and tugged at the bodice. "I think I've gained a couple of pounds since the last time I wore this. I don't remember it being quite so…"

"Glorious? Incandescent? Ravishing?"

Her expression was an odd mixture of pleasure and disbelief. "I thought it was Irish men who kissed the blarney stone."

"If I were going to stick around for any length of time, I'd prove to you how beautiful you are."

A heartbeat passed. Then two. "If you were going to stick around, I might let you."

Duncan felt a shift between them, a bittersweet acknowledgment that they had come close to having something special. The prospect of leaving Abby was physically painful. It was a reality he would have to address, but not tonight, not now.

"Let's head downstairs," he said gruffly.

The dining room of the Gloucester Park Inn was blacktie only. Its centerpiece was an enormous antique chandelier that cast light in a million rainbows across the elegant space. Beneath was a highly polished dance floor. Dinner tables, staggered several deep, ran around all four sides of the rectangular room. French doors opened out onto a terraced patio for use when weather permitted.

Duncan had requested a corner table that afforded a modicum of privacy.

Abby's obvious enthusiasm pleased him. "I see now what all the hype was about," she said. "No wonder couples save their pennies for a night out."

"Indeed." The crowd was eclectic, but no children in sight.

The waiter arrived and handed them menus. Abby studied hers with charming seriousness. "I believe I'll have the salmon and asparagus," she said.

Duncan decided to try the prime Angus steak. When they had ordered, he held out his hand, no longer willing to wait. "Let's dance."

Abby's beaming smile warmed him to his toes. "I thought you'd never ask."

He led her out onto the dance floor, ruefully conscious that his height and hers did not make for perfect partners. Nevertheless, he folded her into his arms, smiling when her cheek rested over his heart. She had worn sexy shoes with stiletto heels that gave her an additional three inches.

Although dancing was not Duncan's usual recreation, he knew enough to pilot his partner around the dance floor. A six-piece orchestra played beautiful evocative melodies. He closed off the memories of the past week and concentrated on Abby. The music soothed him.

He inhaled her delicate scent. In his embrace, she felt soft and warm and intensely feminine. It was impossible to imagine walking away from this unexpected, visceral connection. And yet what did he really know about her? The woman scarcely talked about herself at all. Was she simply reserved or intentionally secretive?

If Duncan remained in Candlewick, there might be a chance for the two of them, but every time he contemplated staying, his stomach tightened with panic.

Taking Abby to Scotland was no better plan. She had worked hard to get where she was in her career. Starting over in Skye would be virtually impossible.

He splayed his fingers over her bare back, shuddering inwardly as he imagined having her naked again. His body responded predictably. Since he still had to make it through dinner, he reached desperately for something to distract himself. "Tell me about your family," he said. "You know everything about me."

Abby stiffened in his embrace. Noticeably. He felt the tension in her body. It made no sense. "Abby?" he prodded.

Her fingers were white-knuckled at the breast pocket of his jacket. "Not much to tell," she said. The words were nonchalant, her tone anything but.

"Your mother must have been a beautiful woman. I'm assuming you look like her?"

She made a sound in her throat that might have been agreement or denial. "Sometimes I think I have a snippet of a memory, but it might be my imagination. I have a few photographs. She was a teacher before I was born."

"How did she die?"

"Her appendix ruptured. She let it go too long before she went to the doctor. The infection caused sepsis."

He stroked her hair. "It's not right for a bairn to grow up without her mum. I'm sorry you lost yours."

"Thank you."

"You haven't said much about your father."

"And I won't." The words were sharp.

There was a story there, and not a pleasant one, it seemed. "I won't force it out of you. But if you and he don't get along, why have you stayed here? 'Tis a lovely town, for sure. Still, there would have been more opportunities in a bigger city. You're smart and ambitious. What keeps you in Candlewick?"

Abby looked up at him, her gray eyes dark with mysteries he couldn't fathom. "My mother is buried here. I often go to her grave and talk to her about my life. It's not morbid, I swear." Her lopsided smile was self-deprecating. "It makes me happy to think she might be proud of me."

"I'd say that's a fair bet. Ye've done well for yourself, Abby Hartmann."

It was true. For a young woman with little parental support as far as he could tell, Abby had accomplished a lot in her short life. He had witnessed her devotion to her boss's cause. If she was as doggedly determined in *every* arena of her life, Abby might end up running the law firm one day.

Why did the notion bother him so much? He should be happy for her.

The song ended and Abby stepped away from him, smoothing her hair. "Our food is here," she said. "I'm starving. Do you mind?"

"Of course not."

The easy communication between them had been shattered. Duncan marked it to the moment he asked about her father. Abby was keeping something from him. Perhaps it wasn't his business, but her reticence brought more questions than answers.

Twelve

Duncan's innocent questions about her family had erased most of Abby's pleasure in the evening. If theirs was a serious relationship, she would perhaps be obliged to share all the sordid details of her family tree. But this fling, or whatever it was, had *temporary* written all over it. She had no interest in telling Duncan all her secrets.

It was bad enough that he had almost met her father. The incident at her house had embarrassed her deeply and reminded her of all the reasons why she should watch her step around Duncan. He was a client of the law firm that had taken a chance on her, given her a job, kept her from starving in the streets. She was risking her professional integrity by socializing with someone whose business interests were inextricably intertwined with her livelihood. Candlewick was a small town. If Abby made a misstep in her personal life that had implications for her career, everyone would know.

When their food arrived, they ate mostly in silence. The meal was astonishingly good. Abby was hungry. Or at least she had been earlier. Now, the knot in her stomach made it

difficult to eat more than a portion of her beautifully prepared food.

Fortunately, Duncan didn't comment. He cleaned his
plate and downed two glasses of wine. Abby drank spar-
ingly. She was nervous, but she wanted to go into the intimacies of the night with a clear head. Maybe she *was* a
control freak. But that bent had served her well.

She would have skipped dessert, but Duncan ordered
the special without consulting her. The cinnamon and fruit
crisp was made from fresh local apples and topped with va-
nilla ice cream. The scent and taste of the cobbler brought
home the flavors of autumn.

Fall had always been a favorite season of hers, but the
cooler days and longer nights were not without melancholy,
especially now. Winters in the mountains came early and
could be harsh, depending on the year. Duncan would likely
be long gone before the Christmas season. And in his leaving, he would take all the joy and the color with him.

For one bleak moment, she wished desperately that she
had never met him at all. Not when the outcome was fore-
told with such dismal certainty.

He scooped up the last bite and offered it to her, waiting for her mouth to open. She swallowed the sweet dessert
and tried not to let him see how much his casual gesture
affected her.

No matter how many times she told herself he was leaving, a tiny flicker of hope remained. Perhaps he would decide to stay. Maybe he would ask her to go with him. It
was a pleasant daydream, but one with little root in reality.
Duncan still mistrusted her motives for wanting him to sell
the property. It was possible he even thought she was in a
relationship with him to further her career, though to any
woman, such an idea was laughable. Beyond that, he had
almost certainly taken offense at her unwillingness to dis-

cuss her father. Duncan knew she was keeping secrets. He wasn't stupid. And now…very soon… he would be leaving. They hadn't had time to build the kind of relationship that could withstand a physical separation. If Miss Izzy hadn't died…

Duncan lifted a hand for the check and the waiter appeared as if by magic. The Scotsman was a compelling figure in a room filled with other, lesser men. The comparison probably wasn't fair. Abby's judgment had been compromised. Tonight, she had eyes only for her dark, brooding Highlander.

He reached across the table and took her hand in his. "Upstairs?" he asked, his voice little more than a hoarse rumble.

She nodded slowly. "Yes."

When they reached the suite, her nerves increased a thousandfold. She wanted to appear sophisticated and at ease. At the moment, those attributes were as far away as the moon.

Duncan toyed with the strap of her dress, his warm fingers stroking her collarbone. "You're jittery, lass. Why?"

His plain speaking demanded an honest response. "I like you, Duncan. And I care about you. But I don't want to have my heart broken."

Was it her imagination, or did he go pale beneath his tan? "Is that a possibility?"

She looked up at him, her smile wry. "Well, look at you. You're tall and smart and handsome as sin, and you have a wicked sense of humor. I'm not immune."

He ran the back of his hand across her cheek, his expression hard to read. "I'm not immune either. I wish our timing were better."

Even now, he acknowledged the truth of the matter. They were too new to survive his leaving. But the sexual attraction was strong.

Somewhere, she found the courage to ask the next question. "Are you going to sell the business?"

He grimaced. "Probably."

She nodded, feeling the sting of disappointment. Doggedly, she shoved the emotion aside and concentrated on the moment. "We may not have forever, Duncan, but we have tonight. Why don't you show me how a Scotsman seduces a lady?"

"That I can do," he said. His expression lightened, and in a heartbeat, the mood went from wistful to carnal. He dragged the straps of her dress down her shoulders, trapping her arms at her sides. Her breasts, unconfined by a bra, spilled out into the light. Duncan looked as if he had been poleaxed, though he had seen her naked now on multiple occasions. "Damn, you're glorious," he muttered, cupping her pale flesh in his slightly rough palms.

She had never considered her breasts as particularly sensitive. But with Duncan holding them and playing with them, her skin tightened and she shuddered inwardly. He was confident and sure. Seeing his tanned fingers against her white skin was unbearably erotic.

Her legs trembled. Her temperature skyrocketed. Her throat dried. She wriggled, trying to free her arms. "We could go to the bedroom," she said. They had made it only as far as the sitting area.

Duncan thumbed her nipples, sending streaks of fire throughout her body. His touch was both familiar and agitating. Her hunger for him eclipsed her need for self-preservation. Tonight she would give him whatever he asked.

Scooping her up in his arms, he strode through the doorway into the inner chamber. The bed was a king, miles across and laden with a dozen pristine pillows. The remainder of the champagne was still chilled. She didn't care. The soft sheets beckoned. Her head rested on Duncan's shoulder. Beneath the veneer of civilization, she felt the pounding of his heart.

"Don't make me wait," she whispered. "I want you."

Her words galvanized him. With one hand, he tore back the covers. Unceremoniously, he dumped her on the bed and came down beside her. Instead of undressing her further, he kissed her wildly, one large muscled thigh pinning her to the bed. His firm masculine lips tasted of apples. His tongue found hers and stroked it coaxingly.

No other man she had ever known had managed to take her from trembling uncertainty to unabashed arousal so quickly. Her body quivered. Her breath came and went in her lungs so rapidly, she risked hyperventilation.

Clumsily, she tugged at his jacket. He shrugged out of it without breaking the kiss. His desperation was no less than hers. They struggled and strained against each other as if determined to share the same space.

It was no beautifully choreographed ballet, but their mad dash toward nudity was effective. Soon, they were both bare-assed naked and entwined in each other's arms. Duncan's body was hard and warm and unequivocally masculine. The shape of his sex, thick and jutting, probed her hip.

She had never had any particular leaning toward men in Scottish attire, but suddenly her heart beat faster at the mental image of Duncan wearing a full dress kilt. Or even sweaty and rumpled in a working tartan. His thighs were powerful, his body tanned and lightly covered with dark hair.

Something about him was different than the men she had known. He was strong, but other men were strong, too. Perhaps it was his intensity. Duncan's ability to give laser focus to the matter at hand, whether it be sex or anything else, made him irresistible to a woman who had spent her life zeroing in on a single goal.

She had tried so hard to rise above her father's shortcomings as a parent and as a man. Nothing else had mattered to her for the longest time. Her entire focus had revolved around the need to make something of herself.

Now here she was, with a great job, a good reputation and a close circle of friends. But the one thing she wanted most of all was going to slip through her fingers. Truthfully, she hadn't known she needed a man. Things in her world had been clicking along pretty well.

Meeting Duncan had opened her eyes to what she was missing.

He bent over and licked her navel. "I think you left me, lass."

"I'm right here," she protested.

"Aye, but your attention wandered."

It amazed her that he was so attuned to her mood. No man should have that much knowledge of the feminine psyche. It made him dangerous. She cupped his head in her hands and massaged his scalp. His hair was thick and silky soft beneath her fingertips. "My apologies." Her breath caught when he moved lower and kissed her thigh. "Duncan?"

He held her down with ease and probed her intimately with his talented tongue. "Trust me, Abby. I've got you. For once, sweet girl, relax and let the moment take you."

She tried. She really did. But this level of intimacy was still relatively new ground for her. Her sexual history prior to meeting Duncan had been brief and unexceptional. Conventional. Situations where she had been in control. She liked it that way.

Sex with Duncan was different.

He demanded complete capitulation, total trust.

It wasn't easy.

Closing her eyes helped.

Her body went lax with pleasure and then climbed a

sharp peak. "Enough," she cried, suddenly terrified of what he wanted from her.

He lifted one of her legs over his shoulder. "Easy, lass. What are you afraid of, sweet Abby? Let me do this for you. Ye're turning me inside out. I'm so hard I ache. Your sex is pink and swollen. I'm going to take you wild and fast and easy and slow and every way in between."

His naughty words combined with the touch of his hands and his tongue to take her deeper and further than she had ever gone with *any* man. The shattering intimacy was both terrifying and exhilarating. Then Duncan stopped talking and finished her destruction.

The peak, when it came, snatched her from complacency and threw her into a storm of pleasure so pure and hot she whimpered and gasped and cried out. "Duncan…"

He held her close as her body shivered through every last ripple. "That's my girl," he said softly. "I'm here, Abby. I'm right here."

Duncan was losing it. He had promised Abby to protect her, but what he felt at the moment was a raw, unbridled urge to take and take and take. Her body was a siren luring him to disaster. How could he want her so much and simply walk away? His brain shut down. The future was not important. All that mattered right now was how fast he could get inside her.

Fumbling and clumsy, he reached for his pants and found the condoms he had stashed in his pocket earlier. Since meeting Abby, the prospect of sex had filled his head almost constantly.

She watched him with eyelids heavy, lips swollen. The tips of her generous breasts were tightly furled raspberry buds. He wanted to explore every inch of her creamy skin and lush curves, but the refrain in his head demanded action. *Take her, take her, take her.*

"Sorry," he muttered. "We'll go slower next time."

Before she could respond, he filled her with one firm thrust. His vision went dark. The feel of her body clasping his rigid shaft fried his brain. He was so hard his eyeballs ached. Her sex gripped him in damp, soft heat.

Slender feminine arms wrapped around his neck. Abby arched her back and canted her hips. He shuddered, gasping for breath. He was so close to coming, every nerve in his body tensed.

Abby whispered his name. "Duncan…"

Her breath was warm on his cheek.

Some primal urge, hitherto unknown, told him she belonged to him. He wanted to claim her and mark her and keep every other man away. She was *his* Abby, no one else's.

Gradually, he found a measure of control, enough to make love to her without embarrassing himself. His jaw ached from the effort and sweat dampened his brow. But he managed to reign in the beast.

Slowly, he withdrew and lazily filled her again. The rhythm was as old as time and yet new and bemusing. Had he ever wanted a woman so desperately? Had he ever connected with a woman so quickly and so intensely?

The comparisons made him uneasy, so he shoved them away, concentrating instead on nothing but the moment and Abby.

She seemed so small beneath him and infinitely fragile. Yet he knew her vulnerability was only an illusion. She was strong and resilient, and she had given him help when he needed it most.

Tenderness sneaked in, tempering his raw passion. His breathing was ragged, his heartbeat a cacophony of drums. He took her slowly and carefully, cupping her bottom in his hands and driving deep.

Abby's cheeks were flushed, her pupils dilated. When she tried to shut him out by closing her eyes, he shook his head. "Look at me, Abby," he demanded. "Tell me what you feel."

Her blush deepened, her gaze dreamy. "You," she said. "I feel you. And there's a lot of you."

The wry commentary surprised a laugh from him. That was new, too. Humor during sex. He wasn't accustomed to the range of emotions Abby drew from him. One moment he was blind with lust, the next he wanted to cradle her in his arms and protect her from everything and everyone, even him.

Inevitably, his libido wrested control. With his heartbeat slugging in his rib cage and his chest heaving with the effort to breathe, he rested his weight on one hand and fondled her breasts. "I hope you don't really want to sleep tonight," he muttered.

Abby's smile was a mix of bashful small-town girl and newly born seductress. "Don't worry, big guy. I can keep up with you."

The end, when it came, was sheer madness. He thrust wildly, barely in control. "Abby," he groaned. "Sweet Abby..."

And then he hit the peak and lost his way.

A million hours later—or maybe it was only seconds that had passed—he regained his speech, though his tongue felt thick and his head was muzzy. "Are you okay, lass?"

His not inconsiderable weight rested completely on top of her.

Abby wriggled and freed one of her arms. "I'm good."

The prim response made him chuckle. "I suppose we should get some sleep."

"Hold that thought. I need to...well, you know..."

She was cute when she was shy. He let her escape to the bathroom. Rolling onto his back, he linked his hands behind his head and stared at the ornate plaster ceiling. Maybe he should keep her here in this hotel room for more than a single night. To hell with responsibility and expectations.

A man deserved a vacation, right?

Knowing his Puritan-work-ethic Abby, she wouldn't go for it.

When she returned, her feet made no sound at all on the carpet. She was still naked. He took that as a good sign. There were two plush bathrobes hanging on the back of the bathroom door. She could have used one. But she didn't.

In her hand, she held a washcloth.

"What's that for?" he asked, not really caring, but trying to act nonchalant. The sight of her naked body was already having a predictable effect.

Abby's smile was smug and adorable. "I'm going to clean you up, and then it's payback time."

He sat up, mildly alarmed. "That's not necessary."

"Trust me, Duncan. I've got you."

Her deliberate use of his earlier refrain told him that Abby was intent on a bit of *quid pro quo.*

When she sat on the edge of the mattress at his hip and calmly removed the condom, he quaked inwardly. Already, his erection showed signs of new life. Then Abby took him in her hand and soaped him up, and he fell back on the bed, groaning.

Moments later, he gasped. "I think you can stop now," he said.

"Just rinsing," she said airily.

His erection was hard as stone and throbbing. "Please stop," he croaked.

Abby tossed the rag on the floor and leaned over him, bracing her hands on either side of his head. She kissed him softly. "I didn't know you were such a baby. Was I being too rough? Too hard on you?"

The prospect of his Abby being rough with him made him insane. He curled one hand behind her neck and dragged her down for a kiss. "You have a competitive streak. How did I not know that?"

She nipped his bottom lip with sharp teeth. "There's a lot you don't know. Shall I begin, or do you want to talk some more?"

He was torn between laughter and arousal. "You're scaring me," he said, only half-joking.

Abby gave him one last kiss and scooted down in the bed. "I'm only getting started."

Thirteen

Abby had never been uninhibited in her sexual relationships. Cautious by nature, she preferred to guard herself against hurt and the possibility of appearing naive or clumsy.

With Duncan, all her usual reservations vanished in the euphoria of being with a man who made her feel like a sexual goddess. The Scotsman *wanted* her. He couldn't hide it. His passionate need pushed her past her hang-ups and made her want to match his erotic expertise.

She hoped her enthusiasm would make up for anything she lacked in experience or technique.

At the moment, Duncan looked like a man being stretched on the rack. His fingers gripped folds of the sheets. His jaw clenched. She brushed her thumb over his closed eyelids. "Relax, Duncan. I won't bite…much."

Hot color swept from his throat to his hairline. His broad, hair-dusted chest heaved. "Ye're cruel, lass. Don't tease me. I'm on a hair trigger."

Since the man had enjoyed a prolonged and impressive orgasm very recently, she took his protests with a grain of salt. "Try counting sheep," she said. "Or reciting the multiplication tables. I'm in a mood to play."

Scooting down in the bed, she reclined on one elbow and studied her lover's body. His abdomen was taut and firm. She stroked the silky hair above his navel and smiled when he flinched.

His penis was both beautiful and masculine. It reared against his belly, full and thick and long. Lightly, she circled the head with her fingertip. A single drop of fluid leaked from the slit. She spread the moisture, her heart thumping as she imagined him entering her again.

Having him momentarily at her mercy was a novel experience.

Then, giving him no verbal warning at all, she went down on him, taking all of him that she could manage in her mouth and tasting his essence. A lingering bit of soap remained. But that was the least of her worries. Now that she had him, what was she supposed to do with him?

Duncan's entire body went rigid. He muttered something in Gaelic that was either a prayer or a curse. Between her lips, his erection flexed and thickened a millimeter more.

More than anything, she wanted to give him the blissful intimacy he had shown her. Gently, she scooped his testicles into her free hand and stroked him. The effect on Duncan was electric. He tried to sit up, but she snapped out a warning. "Don't move."

He fell back onto the mattress, groaning deep in his chest. He was caught now, his vulnerability trapped in her grasp. With one hand below and the other wrapped around the base of his erection, she moved her mouth up and down, learning intimately the spots that made him shudder with pleasure.

Unfortunately, Duncan was too primed for much of her gentle torture. She could actually *feel* the urgency in him, the need to come. With one last carnal kiss, she released him. "Please tell me you have more condoms."

"Wallet," he croaked. "One more."

Abby found what she was after and fumbled to tear it

open and roll the latex onto Duncan's shaft. "There," she sighed. "We're good to go."

What happened next was so fast, Duncan's movements were a blur. He dragged her to the side of the bed, bent her over and pressed her cheek to the mattress. Then he entered her slowly from behind. With this angle, he felt bigger still. Or perhaps her body was sensitive from his earlier lovemaking.

Now *she* was the one pinned and helpless. The feel of him surrounding her, dominating her, ignited her own fuse. She had been on a slow burn, never entirely sated. The way she felt at the moment, one night was never going to be enough. Could she fight for him? Was there any chance at all?

Duncan slowed his thrusts, backing her away from the precipice. She didn't want to savor. She wanted the hot flame, the blind rush. "Don't stop," she begged. He had one hand on the back of her neck. Her nape tingled.

"I'm in charge now, Abby," he said, the words guttural. "You had your chance. Now we'll do this my way."

Duncan was drunk with lust and testosterone. He wanted to pound his way to the end, but he also craved the chance to make Abby fly…to scream out his name…to know that in bed, at least, they were perfect together.

Her heart-shaped ass curved upward to a narrow waist. The line of her spine was feminine and delicate. Her reddish-blond hair made a cute wavy halo around her head.

"Give me your hands," he said.

She shot him a confused look over her shoulder. Her arms were above her head.

He clarified. "Put your hands behind your back."

Slowly, she did as he asked. Now he could manacle her wrists with one hand and steady his other hand on her rounded butt. It was a win-win for any man.

He gripped her wrists and pumped his hips. Reaching beneath her, he found that one, tiny sensitive spot and stroked it firmly. The keening sound from Abby tore through him like a shot of adrenaline. He kept up his carnal assault until he lost control and had to release her wrists. Now, with both hands caressing her sexy-as-hell butt, he groaned, picked up the pace, and shot them both over the finish line.

When it was done, he slumped on top of her, wondering what the hell had happened. He'd never gotten off on dominating a woman. Something about Abby made him want to play that game. Perhaps it was the absolute certainty that she was woman enough to meet him halfway and match his brash, demanding love play. How could anything as powerful as this be temporary, or even worse, a female game to manipulate him?

He tried to breathe, but he had forgotten how. Slowly, moving like an old man, he dragged himself and her up onto the bed and retrieved the covers. "Sleep," he mumbled. "We need sleep."

When he surfaced the next morning, it took several long minutes for the fog to clear. He and Abby had found each other twice more during the night. The memories of sex were dreamlike, but the pleasurable aches in his body were very real.

He squinted toward the window where a weak ray of sunshine peeked in around the curtains. An hour ago, barely conscious, he had stumbled to the bathroom and taken care of urgent business. Afterward, he had fallen immediately back into bed.

Now, Abby was curled into a ball with her bottom pressed to his pelvis. He stroked her hair lazily, trying to process what had happened. Yesterday had encompassed a wealth of emotional turmoil and difficult experiences. His deep gratitude for Abby's support didn't come close to explaining why he had just experienced the most amazing night of sex in his life.

She opened her eyes, shifted onto her back and looked up at him. "Hello."

He cupped her cheek and kissed her nose. "Hello, yourself." He liked her like this, all drowsy and vulnerable.

"What time is it?"

He rolled away momentarily and glanced at the clock on the bedside table. "Ten."

Abby squeaked. "Please tell me you hung out the Do Not Disturb sign."

"I did."

"We have to check out."

"Yeah." The reluctance he heard in her voice mirrored the feelings in his gut. "What if I order room service? I'll let you have the bathroom first."

"That would be nice."

"What would you like? Eggs? Pastries?"

Her lips quirked. "At the risk of sounding unladylike, order it all. I'm starving."

"Well, you *did* work off quite a few calories last night." He said it with a straight face.

A tiny frown appeared between her perfect brows. "Are you mocking me, Mr. Stewart? How rude."

He nuzzled her neck and cupped the closest breast, closing his eyes and breathing a sigh of bliss. "No mocking, lass. Only a reminder." He took her chin and turned her to meet his lips. "I'm verra grateful for all the aerobic activity. You keep a man on his toes, wicked girl."

Abby smirked and kissed him warmly. "You're not so bad yourself."

When he tried to slide his hand between her warm thighs, she batted it away. "No time for that. You promised me food."

With a long-suffering sigh, he stood up and stretched. "If you insist."

For the second time, he availed himself of the facilities in the sitting room. Grabbing jeans and a navy knit Henley, he made short work of cleaning up and getting dressed. Fortunately, he was close enough to the front door to hear when the bellman delivered the meal.

Abby appeared just as Duncan was tipping the hotel employee. Like Duncan, she had opted for jeans and a knit shirt. Hers was pink. A pale pink that clung to her breasts and made him want to say to hell with the meal and take her straight back to bed.

He had ordered an obscene amount of food. Between them, they devoured it all.

His breakfast guest stared at the empty tray as she drank her second cup of coffee. "Wow. I think I'm embarrassed."

"I like a woman with a hearty appetite…for everything."

Now her cheeks were pinker than her shirt. "The sun is up. We shouldn't be thinking about sex."

"Well, you're out of luck, because I'm always thinking about sex when I'm around you."

"Really?"

It occurred to him that she thought he was kidding. He leaned over, put a hand behind her head and pulled her close enough to give her a hungry kiss. "Really, Abby."

When he released her, they were both breathing hard. "Stay at the house with me this week," he said impulsively.

Abby bit her lip. "I don't think that's a good idea. I *will* help you every day. I promised you I would. But I'll go home in the evenings."

He scowled, feeling remarkably surly for a man who had spent the better part of the night in nirvana. "Why?"

She shrugged, her expression hard to read. "I'd rather make the break now. You're leaving soon. This is hard enough already, because I care about you. Not to mention the fact that you're going to have people in and out of the house this week. I can't risk the gossip, Duncan. When you're nothing but a memory, I still have to live and work here. My job and my reputation are important to me."

His temper skyrocketed. "So this is it?"

"What do you want from me?"

Only the pain in her eyes kept him from yelling at her. He tempered his response with difficulty. "Maybe you could give me a chance to figure a few things out."

"To what end? I live here. You live there. We've had great sex, and that's about the only thing we have in common. I don't want to talk about this anymore. Take me back to Candlewick, please."

The hour-long trip home was awkward at first, neither of them speaking at all. Eventually, he decided he was too tired to stay mad. Abby's rules made sense, even if he didn't like them.

He reached across the space separating them and took her hand. "We'll handle this however you think is best. And I won't hold you to your promise to help."

She squeezed his fingers. "You need me for a few days. You can't simply let a company come in and take it all. I know you think you don't want anything, but there might be valuables we need to find…if not for you personally, then perhaps for Brody's kids. Or yours."

"I don't plan on having kids," he said, putting both hands on the wheel.

"Oh?"

"Too much responsibility. And it's not fair to the kids when the parents break up."

"You speak from experience."

"Yeah. I told you before that I don't like secrets. That was the problem with my parents. They thought they were protecting Brody and me by shielding us from the problems they were having. They kept up appearances…never argued and yelled in front of us. I suppose on the surface that seemed like the civilized thing to do."

"But it wasn't?"

"Hell, no. Brody and I were completely blindsided when they split up. It tore the ground from beneath our feet. We felt stupid and betrayed. I don't know what we would have done without Granny and Grandda to look after us in the midst of all the nastiness when everything imploded."

"Not all marriages end."

"But a lot of them do. So I'd just as soon not take the chance." He took a deep breath, his hands white-knuckled on the steering wheel. "Can we change the subject, please?"

"Of course."

Several miles passed in silence before Abby spoke again. "Tell me about working for your brother," she said. "Do you enjoy it?"

"I do." In fact, he missed being at his desk with the view of the loch more than he realized he would.

"And are water and boats your passion like they are for Brody?"

Duncan chuckled. "Not entirely. I love Skye. 'Tis a beautiful place to grow up. But for me, it's the mountains that call. A couple of years ago, I began climbing the Munros in Scotland. I've managed twenty-three so far."

"Munros? I don't know what that means."

"In Scotland, it's the term we use for any summit that's over three thousand feet. There are almost three hundred in all. So I've quite a way to go. When I thought I'd be living here with Granny, I had explored the idea of hiking in the Blue Ridge. I fell in love with your mountains when Brody and I spent summers here as kids."

"We do have some spectacular ones. Very different from Scotland, I'd say."

"Indeed. Ours are mostly bare and windswept. Here, you have peaks twice as tall and very hard to get to."

"Well," Abby said with a cheerfulness that was clearly forced, "maybe you'll find time to take at least one hike before you leave."

After that, they were both silent again. The easy intimacy they had shared during the night didn't hold up in the light of day. Plus, Abby seemed determined to remind him he was leaving.

When they arrived in the outskirts of Candlewick, Duncan steered the car up the mountain. He wasn't about to give Abby an opportunity to ask if he would drop her off at her house.

His grandparents' home already looked sad and abandoned. It made no sense, really. Nothing had changed except for the inhabitants.

Duncan unloaded their bags. Someone had left two flower arrangements on the front porch. While he read the sympathy cards, Abby kept her distance. After last night, the walls she was trying to erect between them pissed him off, even though he didn't really know what he wanted from her. Was he afraid that she was angling for marriage and children?

Inside, he stared at her. "Lunch?"

"I won't need anything until dinner," she said, her gaze not meeting his. "I think I'll get started on that first bedroom."

"Fine. Suit yourself."

"What will you do?"

"I suppose I'll tackle the office. Granny tried cleaning it out when Brody and Cate were here with her, but it was too much. She made me promise to do it with her."

Abby came to him then and put her arms around his waist, resting her cheek on his chest. "I'm sorry she's gone, Duncan."

He held her tightly. "Aye. She was a hell of a woman. I hope she and Grandda can't see what I'm about to do."

"You have to decide what you think is best for you and your family. That's all anyone can ask."

She took a step back, and he was forced to release her. "I found trash bags in the kitchen yesterday," she said. "I'll use white ones for things we're donating and the black ones for stuff that needs to be thrown out. Is that okay with you?"

Suddenly, the whole damn situation suffocated him. His grandparents' business empire. Abby's expectations of him, both personally and as a lawyer. His own ambivalence about everything. "Do what you want," he said curtly. "I don't really care."

When she turned on her heel and walked away from him, he wanted to drag her back and apologize. But maybe it was better this way. If she thought he was a jerk, she wouldn't want him to hang around…right?

Though his heart wasn't in it, he went to his grandfather's office and began the daunting task of separating wheat from chaff. The detritus of decades-filled drawers and covered tabletops. There were hundreds of maps and architectural drawings. He felt comfortable pitching all that because the important ones could be found downtown at Stewart Properties headquarters.

It was galling to admit that Abby had been right. Almost immediately, he had to begin filling a box with small items that were too valuable or too historically significant to pitch. Maybe a local museum would like to have the knickknacks and programs from the 1950s and 1960s. All of it was interesting, but if Duncan began reading each little pamphlet and check and receipt, he'd be here until the end of time.

A second, larger box was required for the cloth-bound notebooks. His grandparents had both kept journals, particularly from the years when they struggled to establish their business. In the prosperity of post–World War II, Isobel and Geoffrey's foresight in predicting the upcoming tourist boom had given them an edge in the empire they began so modestly.

One glance at a few of the entries was enough to tell Duncan that his brother and sister-in-law would want to see these. Once he had them all together, he could seal the box and ship it to Scotland. It would cost a fortune, but it would be worth it.

After a couple of hours, be began to feel a sense of accomplishment. He worked quickly but methodically, ignoring the urge to go down the hall and see how Abby was faring.

If she wanted distance between them, he would try to comply, even if it killed him. She was right about one thing. It would be damned easy to fall in love. And there was nothing for her in Scotland. Her career was right here in Candlewick. Reading between the lines, Duncan felt certain that her boss planned for Abby to take over one day. Why else would the man have devoted to much time and attention to her schooling?

Duncan tucked the last two journals in the box but left the top open in case he found more. As he bent to set the heavy carton on the floor in the corner, he spotted the edge of something sticking out from behind the large oak filing cabinet.

It was a large, heavy vellum envelope. His grandfather's scrawling handwriting was immediately recognizable. Clearly, the envelope had never been opened. On the front were the words *My Dearest Isobel.* The salutation was innocuous enough, but for some reason, dread slithered through Duncan's veins. What could his grandfather have written that was only now coming to light over a year after the old man's death?

Fourteen

Abby straightened, yawned and stretched to get the kinks out of her back. She had carried multiple armloads of clothing from the closet to the bed so she could go through the pockets. Even so, she'd done a lot of bending and lifting. Her nose itched, probably from the scent of all the mothballs. Isobel had been determined that no feckless moth would ever get a crack at her and Geoffrey's winter wardrobes.

In two hours, Abby had made a huge dent in cleaning out this particular guest room. The closet was now empty, as were all the drawers in the furniture and in the bathroom. All that was left was to strip the bed.

Sadly, Duncan had been right about the fact that most things would end up in the rubbish bin. Much of the clothing was too dated to donate but not old enough to be of interest to a museum. Hence the fact that Abby now had a dozen huge trash bags ready to go to a Dumpster when the time was right.

When it came to finding valuable things to keep, so far she had collected seven sticks of spearmint chewing gum, four orphaned buttons, and a *Carter for President* button.

The only possible standout in her collection was a small gold tie tack in the shape of a fleur-de-lis.

She put the odds and ends on the bedside table and went into the bathroom to splash her face with cold water. Her lack of sleep the night before was beginning to catch up with her. In the mirror, her eyes were bright. Despite the hard work, she was happy to be here with Duncan.

Making a face at her reflection, she sighed. "Stupid woman. You should run. This isn't going to end well for you."

Mirror Abby didn't seem any more sensible than her flesh-and-blood twin. She returned to the bedroom and found Duncan standing in the doorway. When she smiled at him, he didn't seem to notice. His face was dead white and his hands clenched an envelope.

Alarmed by his pallor and his demeanor, she went to him immediately. "What is it? What's wrong?"

The muscles in his throat worked as he swallowed. "I found a note. From my grandfather. To my grandmother. One she apparently never saw. It's dated ten days before he died."

"Oh, Duncan. How sad. I'm sorry. But they're together now, so if you think about it, the note isn't really that important, is it?" She was trying to cheer him up, but it wasn't working.

"It's bad, Abby."

Her stomach clenched. "Bad how?" Geoffrey hadn't committed suicide. She knew that. Such a thing would have been impossible to hide in a small town. From what she remembered, the old man died of a stroke.

Duncan hadn't moved from his position in the doorway. His eyes were pools of misery and shock. "Read it," he said gruffly. "I don't know what to do."

Now she was frightened. What could possibly be so terrible? Duncan's grandfather had been married to his grandmother forever. This couldn't be one of those scenarios where he had a secret family. No other possibility came to mind. Unless he had been unfaithful and wanted to clear his conscience. Surely it wasn't that.

With trembling fingers, she took the envelope and extracted the single sheet of eight-and-a-half-by-eleven onionskin paper. Geoffrey Stewart had typed his note, presumably on the old Royal manual machine Abby had seen in the office. She took a breath and started reading…

My dearest Isobel—

If you are reading this, I'm guessing that I have passed on and you are left to unravel the mess I have made of things. My only excuse is that I believe I have been experiencing the onset of dementia. Much of what I am about to tell you refers to events of which I have no real memory. I suppose that sounds like the worst of excuses, but it is true.

Some weeks ago, a gentleman came to me with an investment proposal. He was very persuasive, and apparently I agreed to let him make a purchase on my behalf. I do not even recall the nature of the business proposition, but I took five million dollars out of our account and gave it to him.

All the money is gone, Isobel. All of it. I am an old fool, and I should have handed over the reins of the company long ago. The auditors were here only last week, so it will be a year at least before anyone finds out what I have done. I did not mortgage our business, thank the good Lord, but I have made such terrible inroads into our liquid assets that it will be difficult to recover.

My hope is that I will be able to somehow replace the money. If that is the case, you will never have to know, and I will destroy this note. I am frightened and distraught. You put your faith in me, and I have betrayed you terribly.

I find that my grasp on things is tenuous some days. I want to tell you the truth. I want you to know that my mind wanders. I am so ashamed, and I find it difficult to speak of these things. A man is supposed to care for the ones he loves. How can I do that when I don't always remember how to find our home at the end of a long day?

In case there is the slightest chance that our funds might somehow be recovered, I am enclosing the business card I found in my suit pocket. The man's name is Howard Lander...

Abby gasped and dropped the letter, her hands numb. *No. Please, God, no.*

Duncan misread her shock. "I told you it was bad. Five million dollars, Abby. I won't even be able to sell the company now. With the assets decimated, people may lose their jobs. This was going to come to light soon enough. I don't know how to tell Brody. And what about the employees? How do I explain that my grandfather was senile?"

He shouted the last question. His face was stark white.

Abby could barely speak. "We'll figure something out, Duncan. You could sell a few of the cabins. Restructure. My boss will help you, I'm sure."

Duncan's lips thinned and his scowl sent ice down Abby's spine. "Or I could hunt down this Howard Lander fellow and make him wish he had never been born."

Already Abby was wishing the very same thing. She swallowed hard. "Give yourself a moment to breathe. It may not be as bad as you think."

"I appreciate your attempt to comfort me, Abby, but all the positive thinking in the world isn't going to make five million dollars magically appear."

His cynical response crushed her. First his grandmother's unexpected death, and now this. She had to tell him the truth, but the words stuck in her throat. She knew exactly who Howard Lander was and where to find him. If she told Duncan that Howard was her father, Duncan would eye her with contempt and distrust. He would never believe she'd had nothing to do with the scheme to defraud his grandparents. He would think she had kept this horrific secret. But she hadn't. It wasn't true. She was as shocked as he was.

Nausea flooded her stomach. "Would you mind taking me home, Duncan? I think I've done all I can for one day. I'm really tired, and I just remembered an appointment I shouldn't miss."

A frown appeared between his brows. "You're not staying?"

"I'll come back in the morning."

He reached for her hand. "I'm sorry if I've upset you. Please don't go, Abby."

His sweet, weary smile tore the heart out of her chest. Her terrible secret choked her. She wanted to console and comfort him, and yet she was the last person who should be with him at this moment. Now it was far too late to wish she had told him all about her father and his failings. Her silence on the subject would condemn her when the truth came out. Before that happened, she had to at least try to find a solution.

She allowed herself the luxury of leaning into him for one blissful second and then another. At last, she forced herself to step away. "It's not you. It's me. You haven't done anything wrong. Not at all. But I do need to go home for a bit. Please. Or let me take your grandmother's old car."

He shuddered. "Not that. It's a piece of junk. I'll take you down the mountain if that's what you want."

It wasn't what she wanted. But she had no choice.

Twenty minutes later, they were back in the car. Abby

had her suitcase and her shattered dreams. Once the truth came to light, Duncan would look at her with disgust and scorn.

More important than her own sorrow was Duncan's terrible situation. Abby had to do something—anything—to undo the damage that had been done. To right the wrongs.

She and Duncan didn't speak during the drive down the mountain. Eventually, an icy calm replaced her near hysteria. She had faced difficult situations before. This was no different.

Liar. Her conscience screamed condemnation. It didn't matter how very hard she tried not to be her father's daughter. His blood ran in her veins, and his transgressions were written in indelible ink on her ledger sheet. How would she ever make it up to Duncan?

At her house, he kept the engine running. "Thank you, Abby," he said.

His gratitude was a slap in the face under the circumstances. She managed a small smile. "Are you thanking me for sex?"

"It's a blanket thank-you," he said, leaning over to kiss her forehead. "I couldn't have survived all this without you."

The protective ice around her heart began to melt, allowing the gargantuan pain to return. "I wanted to be with you, Duncan. I still do."

"I'll text you in the morning. Does that work?"

She searched his face, looking for some sign that the intimacies they had shared were more than commonplace for him. "Will you be okay tonight?" *Alone...*

He nodded slowly. "I'll have an early night."

"Don't brood about the money."

"That's like telling the sun not to come up. Don't worry about that, Abby. It's not your problem."

She fled the car and escaped into her house, barely closing the door behind her before she collapsed onto her bed.

For half an hour, she sobbed. Already she missed Duncan with a dreadful ache that was like a black hole sucking her into oblivion...

When she was too empty for tears anymore, she lay there and tried to breathe. Her chest hurt. Her head hurt. Her stomach hurt. But she didn't have the luxury of wallowing in her grief.

Feeling light-headed and sick, she got to her feet and went into the bathroom to wash her face. Then, before she could lose her nerve, she grabbed her car keys and walked out of the house.

Her father lived on the fringes of Candlewick in a trailer park that had seen better days. The police regularly made meth busts in the area. Surprisingly, her father had never dabbled in drugs. He seemed quite happy with his whisky and his cigarettes.

She parked in front of his rusted mobile home and got out. This was the first time in more than six years that she had actually sought him out and not the other way around. When she pressed the peeling, discolored buzzer, she had to battle the urge to run.

Howard Lander flung open his door and stared at her, his mouth slack with shock. "My baby. Abby. I'm so glad to see you."

When he went to hug her, she held him at bay with a hand to his chest. "Save it, old man. This is business." She pushed past him into the tiny living room and began to have doubts. Her father lived in near poverty. His furniture was made up of mismatched thrift store finds.

Could the note Duncan found have been no more than the ramblings of a very sick man? *Please, God, let it be so.*

She couldn't bring herself to sit down, so she stood. Her father sprawled in his recliner and hit the mute button on the TV. "To what do I owe the pleasure?" he asked, grimacing.

"What did you do with Geoffrey Stewart's money?"

Even then, she hoped her father would look blank.

Unfortunately, his response left no room for misinterpretation. His puffy face turned red. Fear filled his eyes. His expression was equal parts haunted and terrified. "I don't know what you're talking about."

She wrapped her arms around her waist to keep from shattering into pieces. "I know about the five million dollars. I want it back."

Howard switched from guilty fear to bluster. "Do I look like a man who has five million?"

"Maybe you're hiding it so no one will be onto you. But I know. Duncan knows, too. Geoffrey Stewart left a note. And he admitted everything. Your business card was in the envelope. How could you, Daddy?"

Her voice broke on the last word. How many times could a man disappoint his child before the relationship was irrevocably destroyed?

Howard switched to attack mode. It was a familiar pattern whenever life backed him into a corner. "The old coot had more money than he could ever spend in a lifetime. I didn't do nothin' wrong. He gave it to me of his own free will."

"The man had dementia," Abby yelled. "You took advantage of him."

"It's not like he was gonna miss the money." Howard sulked.

"I want it back. Where is it?"

"It's gone."

"Gone where?"

"I had a run of bad luck at the craps tables in Biloxi. I thought I could double the cash. Make five mil for myself and pay the old boy back. But it didn't go my way."

Abby thought for a moment she was going to be physically ill. "We have to make this right," she said desperately.

Howard shook his head. "Are you out of your mind? We could sell this trailer and your house, and that wouldn't even be a drop in the bucket. The cash is gone. End of story. Those Stewarts are richer than God. This is a blip on their radar. You worry too much about nothing, girl."

Anger seared through her veins. "And what if Duncan Stewart sends you to prison? What then?"

Her father gaped at her. "You wouldn't let that happen. I know you, Abby. You're my kid. I'm the only thing you've got."

She backed away from him, sick and heartbroken. Her naïveté was astounding. She had worried that being in a relationship with Duncan was dangerous. That the temporary affair might mean losing her job, her reputation. Even worse, her heart.

But all along, her blood, her family sins, were the real ticking bomb. Like Duncan, she had been blindsided by a secret. And like Duncan, she felt stupid and betrayed.

And all because she wanted so badly to have a parent, any parent, to love her.

"You're not anything to me," she said dully. "Don't ever come near me again. As of Monday, I'll have a restraining order in place. You no longer have the right to call yourself my father. How does it feel to know you gambled that away, too?"

She jerked open the door and stumbled outside. Curious neighbors watched her climb into her car. Abby ignored them. With trembling hands, she sent Lara a text. Can you meet me at my house? It's an emergency. The bank had closed fifteen minutes ago. She was counting on the fact that her friend would be free.

When Abby pulled into her own driveway, Lara was already sitting on her porch. Abby walked up the steps and into Lara's arms. This time, the tears were far beyond her control. She lost it completely.

Lara hustled her inside and into the kitchen. Abby sank into a chair and buried her face in her arms. Her friend didn't say a word. Instead, she put the kettle on to boil and found Abby's favorite tea bags.

"Here," Lara said some time later. "Drink this."

"I don't think I can." Abby choked out the words. Her stomach heaved, but after a few cautious sips, the scent and the taste of the familiar drink helped calm her. In the silence of the kitchen, she could hear a clock ticking. Her life was in ruins, but the world went on.

Lara wet a paper towel and handed it across the table. "Wipe your face and take a breath. Then tell me everything."

The whole sordid tale came tumbling out. Abby glossed over the trip to Asheville after the funeral, but Lara read between the lines. When Abby arrived at the part about the note and the money and her father's involvement, Lara got quiet and her frown deepened.

Abby clenched her hands on the table. "So that's it. Do you think I could get a loan at the bank? It might take me a lifetime to pay the money back, but I have to do something."

Lara grimaced. "Here's the thing, kid. You have excellent credit. But no one in his or her right mind is going to loan you five million dollars. Speaking as a banking professional, I'm telling you that's not going to happen. I'm sorry."

"Oh." Abby absorbed the blow. "How much *could* I borrow?"

The other woman reached across the table and took Abby's hands in hers. "Look at me, love. It's your father's debt. Not yours."

"You don't understand," Abby muttered.

"I understand more than you think. That asshole has been a millstone around your neck for most of your life. But he's not *you*, Abby. Everyone in this town knows who you are. They see your honor. Your integrity. As much as this hurts, you're going to have to find a way to let it go. A terrible wrong was perpetrated on the Stewart family. But they're not destitute. They'll recover."

"I have to tell Duncan the truth."

"Of course you do. And sooner rather than later. But if the Scotsman is half the man you think he is, he'll accept the fact that you aren't responsible for your father's way of life."

"I'm scared."

Lara came around the table and put her arms around Abby. "I would be, too, if I were in your shoes. But the truth is always best. Call your Duncan and tell him everything."

Abby wiped her face with her hands, unable to entirely stem the tears that came and went. Her throat closed up. Regrets strangled her. "I know we didn't have much of a chance. Everything was temporary from day one. He was going to leave. But I didn't want it to end like this."

"No matter what happens, I'm here for you, Abby. You're my best friend in the whole world. You don't have to do this alone."

The other woman's affection threatened Abby's hard-won composure. She stood up and hugged her friend. "I'm okay now. I'll keep you posted."

Lara cocked her head and stared. "You sure?"

Abby nodded, her lips numb and her heart aching. "I'll have an early night. Things always look better in the morning. Isn't that what they say?"

"The good news is they couldn't look much worse."

"Go home," Abby said, actually managing a genuine smile. "With friends like you, who needs enemies?"

When Lara was gone, Abby took out her phone and sent a text. What time do you want to start in the morning?

Duncan's reply was immediate. Let's wait until Wednesday. I have several things to deal with in the morning.

Her heart sank. Was he putting her off, or was he really busy? She tapped out another message. Would you like to come to my house for an early dinner tomorrow night? We need to talk about a few things.

This time his response soothed her nerves. I'd like that. What time?

Five thirty?

I'll be there.

She hesitated but took the risk. I miss you...

I miss you, too, lass.

Fifteen

Duncan spent a largely sleepless night searching for answers. He hadn't called Brody yet. It seemed pointless to upset the rest of the family until Duncan had some answers and a plan for a way forward.

In between worrying about his grandparents' business and legacy, he thought about Abby. His bed had never seemed emptier than it did right now. Twenty-four hours ago, he and his curvy playmate had been burning up the sheets. One reason he had waved her off for tomorrow was that he wanted to get a handle on his feelings.

When he was with her, everything seemed right. Without asking, she had inserted herself into his tragedy and cared for him at a time when he was most vulnerable and alone. The past few days would have been virtually unbearable had he not had Abby at his side.

But something bothered him still. Her refusal to talk about her father for one thing. It seemed an odd omission. And when Duncan had showed Abby the letter from Howard Lander, she went white, her expression beyond distraught. Was she really that empathetic, or was there something she wasn't telling him?

Now, he lay awake…on his back…staring up at the ceiling. Wishing he could hold her and touch her and kiss her and bury himself in her welcoming warmth. Abby had told him she didn't want a broken heart. Is that what was happening? Were the two of them falling in love? Against all odds, had Duncan come to America and found a missing piece of himself?

He doubted his own instincts. He'd been drowning in family drama for days now. Everything was magnified. The good. The bad. Maybe sweet Abby was an attractive life raft. A distraction.

After 2:00 a.m., he managed to sleep for an hour at a time. But at sunup, he was out of bed and in the shower, determined to get his life back on track. Tonight, he looked forward to spending time with Abby. The prospect was the dangling carrot that would propel him through the day.

When his grandparents' bank opened at nine, Duncan was on the doorstep. Five minutes later—despite the fact that he didn't have an appointment—he was sitting in the bank president's office.

The man seemed curious, but welcoming. "How can I help you, Mr. Stewart?"

Duncan drummed his fingers on the leather-covered chair arms. "Just before he died, my grandfather made an extremely large withdrawal from one of his accounts. Were you aware of that?"

The man nodded. "I remember. An amount like that is hard to forget."

"And you didn't try to stop him?"

A frown appeared on the dignified president's face. "We are not in the business of keeping customers *away* from their money, Mr. Stewart. Your grandfather filled out the appropriate paperwork, and he made the transfer to a bank in a nearby town. I assumed he was opening another account. Not my business to interfere."

Duncan ground his teeth. "Were you also aware that my grandfather was experiencing signs of dementia?"

The man paled. "I was not. Your grandfather was a well-respected businessman. It would never have occurred to me to interfere with his transaction."

"Even for his own good?"

"We're not social workers, Mr. Stewart. We're bankers. Did others know about this?"

"Unfortunately, no. Or if my grandmother did, she never admitted it to any of us."

"Then how are you making this assumption?"

"It's not an assumption. It's fact." Duncan reached into his coat pocket and extracted the crumpled letter. "Take a look."

Duncan saw the man's face change as he absorbed the contents of the letter. His shock and dismay were much the same as Abby's had been. "I'm very sorry," he said. "This is dreadful."

"Aye. Have you heard of this fellow?"

"Oh, yes…unfortunately. He's lived in Candlewick for many years. And you know his daughter, I'm sure?"

"His daughter?" Duncan's stomach clenched the moment before the words were spoken aloud.

The bank president nodded. "Abby Hartmann. Poor girl has had to deal with her father's transgressions her entire life. He's a grifter and a con man. I'll admit, though, this is the first time I've ever known him to attempt something on this scale."

Duncan had gone blind and deaf. The other man was still talking, but none of it made sense. Outside the bay window, a storm lashed the streets, ushering in the first serious cold front of autumn. Colorful leaves fell like rain. Duncan studied a rivulet on the glass and watched it slide from top to bottom.

The only two words echoing in his head were the most unbelievable. *Abby Hartmann*.

The feeling of shock and betrayal was absolute. Suddenly, every word she had ever spoken to him was suspect, his worst fears realized. He'd been worried about her attempt to sell Stewart Properties. That seemed laughable now. He had told her more than once how much he hated lies, and all the while she had been as duplicitous as a woman could be.

He lurched to his feet. "Thank you for your time," he muttered. The gaping hole in his chest made it hard to breathe.

"If you decide to pursue legal action, I'll cooperate in any way I can. I am very sorry, Mr. Stewart. Sorrier than you know."

With a curt nod, Duncan managed to find the door and escape. Outside, he hovered on the stoop and watched the driving sheets of rain. He was cold to the bone, but he stepped out into the deluge anyway.

There was only one destination left. And he knew the way.

Abby hummed now and again as she diced and chopped vegetables for the soup she was making. Morning had brought a modicum of peace. Every family had skeletons in its closets. Surely Duncan would understand that her father was not under her control. No matter how hard she tried, she couldn't keep her blood relation from wreaking havoc.

Even so, she dreaded the moment of truth. Having to confess her connection to the man who had robbed the Stewarts was going to stick in her throat.

Pride was partly to blame, but it was more than that. She ached for the upheaval in Duncan's life. Izzy's death was shockingly sudden yet inevitable. But Howard Lander's perfidy was the equivalent of the sports term *piling on*.

Duncan was already having a hell of a month. Now, he

had even more to bear. The weight of his responsibilities to Stewart Properties and to his family must be daunting.

When her doorbell rang, she turned the soup pot on low and wiped her hands on a towel. As she approached the front door, she saw the outline of a man's head through the small fan-shaped piece of glass.

Her heart beat faster.

She yanked open the door. "Duncan. Good grief. You're soaked. What are you doing here? Let me get you some towels."

He didn't say a word, but he waited obediently until she returned with a handful of her thickest terry cloth. In another situation, she might have helped dry him off, but something about his body language warned her not to touch.

When he was no longer dripping, they moved to the living room. Abby switched on the gas logs and sat down on the sofa. Duncan remained standing, his big frame rigid. His expression was impossible to read.

"The soup won't be ready for a few hours," she said. "but if you're hungry for lunch, I make a mean grilled cheese."

Her attempt at humor fell flat. Duncan's face was stark and pale. His dark eyes glittered with strong emotion.

He jammed his hands in his pockets and paced. "Tell me this, Abby. Were you in on it? Was all of this a grand scheme to devalue the company so that you or someone else could waltz in and snap it up for a song?"

If he had slapped her, the shock couldn't have been any greater. "You don't mean that...surely."

His scowl frightened her. "Look at it from where I'm standing. You had an inside track with my grandparents' lawyer from the beginning. No sooner did I move into my grandmother's house, than there you were, metaphorically holding my hand, making yourself indispensable. You even admitted you thought I should sell everything. How convenient for you and your father that I wanted to go back to Scotland."

Tears clogged her throat, even as her heart shredded. "*You* were the one who asked me out, Duncan. Are you forgetting that? I told you it wasn't a good idea. Now that's coming back to bite me. But I never did anything to harm you or your family. I wouldn't. I couldn't."

"Five million dollars." He looked around her modest house. "Where is it now, Abby? Where's the money? Tucked away in a Swiss bank account somewhere? Waiting for me to leave North Carolina so you can swoop in and take over everything my grandparents worked for all their lives?"

How could a man who had made love to her so tenderly stare at her with such visible disgust?

Her chin wobbled. "It's gone. I went to see my father yesterday afternoon. It's gone. He gambled it all away."

Duncan's gaze narrowed. "You lied to me, Abby, and so damned convincingly. You stood in my house and read the letter I handed you and yet you never bothered to mention that you knew the charlatan my grandda was describing. Howard Lander. Your father. Why don't you have the same last name he does? Is there a husband waiting in the wings? Is he in on this, too?"

She knew Duncan was hurt. She knew he was lashing out in his pain. But knowing didn't make the insults any easier to bear. "I legally changed my name five years ago, because I was ashamed Howard Lander was my father."

"A convenient answer."

"It's the truth."

Duncan shook his head slowly. His face was an open book for once. Disillusionment. Pain. Deep regret. Gut-level sorrow. "You were good, Abby. I have to hand it to you. I suppose it helps when your father is a con man. I actually considered the possibility that I might be falling in love with you. Ridiculous, isn't it?" He paled further. "That's why you didn't want me to meet him the day I was here with you and you were picking out dresses. You were so upset. I thought he had done something to hurt you. But it was far more sinister than that. You didn't want to risk me finding out about the money."

"I didn't *know* about the money," she shouted, tears streaming down her face. "When you showed me that letter yesterday, I wanted to die."

"And yet you didn't say a word." He threw the accusation at her without remorse, his tone flat and cold.

Silence reverberated in her little house. She scrambled for a way to make him listen.

"I was in shock. It stunned me. But that's why I invited you to dinner tonight. I was planning to tell you everything, every last wretched detail. You have to believe me."

His expression never changed. No matter what she said or did, Duncan was going to think the worst of her.

It was a hell of a moment to realize that she loved him, body and soul.

She took three steps in his direction. If she could touch him, they might be able to break through this agonizing impasse. When she laid a hand, palm flat, on his chest, he didn't flinch. His icy gaze was painful, but she bore it bravely.

"Think, Duncan," she said. "Think of what we had Monday night. That was special. You felt it, too. I gave you everything. I held nothing back. Tell me you know how much I care about you."

Beneath her fingertips, his heart slugged in his chest. He was living and breathing, his skin hot to the touch, even through his crisp dress shirt.

But the ice that encased him never cracked.

If he had been hotly furious, she might have reached

him. Instead, the man she had come to know so intimately was locked away somewhere he couldn't be reached.

With two fingers, he lifted her arm away from his chest and dropped it.

"Too little, too late, lass. I'll clean up this mess. Somehow. And if I find solid evidence that you conspired with your father to defraud my family, I won't have the slightest compunction about putting you behind bars right alongside him."

The remainder of Tuesday was a blur for Duncan. He left Abby's house and went straight to his grandparents' empty mansion on the mountaintop, because it was the only place he had to go.

He'd forgotten that the minister had promised to come by with a potluck lunch. The containers were stacked neatly on the porch. With a guilty grimace, Duncan carried them inside and called the pastor to apologize and say thank you. The man's genuine concern bolstered Duncan in spite of the hellish day he was having.

The food smelled amazing, but Duncan had no appetite. He roamed the house moodily, feeling angry and off-kilter and so much more.

The rooms mocked him. He had seen Abby in almost all of them. Her presence was everywhere. Her scent. Her ghost. How could he have been so wrong about her?

Already, remorse flooded his gut. He had been cruel, harsh. What if he were wrong? The facts seemed crystal clear. Then again, his world was in such turmoil, he scarcely knew down from up. It was not hyperbole to say that Abby had been his salvation in recent days. Could her kindness be motivated by a mixture of greed and guilt? Or was she genuinely innocent? Was she speaking the truth when she said she didn't know what her father had done?

He wanted that to be true. God how he wanted that to be

true. But his own parents had fooled him completely once upon a time with convincing lies. How could anyone ever know for sure what was in the heart of another person?

He contemplated going to a hotel, but that required more energy than he possessed at the moment. Sometime around six, he dug out a bottle of his grandfather's best scotch and opened it. If he was going to wallow in his own misfortune, he needed company. Right now, the whisky was the best he could do.

By the time the sun rose again, he was no closer to a solution for his problems, but he had a hell of a headache.

When the doorbell rang midmorning, his heart lurched. *Abby...*

He strode down the hallway, yanked open the door, and felt his heart fall to his feet. The woman standing on his porch was a stranger.

Before he could speak, she poked him in the chest with a sharp finger. "What did you do to her, damn it?"

The blonde with the runway body and the street-fighter attitude backed him into the house.

"Could you please not shout?" He put his hand on the top of his head and tried not to throw up.

The woman slammed the door...with her on the inside now. "I'll ask you again. What did you do to my friend?"

"Have we met?"

"Don't play coy with me, Duncan Stewart. I'm talking about Abby. What did you do to her? She's not answering her phone. Her car isn't in her garage, and she's not at work."

He cherry-picked the questions. "She took some time off. I'm sure she's fine." Even as he spouted the lie, all he could think about was the way she looked when he walked out of her house. Devastated. Defenseless. Shattered.

"Where's your kitchen?" the blonde asked, her voice curt.

Duncan pointed. "Through there."

She took his arm and force-marched him down the hall. In the cheery breakfast nook, she shoved him into a chair and turned to the counter to fill his coffee maker.

Duncan began to wonder if this was some kind of bizarre nightmare. "Who are you? What are you doing in my house?" he asked. "And do you have any acetaminophen?"

The blonde scowled. "My name is Lara Finch. I'm here to sober you up, because I need your help. I'm worried about my best friend." She reached in her purse and tossed a plastic bottle in his direction.

At this point, it seemed easier to go along with the crazy woman. Duncan swallowed two capsules. Without water. And waited for the coffee. When the blonde handed him a steaming cup several minutes later, he almost wept.

She poured herself a mug as well and took a seat across the table from him. "When was the last time you saw her? Last night?"

He shook his head. "No." He glanced at his watch. "It's been a long time. Almost twenty-four hours."

Lara frowned. "She told me she was fixing dinner for you last night."

"Well, she didn't. I was here. Alone."

The blonde shook her head as if clearing bad information. "Okay. Let's start again. What did you do to her?"

Duncan sighed, wondering how long it would be before his head stopped pounding. "Abby and I had words yesterday morning. At her house. I left. That's it."

"You were at the bank yesterday, weren't you?"

"I'm not sure my whereabouts are any of your business."

Lara ignored him. "The bank president told you that Abby Hartmann is Howard Lander's daughter. So you put two and two together and came up with five."

"What do you know about all this?"

"She came to me Monday afternoon. She was distraught."

"Because she knew the ax was about to fall."

"Oh. My. God. Listen to yourself. *You* don't even believe what you're saying…do you?"

He stared at his coffee. "No." Suddenly, his heart jerked. "Why are you worried about her?"

"She's disappeared."

His heart stopped. "Then we have to find her." Now, in the light of day and with a few hours' sleep under his belt, the truth came to him. He was a fool, plain and simple. It didn't matter if Abby had lied or not. He wanted her. He needed her. It was as simple as that.

"We're wasting time," he said. "I'll be ready in five minutes. You're familiar with Candlewick and the surrounding area. Start making a list of any conceivable places she might have gone."

When he returned in less time than he had promised, Lara stood and crooked a finger. "Give me your keys."

"Oh, hell no."

She grinned. "Well, it was worth a try. Come on, Mr. Tall, Dark and Gorgeous. We'll take my car, then, 'cause I know all the back roads. Let's go find our Abby."

Sixteen

Duncan hated being a passenger. But he would have done anything to find Abby, even if it meant tolerating the kamikaze driving of her best friend.

Not only did Lara have a death wish on the narrow two-lane roads, she relished the chance to berate him. "You know Abby is pure gold."

"Yes." He opened his mouth to defend himself, but no words came out. He'd made the biggest mistake of his adult life and that was saying something, because he pulled some boneheaded stunts in his time. "I was upset. I felt betrayed. She saw the name in the letter. I showed it to her, damn it. Why didn't she say something then?"

Lara shook her head slowly, her expression bleak. "I'll tell you why, Duncan Stewart. Because I think my sweet friend was falling in love with you, and she couldn't believe that yet again her son-of-a-bitch, worthless father was ruining her life."

"You seem to know a lot about him."

"I should. Abby and I have been friends since we were in first grade. When I met her, she had already been without her mother for three years. A kid needs her mom, Duncan."

"Aye."

"I've watched that woman work twice as hard as everyone else for years. She always has to be the best. The smartest. The most prepared. She's loyal to a fault, and she would do anything for the people she cares about. For some reason, Duncan Stewart, that list most recently included you."

Duncan tasted shame, and his spirits sank lower. They had been driving for an hour already and had nothing to show for it. "Tell me about Howard Lander," he said. "We were at Abby's house one day, and she hid in the kitchen so she wouldn't have to answer the door."

Lara winced. "I tried to convince her to get a restraining order against him. She changed her name, but the legal action was a step too far."

"Maybe not now."

"True."

"What's wrong with the man?"

"Honestly, I don't know. He's too smart for his own good, for one thing. Abby has always tried to give him the benefit of the doubt. She thinks that losing her mother broke him."

"Or maybe he was always a jerk."

"Possibly. For years, he's been a functioning alcoholic. But lately, the act has worn thin. Did she ever tell you about last Christmas?"

"No. I've asked about her parents, but she didn't have much to say."

"It's no wonder. And for the record, my family has adopted her. We all love Abby, and if you mess with her again, we'll hurt you."

Duncan hid a faint smile. "Last Christmas? You were saying?"

Lara took a corner on two wheels. "Christmas Eve. Abby and I had been out to dinner with friends. We were on our way home when we cut through the town square in front of the courthouse. Howard was standing in the middle of the road wearing nothing but boxers, drunk out of his skull, singing Christmas carols."

"Hell."

"Yeah. It was pretty awful. The police carted him away, but the damage was done. Abby was humiliated. It was a human interest story, so one of the stations in Raleigh picked up the video footage and ran it on the evening news."

Duncan cursed. "I should press charges...send the bastard to jail. Would that make things better or worse?"

"I can't speak for Abby. Maybe that's something the two of you need to talk about."

Abby rotated her straightened-out coat hanger ninety degrees. Years ago, she had learned how to make the perfect s'more. The key was in a perfectly browned marshmallow. Her campfire was just right. Big enough to keep her warm. Not so big that she was risking a conflagration.

She knew Lara was worried about her. The texts had come fast and furious until Abby had been forced to turn off her phone. For the last twenty-plus hours, she'd been here at this campsite, hiding out. It was cowardly. She'd be the first to admit that. Even so, she needed time to recover.

Remembering the look on Duncan's face when he accused her of fraud still made her want to dive into a deep, dark hole. Forget having her heart broken. This was several levels worse.

She had the campsite mostly to herself. It was midweek. The weather was nasty. Most of the tourists had moved on to other pursuits. Other than the fire, her only accoutrement was the portable awning that gave her a modicum of shelter from the elements. Fortunately, she had been able to snag the closest site to the bathhouse and the facilities.

Abby was car camping. It was something she and her

dad used to do a lot when she was a kid. The childhood memories were happy ones. It was only much, much later that she realized they had been homeless for a time.

A gust of wind blew sideways, bringing a raw sluice of rain. She pulled her coat more tightly around her neck and stared into the flames. Her brain was blank. For the first time in many years, she had no clue how to move forward. Should she turn her father in to the authorities? Would that mean anything to Duncan?

The money was gone. No matter how many ways she tried to find a feasible solution, she hit a wall. She could work for the rest of her life and never be able to repay the Stewart family.

A sudden rustle of footsteps in the gravel brought her head up. Lara stood there, hands in the pockets of her raincoat. "You scared me, kid."

Abby grimaced. "Sorry."

She couldn't bring herself to look at the man beside Lara. But she glared at her friend. "Traitor."

Lara shrugged with an unrepentant smile. "I needed backup. He was available."

Duncan squatted and peered at Abby's dessert. "I'm no' an expert, but that looks revolting."

Lara thumped him on the shoulder. "When in Rome…" She leaned down and ruffled Abby's hair. "You want me to sit in the car? In case you need a referee?"

Abby grimaced and handed the coat hanger to Duncan. "No. You can go home." She stood and hugged her friend. "I don't know what to do," she whispered in Lara's ear, already close to tears again. And she *hated* that.

"*You* don't have to do anything, honey." Lara spoke softly so the words wouldn't travel to Duncan, especially with the rain pelting down. "The ball's in his court. If things get bad, call me and I'll be back in a flash."

Abby nodded, feeling nothing but a dull sense of dread. "Okay."

With nowhere else to go, she sat back down on the tarp.

Duncan shot her a sideways glance. "What am I holding?" he asked, staring at the sugary blob.

"Don't they have marshmallows in Scotland?"

"Aye. But we put them in cocoa. We don't incinerate them."

Abby reached in her waterproof tote and pulled out the graham crackers and Hershey's bars. "Give me a sec." She took the makeshift cooking utensil from him and held it over the fire again...only long enough to bring the marshmallow back to full heat. "Now, watch. Graham cracker. Chocolate. Hot marshmallow. And one more graham cracker. Voilà. A s'more."

"I'm missing something."

"It's a fun, gooey treat. And everyone always wants *some more*. Here. Try it."

Duncan's fingers brushed hers as she handed over the messy concoction. With a dubious expression, he opened his mouth and took a big bite. His eyes closed. She saw the moment the mélange of flavors hit his taste buds.

"Well?" she said. "What do you think?"

He wiped his mouth with the back of his hand. "You Americans have the weirdest and best ideas."

"So you like it?"

He nodded solemnly. "I do. But what about you? Shall I share this one?"

"I'll make another." She wanted something to occupy her hands and give her an excuse not to look at him. After threading a second fat marshmallow onto the coat hanger, she concentrated on her cooking.

Duncan finished his s'more and sat down cross-legged beside her on the tarp. He'd been squatting the entire time up until now. The man must have incredible thigh muscles.

Thinking about Duncan's thighs was not a good idea.

With her marshmallow nicely browned, she assembled her own dessert and took a bite. The knot in her chest relaxed as she stared into the flames. The scents and sounds of the fire made up for the fact that she couldn't feel her frozen feet. She'd been too upset to eat anything yesterday. Now she was starving.

Having Duncan with her here in the forest was both comforting and unsettling. Because she didn't know what to say, she kept quiet. He was quiet, as well.

The rain drummed on the tarp, providing an intimate, if somewhat damp, bubble of privacy.

Finally, Duncan sighed. He poked at the fire with a small stick, rearranging the coals and sending a geyser of sparks into the air. "I owe you an apology, Abby. I said things yesterday that I deeply regret."

She licked her fingers. "It's understandable. You were shocked and upset. And still grieving your grandmother."

He cursed beneath his breath. At least she thought it was a curse. The Gaelic word was unfamiliar.

He turned sideways and stared at her. "Are you always so quick to give people the benefit of the doubt? I'm sorry, Abby," he said. "Deeply sorry. I was angry with you for not telling me the truth, but it was more than that. From the beginning, I was conflicted about the fact that your firm had a client who wanted to buy the business. On the one hand, it seemed like my way out. But that felt disloyal to Granny. And then when I found out you had lied by omission, the whole thing seemed sinister."

"I'm sorry, too," she muttered. "My father—"

Duncan put a hand over her mouth. "We're not going to talk about him, Abby. He has nothing to do with you and me. His sins are his own. You have nothing to be ashamed of, nothing at all. It's not your fault."

"Then why do I feel so terrible?" she croaked. There

was nothing she could do about the tear that rolled down her cheek.

Duncan scooted closer and put his arm around her. The heat from his big body was more comforting than the fire. "It's time for me to talk and you to listen, lass. Can you do that?"

She nodded. Whatever he was going to tell her was bound to be painful, but she was a big girl. Closure was good.

Duncan took her chin without warning. "Ye've got marshmallow on your cheek. Hold still."

She held her breath as he bent and kissed away the sticky, sweet residue. His lips never touched hers. But he was so close she could feel the stubble on his face. The man hadn't shaved. And now that she thought about it, he looked like someone who hadn't slept in days.

Her heart raced. Her blood pumped.

Maybe she was experiencing a sugar high. That's all.

Duncan retreated and tucked her more firmly against his side. "I've not been entirely honest with you, Abby."

Alarm skittered through her veins. Was there a woman in his life after all? "Oh?" she said, trying not to sound as freaked out as she felt.

"I resented the hell out of the fact that I had to be the one to come here to the States and help Granny run Stewart Properties. I felt backed into a corner by circumstances beyond my control."

"I see."

"My life in Skye was good. *Is* good," he said firmly. "I like my job and my friends and the vast, wild beauty of the land where I grew up."

Her heart sank. "I see." It was the only response she could come up with, at least the only one that didn't reveal too much of her own distress.

"I don't think you do," he said slowly. "My life in Skye

is great. It's *comfortable*. But here's the thing, Abby. I'm thirty-two years old. I don't think *comfortable* is the end-game for a man my age. That's for people who are fifty or sixty or, hell, I don't know. Maybe even eighty."

"What are you trying to say, Duncan?"

He ran a hand through his hair. "The TV shrinks tell us that personal growth only happens when we're pushed outside our comfort zones. Well, I'm here to tell you that these last couple of months have been *way* the hell out of my comfort zone. And what's worse, even after I made the decision to move to Candlewick and help, suddenly Granny was dead. And the business had lost five million dollars...and—"

When he ground to a halt, she saw the muscles in his throat work. Against hers, his body was rigid.

"What, Duncan? And what?"

He turned and pressed a kiss to her temple. "And then there was you."

To be included in his list of tragedies stung. "I'm sorry I made your life difficult," she said.

His rough laugh held little real humor. "You were the only bright spot in a very traumatic season for me. You were charming and funny, and then later... Well, you were my friend, Abby. And finally, my lover. My feelings for you have been all wrapped up in the upheaval of my comfortable life, and I haven't had a clue what to do about you."

Her heart sank. Duncan's honesty was hard to bear. She was glad he didn't blame her for the missing money, but the man was not exactly pledging his undying love. How could he? They'd known each other less than a month.

Suddenly, the rain went from gentle showers to a deluge. Huge, fat droplets pummeled the fire, making it sizzle and pop.

Even the overhead canopy wasn't sufficient to keep them dry.

Abby took his hand. "We need to get in the car," she said. She made a dash for the vehicle, opened it and scrambled into the back, waiting for him to follow. Duncan was right on her heels. He slammed the door and sprawled in the seat with a sigh. "Where's your tent, lass?"

"Don't have one. I slept right here last night." She pulled a tissue from her pocket and dried her face. There was nothing she could do about her hair. From past experience, she knew her curls were running wild. She didn't have on a lick of makeup, and her T-shirt and jeans were ancient. This might be the last time she ever saw Duncan Stewart, and she looked like hell.

With all the car doors shut, the windows soon steamed up from their breathing. A big man like Duncan Stewart put off a lot of body heat.

Despite being wet and exhausted, he looked ruggedly handsome. It really wasn't fair.

She summoned her courage. "There's no need to worry about me, Duncan. I knew when I first kissed you that we were having a fling. I guess since it's you, that makes it a Highland fling?" She was getting punchy from lack of sleep and grief and the strain of not begging him to stay.

He frowned. "Listen. Don't talk. Remember?"

She mimed zipping her lips.

Duncan's lips quirked in a half smile. "So to sum up, these last few weeks have set me on my heels. Every time I thought I had found solid ground, something else happened to shove me on my ass. When I thought Granny was leaving the company to Brody and me fifty-fifty, it was bad enough. But then you told me about the damned will and all the changes, and suddenly all of this was *my* responsibility. The business. The house. The family heritage."

"Well, not to beat a dead horse, but with a few strokes of a pen, you can be done with it all. You can be home in

Scotland before you know it. No more responsibility. No more ties."

"And no more you." He said it soberly.

Her eyes stung. "This is a really long speech. And my clothes are wet. Could we speed this up, please?"

Duncan laughed out loud. "God, I adore you."

"You do?" She blinked at him, wondering if the water in her ears had affected her hearing.

"Come here, my sweet, wet Abby." He pulled her into his embrace and stretched out as much as he could with her on top of him in a very compromising fashion. "Kiss me, love."

Then his hand was on the back of her neck and their lips met and every inch of her body that had been cold and shivering moments before was now on fire.

Duncan tasted like chocolate and marshmallows and everything she had ever wanted in her life. His tongue teased her lips, stroking and thrusting and taking her breath.

"I don't know why we're doing this," she said, half-panicked.

"I do," he groaned. He slid a hand under her shirt and unfastened her bra. His fingers teased her taut nipples. "You gave yourself to me, lass. Body and soul. I took the gift, and I didn't treasure it, but I won't make that mistake again." He cupped one of her breasts and squeezed gently.

"Finish your speech," she said, breathless with hope.

He smiled and kissed her nose. A giant sigh lifted his chest and let it fall again. He tucked her head against his shoulder. "I'm not leaving Candlewick, Abby. I'm not leaving you. It finally dawned on me that what I really want is to carry on my grandparents' legacy. I think it's my purpose. The missing money may be more of a blow than I realize, but I'm not afraid of hard work. And there's one more thing…"

She held her breath, playing with his collarbone where she had unbuttoned his shirt. "Yes?"

"I want you to do it with me," he said firmly. "Either formally or informally. If you want to continue your job at the law firm, I certainly understand. But I would think a company like ours could use professional legal counsel in-house. Under the circumstances, I'm not sure what kind of salary I can offer you, but the benefits package would be significant."

She stroked him through the heavy, damp denim that was not thick enough to disguise the eagerness of his erection. "I'm impressed by your package already," she teased. The reality of what he was saying overrode the humor in the situation. Her chin wobbled. "You're serious about this?"

He held her chin with two fingers, tilting her head so he could see her face. His gentle gaze held so much pure emotion, her heart contracted. "I've never been more sure of anything, Abby. I want you to be my wife. I love you body and soul. And before you even have to ask, that means children, too."

Suddenly, everything she had ever wanted was a breath away. It seemed too good to be true. Her entire body trembled with a mixture of fear and delight. "You love me? Truly?"

Seventeen

Duncan stroked her hair, feeling the silky, bouncy waves. "To my very bones. We're going to call this a practice proposal. It's too soon, and I want you to know you can trust me for the long haul." He paused and winced. "Not to mention the fact that I'd prefer a more romantic setting."

"Ah, a Scotsman with a heart for romance. If we ever get married, will you promise to wear your kilt?"

He pinched her butt. "No *ifs* about it, lass. You're mine now. No going back. And yes. I'll be delighted to wear my kilt if it will make you happy."

She lifted up, bracing her hand on his chest. "*You* make me happy, Duncan. I love you."

"Even though I was a damned fool yesterday? I let my pride and my prejudices get in the way, and I nearly lost you. I'll no' ever get over that. I was arrogant, Abby. I thought I knew how to handle Granny, how to handle the business, hell, even how to handle you. I thought all I wanted was a temporary affair. But I was wrong on so many levels."

"That's in the past. We're looking toward the future."

He raked a hand through her curls, toying with them as they wrapped around his fingers. "Our vehicles are smaller in Scotland. But I've heard 'tis a rite of passage for an American lass to give herself to the man she loves in the back seat of a car."

"Not at our age. We have two perfectly good houses at our disposal."

His breathing came faster. He unbuttoned her jeans and slid his hands inside. "Can't wait."

Duncan recognized the complicated logistics. But he had Abby in his arms again, and it felt as if it had been weeks since he last made love to her. He nuzzled her neck. "What if I sit up and you straddle my lap?" The rain was a torrent now, ensuring that no prying eyes would spot them, not to mention the fact that Abby's car was the only one anywhere around.

Her eyes widened. A pink flush suffused her throat and cheeks. "I don't know…"

"Don't be bashful, sweet girl. I won't let anything happen to you."

His proposition meant that Abby had to shed her clothing completely, at least from the waist down. He helped her undress with barely controlled impatience, pausing to kiss and stroke and fondle until they were both shaking and clumsy with hunger.

When everything was right, Duncan found the single condom he'd had the foresight to bring along and rolled it on. Steadying Abby with his hands at her waist, he eased her down on top of him. Her body accepted his urgent possession. He filled her with a ragged thrust and a groan.

She rested her forehead against his. "I would go to Scotland if you asked me, Duncan. I don't want you to have regrets."

He wheezed out a laugh, barely able to breathe. "Don't be daft. *This* is what I want. As long as I have you, I have everything."

That she could forgive him so easily for his cruel accusations the day before made him want to be a better man. God willing, he had years ahead to prove to her that her trust in him was not misplaced. With everything he had, he would honor and protect her.

A family would be nice. A boy. And then a girl.

His orgasm bore down on him, demanding, importunate.

Duncan gritted his teeth and concentrated on Abby. He reached between them and touched her intimately. The sight of their joined bodies affected him profoundly. Whatever his sins in the past, he must have done something right to deserve this woman.

Abby clung to his neck. Her breasts mashed up against his chest, making him dizzy. She bit his earlobe, her breath tickling his ear. "I'm close," she whispered. "Give me everything. Send me over."

She didn't have to ask twice. With a roar of exultation, he braced his feet against the floor of the car, gripped her hips and thrust again and again until his vision went black and Abby cried out his name.

Eons later, he realized that his lover's cute bottom was cold. He didn't want to move. His body was lax with pleasure, his brain clearer and more calm than it had been in months.

He blew a curl out of his face. "Anybody awake in there?"

Abby pulled back, sending delightful aftershocks through his sex. Her smile was tremulous. "You do that really well."

"I don't know what you mean," he said, straight-faced. "This is my first time to shag in a car."

"Very funny."

"I try," he said modestly. He sensed the moment when her mood changed.

She sobered, her hands braced on his shoulders. "Things always seem perfect when we're having sex, but our world is complicated, Duncan. My father will always be my father. I can't make him go away. If you're living in Candle-wick, you'll be bound to run into him sooner than later."

Instead of answering, Duncan eased Abby off of him and helped her deal with her clothes. When they were both decent again, he caught her close for a hard kiss. "It doesn't matter," he said. "And for the record, I won't be pressing any charges. For one thing, it would be difficult to prove anything in court. My grandfather withdrew the money of his own free will. But more than that, legal action would be pointless because there is no money to recoup. And it would hurt you. We can see him or not see him. He helped give birth to you, so I'm feeling remarkably mellow about all that right now. But it's your call."

Abby leaned her head against his shoulder and reached up to kiss him. "Thank you."

Her gratitude bothered him. "Don't thank me." His throat tightened. "I don't know if I can forgive myself for attacking you yesterday. I knew in my gut what kind of woman you are. You never lied to me about anything that truly mattered. I was hung up on my pride and my fear of betrayal. I let myself be blinded by evidence that didn't add up. I won't ever do that to you again, I swear."

"Stop it, Duncan," she said firmly. "It was a crisis, and we all make mistakes under pressure. I should have told you immediately that he was my father. So I screwed up, too. No more sadness. Not today."

He held her close, marveling at what life had given him. "I wish Granny had lived to see you and me together."

"I like to believe she *does* know. She and your grand-father both." She smiled against his chest, her cheek rest-ing right over his heart. "I think I'm going to like being a Stewart."

"Well, lass, the Stewarts are the lucky ones. Because they have you." He tilted her chin up and found her lips with a kiss that threatened to start round two. "And so do I…"

Epilogue

Duncan ran both hands through his hair and tried to swallow the knot in his throat. "Well, how do I look?"

Brody snickered. "I've never seen you like this, little brother. It's pretty damned funny."

"Shut up and help me. We have to walk out there in about a minute and a half. Is my jacket collar straight?"

Both men were wearing full dress kilts at Abby's request. In the same church where the Stewart funerals had been conducted, Duncan would now pledge eternal devotion to his bride.

In the distance, the plaintive sounds of a bagpipe echoed.

Brody, taking Duncan by surprise, hugged his brother tightly. "I'm going to miss you, damn it. But I know you're doing the right thing. Granny and Grandda would be delighted and proud."

Duncan nodded, his throat tight. "Ye know I'm not staying here in Candlewick out of obligation...right? I want this. For me. For Abby. For future generations of Stewarts."

"I can't think of a better way to start your life together."

The door adjacent to the altar opened, and the minister

gave them a nod. The men strode into the sanctuary, barely registering the rustle of response at their appearance.

The church was decked out for Christmas with poinsettias in the windows and swags of fragrant balsam everywhere.

Down the center aisle, a local piper strolled, playing a traditional tune. Behind him, clad in dark green velvet, Abby's friend Lara walked slowly. At the back of the church, framed in the doorway, stood the only person Duncan wanted to see.

Abby was wearing a traditional wedding gown. Knowing how much she had missed in her young life, Duncan had insisted she have all the bells and whistles for this wedding. She carried a bouquet of crimson roses and eucalyptus.

Her dress was strapless and cut low over her beautiful breasts. An antique lace veil flowed from a diamond tiara that had been part of Duncan's wedding gift to her, along with a simple teardrop necklace that matched the headpiece.

As she walked down the aisle toward him, everything in the room faded away until all he could see was his Abby. Beautiful gray eyes met his. Everything she was—her spirit, her integrity, her huge caring heart—shone in that gaze.

Lara took her place opposite Brody.

Then it was time for Abby to ascend the shallow steps. Duncan gripped her hand to help her, kissed her cheek and wrapped her arm through his as they took their assigned places. "I love you," he said, going off script.

The chuckle that ran through the crowd barely registered.

Abby looked up at him, her eyes bright with tears. "And I love you, stubborn Scotsman. Now hush and let the minister do his job. We have a lifetime ahead of us for kissing."

Duncan glanced at Brody and grinned. Then he took a deep breath and squeezed his bride-to-be's arm, focusing obediently on the officiant. "Aye, love, that we do."

* * * * *

COMING SOON!

We really hope you enjoyed reading this book. If you're looking for more romance, be sure to head to the shops when new books are available on

Thursday
12th July

To see which titles are coming soon, please visit
millsandboon.co.uk

MILLS & BOON

LET'S TALK
Romance

For exclusive extracts, competitions
and special offers, find us online:

facebook.com/millsandboon

@millsandboonuk

@millsandboon

Or get in touch on 0844 844 1351*

For all the latest titles coming soon, visit
millsandboon.co.uk/nextmonth

Want even more
ROMANCE?

Join our bookclub today!

'Mills & Boon books, the perfect way to escape for an hour or so.'

Miss W. Dyer

'Excellent service, promptly delivered and very good subscription choices.'

Miss A. Pearson

'You get fantastic special offers and the chance to get books before they hit the shops'

Mrs V. Hall

Visit millsandbook.co.uk/Bookclub and save on brand new books.

MILLS & BOON